THINGS THAT NEVER WERE

monkeybrain, inc.

THINGS
THAT NEVER WERE
FANTASIES • LUNACIES & ENTERTAINING LIES

MATTHEW ROSSI
INTRODUCTION BY PAUL DI FILIPPO

For Scott Vice

who believed more than I did

And Geoff Clark

who taught me how to think

Table of Contents

The Prince of Paradox
by
Paul Di Filippo

Matthew Rossi may have invented an entire new art form in *Things That Never Were*. Call it speculative nonfiction, or cryptojournalism, or historico-literary ranting, or guided daydreaming, or collective-unconscious channeling, or edutainment disinformation, or fabulaic mimesis, or polymorphously perverse media-jamming, or any other semi-oxymoronic term you care to employ, so long as the new phrase conveys the proper sense of daring, erudition, obstinate refusal to accept consensus reality, playfulness, willingness to go out on a limb then saw the limb away, and all the other qualities traditionally associated with humanity's greatest rebels, outcasts, eccentrics, visionaries, saints, madmen and plain old bullgoose loonies.

On the other hand, Rossi might just be transcribing without embroidery the unadorned yet nigh-ineffable history of our race and planet. In which case, we had all better stock up on lead underwear, taco sauce, anti-telepathy rigs, nose glasses, pscilocybin suppositories, and alien condoms, before heading for the nearest, deepest cavern or remotest hidden alpine valley.

But in either case, what the discerning, open-minded, suitably starry-eyed reader will find here is hours of mind-blowing, gonzo entertainment, scores of small essays (perfectly shaped for the postmodern attention span) which will insure that you never view the past, present or future the same again. (And as Rossi might maintain, who's to say these three terms are not synonymous?)

At heart, Rossi is a storyteller. He is a fount of ideas which in lesser hands would be used to populate about two hundred novels. He has the ability to compose plots which embody all the traditional virtues of hooks, suspense and climaxes. He boasts an engaging, colloquial style which sucks you in, making it seem as if Rossi is speaking to you alone, as the two of you hang out on his back porch with a view of Shangri-La, or perhaps in a cloaked orbital observatory, beaming pink rays of enlightenment down to the unsuspecting populace. But what Rossi doesn't have—and this is his essential virtue—is the patience to play the storytelling game in the standard manner. He has absolutely zero interest in creating fictional mouthpieces for his tropes, then inventing actions to illustrate his themes. (And I suspect that Rossi would also feel frustrated in trying to get any hypothetical finished stories he wrote past the censorious, unsympatico editorial establishment, into magazine or novel form.) For Rossi, the world and its recorded personages are supremely weird as they stand, without his having to invent new beings to season the mix. Instead, he'll start from a basis of verifiable events and actors before soaring off into the stratosphere of counterfactual, nonintuitive lunacy.

This is not to say that Rossi doesn't like fiction. Far from it. Plainly, he loves many of the classics of SF, fantasy and horror, and draws inspiration from them. He loves them so much, in fact, that he ramps up their ontological status to be equal to that of, say, Napolean or Jesus. Then they can become equal tokens in his recombinatory game.

Rossi's uniqueness does not mean that he does not honor his literary ancestors, those who have preceded him and inspired him on his path. He cites them often and copiously, and the result is the creation of a fraternity of like-minded savants, distributed through time and space, all working toward elucidation of eternal mysteries. Charles Fort, Robert Anton Wilson, H. P. Lovecraft, Colin Wilson, Michael Moorcock, Edgar Rice Burroughs, Robert Graves, Sir James George Frazer, Jack London, W. B. Yeats, Philip K. Dick—these are just the first names that come to the tip of the tongue when cataloguing Rossi's compadres. And although he doesn't cite them specifically, I'd have to add such figures as R. A. Lafferty, Bill Griffith (of *Zippy* fame), Avram Davidson (especially for his *Adventures in Unhistory*), Rudy Rucker (whose recent *Saucer Wisdom* would make a perfect companion to Rossi's book), Philip Jose Farmer, and James Burke, the fellow who did a TV show and books under the *Connections* rubric, in which the most unlikely sequence of facts conspired to create odd tapestries of nonobvious history.

But Rossi is hardly a literary elitist. He'll take his intellectual fodder wherever he can find it, whether in the hokiest New Age tomes, or *Reader's Digest*-style compendiums of "unexplained" events, or from the crumbling pulp pages of, say, Ray Palmer's *Amazing* magazine. Rossi is a true democrat, a quintessential American, willing to consider that the truth of existence, the secret of the ages, might just as likely be in the possession of some hick redneck farmer as it would reside in the vaults of some periwigged society of Illuminati.

Reference to Rossi's Americanness brings up a vital quality of his work. It's simultaneously cosmopolitan—Rossi's imagination ranges all time and space—but also anchored in the present-day USA. As Rossi maintains in the essay titled "Et in Lemuria ego," America stands as a Borgesian construct formed of Old World desires for an Arcadia where strange magics could be unleashed. I highly doubt that Rossi or his book could have emerged from any nation where daily living was less fantastic than America.

And, like that archetypical American sage and sensitive genius, Walt Whitman, Rossi is large enough to contain multitudes and not live in fear of contradicting himself. *Things That Never Were* is guaranteed to create beautiful and fertile psychic whiplash in the reader. Your brain will be ping-ponging back and forth between the mutually exclusive narratives which Rossi offers. This book is a kind of internally writhing and self-devouring organism whose parts seem to be at war. But don't be fooled by the ostensibly internecine warfare: Rossi's several incompatible mindchildren are not fighting, they're violently *screwing*, and out of this brain-intercourse is going to arise an unpredictable hybrid of startling portent.

Learning in an aside that Rossi, like myself, has connections with Providence, Rhode Island, that turf sacred to Chthulu, I am inspired to close with my own little Rossi-style riff on the probable origins of this mystery man.

The Prince of Paradox

Of course the infamous seventeenth-century vampires
of Southern Rhode Island had to have their nemesis, an

alliance of men and women determined to eliminate the bloody plague from the state. Chief among these righteous families was the Rossi tribe, descended from Sardinian white magicians. Having emigrated to the New World and interbred with Native Americans, the Rhode Island Rossis were heir to twin strands of supernatural puissance. After the total defeat of the undead hordes, the Rossi clan continued to guide the fortunes of Rhode Island from behind the scenes, eventually helping the state achieve its status as an industrial powerhouse during the nineteenth century. (Funding for the development of the famed Corliss steam engine came from the sale of certain Atlantean artifacts long kept in the Rossi coffers.) But with the arrival in Rhode Island of competitive black sorcerers from Sicily, the Rossis found themselves fighting for their very lives in a kind of proto-Mafia war. As elder members of the clan were killed off in supernatural battle before they had a chance to transmit their knowledge and skills, the Rossi line degenerated in the twentieth century into mere mortals. It was not until the birth of one Matthew Rossi, rumored to be the offspring of a mortal mother and a winged and be-webbed citizen of Unknown Kadath, that the legendary blood of the Rossis resurged. Upon attaining his maturity, Matthew Rossi was soon dubbed the "Prince of Paradox," for his extreme cognitive dissonance faculties. Seldom seen by the average citizen, nowadays Rossi is rumored to inhabit an aeyrie high on Mt. Tamalpais, staffed by retainers half-zombie, half-nightgaunt. Currently, Matthew Rossi is working on a plan to halt and reverse the Mayan Apocalypse of 2012. Donations gratefully accepted.

The Good Citizens of Sodom

Okay, weird stuff in my head must be shared with the world.

On June 30th, 1908, a violent blast from space flattens a whole lot of Siberian taiga near the Tunguska River. By itself, that would be pretty dramatic, a violent explosion wiping out a whole forest. However, it didn't happen by itself. According to the Journal of the International Meteor Organization, WGN's 1995 edition, it happened at least twice more within the past one hundred years. Both on August 13, 1930 and on December 11, 1935, violent explosions on a scale usually associated with nuclear weapons or volcanic eruptions wiped out hundreds of square miles of jungle. The latter blast, in the Rupununi region located in British Guyana, is thought to have been even more powerful than the Tunguska blast itself. Of course, people will tell you that these were the death throes of comets bursting in our atmosphere, or asteroid fragments, or what have you.

What if, however (the most dangerous phrase in English, my friends), they were something else? No, not spaceships or antimatter; far too prosaic. What if they were the inevitable explosions caused by abortive time travel experiments?

Bear with me; if you try to send something back into the past, besides all the problems inherent in the process (like the fact that the place you want to go, namely the Earth in the past, wasn't at that time where it is now), one salient fact remains. You are introducing matter into a place where there was no matter before, forcing the matter that was there to move or be annihilated. If you try to introduce a human being into a space where there was but air before, some of the air molecules and some of the human's molecules are going to try to take up the same space, and an explosive release of energy is most likely the result. Boom. No more Mister Time Traveler, and most likely, no more Tunguska forest.

Even assuming they could somehow generate a concussive wave to part the air a microsecond before the capsule appears (and they're gonna need a capsule; I'm not sure you want to think about what's going to happen to frail human flesh when the concussive wave folds back on the traveler) and thus prevent the explosive death of the Chrononaut, the wave itself will be more than enough to generate a massive explosive burst. Plus, just as the introduction of matter where there was no matter will have consequences in the past, the removal of matter in the future where there was matter will also have consequences. Since matter and energy cannot be destroyed, merely converted into each other, a toll is gonna have to be paid just to get the traveler gone.

At this point you are probably thinking to yourself: *Then why don't they just do it in space, smart guy?* Indeed, this occurred to me too. And sure, assuming that there's no trace hydrogen or messy nonbaryonic particles to worry about, this may be the best way to go.

Assuming they manage to work all the kinks out and get this sucker up and running, why then don't they do it all the time, so to speak? Well, maybe the calculation of the exact implosive energies needed to generate the concussive wave in the past is so difficult that even with advanced 352nd century Quantum Molecule Replicating Helix computers, they still only get it right one trip in every ten million. Or maybe, just maybe, they tried it once, and wiped themselves out.

Take the story of Sodom and Gomorrah. Imagine, if you will, that these cities were not sickening fleshpots but rather the height of early civilization, burgeoning proto-metropoli that put Babylon to shame and made Heliopolis look like a shoddy trailer park. In time, from these two majestic cities would rise a culture of elegance and grace that would master physics, and despite world-wide conflicts that caused much historical knowledge to be lost, they managed to bring all of mankind together in peace and brotherhood and unity. Now, of course, being human, they were curious about their long-vanished forebears and they decided to try to observe them with a new technology. They decided to send back a camera in a time-pod, did the intricate math, and sent back the camera without generating the concussive wave first, because it was their first test.

BOOM.

You guessed it. The molecules in the camera and the molecules of the air explosively released their full energy, in a blast just shy of the power of a matter/antimatter bomb. Sodom and Gomorrah were wiped off the face of the earth, that whole timeline was destroyed, and the neighbors of those vanquished titan cities decided that they must have done something really, really bad to piss off God. So the course of civilization on Earth is hideously set back as the paragons of culture and refinement are transformed into the archetypes of depravity in order to explain a time-travel mishap.

No, I really do think like this, I swear.

Al-Aurens! Al-Aurens!

In the 1990s, a team consisting of ethnologists, space scientists and archaeologists set out through the trackless wastes of the Arabian desert looking for the "City of Brass," a lost metropolis known by many names throughout history. To the natives who guided them, it was Ubar, land of the 'Ad, and it had been a land of mystery for centuries. They found it, with the aid of an American space shuttle, the writings of Bertram Thomas and Claudius Ptolomaeus, and the luck of those who were finally in the right place at the right time.

But were they really the first? Or had others- perhaps many others- who were there before them on the quest for the "Atlantis of the Sands" been more successful than they dared reveal?

> Lawrence was certainly the most likely candidate to take up the search for Ubar. An erudite Arabist, he was also a trained archaeologist with field experience in Syria. He had a deep, near-mystical feeling for Arabian lore: indeed, the white-robed, blond figure known to the tribes as 'al-Aurens' ("Lawrence") had become part of it... If he revisited the scene of his exploits, Lawrence indicated, it might well be to search for archeological remains in the Rub'al-Khali.
> *Nicholas Clapp,* **The Road to Ubar:- Finding the Atlantis of the Sands**

> He claimed to have seen fabulous Irem, or the City of Pillars, and to have found beneath the ruins of a certain nameless desert town the shocking annals and secrets of a race older than mankind.
> *H.P. Lovecraft,* **The History of the Necronomicon**

T.E. Lawrence died in a motorcycle accident on April 2, 1935. Really. He certainly did not fake his death to escape the monotony of his life in Dorset and his feelings of shame at the treatment of his Arabian allies at the hands of his country, oh my no. And he most certainly did not follow in his close friend Bertram Thomas' tracks, and head deep into the Crimson Desert in search of lost Ubar, or Omanum Emporium as Claudius Ptolemaeus (better known to us as Ptolemy) called it, or Iram as the Quran called it ("Do you not know how Allah closed his hand upon 'Ad? The ones who infested the pillars of Iram, whose sight has not been seen again in the whole world?") or, for that matter, the very same Irem that Lovecraft embroidered into the tapestry of his *al-Azif,* the book which became better known by its bastard Greek name, *Necronomicon.*

No, Lawrence died that April morning. Better that by far than to suppose that he disturbed the realm that God declared forever swallowed by the sand, don't you think?

> In 1934, the young French journalist Andre Malraux claimed to have discovered her white city while flying over the desert of southern Arabia. In a cable to his Paris newspaper, he described sighting twenty towers or temples still standing... on the north boundary of Rub'al Khali.
> Alex Mantoux, **"The Land of the Queen of Sheba"** *(from* **The Reader's Digest The World's Last Mysteries)**

Ah, now we drag in the queen of Sheba. And where there's the queen, can the sorcerer-king Solomon be far behind? Were the 1930s a significant time for the dream-haunted city of Irem, capital of the lost kingdom of Sheba? Perhaps. And perhaps it isn't merely coincidence that Sheba sounds like an elision of Shub-Niggurath, also known as the Black Goat of the Woods with a Thousand Young. In many of the Medieval tales, the queen comes to Solomon with thick, goatish hair all over her body... and yet the Wizard King is seemingly unperturbed by this. Could this be due to the striking similarity between the Seal of Solomon and the Elder Sign? Yet again, Lovecraft and the ancient Hebrews seem to be heading down the same trail and merely disagreeing on the view. Is it just that Howard Phillips was a glass-half-empty type, or is there even more to the story? The queen is identified with the moon by some Yemeni nomads, and her name there is Bilkis the Queen, linking her to the Haram bilkis ruins in Marib. These are also in the south of Arabia-possibly an outlying part of her empire?

The Kaaba is a rock that fell to earth, a star-stone, the *lapis ex caelis* also referred to as the Holy Grail. For seven millennia, the region known now as the Middle East has been home to countless events that are variously described as miraculous, magical, or fictional, depending upon your belief. Things stellar make themselves felt in the Middle East all the time. Stars appear in the sky over Bethlehem, fall from the heavens and land in Mecca, descend in the form of a wheel within a wheel and make off with Elijah... Imagine, if you will, that a young Englishman with a deep, nearly-mystical feeling for the area discovers too late that the government he serves intends not to help free this great and glorious land from oppression, but rather to become the oppressor, as the Mahdists learned at Khartoum? Might not "al-Aurens" find himself forced to make his way through the trackless wastes of the Crimson Desert, depending upon that same ancient voice that once beguiled Solomon himself to draw him ever nearer to the ancient well of the mysteries, the city that only exists in dreams? Malraux saw it, and he was hardly given to fancy. Imagine, then, how much more real it could have become for the man who envisioned an Arabia free of the Turks, and who somehow forced that dream into reality. Perhaps the reason no one ever found Irem before the Challenger flight was because it wasn't there. (Also, it's interesting to note that it took a ship voyaging through the heavens to pierce whatever it was between Irem/Ubar and the world. Was the shield weakening, or was this a condition of its fall?)

> Whoever shall find and enter Ubar will be driven mad with fear.
> Rashid al-Din, **The World History**

> God's angel Gabriel said, "O cloud of the Barren Wind, be a torment to the people of 'Ad and a mercy to others!"
> Muhammad ibn Abdallah al-Kisai, **The Prophet Hud**, Lines 148-150

Imagine, if you will, a mage-war. On the one side, the beautiful but evil queen of Sheba, consorting with the hideous Shub-Niggurath and her Black Young. On the other, the wise and sybaritic King Solomon of Israel, who inlaid the very walls of the temple with gold, placed a glass floor inside his own chambers, and who practiced the conjuration and summoning of "angels." Eventually, acknowledging the enormous power and wisdom of the king and seeking an alliance, the queen comes to Israel with her treasures, and despite the fact that she is covered with hair that marks her as an ally of Lillith (another female of enormous power and dark beauty- Cybele/Shub-Niggurath again?) Solomon simply summons some "genies" who depillate her, and they get married (according to the Quran, anyway, which also has Solomon convert the queen to Islam. Which didn't exist yet, but let us not get bogged down...) and unite their kingdoms.

Following which, Solomon dies, the queen skedaddles and the Israelites go on a tear of destruction, rebelling against Solomon's (and Bilkis'?) son Rehoboam and dividing the kingdom in twain. This was followed by an attack by the Egyptian pharoah Shishak (possibly Ramses II, possibly Shoshenq, nobody knows for sure; see Isaac Newton's *Chronology of Ancient Kingdoms* if you can find a copy) and the whole shooting match went to hell. Did Solomon anger Yahweh (not too tricky in the Old Testament, anyway...) by marrying a non-Jew who may or may not have been a servant of Lillith/Cybele/Shub-Niggurath? Is that why Gabriel (the same Gabriel who supposedly tells the Virgin Mary that to her, a son will be born, and who reads the Quran to Mohammed; Gabriel's kept busy) is sent to Ubar/Irem, to teach a rival god a lesson in poaching on Yahweh's turf?

> He felt when all was said and done, he had betrayed the Arabs.
> He lamented his "mantle of fraud in the east," yet he considered
> returning to Arabia. The mantle "might be fraud or might be
> farce: No one should say I could not play it."
> *Nicholas Clapp,* **The Road To Ubar**

Flash forward yet again to 1935, when Yahweh's flock is facing devastation in Europe and his attention is wandering. Did something out of many-pillared Irem try and force a way back, first through the mind of a receptive French journalist and then through the iron will of the greatest dreamer of his generation? Keep in mind that T.S. Eliot and Aleister Crowley were among that generation, as were H.D. and Gertrude Stein and Ezra Pound and Antoine de Saint Exupery and Jean Rhys and the aforementioned Lovecraft.

This was a whole world full of dreamers, yet Lawrence stood above them all, an Arthurian madman who could impose his will on the Turks and British alike. Did Lawrence really crash that motorcycle by accident, or did he sense a call too powerful to ignore and yet too terrible to answer, and know that it was his life against a world bound in the fecund claws of the Dark Goat of the Wood with a Thousand Young? Or worse, did he answer? Does "al-Aurens" wait patiently in the true Irem, the one on the border of dream, to lead Lillith's army forward to conquer the pale world of man?

> That is not dead which can eternal lie,
> And with strange aeons, even death may die.
> *H.P. Lovecraft,* **The Call of Cthulhu**

> We saw that while on one hand they, by prayer and supplication, threw themselves upon the mercy of the Divinity, who, in their belief, was responsible for the granting, or withholding, of the water, whether of rain, or river, the constant supply of which was an essential condition of such ordered sequence, they, on the other hand, believed that, by their own actions, they could stimulate and assist the Divine activity. Hence the dramatic representations to which I have referred, the performance, for instance, of such a drama as the Rishyaçriñga, the ceremonial "marriages," and other exercises of what we now call sympathetic magic.
> *Jesse L. Weston,* **From Ritual to Romance**

However, it doesn't have to be all darkness and destruction. It's very easy to take young T.E. Lawrence and the queen and weave a romance of reincarnation around the dashing young commander with a fire to command and the beautiful Bilkis, whose first love was lost to her more than two millennia ago. Think Avalon in the desert, rather than Atlantis. Lawrence the dreamer could easily be seen as an Arthurian figure, come out of the British Isles when his kingdom and the Holy Land itself needed him (see Tim Powers' excellent *The Drawing of the Dark* for another take on this kind of thing, as well as his gloriously numinous trilogy of *Last Call, Expiration Date* and *Earthquake Weather*) and meeting up with the queen herself, the gateway to the land and the manifestation of the moon. Another good source for this take on the return of Ubas/Irem and the love story between the Sacred King and Divine Queen is Weston's *From Ritual to Romance* or Sir James Frazer's The *Golden Bough*. Imagine the sweeping desert sands, the lone man standing against the power of his own people and the Turkish nation, leading the Arabs to their destiny while forever driven by his love for this presence from Biblical times. It's kind of *The Mummy* in reverse, now that I think about it.

In this version, of course, when Lawrence falls off that motorcycle, his friends (being anthropologists and archaeologists) know enough to immure his sacred flesh quickly and send him off to Arabia secretly, where he is buried in Ubas, awaiting the return to this world of his queen, who will call him forth to once again defend his beloved Arabia from all harm. Hell, as I pointed out before, the *lapis ex caelis*, the Holy Grail, lies in Mecca awaiting the king. Perhaps even now, "al-Aurens" walks the streets of the land he so loves, at last reunited with his queen in the city which is all cities at once. Which is a rather upbeat ending for one of my rambles, and a good place to stop.

Chaos

Verily at the first Chaos came to be.
Hesiod, ***Theogony***

Wild patterns disrupt the boundary between fluid and solid. Energy drains rapidly from large-scale motions to small. Why? The best ideas came from mathematicians; for most physicists, turbulence was too dangerous to waste time on. It seemed almost unknowable. There was a story about the quantum theorist Werner Heisenberg, on his deathbed, declaring that he will have two questions for God: why relativity, and why turbulence. Heisenberg says, "I really think He may have an answer to the first question."
James Gleick, ***Chaos - Making a New Science***

Truly, without lies, certainly, and most definitely, that which is Below is like that which is Above, and that which is Above is like that which is Below, for the accomplishment of the miracle of one thing. And just as all things have come from One, through the mediation of One, so all things have been derived from this one thing, by Analogy. Its Father is the Sun; its Mother is the Moon. The Wind has carried it in its belly. Its nourishment is the Earth. It is the Father of every completed thing in the whole world. Its strength is intact if turned towards the Earth. Separate the Earth from Fire, the Fine from the Gross, gently and very carefully.
Hermes Trismegestus, ***The Emerald Tablet***

As I write this there are less than five months left in the Twentieth Century, which ends on December 31, 2001, due to the artificial nature of the origin of our calendar. In this century, two scientific paradigms have done much to restore the mystical and medieval to modern thought. One of them is quantum physics, and the other is chaos. Less a science than a metaphysic, chaos is many things to many people, but to me it is hope. Chaos began in mathematics (shades of Pythagoras) and is, at its heart, the study of the wildly disparate; from weather patterns on Jupiter to the crystallization of snow, chaos tries to answer real questions. Why does water make the patterns it does when it flows? Why do systems in nature from the smallest observable (the atom) to the largest (the galaxy) have an underlying symmetry that would seem more at home to a medieval cosmologist than a modern physicist?

Erwin Schrodinger saw the writing on the wall for the strict rationalist. Besides giving us his famous cat thought-experiment (and thus inadvertently inspiring one of the greatest books of twentieth-century magick, Robert Anton Wilson's *Schrodinger's Cat*, written in San Francisco, where, as I have elsewhere postulated, Ormazhd lurks, waiting for the final battle; but I'm getting ahead of myself again) it occurred to Schrodinger one day that the reason that physics seemed to contribute so little to the understanding of biology was that their focuses differed so wildly. Biologists had been forced by the wild fervor of life itself to recognize the irrationality, the dynamic chaos of life itself, whereas up to that point physicists had remained strictly rational, busying themselves with such minutiae as periodic crystals and atomic weights. But deoxyribonucleic acid is an aperiodic crystal, many orders of magnitude more complex and intricate than even the most elaborate periodic.

What Scrodinger was proposing had more to do with alchemy than anything his fellows recognized at the time as actual science. But in fields from neurochemistry to meteorology, Schrodinger's ideas are being felt like the proverbial butterfly wings proposed by Konrad Lorenz (or, for that matter, the ones proposed by Ray Bradbury in his awesomely visionary "A Sound of Thunder") with the first stirrings of modern chaos theory.

All of this should seem quite familiar to us students of mythology, or poetry, or dramaturgy, or what have you. The mingling of order and disorder to create a meta-order is nothing new, and is one of the grand lynchpins of almost all myth systems, hence the by now familiar quote from Hesiod, which I really prefer to almost any other myth-system's similar pronouncements for its sheer poetry (look at the Sumerian myth of Apsu and Tiamat, or the opening of Genesis, or the Vedic creation cycle, or the Chinese pronouncements of the Way, and you find the nonlinear flow of chaos waiting for you). Poetry, in fact, is a very large part of the inspiration for modern chaos theorists like Feigenbaum and Libchaber. And one poet in particular, who was far more than a mere poet (as if being a poet was ever a mere thing), could truly be said to be the father of chaos theory.

> In his novel *Doctor Faustus* Thomas Mann has the narrator play on the common root in the German words *veruschen*, meaning to try or test, *Versuch*, experiment, and *Versuchung*, temptation-all by way of evoking the alchemist's suspect trade.
> *Peter Salm,* **Introduction to Goethe's Faust**

Chaos could well be called Goetheian physics. Feigenbaum's experiments into the nature of strange attractors and universal theory were inspired by Goethe's Theory of Colors, which argued that color itself was the result of the interaction between light and the human perceptive apparatus. Libchaber was inspired in turn by Goethe's masterful "On the Transformation of Plants," which was the poet's disguised polemic against the way physicists, following Newton's lead, were heading towards the study of minutiae and static physical phenomenon and away from a syncretic theory that would explain the forces of dynamism and flow that Goethe saw as vital to an understanding of physics in general, and existence in particular. While Newton's followers certainly won the battle (which is ironic, inasmuch as Newton himself was a deist, an alchemist, and the writer of *Praxis*, which was jam-packed with as much half-baked mysticism as he could fit in) it seems that in the late twentieth century the followers of Goethe managed to jam their feet in the door, and then blew it wide open again. Like D'Arcy Wentworth Thompson (whose *On Growth And Form* is devilishly difficult to find, but well worth it), Goethe saw all things, including life itself, as a combination of dynamic forces which must be studied in their entirety. These people argued for a real metaphysic, not a series of magical hoaxes for the credulous, but an actual overarching system that could combine all of the fields of human endeavour from art to botany, just as the Persian magi and the Alexandrian Hermeticists sought to create-just as chaos threatens to create now.

When John von Neumann, just before his death, noticed the dramatic similarities in overall function between the human brain and a hurricane (he was working on meteorology and neuroscience at the time, and if it were not for his death, well... who can say?), he was making an observation that would later inspire Konrad Lorenz and Mitchell Feigenbaum in their individual struggles to understand the nature of systems. And he was also making an observation codified in the ancient Emerald Tablet of Hermes Trismegistus. As above, so below. At every stage of the Mandelbrot set, similarities recur, just as the atoms in our brains and the whirl of our galaxies follow similar designs, guided perhaps by one single set of forces as widespread and unknowable as God. Is it a coincidence that the chaotic idea of self-similarity and the quantum idea of synchronicity so eerily replicate the basic underlying principles of almost every magickal system since the first primitive hex began? Can our will create rain? And why not, if our brains are so similar in function to hurricanes? Might storms have minds with which we can communicate? If not, then how is it possible that each atom in a magnet seems capable of communicating with all the others, informing them of which charge to manifest in which direction? As above, so below.

In the late sixties, while a lot of this thinking was going on but few outside the scientific community had any inkling of it, chaos ran rampant in our culture. A period of extreme disorganization seemed evident. Was this a reflection of the new ideas making themselves felt in science? Michael Moorcock's Lords of Chaos seem to me fit avatars of this idea, serving as impetus for the creation of a new world, one where the line between science and magick is gone. In the future, a sufficiently advanced technology may not merely be indistinguishable from magick; it may incorporate it.

This is my dream, anyway.

> You study through the great and little world,
> In order in the end to let things be
> Exactly as the Lord desires.
> In vain, that scientific rambling everywhere,
> Each one of us will learn what he can learn, no more.
> But he who takes the moment by the tail,
> He proves himself the man of the hour.
> *Johann Wolfgang von Goethe,* **Faust Book I**

When we have learned to stop inventing order and understand disorder, perhaps then we will finally apprehend what is meant by the old longing to understand the mind of God. Or, even closer to my heart, to replace God. Because children are supposed to take their parents' place, aren't they? Forgive me my hubris, as I have forgiven those who have considered themselves my superiors, amen. Who can say what the ultimate goal of a nonlinear system is? It expands in all possible directions, and for that, I shall always be grateful.

The Dragon and Marduk

On this date a vigorous attack was made upon one of the Boer forts on the north. There seems to be little doubt that the enemy had some inkling of our intention, as the fort was found to have been so strengthened as to be impregnable without scaling ladders. The attacking force consisted of two squadrons of the Protectorate Regiment and one of the Bechuanaland Rifles, backed up by three guns. So desperate was the onslaught that of the actual attacking party a forlorn hope, if ever there was one fifty-three out of eighty were killed and wounded, twenty-five of the former and twenty-eight of the latter. Several of that gallant band of officers who had been the soul of the defence were among the injured. Captain FitzClarence was wounded, Vernon, Sandford, and Paton were killed, all at the very muzzles of the enemy's guns. it must have been one of the bitterest moments of Baden-Powell's life when he shut his field-glass and said, "Let the ambulance go out!"
Sir Arthur Conan Doyle, **The Siege of Mafeking**

So I was talking to my friend Pete about mystical conspiracies the other week, and he said "Do you remember all of those weird commercials a few years back where various famous and powerful people, like Gerald Ford and Sam Nunn and Jim Lovell all admitted to being Eagle Scouts? You don't suppose there's anything hinkey about that, do you?" I responded with something along the lines of "Just ask the Kindred of the Kibbo Kift about hinkyness and Boy Scouts, my friend," and from there, we got to thinking. William DeVries, the first doctor to transplant a Jarvik 7 artificial heart, was a Scout. Lloyd Bentsen was a Scout. Ross Perot, Steven Spielberg and Bill Bradley were all Eagle Scouts. On the official Scouting website, they talk about their conservation efforts, their recruiting among Buddhists and Lutherans and their special awards; make no mistake, my friends, the Scouts are not just messing about. There's even a special Boy Scout Space Exploration Badge!

Lord Robert Baden-Powell (1857-1941) was no fool, and no

dilettante. He was a typical Victorian hero in many ways, brave, dashing, popular, and willing to play in fields of study that brush the edges of what we might consider strange and unusual. He saw military service all over the African continent, and was instrumental in many aspects of English policy in the Boer War. He was a friend of Rudyard Kipling (which is where the weird animal badges in scouting come from, as Baden-Powell freely used *The Jungle Book* as a kind of mysterious background for his fledgling organization, something Kipling seems not to have minded) and while there is absolutely no evidence that Baden-Powell was a Mason, many Masons today are initiated into the secret world of Freemasonry via the path of the Eagle, by following in the footsteps of earlier Eagle Scouts and members of the Order of the Arrow. (I should point out that at least ninety-nine percent of these Freemasons are completely harmless, and hardly world-shaking types, unlike, say, the head of the Marriot Corporation, who is an Eagle Scout.) And, of course, there is the simple fact that Baden-Powell was a legend in his homeland at a time when it was not exactly sparse for legends.

> No one had ever believed Mafeking could hold out half as long. A dozen times, as the siege dragged on, the watching nation had emerged from apprehension and despondency into renewed hope, and had been again cast down. Millions who could not follow closely or accurately the main events of the War looked day after day in the papers for the fortunes of Mafeking, and when finally the news of its relief was flashed throughout the world, the streets of London became impassable, and the floods of sterling cockney patriotism were released in such a deluge of unbridled, delirious, childish joy as was never witnessed again until Armistice Night, 1918. Nay, perhaps the famous Mafeking night holds the record.
> *Sir Winston Churchill,* **Great Contemporaries**

But why did Baden-Powell leave the army to weave his vast web of children? Perhaps because he had done all he could for England (indeed, if Mafeking had fallen, it's hard to imagine the English overcoming the loss to continue on in their role as conquerers in Africa) or perhaps it was for another reason. To me at least, the Boy Scouting movement has always evoked another, darker crusade. Yep, the Children's Crusade, where a whole bunch of kids listened to a powerful visionary and ended up as slaves in African Islamic nations. However, it would be extremely unfair to mention that here, inasmuch as to my knowledge the Boy Scouts don't go around preaching that the oceans will part for them or what have you. They do, however, have the distinction of having at least one acolyte get a lot closer to the Moon than most of us will (Jim Lovell, while he didn't get to land on it- or so we're told, anyway- did orbit it) and we all know how sacred the moon is to Islam, especially the Mahdists who Baden-Powell battled during the African campaigns. Was Scouting acting as his arm in a little mystical joke, thumbing its nose at the enemy?

Of course, I haven't even really gotten to the good weirdness yet. I mentioned the Kindred of the Kibbo Kift founded by John Hargrave in 1920 (and please, don't even bother searching the Scout pages for him, because they actually *excommunicated him from scouting.* I bet you didn't even know they could do that, huh?) and elucidated in his book *Lonecraft.*

Look, don't stare at me here, I'm not the one who named the damn book.

Like Harry Crosby and H.P. Lovecraft's Herbert West, Hargrave went a little buggy during WWI and began to think that the world as we knew it was over. Soon, he got himself tossed out of the Scouts for arguing for the ideas of noted racist crank C.H. Douglas (the same one who made so much sense to Ezra Pound that the poet ran away to Italy and supported the Fascists), started a horde of Green Shirts, and began trying to integrate weird mystical rites into Scouting (as if it needed any) in an attempt to improve the white race.

That's right, the Kindred of the Kibbo Kift were sorta-kinda racist. Big surprise, huh? While Hargrave failed in his attempt to, as Kenneth Hite puts it, return Scouting to its edenic, nature-worshipping roots, he did manage to bring to his KKK the dragon dances of the old Dragon Society, Francis Bacon's old goddess-worshipping occult colonial company headquartered in Quincy, Massachusetts. The Dragon Society experiment, centered in the old Merry Mount colony, lasted just long enough for the Pilgrim Fathers to arrest Thomas Morton in 1644 and drive the rest of them away with torches and such... which fits in nicely with what we know about Pilgrim tolerance for the strange and different, eh?

And as an aside, what's with those initials?

It must develop a technique of life in the midst of a chaotic
civilisation ...
It must have an epic quality of thought and action ...
It must fire the imagination, hold the attention and liberate
the will.
It cannot look back for a historical counterpart, it is a new
thing.
It cannot be amusingly mystical in the half-shades; it must
stand four-square in the full white light of the morning.
We have need of this instrument - this living thing - now ...
We have need of it, however feeble and halting its embryonic
emergence may be ...
because it already exists dumbly, incoherently, within the hearts
of millions of human beings ...
Because of this dire need such an instrument will take shape.
John Hargrave, **The Ritual of the Kibbo Kift**

I believe that certain
physical changes in the brain
result in a given word-this
word having the distinguished
characteristics of unreality
being born neither as a result
of connotation nor of conscious
endeavor
Harry Crosby, **A Short Introduction to the Word**

So from Hargrave, one of Baden-Powell's confidants and a
Quaker (and boy, the Pilgrims loved Quakers, didn't they?) who
ended up going crazy after being a stretcher-handler during the WWI
(shades of Crosby, who received his Black Sun revelations while an
ambulance driver in the same war, and believed that so many dead
could well have attracted the attention of some entity- perhaps a
dragon?) we get this weird occult Green Shirt faction which tried to
do in England in the 1930's what the Fascists did in Italy, and the
Nazis did in Germany (isn't it interesting that a mere year after Baden-
Powell went on his peace expedition to Europe to found Boy Scout
organizations, Hitler nationalized the German chapter of the Boy
Scouts with nary a whimper from B-P?) yet with, fortunately for us,
less success.

One wonders just how much Baden-Powell objected to all this. The man died in 1941, so it isn't as though he wouldn't have witnessed his own appointee to the position of Boy Scout Commissioner for Woodcraft and Camping's slide into megalomaniac behavior. It's obvious as well that Baden-Powell was no stranger to war and death; his experiences in the famous Mafeking siege alone pitted him against almost certain death. But unlike Hargrave and Crosby, Baden-Powell was a career soldier, inured against death and pain and madness. Is it possible that Baden-Powell and Hargrave were listening to the same occult message of destruction, the same music of a mad god, but that Baden-Powell was more inured to the sanity-shattering message of this world-eating Dragon, this Black Sun, this Messenger of the Elder Gods?

Is it possible, furthermore, that the reason Baden-Powell was so afraid of the release of the ambulances is that he knew the men driving those carts would be interrupting his sacrifices to the Old Gods, and in so doing might well be exposed to those malign and powerful ancient ones from beyond time and space, without the mystical protections he himself had learned from long association with Qabbalists and mystics in higher Victorian society?

Are the Boy Scouts a conspiracy dedicated to the slow path, the gradual maturation of the kine of humanity into a proper sacrifice for the beings from outside? Is that why Scouting is still here, whereas other groups with magic rituals and strange orders go by the wayside? And, if every member of the Boy Scouts is expected to take part in some kind of mass sacrifice as laid out by Baden-Powell himself, is that the reason the Scouts are so dogmatic on the subject of homosexuality? (After all, a gay man cannot be sacrificed as Dumuzi, beloved of Innana;such would be sacred to Gilgamesh and Enkidu instead, rather than the capricious Goddess of the Morning Star, sometimes-ally to Marduk, whose symbol was the dragon, and who was known as the Lord of the Eclipse- the Black Sun.) Were Hargraves and Crosby unfortunates who stumbled upon a horror that battened upon the great death of the War to End All Wars and were blasted into insanity for their interference? Did Baden-Powell promote Hargraves upon his return from the war due to his sense that the man was a kindred spirit, only to see him degenerate and fall away in a few short years, and so force an excommunication?

Remember, they're everywhere, in every political party, in every walk of life. They intend to colonize space and explore all the world. They probably don't know that they are intended to be sacrifices, but the clues are there in Hargraves' *Lonecraft*. *Lonecraft*, indeed. (Note: If you happen to be a Boy Scout, try not to take any of this too seriously, okay? Lord Baden-Powell was a great guy, I'm sure, and remember, I just make all of this stuff up, okay? So please don't loose the Order of the Arrow to slay me dead and make it look like an accident, okay?)

Welcome to the Mountain of Paradise

Welcome to California, the Unseelie Kingdom of America.

California has an undeserved reputation for strangeness. (Or, more accurately, the rest of the nation has an unfair bias against strangeness.) People on the East Coast snicker at Californians as fruits and nuts, referring in no small part to those people who have escaped to the West Coast in order to be free to pursue ideals or lifestyles outside the narrowly defined "norm" of America. What people don't realize is that California is no odder than any other part of the country, exactly; it's just that the rules of reality run a little widdershins there. California is the remnant of a magical experiment, heir to the fantastic energies of the native people of the American continents welded to the visionary mysticism of men like Lope de Vega, Cervantes, and Garcia Ordonez de Montalvo. California is Aztlan melded with Avalon, and it all began with the magi of Persia, before the birth of Christ.

> "Rollant, my friend, fair youth that bar'st the bell,
> When I arrive at Aix, in my Chapelle,
> Men coming there will ask what news I tell;
> I'll say to them: 'Marvellous news and fell.
> My nephew's dead, who won for me such realms!'
> Against me then the Saxon will rebel,
> Hungar, Bulgar, and many hostile men,
> Romain, Puillain, all those are in Palerne,
> And in Affrike, and those in Califerne"
> **The Song of Roland**, Lines 2915-2924, Translated by Charles Scott Moncrief

The world *California* is of ancient origin, entering the Spanish language via the Muslim conquest of the Iberian Peninsula (which is how it entered into *Le Chanson de Roland* as well), and its roots run deep. *Kar-i-Farn* is the legendary Mountain of Paradise in pre-Avestic Zoroastrianism, where Ormazhd and Ahriman will do battle for the souls of humanity and the world as we know it will come to an end. It has been preserved for us in many ways great and small throughout history: Alamut of the Hashish Eaters, that sect of killers who slew under the orders of the great Hassan I Sabbah, is but a pale reflection of paradise's glory. The poet Omar Khayyam, an initiate of Sabbah's, wrote the *Rubiyaat* about the paradise on earth which entered into Islamic thought via the conquest of Persia, now Iran.

But how, you may ask, did California get from Persia to the Americas? One of Hassan I Sabbah's titles was *Sheik-al-Gebel*, the Old Man of the Mountain, and we know that the Hashish Eaters believed in using chemicals to alter the perceptions; while the first rank of initiates were simple killers, obviously there were higher ranks, maintained by poets and scholars like Omar Khayyam. When Islam conquered Iberia, Moorish and Spanish blood intermingled, and the mystical understanding of the Hashishin entered into the magickal thought of the peninsula.

In 1510, Spain was a rising power, its domination of the new source of gold and slaves swelling its influence over Europe. At that time, Garcia Ordonez de Montalvo wrote a book entitled *Las Sergas del Esplandian*, which portrayed a magic island named California swarming with griffins and with Amazons who were rather loose with their affections. It resonated with an earlier work by the Englishman Sir John Mandeville, the infamous *Travels*, which portrayed the Amazons as living between modern Azerbaijan and Persia, in the mountains on the Silk Road to India. Now, why would Montalvo (yes, again, the name derives from 'mountain') displace the Amazons? Because the very mountains they lived amidst were the mountains of Alamut, where the Persian paradise is located. In magick, transference is a powerful tool, especially when attempting to create a bond between the Old World and the New. But while the School of Night would later seek to conquer the magic of the natives with their own, the people of the Californian conspiracy were after synergy. They wanted to fuse the power of the old with the new.

In California today, Mount Shasta stands as a monument to the old merging with the new. Hollow Earth enthusiasts believe it to be where the Agarthan Secret Masters ascend to speak to select humans. The Heaven's Gate cult thought it was where the Hale Bopp aliens would land to pick them up. The native tribes called it *Wyreka*, the "Mountain to the North." From Lemurians to aliens to Gitche Manitou to Bigfoot sightings, Mount Shasta's seen it all. In 1934 (the same year that Flash Gordon was blasting off to Mongo, oddly enough), Guy Warren Ballard published *Unveiled Mysteries*, wherein he alleged that he met a mysterious old man on the mountain (a Sheik-al-Gabal, perhaps) who gave him a "creamy liquid to drink" and then revealed himself to be the Comte de Saint-Germaine, the supposed immortal magus of indeterminate origins who seems to have had a hand in everything from Transylvanian succession (a lot of mountains in Transylvania) to the mystical education of Cagliostro, the Masonic master (and possible con man) who was born Guiseppe Balsamo, and who may or may not have taught Thomas Jefferson how to transmigrate his soul. As you can see, an impressive amount of weirdness swirls around Mount Shasta. Is it *Kar-i-farn*? I believe it is, as Mount Olympus was the divine heart of Greece. Shasta is *El-Gabal*, the Mountain God, home of the Old Man. Yet Greece had two other hearts, and so does magical California. The Iberian mages planned it that way.

> **Paradise:** From old Persian (Zeud) *pairedaeza* an enclosure, a walled-in-place; Old Persian *pairi*, around, *dig*, to mould, form, shape (hence to form a wall of earth.) *Paradise* has been sought for or located in many regions of the earth. In Tartary, Armenia, India and China: on the banks of the Euphrates and of the Ganges; in Mesopotamia, Syria, Persia, Arabia, Palestine and Ethiopia, and near the mountains of Libanus and Anti-libanus.
>
> *Lewis Spence, **An Encyclopedia of Occultism***

Imagine, if you will, that California is a very deliberate attempt to harness the awesome magical power of the American continents and channel it along lines of thought brought to Spain centuries before, when the first Moorish armies flooded across the Pillars of Heracles in A.D. 711. By utilizing the principles of contagion and similarity, a link was to be forged between Alamut and the Pyrenees to create Calyferne as a ink for the *Hashishin* to use. With Roland's sacrifice, however, a backlash eventually allowed that warrior's soul to re-enter the world in the body of Rodrigo Diaz, known as *Sayyid*, the Lord by the armies of Islam and *El Cid* to the Spanish. If at first you don't succeed, however, you try again. Assimilated into Spanish culture, these neo-Hashishin were willing to attempt a similar feat in this new world. They were helped by their enemies' ignorance of their design. (Similarly, when the English learn of this magickal working, they will attempt one of their own on Roanoke Island.) By taking elements that were already present, like Mount Shasta, and grafting elements of their own onto them, like Kar-i-farn, a true alchemical nation could be created.

Mount Shasta is the divine heart. Where, then, is the mind of the Californian dream state? San Francisco is home of the Emperor Norton I, Fisher King of the West and Discordian Maimed King par excellance. Norton symbolizes the insane meta-sanity of the Californian experiment. He declared himself emperor, and nobody minded. It has long been pointed out that in Islam, the mad are considered divine, and so too with the Iberian descendants of the Hashish Eaters who carefully constructed California. Norton is Quetzalcoatl, the bearded white god from the east, born in Deptford, England (where Chris Marlowe was assassinated- a connection to the School of Night? An English attempt to usurp the magick, or perhaps the Sheik-al-Gabal thinks further ahead than we can imagine, and in Norton saw a perfect chance to combine two magical empires in one) and intimate with the sea and with pirates (at one time, he owned a great shard of the Barbary Coast) as well. One might say that San Francisco is the Athens of California, and Norton was its Solon. From the gleeful Discordians of Robert Anton Wilson fame to the airships of the 1890's onward to the present, with every bend and twist along the way, San Francisco has survived earthquakes and the 1960's and the death of Harvey Milk. In San Francisco men like Terrance McKenna argued for the chemical liberation of the unconscious mind, which surely must have led the Old Man of the Mountain and his Hashish Eaters to grin knowingly. San Francisco is the Sacrificed City, the Mithras of the West Coast, where Ormazhd weeps mad with mourning for his dead son.

> Father, O father! what do we here,
> In this land of unbelief and fear?
> The land of dreams is better far

Above the light of the Morning Star.
*William Blake, **Songs of Innocence***

Los Angeles, of course, is the Smoking Mirror, where the defiled spirits of the dethroned Aztec gods refuse to die. It is the Waste Land of Eliot, the Inferno of Dante, and yet... there is power here too, a power ripped from the desert by sheer will and influence. The Bright Son of Morning has gilded his half of the Californian paradise, for we mustn't forget that paradise is where the final battle will be waged. Please don't think I view Los Angeles as evil, however; I quoted Blake for a reason. An act of magick such as the creation of California, a theft so brazen as this, must have its backlash. The outrage must be addressed; there must be a city to evoke this experience. A city which shows us the penalty for hubris and encourages it. A Sparta, a Rome, a Constantinople, the black dot in the white to San Francisco's white dot in the black. Call it yin and yang, call it balance, call it the Ouroboros facing itself. Ahriman waits among the gilded streets of Los Angeles.

The state of California throbs with concentrated dream energy, crackling and burning as it slams into the bowshock of the American zeitgeist. The combination of the East and the West has created a mad empire, a burning land of gunmen and poets, con-men and Christs. If America is Arcadia, then California is *Tir Tairngiri*, the Land of Promise. The Old Man of the Mountain wrought better than anyone understood when he shaped paradise in the New World, for in Los Angeles and San Francisco, you can see Ahriman and Ormazhd gearing up for the final battle. But the old tempter has grown wise and cunning and the great white lord is demented and brilliant, and who can say who the winner should be?

Not me.

Green Children and the Caul-Born

> According to William of Newburgh, the children were "clad in garments of strange color and unknown materials." They could speak no English and refused all food offered to them. A few days later, on the brink of starvation, they were brought "beans cut off from the stalks," wrote Abbot Ralph of Coggeshall, who allegedly had the story from de Calne himself. The children "broke open the beanstalks, not the pod or shell of the beans, evidently supposing that the beans were contained in the hollows of the stalks. But not finding beans within the stalks they again began to weep, which, when the bystanders noticed, they opened the shells and showed them the beans themselves. Whereupon, with great joyfulness, they ate beans for a long time, and would touch no other food." Soon the children were baptized, and not long afterward the boy weakened and died.
>
> *Jerome Clarke,* ***Unexplained!***

Green Children. They appear at the strangest times, they disturb and dismay us, and then they merge seemingly seamlessly into the fabric of history. The Greenlings are a mystery, all right, an enigma so terrifyingly vast in their implications that we need to begin examining them with great care and seriousness. After all, somebody has to.

There are stories of the Green Children that serve as templates for the rest. Generally speaking, there's the English appearance of the twelfth century and the Spanish incident of 1809. Each is a mirror of the other; green children supposedly appear out of nowhere, wandering in a field, and are taken into a town. At first, they are impossible to care for. Eventually, a kind of plant matter (beans in the English report, seeds in the Spanish) is found that they consider palatable. In all three cases, after baptism the boy dies, and the girl is assimilated, her skin tone returning to the normal hues of European humanity. Thereupon, it is remarked that the girl grows up to be loose and wanton in her conduct, as Ralph of Coggeshall wrote of the English child.

> She asserted that the inhabitants, and all that they had in that country, were of a green color; and that they saw no sun, but enjoyed a degree of light like what is after sunset. Being asked how she came into this country with the aforesaid boy, she replied, that as they were following their flocks they came to a certain cavern, until they came to its mouth. When they came out of it, they were struck senseless by the excessive light of the sun, and the unusual temperature of the air, and thus they lay for a long time. Being terrified by the noise of those who came on them, they wished to fly, but they could not find the entrance of the cavern before they were caught.
> *Ralph of Coggeshall's Testimony*

Perhaps they could not find it because it didn't exist on this side? The story of the Green Children brings to mind almost inexorably the possibility of Gentry involvement. For years, the people of Suffolk have been finding the flint arrowheads modern archaology defines as Beaker-Folk and which the villagers call Elfshot. What if they're both right? What if the pre-Celtic inhabitants of Britian saw that these newcomers (the people of the Goddess Donu, as transmitted in variant form by Irish Celtic sources) were going to overwhelm the islands with their powerful war craft and strange magics? Rather than fight, perhaps the Beaker-Folk climbed into a fae mound and closed it up after them. Is it possible that the paleolithic peoples of Europe exist in a tesseract network under the soil of the Eurasian continent, invoking ancient totemic magics to align themselves to various vegetation spirits (which explains why they cannot eat any but a chosen plant; it's a *geas*, similar to the idea the Celts maintained, a kind of taboo) in order to lock their lifeweb in place? Perhaps, as the overlanders grow more numerous and plant over fields that were once free range, they disrupt the totem magics and cause mystical feedback, bending and twisting their grains in the odd formations we call crop circles. (This would be dire indeed for the Beaker-Folk inside their tesseracts, for every disrupted totem spirt would mean the shrinking of their pocket realm.)

This would also explain why the sightings of Green Children coincide with great tumult in the world above. In short, war fucks up the earth, which shrinks the totem web, which creates openings to the surface that weren't there before. Children stumble through them, and are found. Simple.

Maybe too simple. We all know the stories about fae kidnappings of children. What if the Green Children are in fact an example of human kidnappings of fae children? Reverse changelings, if you will. Perhaps, in order to make the human kidnap victims suitable for life in the tesseract, they must be bonded to one of the offspring of the Beaker-Folk. Then, like mystical siamese twins, they are always together, and what affects the one affects the other.

A sect of mystics with, perhaps, great connection to the power of vegetation, the mysterious Benandanti, the caul-born dream witches who fight on every solstice to prevent the death of the natural world from darkness and evil. Allies to werewolves and sorcerers, the Benandanti know the otherworld very, very well. It's possible they are attuned enough to the plant kingdom to sense the breakdown of the totem web, and take advantage of it when it happens. Isn't it odd that there are always pursuers close at hand whenever the Green Children step forth from the interstices between worlds?

As to why the Benandanti would concern themselves, first off, they are somewhat vain and proud, like all good self-appointed heroes, and might well see the theft of human children as wrong. Secondly, they would see the Beaker-Folk as overstaying their welcome; connected as they are to the powers of the natural world, the Benandanti know that all things change, and all things die. But why, you may ask, do the boy children always die? Good question. Because they aren't boy children at all. They are vegetative homunculi, created in order to ensure that the plant spirits can continue their bond with these new adoptive Beaker People. Benandanti would know this, and would know how to sever this plant-bond.

Perhaps the women who grow to adulthood in this fashion, freed from slavery and loose and wanton of character, in other words free spirited, make excellent Benandanti. Of course, we still haven't discussed another possibility, one that connects with these others....

> Sharpe alleged that for years evil creatures known as "Deros"- short for "detrimental robots" (who were not robots as the term is ordinarily understood but "robots" in the sense of being

slaves to their passions) had tormented him. Deros were the degenerate remains of the "Titans," the people... who 12000 years ago were forced to escape into great caverns under the earth... (Some Titans, however, stayed on the surface, adjusted, and became the present human race. Others fled to distant planets.) Deros- demons in all but name and close to it even there- were sadistic idiots who had access to the advanced Titan technology, which they used to increase sexual pleasure during the orgies to which they were addicted. They also used the machines in marathon torture sessions on kidnapped surface people and on the "Teros" (Integrative Robots, also not robots but good Titans who, though vastly outnumbered, were fighting the deros); they also used the machines to create accidents, madness and other miseries in the world above the caves.

Jerome Clark, **Unexplained!**

Here we go, then, into the Hollow Earth. Imagine this interconnection; the nanotechnology of the Titans I have mentioned elsewhere, and their grand civilization on Minoan Crete. After the war between the Titans and the Olympians, the Olympians rule the world while the Titans flee into the great caverns beneath the earth. Then, after the war between Typhon and Zeus, the Olympians flee into outer space and Typhon descends with Echidna, his Egyptian sphinx-bride, into the caverns of the Titans. What he finds sickens him; the Titans have degenerated into squat pleasure addicts, monstrous creatures unfit to be called Titans. Thus the formation of what Richard Sharpe Shaver (a shithouse rat crazy bastard who probably got the dates wrong anyway and had little understanding of nanotechnology, hence his pell-mell definition of everybody involved as "robots;" he was unable to understand that they weren't robots, but merely contained millions of microscopic robots inside them) calls the "Deros" and the "Teros." The Beaker People and their later Celtic successors most likely called them the Unseelie and Seelie camps of the fae folk. When the Beaker People created the totem web, they didn't realize they were heading straight into a trap set by the Unseelie, who enslaved them, used them for sport, and forced them to kidnap others for their amusement.

Therefore, the Benandanti (who are probably being fed information by the Typhonian Seelie) are working to free the Beaker

45

People from the clutches of their dark masters, who lurk in the bowels of the tesseract web, in the heart of the endless hollow earth. For as we know, for some strange reason the Titans have always thought kindly of humanity. Perhaps it's as simple as a mother's love for her children? Who knows? Whatever it is, this is but one manifestation of that endless war, one that encompasses many fronts on the small blue ball riddled with holes we live on.

Well, it's one explanation, anyway.

The Peal of the Bell

Imagine a world where one man could nearly bring about the end of a civilization by means of his terrible brilliance and an invention unfathomable to science. A world where a father could kill his own son in order to test a device's ability to ressurect him, not once, or twice, but a thousand times. Imagine over a billion Chinese annihilated by the Western powers in a bacteriological holocaust in the far-flung future world of... 1976.

If you were to imagine this world, you would be too late. One man already did it for you. That man was Jack London.

> The madness of magic was in the air. With the people it was as if all their gods had crashed and the heavens still stood. Order and law has passed away from the universe; but the sun still shone, the wind still blew, the flowers still bloomed- that was the amazing thing about it. That water should continue to run downhill was a miracle. All stabilities of the human mind and human achievement were crumbling. The one stable thing that remained was Goliah, a madman on an island.
> *Jack London,* **Goliah**

Most people who know London know him from being forced to read *The Call of the Wild* in junior high and possibly *The Sea Wolf* in college, if they took the right (or some might say the wrong) courses. But while London the naturalist writer had a head full of socialism and a heart burning with rage at the poverty he was born into and the assumptions others made about his brawny frame, London the mad fantasist didn't have time to preach in his works. He was too busy predicting that someday it might be possible for the planet earth to be sealed off and unfettered from the gravity of the sun, transforming our world into a wandering starship, or warning of the dangerous plagues that might arise from human beings packed like freight in an overpopulated world (keep in mind, this was penned in

1902... The Hot Zone wasn't even a hinted at in the most dire predictions of medicine at that time). He also foreshadowed the barbarity and mindlessness of a mankind degraded through economic slavery and information sequestration, when he wasn't waxing rhapsodic about anti-agathic drugs and coolly stating cryptozoological heresies years before any other writer would take such notions to heart.

London seems, in fact, to have created at least three alternate timelines, all of which branch off from the main root of his initial idea. In one, the mad anarchist and wronged genius Professor Emil Gluck develops a device which can detonate gunpowder at long range by means of electromagnetic energy projection. (Shades of Nikola Tesla's broadcast power, you say? Why, that never occurred to me, your narrator grins wolfishly...) Gluck sets off a war between Europe and America that only ends with his execution on December 4, 1941. From this timeline, we seem to have three possible options.

One leads to 1976 and the Chinese holocaust, as the world's fear of a "Yellow Peril" from over a billion Chinese leads the nations of the world to unleash a host of bacteriological weapons upon China, causing the extinction of all the peoples of Asia. (London had little respect for others when writing... in a note to a friend while writing *Goliah*, he said with glee, "Yesterday, I annihilated the Japanese Navy. Today, the Americans get it! I haven't a bit of conscience when my imagination gets to working.") And, seemingly as a result of these weapons, the eventual creation of the Scarlet Death which kills off practically everyone else, leaving one person in ten million alive. If this reminds you of *The Stand* you aren't alone. The great wheel spins round at the end of London's *Kali Yuga* and man prepares to pick up the old ways again, as his numbers increase and tensions begin to reassert themselves.

Also leading from the nexus point of Gluck's anarchistic rampage is the timeline of *Goliah*, where a little old man named Percival Stultz manages to so terrorize the world that he forces it to disarm and rules as a semi-Socialist dictator. Some see this as London's great wish fulfillment, the world as Socialist paradise, but a closer reading will in fact see a dreadful warning in the tale, a harbinger of fascism at its worst. London had no sympathy for his pathetic, dreary little tyrant. The far future of this world is that of Asgard, which was

London at his most scientifically fantastic, a kind of wonderworld that would inspire George Orwell in his writing of *1984*.

Finally comes the nightmare of nightmares, London's greatest fear- the dictatorship of the bourgoisie. The owners continue to own, and prevent others from profiting from their own work. Eventually, financial and economic servitude become full-fledged slavery again, as those who are not owners are declared herd animals and have literacy stripped away from them. Itinerant song-singers and tale-tellers are used as controls, spinning fantastic yarns to keep the ignorant happy. But these same tellers of stories are the ones who have kept the written word alive, and they slowly spread the dangerous fever of independent thought, and the secret magic of deciphering the squiggles that have meaning.

Capering in the vast shadows thrown by these three pillars of foreseen futures come other forms: a dead man back from the grave to enact his wedding vows; a hunter whose exploits in the frozen Yukon have led him through a strange gap in time and space; a man who by day is a mild-mannered businessman and yet is a shell within which beats the heart of a beast-man from long ago savage enough to kill a bear with his bare hands; two men alike in interest and aptitudes, who both seek invisibility and would kill to possess it, and do; and a starstone which may contain the last words of an angel cast from heaven. None of these are necessarily connected, yet all connect, and all are obviously cut from the same cloth. The question is, however, is that cloth one of London's imagining, or did he receive it from somewhere else?

> London's idealistic and imaginative preoccupations seem decidedly out of tune with the presumably rational and scientific approach to things he found and embraced in his self-educational steeping in Darwin, Spencer, and Karl Marx. But London was forever a man of philosophical contradictions (his individualism versus his socialism being the most critical in any thorough examination of his career) and his periodic experimentation in fantasy fiction is perhaps not so extraordinary as it is a neglected aspect of his contribution to American Literature.
> *Dale L. Walker, **The Alien Worlds of Jack London***

Not extraordinary. That a man of a literary generation that prized naturalism, the rendering of things as they were believed to actually be, above all else, would write about time-lost mammoths, atavistic barbarian bankers, planets that could be detached from their stars, the annihilation of ninety-nine percent of the population of the earth, and so on in the most rational, ordered and logical way? Well, no, it really isn't all that extraordinary. I actually have no difficulty believing that.

Yet let me play Lucifer's advocate for a moment (as I often admit that I am) and sing a song of something else. London traveled far in his life, from the West to the East, to the wide open Yukon of his most famous tales and the south sea islands he so enjoyed. Who is to say this young dreamer, disinherited by his father, cursed by a body belonging more to a war god out of myth than the poet he sought so hard to be, didn't find a bit of magic on his travels? He strode the world from the great wound of the meteor impact in Hudson Bay to the warrior natives of the Pacific... there were secrets to be learned, if he was of a mind to. And I believe he was. I believe London learned how to pierce the barrier between our world and the *eigenstate* of quantum physics, staring forth into alternate realities first at the feet of an Inuit shaman, and then among the mad and respectful Amok of Polynesia. He saw other worlds, other sciences, other ways of living. The strain was, of course, terrible, for as was pointed out at the very year of his birth by Friedrich Nietzsche, staring across such gulfs could allow them access into your own.

Imagine that London and a few other souls of his era with minds broad enough to handle such gulfs, men like Ambrose Bierce and Stephen Crane, all took up arms against these otherworldly invaders, as was well within their ability and natures. Crane's death in 1900 may well have been a warning from extradimensional invaders, mad inventors like Emil Gluck and the deranged narrator of London's "A Thousand Deaths" who sought to breach the barrier between worlds. So attacked, our world's defenders would have struck back, but while we have so far escaped the tyrants and germ warfare London foresaw, it cost him his life in 1916, and Bierce disappeared in 1914 while on a trip to Mexico which was certainly the end of him, one way or another. Bierce's disappearance led Charles Fort, that indefatigable investigator of the bizarre, to ruminate, "Is someone collecting Ambroses?" after another one vanished in New York later.

Perhaps Bierce's otherworldly enemies didn't know it wasn't him?

Very often writers of weird and fantastic tales die young, or in conditions of mystery or tragedy. Robert E. Howard was not yet thirty when he shot himself, H.P. Lovecraft died barely out of his forties, as did Poe; Guy De Maupassant went mad and died in a Paris sanatarium, hopelessly syphilitic; Rene Descartes (who wrote amusing fantasies as well as philosophical texts) was apparently poisoned while attending the Swedish court and his head taken from his body... the list goes on. Has our world been under consistent threat of invasion from other mindsets, warded off only by the sacrifice of our most unconventional and brilliant explorers of the uncharted depths of language?

Well, probably not. But tonight, before you go to sleep, I challenge you to read Jorge Luis Borges' *Tlon, Uqbar, Orbis Tertius* or for that matter any of London's tales of cosmic hostility and human indomitability in the teeth of such. (The text I have is named *Jack London's Fantastic Tales*, which is fairly accurate if not especially creatively titled- London would have done better.) I promise that thoughts you may not want to have will be yours.

Which, as always, is the best gift I can give you.

The Killer of Gods

> After Zeus had driven the Titans from the sky, monstrous Earth
> gave birth to her youngest child Typhoeus, after being united
> in love by golden Aphrodite with Tartarus. Typhoeus is a god
> of strength: there is force in his active hands and his feet
> never tire. A hundred snake heads grew from the shoulders of
> this terrible dragon, with black tongues flickering and fire
> flashing from the eyes under the brows of those prodigious
> heads. And in each of those terrible heads there were voices
> beyond description: they uttered every kind of sound;
> sometimes they spoke the language of the gods; sometimes
> they made the bellowing noise of a proud and raging bull, or
> the noise of a lion relentless and strong, or strange noises like
> dogs; sometimes there was a hiss and the high mountains re-
> echoed. The day of his birth would have seen the disaster of
> his becoming the ruler of men and gods, if their great father
> had not been quick to perceive the danger.
> Hesiod, **Theogony,** Book XII

Call us Legion, for we are many. When considering the last and
strongest of the Titans, we must take care to remember that his was
no ordinary birth; unlike the other Titans, his father was not Sky but
Hell itself, and his mother gave him life to vent her rage at the abuses
of the Olympians. Typhon was not as others were. Of all the enemies
of Zeus Sky-Father, only Typhon could match the Thunderer in
power. (And indeed overmatch him; Typhon tore Zeus' tendons out
of his immortal flesh and used them to tether him to the very rock of
Mount Olympus itself. If not for the other Olympians, Heracles, the
Cyclopes and the Hundred-Handed Giants, Zeus would have lain on
that mountain longer than Prometheus lay on his.) And of all the
divine beings of the Hesiodian imagination, only Typhon could match
Zeus' prolific shape-changing and fecundity. (Indeed, it was Typhon
who fathered the great three-headed hound Cerberus, the Nemedian
Lion, the Symphalian Birds, the Hydra, and other such terrors.)
Unlike Zeus, however, Typhon was faithful to his monstrous bride

Echidna, and all his offspring were hers as well.

So let's look. Typhon didn't shapeshift and rape mortal women. Typhon stayed loyal to his wife and loved his children. Typhon opposed cruel bloodthirsty Zeus, who drowned all the men and women of the Earth, who slew Aesculpias the healer, who unleashed the curses of Pandora's box upon the world, whose violent storms slay unwitting mankind and who crucified Prometheus on a mountaintop for the crime of worrying about mortals so much that he would dare give them fire. Hesiod himself described the reign of the Titans over the Earth as a golden age where mankind never sickened or died. Why, pray tell, were the Greeks rooting for Zeus? What was Typhon, mightiest of the Titans and the children of earth, and why did the Titans care more for mankind than the Olympian gods did?

> Of all the children of great Earth and Sky these were the boldest, and their father hated them from the beginning. As each of them was about to be born, Sky would not let them reach the light of day; instead he hid them all away in the bowels of Mother Earth. Sky took pleasure at doing this evil thing.
> Hesiod, **Theogony,** Book III

Sky perpetrates outrages upon Earth, and she asks her children the Titans for help. Only one of them, Cronos, dares to do as she asks and castrates his dark father, the rapist and abuser Uranos. Then, apparently drunk with power, Cronos emulates his father to an extent and refuses to allow his own offspring to be born in response to Uranos' curse that a son of Cronos shall do to him what Cronos has to Uranos. Now, we only have Hesiod's, and the Greeks', word that Cronos was doing this out of evil intent, and considering how willing they were to go along with Zeus and the Olympian order, we can't trust them. (Even though they themselves admit that under Cronos, mankind lived in a golden age, an edenic paradise.) Befire turing our attentions to Typhon, let us first examine Cronos... the Titan of Time.

Cronos is the being we also know as Saturn, and who we mean when we think of Father Time. Cronos knew past, present and future. Before the Fates, or the Furies, it was Cronos who with his sickle reaped the strands of destiny, and you'll note that under Cronos no one sickened and died. Now, what does this mean? Let us assume that to every myth, there is a kernel of truth. Was Cronos the king of Crete? Was he the one who found the secrets of the Earth Power that allowed the Cretans to rule in the Mediterranean? Or perhaps he was the first to find the alien starship with the nanotechnology that allowed his people to become as gods. Whatever Cronos was, if you weren't an Olympian he seems to have been a fine fellow. Did he forsee that the same nanotechnology that made him and his people Titans would have a less salutary effect on their offspring, and in exchange for immortality forced them to agree to end their reproductive roles?

Imagine, if you will, a fallen starcraft in the Cretan mountains. It is damaged beyond recognition, and fragments of it (perhaps the same fragments that will transform the Scythians into vampires) have broken away and rained down on the distant corners of the Earth. However, one tribe finds it and manages to get the nanotech assemblers on-line, and with those engines of creation can create wonders that transform the human body into examples of inhuman perfection. Cronos, the first discoverer of the device, has literally freed his people from the bowels of the earth via his usurpation of this skyborn device. But while these Titans (Greek for "tighteners," for as they tightened the noose around Uranos, so did he wrap his curse taut about them) still remember what it is to be mortal, all the shocks and pains that flesh is heir to, Cronos' new advanced mind can act like a supercomputer, and it tells him that if he allows his people to breed, their children will not remember what it was like to be merely human, and they will plague humanity, seeing their unimproved cousins as playthings. He therefore forbids it. (Perhaps he even senses that the offspring must always go further than the parents, as a form of rebellion- cruelty and madness as a sign of superiority to their progenitors, as a kind of metaphysical rebellion? Shapeshifting as the ancient equivalent of that devil-horn implant craze?)

But his wife Rhea disobeys. Unconvinced by Cronos' arguments (perhaps foolishly, he has kept the mental enhancement that allows his brain to act as a supercomputer to himself) she manages to conceive and hide the fact from him. Thus, she gives birth to her eldest child, Hades. Cronos is horrified by how thoroughly the infant is infiltrated by the nanites, and uses the fallen ship's stasis pods in an attempt to permanently imprison the child. But others among the Titans follow Rhea's lead... and the Titans are doomed, as their offspring come darkly into the world, with giant eyes and twisted, many-handed bodies and bestial forms and the ability to warp their bodies at command. These new beings overthrow the Titans, abandon Crete (after burying the craft in one of the area's common earthquakes) and set up a reign of blood and death on the Greek mainland. The site of the ship's burial is called Tartarus after the sufferings of the imprisoned immortals buried forever in the stone. This reign of the Olympians precipitates the Mediterranean Dark Age, as the ancient civilizations either fall before their might (the Hittites, Akkadians and Cyprus/Palestine) or battle with their own strange magics which may or may not have been born from that crashed stellar vessel (the Scythians, Etruscans and Egyptians).

Till the coming of Typhon. Most likely, Typhon was simply a villager from one of the Cretan communities devastated by this strange mythic war of the gods on earth, and he stumbled upon Tartarus, an area rife with the transformative power of the nanotechnology of the Titans, who were trying desperately to find some way out. And they did, each of them infecting Typhon in turn, until he basically became a seething pool of molecular machines, each from a different Titan, each giving him a different power and a hybrid form which, while hardly pleasant to look at, matched the demonic visage of the Olympian's hundred-handed shocktroopers and their cyclopean weaponsmiths.

Seeking allies, Typhon went to Egypt (it's worthwhile to point out that the Egyptians had no problem at all identifying Typhon with Set, the God of Foreigners; perhaps it was this visit that inspired the legend) where he recruited beings like himself, strange inhuman monstrosities born from Egyptian experimentation combining the nanotech with the recently slain bodies of beasts and men. This army of creatures would become the inspiration for Typhon's brood of monsters. Perhaps the resemblance between the Echidna of ancient Greek myth and the statue of the Sphinx isn't a coincidence? (It's worth noting that the Greeks had sphinxes in their mythology as well, and the Nemedian Lion was the offspring of Typhon and

Echidna... another sphinx?) If Typhon's mate was a creation of the Egyptians' desperate resistance to the rule of Ammon (the Bull of Heaven, the Egyptian diety most often compared with Zeus), then Typhon/Set's murder of the pharoah Osiris makes sense, as the God Emperor of the Nile could well have been a puppet of the Olympians. (It's worthwhile to note that Isis and Osiris belong to that order of Egyptian dieties who lack the bestial attributes of the earlier gods like Ra and Set. It's also interesting that Isis is well known for having tricked Ra into giving her his magical knowledge- perhaps the science that allowed her to infuse her husband's corpse with nanites, bringing it back from death.)

This, of course, leads us to the war of Typhon and Zeus, the destruction of Mount Aetna, and the end of the Greek Dark Ages. I suspect we'll never know who won. The Greek sources, of course, say that it was Zeus, although they differ greatly as to how. Hesiod argues that Zeus did it by himself, while the cult of Olympian Zeus wrote that he required the aid of all the gods and Heracles, as Robert Graves pointed out. At any rate, Zeus was unable to kill Typhon in this version and had to settle for imprisoning him in an active volcano. The Egyptian and Hittite sources argue that the great serpent Apophis (in Hittite myth, he doesn't really have a name) will eventually swallow the barque of the sun or crush the Thunder God once and for all. If Typhon and Set are the same, then the fact that he was available in Egypt to fight with Horus implies that he at least stalemated Zeus and returned to the land of the beast-gods. While he loses to Horus in most versions of the Egyptian myth, it's telling that the pharoahs Seti and Ramses both considered Set to be their patron and the leader of their resurgence into prominence on the world scene.

Did Typhon/Set, having checked the ambitions of the Olympians, settle gracefully into divine retirement? He would be as immortal as any of these nanotech gods, with total control over his form and perhaps the ability to alter the very character of his thoughts. In the stories of his battle with Zeus, the two gods threw lightning and mountains at each other, implying that they were powers unlike anything the world ever saw. However, following the Dark Ages, it's telling that very few godlike events seem to have happened. Did the destruction of Aetna serve as a cover for an atomic detonation, the EMP of which would wipe the delicate programming of the divine nanotechnology and slowly return the gods to normal humanity?

Of course, this is only one possible divine history. It doesn't have to be nanotech at all. Replace the word nanite with the words blood sacrifice or geomancy or what have you, and it will still work. The Titans could be aliens, faerie, sorcerers, an elder race of man... The thing to keep in mind is this essential paradox: if the Titans were so bad, why did they like the human race? Did they know something about us we don't?

And is it a grand secret or a sinister one?

Quantum Britannia

Napoleon loved science; at one point in his life it seemed likely that he would make it his profession. He was especially fascinated by the attractive force of gravity, and accumulated notes all his life for a thesis he hoped to write extending Newton's work to the interaction of gravity on the microscale. Much has been made of his error in invading Russia, despite his knowledge of history (he was well versed in the subject, as he was in mathematics as well as physics, having been an artillery commander) and of how the tactic had so utterly backfired on Charles XII of Sweden in 1712. Yet he did it anyway, and undid himself. (A hundred years later... What was the significance of that century? Why did Napoleon wait until 1812 to invade Russia?) What if he had not? Would he have remained on the throne of France? Let us imagine, for just a moment, that an event occurred that would have made such an outcome possible.

> The authorities searched first the inn and then all of Perleberg. Inquiries from the British Foreign Office brought a denial from Napoleon that his agents had been involved. Stories circulated that Bathurst had been robbed and murdered, that he had secretly gone on to a port and been lost at sea, and so on- but all that is known about Benjamin Bathurst's disappearance is summed up in the words of Charles Fort, that tireless collector of events that have no rhyme or reason: "Under observation, he walked around to the other side of the horses."
> Reader's Digest's *Mysteries of the Unexplained*

Napoleon is so obviously a suspect in the disappearance of Bathurst that I reject him out of hand. Bathurst was in Austria attempting to gain Austrian support in the chaotic melange known as the Peninsular War, where the French, Spanish, and English battled in a constantly shifting web of alliances. Napoleon created this mess for himself by placing his brother Joseph on the throne of Spain, and when the Austrians did as Bathurst suggested, Napoleon defeated them at Wagram and forced them to hand over Austrian lands. So it's just possible that the Austrians decided to take out their frustrations on Bathurst, knowing that it would appear to the British that the French had captured him. After all, Bathurst disappeared in German territory, not in Napoleon's demesne.

But what if Bathurst had arrived safely in Britain? The Austrians who had once attempted to cement an alliance with France by means of marriage might well have tried again. After all, the year before, Napoleon had divorced Josephine and married Marie Louise, an Archduchess of Austria who would eventually give birth to Napoleon II. If the Austrians had taken out their frustrations with their (seemingly) impotent ally by exchanging alliances with the (seemingly) superior French, a kind of triple detente might have resulted. England supreme on the seas, France holding the cards in Europe, and Russia on her frozen steppes immune to attack. For that matter, with Austrian support, he may well have invaded Russia earlier in the year. With General Winter not a factor, could Alexander I hold out against Napoleon? (Keep in mind that Alexander actually believed in the Hollow Earth and may well have faked his own death in order to take up the life of a hermit named Feodor Kuzmich, whereas Bonaparte was the acknowledged master tactician of his time... and even with the winter, he did get as far as Moscow.) What would come of a world with France and England facing each other with jaundiced eyes for another decade or two, each gaining strength and waiting for the opportunity to strike, a cold war a century and a half earlier than the one we experienced?

Would you believe a train to the moon?

> Do you know how long it would take an express train to reach the moon? Three hundred days. No more! A distance of 86, 410 leagues, but what is that? That is only nine times around the earth, and any sailor or traveler expects to do more than that in his lifetime.
> *Jules Verne, **From the Earth to the Moon***

It's a fact: war brings technological progress, and cold wars tend to bring about massive projects intended to demonstrate a nation's preparedness to wage war without actually doing so. In our own history, we saw a series of missile launches as each side tried to psych out the other, leading to SDI and the bankruptcy of the Soviet empire. Now, imagine our English/French cold war projected forward some twenty years to 1835.

An aging Napoleon I spends most of his time with the French Academy of Sciences studying the mechanical computer schematics left behind by Blaise Pascal when he found religion, while in England men like Michael Faraday and Charles Babbage, as well as Augusta Ada Byron, work to counter the French. Byron's father did not have time to travel Europe or involve himself in the problems of the Greeks; instead, Byron the elder was shocked to see the French Revolution toss away all its high ideals to become an Imperial power, and he focused more on his career in the House of Lords than his poetry, even though his childhood flirtation with Goethe's *The Sorrows of Young Werther* will have a great impact later.

Since both nations are embroiled in war, and have been for decades, funds are made available and the great machines are created. The French device is a pure steam creation, a mere refinement of the device Pascal left behind. But the English have Faraday, and later William Thomson, Lord Kelvin: their calculating engine is built with electromagnetic principles in mind. They begin to race ahead of the French, who respond with espionage; using Ada Byron's family connections, and the former young radical Percy Bysshe Shelley, they manage to steal the plans to the Brabbage-Faraday Electrical Mathematician. It proves replicatable, especially once the emperor himself applies his own brilliant mind to the problem, and in a flash of insight (inspired perhaps by James Mill's *Analysis of the Phenomena of the Human Mind*), he decides on a few ways to improve it, devising what he comes to call Mask Theory, a means to simulate human personality through mathematical prediction. In effect, the Napoleonic Oracle can predict, to a certain limited degree, what human beings' reactions to situations would be well enough to emulate one. Although the term would not exist, they can pass a Turing test. And to the aging emperor, knowing his death is at hand and not trusting anyone to rule the empire as well as he, this suggests something intriguing about the nature of math and thought.

My son could not replace me. I could not replace myself. I am

a creature of circumstances.
Napoleon Bonaparte

The English are horrified to watch as the Napoleonic Oracle becomes the de facto ruler of Napoleon's empire. With the Mask of Bonaparte fully installed, the machine seems to behave exactly as Napoleon himself would, so much so that when the emperor dies in 1844, it takes a month for the news to reach London. But while the Mask rules the continent, the British Empire has made use of the Electrical Mathematician and the programming brilliance of Augusta Ada Byron (in this world, her father's respectability keeps her mother from dominating her life, allowing her relationship with Babbage to continue) to create machines along a different design philosophy. The Mask runs in an Oracle, an electric and steam computer the size of a factory that must constantly resolve extraordinarily complex equations in order to keep the pretense of its being Napoleon alive, but since the British eschew such, their computers are free to specialize.

The E.M. becomes a common sight in the ironclads of the Navy, in the rapidly modernizing factories, and throughout the Empire. William IV's death leads his daughter to the throne in 1837, but by the Great Exhibition of 1851, Prince Albert is so taken by the EM (as he calls it) that it soon becomes a common sight in British homes. (Ironically, his support for technical innovation saves his life, as medical advances prevent the death that paralyzes Victoria with grief in our timeline. She and her husband are active monarchs here, but very cognizant of the limits; the example of power run amok across the Channel acts as a brake on any possible tyrannous thoughts.)

By 1860, continental Europe is a repressive gray formula-bound empire ruled by a machine that sees everything in terms of calculation and probability, where one's future is laid out by decree and there is little chance for ambition or personal determination (resisted by a few, rebels like Karl Marx, who live in fear of the scattering of grapeshot Napoleon himself used on Royalist mobs in 1795). Meanwhile the British Empire uses ever more advanced EMs to stay ahead of the Clockwork Dictator, while intuitive geniuses like James Clerk Maxwell (who develops his electromagnetic equation and statistical mechanics into working radio while Tesla is still in diapers and Marconi doesn't exist) and Florence Nightingale (who benefits from the example set by Augusta Byron- in this world, while it will be a long slow battle for equality, a talented woman is too valuable to be allowed to lie abed using her illness as leverage) work to prevent the gray wastes from expanding beyond the continent. The United States never makes the Louisiana Purchase, and French troops constantly encroach upon her border, creating a need for allies that causes the U.S. to ally with the British (in exchange for concessions like the abandonment of slavery; in a world where electrical harvesters are available by 1850 and there is no western expansion, the need for slaves is less urgent in the South), leading men like William Walker and Matthew Fontaine Maury to pit themselves against the encroaching Grey Dominion.

Science progresses along strange paths. While Lord Kelvin's disbelief in heavier-than-air flight retards the development of aircraft, there's nothing preventing Maxwell from developing broadcast power via microwave transmission. Soon giant towers dot islands all throughout the British Empire and its bases in allied nations, providing energy to ships and great war devices derived from a marriage of locomotive and carriage design. Geothermal taps (in essence, the greatest steam engines ever devised) are placed over any spot of volcanic activity possible, including the great vent in the North Atlantic that would have, in our time, raised the island of Surtsey from the embrace of the sea. Electromagnetic sciences are more than a century ahead of our own, with the application of Maxwell and Kelvin's vortex theory to Electrical Mathematicians, which work out the kinks and produce both superstring and chaos theory based on the synthesis of Goethe (who emigrated to England, urged by Byron) and Newton. Relativity is discovered as a by-product of that research. Each side manages to make breakthroughs in these fields, the Grey Dominion often by managing to turn well-placed researchers, or occasionally by suspending all other calculations and using the Mask program to emulate British researchers. This works better at some times than at others, but it is a facility the British at once fear and lack.

The deadlock is intolerable to both sides. So when Louis Pasteur and Jules Verne come to the Mask of Napoleon with an idea to demonstrate the massed power of the Automatic Empire by building an enormous structure- in effect, a series of cables leading up to the moon- it agrees. After all, it really doesn't matter how much it will cost, and could also open up whole new territories to expansion. (And yes, there are the technical challenges of, say, lunar orbit of the earth to overcome.)

> And the Lord came down, to see the city and the tower which the Children of Adam had erected. And he said: "Behold, all are as one people with one language, and this is just the beginning of their undertakings; now, anything which they should scheme to do shall no longer be impossible for them."
> *The Book of Genesis, Chapter 11:5-6*

So far, of course, we've stayed somewhat tame in our musings. We've postulated nothing truly impossible, just improbable. None of it happened, of course, but it is not outside of the realm of conception that it could have. However, that may be because we're playing it safe. Let us stop for a moment and take the governor off of the belching engine of our imaginations and see where this beast takes us.

Imagine the shock to the Anglo-American alliance as the entire Ries astrobleme is evacuated and construction on *La Tour de Babel* begins. This great beast, made possible with oil from the conquered plains of Eurasia, materials mined from all over the world, and the genius of men like the Krupp family, Alfred Nobel, John Ericsson (whose family was not allowed to emigrate out of the Grey Dominion) and others, begins its slow climb to the heavens. This belching skyhook, this railroad to the moon, is a direct challenge to the alliance, yes, but that is not its worst offense.

For when the tripods land all over the world, both sides realize that they have an enemy they had not foreseen, an enemy capable of traversing the void and attacking with great walkers. However, unlike the people of Wells' book, the people of this earth have weapons of great destructive power stockpiled, and they unite briefly to drive off these interlopers, less in peace than an agreement that each will not work to hinder the others. (Richard Burton, the British emissary to Paris, is credited with being able to understand the Mask of Napoleon as well as it understands others, with his strange facility for languages and mimicry... even if they be mathematical languages.)

Vortex theory has yielded devices that work on beam power, and soon the tripods find that they have bitten off more than they can chew in attacking the boisterous, arrogant steam-driven metropolis earth.

As the battles continue, American forces at Grover's Mill, New Jersey manage to capture both a tripod and its landing craft, a self-propelled missile. American visionaries like Pinkerton and Poe realize that unlocking the secrets of the tripods will leapfrog the United States from second-rate ally to important partner in the struggle with the Mask of Napoleon. A young man named Thomas Edison is tapped to work on this project, known as Ares, after the combination of human savagery, unexpected technological prowess and earthly microbes drives the invaders away. Eventually, however, the upstart Americans require British manufacturing aid, but they have the leverage to negotiate for it, and other concessions. By 1872, the war is over, the work on the sky railroad has resumed, and a joint Anglo-American partnership produces the first terrestrial heavier-than-air flying machine, the Phaetheon. But the Phaetheon is more than simply an aircraft. Using Maxwell's radiowave power, it can reach the edge of the atmosphere. The limits of broadcast microwave power, alas, do not allow for more... yet.

The race is on. Will the Mask of Napoleon build a train to the moon before the British fly there? Will the invaders return, with new weapons and tactics, now that they know the level of resistance they can expect? Will an obscure scientist named Cavour accidentally deliver a new element into the hands of the Grey Dominion, or will the British players of the Great Game manage to outwit the master of probabilities?

Those That Fall

By some it is said that they came "out of heaven" and by others that they sprang from four cities, in which they learned science and craftsmanship, and from each of which they brought away a magical treasure. From Falais they brought the Stone of Destiny (Lia Fail), from Gorias an invincible sword, from Finias a magical spear, and from Murias the Cauldron of the Dagda. They were believed to have been wafted to Ireland on a magic cloud, carrying their treasures with them.
Lewis Spence, **An Encyclopedia of Occultism**

The Scythians say they are the youngest of all nations, and the following is an account they give of their origin. The first man to live in their country, which before his birth was uninhabited, was a certain Targitaus, the son of Zeus and of a daughter of the river Borysthenes - I merely repeat the tradition, and do not myself believe it. Targitaus had three sons, Lipoxais, Arpoxais, and Colaxais, the youngest; and during their reign in Scythia there fell from the sky a golden plough, a golden yoke, a golden battle-axe, and a golden cup. The eldest of the three was the first to see these treasures, and as he went to pick them up the gold caught fire. At this he retired, and the second of the brothers approached; but the gold caught fire and blazed, just as before. Lastly, when the two elder brothers had been kept off by the flames, the youngest came along, and this time the fire went out, so that he was able to pick up the golden implements and carry them home. The elder brothers accepted this as a sign of heaven and made over the whole kingdom to Colaxais.
Herodotus, **The Inquiries**

Imagination can be turned in any direction. It can be used to envision paradise, or it can be used to create the devices with which we bring hell to life. The same brain, the same eye, the same hand can fashion devices that are used to rain death down upon London, and then create the engines by which the moon is explored. Humanity, in particular, seems to have a positive gift for this sort of creative dichotomy, this split between creation and destruction, with each tangled in the other. We cannot create without first destroying, and often we destroy with our creations.

What if, rather than simply a consequence of our process of evolution, this very facility was selected for? What if we are exactly what we were intended to be? And now that we have reached our apotheosis, what will become of us?

Various peoples project their own preoccupations onto other groups when they should be examining themselves. The strange tendency of many different explorers to look at other cultures on this planet and see alien intervention rather than natural achievement should be inverted: what, pray tell, is it in the culture that raised an Erich von Däniken that makes him see space aliens everywhere he looks in South America? At least Sitchin looked at his own people and their heritage when he went looking for aliens. But his theories of cosmology seem overly elaborate, and his idea that once they created their humans the aliens were split on whether or not to allow them procreation, self-awareness and even survival seem strange when analyzed deeply. (If the Annunaki were aware that the orbit of their homeworld was going to create tidal waves on its pass by earth, why didn't they just go home?) This isn't to say you can't make a case for some alien intervention on this planet in the past, but even the sources Sitchin uses (*The Enuma Elish*, the *Epic of Gilgamesh*) agree that man existed before the "gods" decided to get involved.

So what, exactly, was their purpose here on earth? Was it anything so mundane as mineral deposits that drew them to our tiny corner of space? It seems to me that the von Dänikens and Sitchins have underestimated the technology needed to make the leap from planet to planet, even if you accept the idea that a rogue world is crossing the orbital plane every 300,000 years or so. And if you don't accept this Velikovskian idea of worlds in collision, it becomes even more difficult to reconcile the kind of time and travail needed to cover interstellar distances just to strip mine a planet- and to do so in such a poor manner. We seem to have mineral deposits left. Did the aliens only take a little, or was this planet so overwhelmingly rich in gold and oil that even after stripping the world of those elements, the traces they left behind were enough to found our civilizations? (Ignoring the fact that a spacecraft from distant worlds might have as much use for oil and gold as a modern nuclear submarine would have for coal. It's hard to imagine a fossil-fuel-powered spacecraft covering interstellar distances.) No, I think whoever our visitors were, they had no such interests.

They were here for us.

> Alas! in committing a great sin are we engaged, we who are endeavouring to kill our kindred from greed of the pleasures of kingship. If the sons of Dhritarashtra, weapon in hand, should slay me, unresisting, unarmed, in the battle, that would be for me the better.
> Sanjaya said: Having thus spoken on the battlefield, Arunja sank down on the seat of the chariot, casting away his bow and arrow, his mind overborne by grief.
> *Barbara Stoler Miller translation of **The Bhagavad-Gita***

Imagine, with that dread facility you possess, a race of people inquisitive and brilliant, who viewed the whole of creation as their intellectual playground to dissect and explore. (Not so hard, huh?) They rose up from whatever situation birthed them to master their physical surroundings while at the same time developing various metaphysical explanations for various behaviors. They held each other as kindred, and yet rivalries developed both among themselves and the other inhabitants of the universe. Feeling that conflict among them had become suicidally stupid as their technology had increased, they sought to find a way to remove the need for it, but they failed. (Or worse, they succeeded, and only then learned that they were but one race in the cold uncaring universe, surrounded by enemies and rivals who were not constrained by the ethical code they had developed. Think of all the myths, from the Greek to the Babylonian to the Egyptian to the Vedic, where the gods make war on one another with devastating results.) Seeking another option, they searched the universe for something they could use.

They found a planet where small biomechanical machines were in the process of creating themselves in ever more elaborate forms, from unicellular up to great colonies. (Note that I am not even trying to apply human ideas of what life is to these aliens, mainly so you can do it for me.) Whether or not this was akin to the process of their own existences is immaterial; what is important is what they could make of such beings. (Perhaps they were forbidden to do such experiments on their own worlds for fear of the consequences, but so far from home it was acceptable.) They set out to make weapons to defend themselves from a hostile universe, weapons that would wield themselves.

Of course, the first experiments would not be perfect. Trial and error led them to what functioned well and what didn't. Eventually, it occurred to them that trying to make beings who were physically powerful yet less intelligent led to weapons that were unable to defend them properly, while too much intelligence led to... difficulties. (Somewhere, a burbling mass of goo is whispering, "Tekeli-Li.") Eventually, rather than creating a new design, it occurred to our intrepid explorers to try something else- to take an existing life form and adapt it. It took them a while to decide which species offered the best potential, but they hit upon an unlikely choice, a being which was spreading across the surface of the planet already.

A being that had very little in the way of natural weapons (which meant that they'd never have to fear those weapons being turned against them) but which was already displaying some nifty trends. Trends like pack hunting and weapon making. With a few tweaks, they should do nicely.

After all, they were just animals.

> It was at this time that the Celts moved south and either destroyed or enslaved the little people already living there. The Celts were themselves later ousted by the Teutonic tribes. From the time of this second invasion, stories began to emerge that not all the diminutive folk had been slaughtered - some had been able to hide themselves away in caverns and holes, emerging only at night to steal their food and carry out occasional reprisals on those that had oppressed them by stealing small animals and even sleeping children. Machen expressed his feeling about the secret race most succinctly: "They are horribly evil," he wrote, "and they are something more - or something less - than human." It was easy to see how the stories of these little marauders had become, with the passage of time, turned into the legends of fairies, goblins, leprechauns and so on.
> *Peter Haining, **Ancient Mysteries***

Once the new and improved killers were completed, of course, there would have to be a test of their capacity to kill. How destructive and vicious were they? So arming the weapons with simple but well-made tools (it wouldn't take much... imagine placing a bronze sword into the hands of a warrior in a Stone Age world) they unleashed their creations into a control region, an isolated section of the main continent where they could be studied and controlled as need be. The killers, for their part, did exactly as was expected of them and killed, driving (as in the Celtic stories) the original inhabitants of the subcontinent away from their lands or killing them outright. Machen's view of these aboriginal Europeans was no doubt tainted by the fact that he was descended from the artifical race that had ravaged them so thoroughly that they were forced into abortive, half-empty gestures of resistance. The Celts, the Teutons, and other races who consider themselves native to the northern reaches of the European continent are in fact imported, having been placed there to destroy and expand... to prove themselves the perfect weapons.

And so they have. There is nowhere on this world that the descendants of the altered humans have not laid the print of their foot, and precious few places where they have not slaughtered any who resisted them. Indeed, it is possible that they grew so puissant in the art of war that they annihilated their creators. (Perhaps with the help of aliens like Oannes and Enki, whoever they were- those that made us and then sympathized with their creations, or entirely different aliens who were offended by our makers' experiments, or some other option I'm too human to come up with.)

> A single projectile, charged with all the power of the universe; an incandescent column of smoke and fire as bright as 10,000 suns, a shaft fatal as the rod of death. Endowed with the force of thousand-eyed Indra's thunder: It was destructive to all living creatures... Hostile warriors fell to the earth like trees burnt down in a raging fire... Elephants fell to earth uttering fierce cries... burnt by the energy of that weapon.
> *John Hogue translation of **The Mahabharata***

Provided with weapons of mass destruction by their creators once they proved themselves to be effective, did the killers turn this power against them? Are the stories of the Tower of Babel and of Sodom and Gomorrah really twisted tales of the living weapons turning their skill at warfare against their creators, who were unused to war? Imagine Arunja at the battlefield, or perhaps the tales of the Nephilim, half-human, half-angelic, who turned their backs on God, or the Tuatha de Dannan's war with the Fomorians, or the story of the Greek gods rising up and defeating the Titans, who in their turn had overthrown Chronus. Blasting themselves back into barbarism in the process, did the warriors destroy those who made them for war? Was it mankind who blasted the Antarctic cities, tilted the poles of the planet, and caused the Deluge that nearly destroyed it? Is it possible that "Tekeli-Li" is the war-cry of the killer angels, the only society on earth that actually required alien help to flourish, the white killers from the north?

Of course, there is another possibility, that the fallout of the wars in heaven in which we were intended to serve as footsoldiers may well have been the stranding of our creators on a hostile earth.

> The Annunaki, great gods, were sitting in thirst, in hunger...
> Ninti wept and spent her emotion; she wept and eased her feelings. The gods wept with her for the land. Overcome with grief, she for beer was athirst. She sat where gods sat weeping, like beasts at a trench convulsed. They burned their lips with thirst, they burned their stomachs with famine.
> **The Atra-Hasis Epic,** *Tablet III*

Whether battling alien rivals of their own race, or of another, or battling their own rebellious creations, disaster may well have struck our arrogant makers. What if the war between heaven and earth was so great that some of them were stranded here on earth, unable to return home? If we were made to resemble them, it is possible that they may have taken wives and husbands and lived out their lives trapped here with their savage creations, directing their violence away from themselves by various means (perhaps teaching them myths that led them to new targets, or bribing them with technologies lost in the conflict, or what have you) and towards the other races of men on the earth. Many gods have been cruel throughout history, demanding sacrifice and conquest, after all. From the smoking mirror of Tezcatlipoca, the still-steaming liver torn from the body, to the demand of Yahweh that not even cattle should survive Jericho, our gods are often wanton with our lives. Is this possibly an act of self-preservation?

I've often wondered if the origin of the vampire legend wasn't in the spread of white men throughout the world, perhaps as far back as the horse nomads at the fringes of the Chinese territories. They had much in common with the Scythians, the horse nomads, as well as having Celtic textiles in their graves. Were they an offshoot of the killer angels?

Did the stories of the Chen Shih and the Penhaligon come from tales of strange white demons from the north and west who were bloodthirsty and who burned in the light of the sun? (Of Celtic and Teutonic stock myself, I have always noticed how badly my family takes sunlight; we all turn bright red and peel within a day of intense summer. It's kind of creepy. Isn't the sun supposed to be the source of life?) Were these nearly-universal human legends spread by the neolithic peoples fleeing the onslaught of the killers across the land-bridges that existed in the Neolithic period? Was the spread of humanity throughout the world the result of rampaging genetically engineered white people going on a killing spree throughout the Eurasian continent? And is it possible that Machen's secret race, the people who inspired our legends of the fae, the unaltered root race of humanity, could have survived by migrating elsewhere?

> Perhaps, though, the strangest of all Lost World stories is that concerning Australia - to most people simply the newest of continents, but to scientists and geographers an enigma, and just possibly the homeland of all mankind. For much of its history the country was completely unknown to the rest of the world, even its nearest neighbors, and while rumors and legends of most great nations existed before they were actually found (for example, America), Australia appeared almost literally out of the blue to the Dutch Captain Jansz in 1606.
> Peter Haining, **Ancient Mysteries**

> They carried their conception of the sacred, of mythic time and ancestral origins with them as they walked. These were embodied in the landscape; every hill and valley, each kind of animal and tree, had its place in a systematic but unwritten whole. Take away this territory and they were deprived, not of "property" (an abstract idea that could be satisfied with another piece of land) but of their embodied history, their locus of myth, their "dreaming." There was no possible way in which

> the accumulated tissue of symbolic and spiritual usage
> represented by tribal territory could be gathered up and
> conferred on another tract of land by an act of will.
> Robert Hughes, *The Fatal Shore*

The Celts freely admit that the Otherworld is not their invention, but the land of the people they displaced, reachable through burial mounds and sacred hills. In all the world, the only belief even approaching the Otherworld (Annwyn, where time and space do not matter and one communes with the ancient heroes) is that of the Dreamtime. Is it possible that, having survived the attack of the killing man-machines, the original people of Europe decided to take advantage when the proto-Celtic/Scythian/Teuton peoples aimed themselves at their makers? Did they walk south and east, crossing the whole of Eurasia, and create for themselves a new Otherworld to replace the one they had lost? Was their voyage, which may well have consisted of the first oceangoing colonization effort in human history, an attempt to survive the devastation that swept their former homeland?

It's possible that the various tribes of Australia migrated there as early as 45,000 B.C., which would put them in line with Sitchin's argument that the reign of Ziusudra began then (Ziusudra is the Sumerian Noah, analogous to the *Epic of Gilgamesh*'s Utnapishtim and, well, Noah) and it's interesting to think that just as the world was supposedly flooding, there would have been boats traveling from Eurasia south and west to Australia. Is Uluru the rock on which Noah landed? Was the main object of the Dreaming the creation of a shield that would turn aside any searching for the last survivors of the great migration, exploiting what the first men had learned about the perceptive defects the Makers had left in the minds of their creations?

Well, probably not. After all, it isn't as if blood-crazed white men somehow broke through a kind of protective barrier and set up a penal colony on their land, using the blood sacrifices of Irishmen to fuel a magical assault that fit hand and glove with the eradication of the natives, now is it? I'm sure it's just a coincidence and not any sort of genetic programming that led the inhabitants of the British Isles to swarm over the Australian continent, in a kind of repeat performance of the neolithic purge of the "Secret Race." No, that would be insane.

But then again, I was born in America, where the sacred marriage between the land and the nation was provided by driving the natives back, back, ever back with rapine and slaughter, so maybe I see things in a slanted way, as if I have inherited perceptive defects from my Celtic and Teutonic ancestors. I hope not.

"Tekeli-Li." Some folks say that white people come from outer space, but I suspect something else; outer space came down into white people, and the rest of the world paid for it. Unfortunately, we've interbred through conquest, through our cultural expansion (which affects the minds of any who attempt to understand it, with neurolinguistic programming) and through sheer brute force of will. One hopes, we can learn from our own mistakes... and from those of our makers.

The King Bears His Wound

He really was a doctor, or at least a fully a fully licensed doctor of dentisty in the state of Pennsylvania. He was also a wanted man, a tuberculosis-ravaged wreck, something of a dandy, and the deadliest man ever to walk the streets of Tombstone, Arizona, not exactly a town shy of deadly men. He was John Henry Holliday, D.D.S., but you can call him Doc. In fact, I recommend it. Be sure to inflect it just right, however, because the Doc's got no patience for fools, and he never, ever loses.

> "Why Johnny Ringo, you look like someone done just walked over your grave."
> *Val Kilmer as the Doc,* **Tombstone**

The bare facts- on August 14, 1851, John Henry Holliday was born to William Burroughs and Alice Martin Holliday. His mother died when he was fifteen, shortly after the War Between the States had ended, and it drove a rift between him and his father, a former Confederate major. (Major Holliday was busy acquiring status in town [Valdosta, Georgia] as mayor and as a member of the County Agricultural Society and the Masonic Lodge, as the secretary of the Confederate Veterans Camp, and as the superintendent of local elections.) John therefore decided to attend dentistry school in Philadelphia, far enough away to ensure a lack of friction between himself and his father, and graduated in 1872. By all accounts he was a fair to talented dentist. However, fate had other ideas. By October of 1873 he was heading west, advised by his doctors that the dry western climate would preserve him a few more years despite the tuberculosis. At least, that's what they tell us. From there, it's not far to his abandonment of his profession (after all, not many people want a tuberculous dentist playing around in their mouths, and the coughing spasms played hell on extractions). He discovered he had two natural talents. He was an expert gambler, and he was a natural killer.

From there, we head to Tombstone, Wyatt Earp, and immortality.

> He was the most skillful gambler, and the nerviest, fastest, deadliest man with a six-gun I ever saw.
> *Wyatt Earp describing Doc Holliday*

After marrying and then leaving Kate Elder (who had saved his life in Fort Griffin, setting fire to the town and bracing a deputy holding him in a cell) after she swore out a statement against him, Doc was at loose ends. He'd been through many of the roughest towns in the West already, and he was justly feared in all of them. Having met and befriended Wyatt Earp in Dodge City, and having nothing better to do than gamble, drink and wait for death, Doc decided to get involved in his friend's problems with a local gang. This was 1881, and it led to the gunfight of all gunfights, the one that didn't actually take place at the OK Corral, but in a vacant lot nearby. Doc was shot in the hip during the fight, but the bullet merely grazed him, unlike Morgan and Virgil Earp, both of whom took serious wounds in the fight. Further trouble with the Clanton gang wasn't especially a problem for Doc, who actually hoped he would get killed. Instead, the following men died after Wyatt's brother Morgan was shot while playing pool: "Old Man" Clanton, Billy Clanton, Frank McLaury, Tom McLaury, Frank Stilwell, Indian Charlie, Dixie Gray, Florentino Cruz, Curly Bill, Johnny Barnes, Jim Crane, Harry Head, Bill Leonard, Joe Hill, Luther King, Charley Snow, Billy Lang, Zwing Hunt, Billy Grounds and Hank Swilling. It's quite possible that Doc shot each and every one of them, inasmuch as he had been the only member of the Earp faction to shoot all three of the dead men at the famous gunfight.

Doc died November 8, 1887, in bed. The tuberculosis got him. He had walked through some of the most violent places in the West, bearing two pistols and a knife and daring someone to kill him, and no one had. They'd tried, but they'd failed. This, more or less, is the life of quite possibly the least vicious dentist in history. (Sorry for the hyperbole, but I hate getting my teeth cleaned.) Now, what can we take from all of it?

Well, it's kind of obvious, isn't it? Unhealing wound, blessed by destiny, excellent with cards, merciless killer... he's the Fisher King. Probably his father, one of those mysterious Masons, groomed him for the role without his realizing it. (For an understanding of the mysticism beneath the Masonic temple, a good place to start is Umberto Eco's *Foucault's Pendulum*.) Scion of a southern "nobleman," John Henry Holliday is touched by destiny in the form of tuberculosis and heads west ("go west, young man") where he learns of his ability with cards (and gambling is a descendant of divination, using the cards derived from the Tarot itself; John Henry may well have been a sorcerer) and his untouchable lethality. What could well have been a fatal wound at the OK Corral is turned aside so that his sacred flesh is but grazed (and, his form is altered by the wound itself, making him a more accurate representation of the Fisher King, struck in the side by the Spear of Destiny), and when Doc is staring death in the face at Fort Griffin, Kate Elder burns the town to the ground and braces the deputy in order to ensure his escape. Kate, a local prostitute, takes the role of the Magdalene in the Merovingian heresy so at the root of the Masonic disciplines, linking the Sacred King to the Moon Goddess via her own body and recreating in herself the role of the Divine Queen (the Lady of the Lake). Together, they are Innanna and Tammuz, Cybele and Attis, Christ and the Magdalene, connecting the ancient sacred prostitutes with the sacrifice of the male. Kate's own fate is uncertain. One source has her dying in a tavern brawl in 1885 after Doc sends her away (and he himself was odd about that; rather than casting her aside, he gave her money and spoke of a "debt still to discharge") while another argues that she lives until November of 1940- still somehow linked to the Doc, who dies on the same day sixty-two years earlier. Was she the tail-end of the sacrifice, a Masonic magic intended to wrest the land from its native inhabitants and graft a western mystical paradigm on it?

Likewise, Wyatt Earp takes on the role of temporal king to Doc's Fisher King, and his crusade at Tombstone against the Clantons takes on a mystical signficance of its own, a re-creation of the war between the Celtic kings in Romano-Celtic Britain before the Battle of Badon. Was "Old Man' Clanton more than he seemed? Remarkably fertile, he either fathered or gathered a vast brood of servants to do his will, a modern Vortigern who needed to be dispatched before the war could be taken to the land and its spirits. Once the killing was over and Destiny had no more need of him, Doc's condition became terminal and he passed on, a blood sacrifice out of the pages of Genesis to bind the West to the mythic west. (And in Genesis, it's interesting to notice that Yahweh's punishment for Cain's act of murder is to mark him as protected and allow him to start and rule a kingdom- hardly the most onerous tithe a murderer has ever had to pay. Apparently, God likes blood every now and again. Doc Holliday certainly provided plenty of that.)

Of course, this is all quite fanciful and probably not true. I'm sure that most men with tuberculosis could have survived fourteen years in the most violent towns of the West, shooting with unerring accuracy and gambling with inhuman skill, never wracked with spasms while engaged in those activities, yet the second they tried to put the guns down they would have had the tuberculosis reassert itself. Of course. That's perfectly acceptable. Honestly. Doc was nothing special. That makes much more sense, I agree.

No, I don't.

Lords of the Scale

The idea that reptilian or dinosaurian aliens created the human race is hardly new. David Icke has been arguing for years that every single power block in human history has has been infiltrated by reptoids (He's especially hard on the British royal family. One wonders what effect Diana's death has on him; he probably thinks it was an attempt by the reptoids to prevent a diffusion of their bloodlines or something, although to be fair I haven't bothered to find out), David Barclay thinks that the dinosaur extinction of sixty-five million years ago was in fact a dinosaur migration to outer space, and that they've now returned to take back the planet from humans, who evolved from a dog-like domesticated dinosaur. (Don't let being a mammal throw you on that one; that's exactly what the dinosaurians want you to think.) Meanwhile, Paul Shockley is pretty sure that he's channeling an extradimensional entity called "Cosmic Awareness" who warns that the reptoids are seeding our culture through kids' shows like "Barney" and "Teenage Mutant Ninja Turtles" for the day when they shall invade in force, because by then our children will have been brainwashed into welcoming them with open arms. (One wonders why the reptile men let shows like "Land of the Lost" and "V" get on the air. Perhaps their control of Hollywood is not total. For that matter, I'm pretty sure that David Icke charges Steven Spielberg with being a reptoid, yet the man made *Jurassic Park*, which is hardly good propaganda for the dinosaurian hordes with its portrayal of raptors as malevolent, intelligent pack hunters who can be granted no quarter. Are some of them traitors to their own species, or are Icke and Shockley just crazy? I'd go with door number two, myself.)

Then there are the "Lucifer spirits" and "Serpent People" of Theosophy, everyone's favorite hodgepodge of plagiarism, invention and eugenic racism. (I suggest reading Madame Blavatsky, if only for the notion that humanity was at one time an egg-laying hermaphrodite species.) I suppose I should mention the Hefferlin Manuscript here, which like the Patience Worth novel was supposedly telepathically dictated, but also like Patience Worth it isn't worth reading.

Of course, the motif is as old as Genesis itself, and can be traced through mythology and history. From the Sumero-Babylonian mythos and Tiamat to Typhon of ancient Greece, from the dragon of the apocryphal *Book of Bel and the Dragon* to the asp associated with the Uraeus crown of Egypt, we see serpents. Including stories such as St. Patrick's banishing snakes from Ireland, the Midgard Serpent girding the world entire in Norse myth, the *Lung Wang* of Asia and their dragon lines of force, the sea serpents reported by Captain Peter M'Quhae and others in the nineteenth century (sightings that did not begin there and did not end there) and our old friends Nessie, Ogopogo, Champ and Morag frolicking in their lakes, we have barely scratched the surface of serpentine imagery on the borderlands between fantasy and reality. Hell, we haven't even mentioned Mokole-mbembe, the sirrush of the Ishtar Gate (again in Babylon), Apophis the Devourer who attempts every night to eat the barque of the sun and consume Ra, the sun god.... Plenty of snakes and serpents and creepy-crawlies in our myths, boy howdy. Not to mention the fictional serpent peoples created by writers like Burroughs and Howard and Lovecraft (whose concept of a mental time traveling race who once inhabited, among others, a race of serpent men is the most blatantly cosmic treatment the scaly folk have ever gotten) or the *marag* of Harry Harrison's *Eden* series. (Which of course takes us to the lake monster of Loch Morar, good ol' Morag.) One thing that immediately comes to mind is that, if Shockley's channelled spirit is to be believed, the reptoids are supposedly engaged in propaganda to convince us of their benefical nature. Well, if that's the case, they need a new publicity hack, because so far almost every single story even touching upon serpents in the whole of human history is blazingly unflattering. Even those stories that admit that they aren't all bad portray them as arrogant and aloof, and many portray them as either hissing mixtures of Machiavelli and Sade with a touch of the Utah Raptor, or mindless and destructive.

Me, I think we should stop and try to see things from the admittedly alien eyes of our dinosaurian kin. (After all, if they're from earth, we are distantly related.) Imagine, if you will, how long it took them from the beginnings of the Mesozoic age some 245 million years ago till the end of the Cretaceous, sixty-five million or so years in the past, to develop from thecodonts to the proud bipedal saurians they are today. Then something happens (more on that later) and they either tunnel into the earth, step into a parallel universe, take off in spacecraft, or whatever. That's some 180 million years of evolution. Whatever happened, from the time it resolved itself to now is a mere sixty-five million years, almost a third of the time it took them to make the climb up the long ladder, and in that time humanity developed from creatures a lot like a tree shrew, up through the ranks of the primates, and into the atom-splitting, god-creating and -destroying, heedlessly progressing and environmental despoiling species we are today. We beat their time, and not just a little, either. Imagine if this was a relay race and we both started on the same starting line. We'd be done, and they'd still be on their second relay. Never mind the fact that, in the millions upon millions of years they've had to work on their society and technology, the best they seem capable of doing is saucers and (again according to Shockley's "Cosmic Awareness") a really bad propaganda push to infiltrate our culture with- I kid you not- New Kids on the Block. I want you to imagine a species that has a sixty-five million-year head start. Shouldn't they be as gods to us, not barely ahead? (And if any of you reading this are reptoids, I'm really sorry about the New Kids thing. I'm sure Shockley is just slandering you.)

What a lot of the alarmists are forgetting is that while the reptoids are very different from us, alien (even if they are of terrestrial origin, they are an entirely different kind of life, with physical and mental characteristics we lack) and strange, we are equally so to them. When dinosaurs ruled the earth, mammals were small, ratlike creatures gnawing at roots and eating the occassional egg. Our minds and theirs are entirely different, our bodies are different; we'd have an easier time psychoanalyzing a crocodile than a bipedal dinosaurian, which is an entirely new order of life somewhere between a reptile and a bird (some modern paleontologists, like Bakker, argue that birds are essentially just modern dinosaurs, in fact) with a mind that may work as well as or better than ours, but certainly entirely differently. We are more like dolphins than like dinosaurs. So it is entirely possible that, to the reptoids, mankind is as frightening as any serpent is to us. Keep in mind, also, that our ideas of how fast technological development should be are based on the past 6000 years of our history, but for a period of time longer than that by a factor of 16,000 we made much slower progress. This is, by the way, a conservative estimate based on the idea that modern *Homo sapiens sapiens* is about 100,000 years old. I'm not even counting all of our anthropoid ancestors. We may be an aberration.

To the R.A. Boulay/David Barclay/Icke crowd, the reptoids somehow either survived their extinction millions upon millions of years ago, or came to earth from another world. Well, there's not much you can say to the otherworldly hypothesis other than to criticize its lack of creativity. (I mean, why saurians? If you're going to postulate alien entities influencing our development, why stay so close to earth fauna? This is my biggest problem with the von Däniken/Sitchin crowds, too. At least with Theosophy, the aliens are ephemeral spirit beings or bizarre root races that made for a great background to Burroughs' Barsoom tales. If you're going to go nuts, go nuts. After Lovecraft, these people seem cravenly unoriginal. I'll take barrel-like masses of sensory input or ambulatory pseudo-fungi colonies over guys in spacesuits anyday.) So I'll be sticking with the idea that the saurians are terrestrial. Let us look at one possible scenario for where they went, and why, and why they'd come back.

Imagine a ray of sunshine illuminating a city on the shores of a sea where Plesiosaurs leap up to try and catch Pteranadon in their jaws, where saurian bipeds live and work in cities probably more advanced than our own, designed for their needs rather than ones we would consider important. So they have hatchery pods where the eggs are laid and fertilized, as an example. At some point, this society realizes that a monster asteroid is barreling down upon them. Being different beings than we are, they devise a solution that may seem unusual to us; rather than attempt to destroy the asteroid or move it, they decide to move themselves. They construct a fleet of ships and blast off to what they hope will be the nearest inhabitable planet. But they don't have lightspeed travel. The best they can do is what we would have to do in this situation... keep accellerating until they hit the relativistic barrier where the energy they expend can no longer increase the speed of their craft. Let's assume they can get up to .5 lightspeed on average (after all, they will have to decellerate for as long as they accelerate in order to stop at their destination). At that rate, it takes them about a decade to get to Alpha Centauri. But the Centauri system does not meet their needs. Imagine a gigantic series of generational systems wandering from star to star, mining resources and looking for a world to colonize. Let's say that it takes them tens of thousands of years of searching to find a suitable world, their entire culture transformed by the experience. Utility becomes the watchword, as does conformity. Their society is stressed to the breaking point; ships are lost, destroyed, cannibalized; occasional disturbances flare up. By the time they reach wherever they finally settle as a people, they are a tenth of what they once were. Still, they land their craft and begin the process of taming an alien world (and remember, at this point they may well have settled on any damn world that looked halfway decent) and building a new home for themselves. We have no idea what technological level they have achieved, how long it would take, what reverses would be dealt them, what resources their new home would yield. Millions of years of history pass. Perhaps they colonize other worlds in the same manner. Lacunae of millennia might pass. Their slower evolutionary rate and tendency to stay at rest as a culture unless spurred onward by something keeps them from pushing forward as fast as we would, not to mention the enormous resources it would cost them to colonize other worlds, limited as they are by lightspeed. Finally, after their existence is assured and their way of life stable, it occurs to someone that it might be worthwhile to send a colony ship back to earth. The arguments back and forth begin. Pragmatism says no. Eventually, enough interest in reclaiming the old homestead makes such a mission (which will require a trip of thousands of years in real space, a true generational trip even with time dilation on their side) a reality.

They brave the dangers of the void again, stopping on all the points they did on the way out, resupplying and refueling whenever possible. And what do they find when they arrive here?

Well, the old homestead is already settled, isn't it? By creatures evolved from the things that they used to eat on a stick. It's as if we went back to the house our grandparents grew up in and found it infested with vermin. Explosively quick-breeding, fast adapting vermin. Vermin who could talk to each other and build cities. Now, the saurians cannot go home. The ones who arrive are in ships that will take thousands of years to get back, even if they try. Now, there are options: try and wipe out the infestation and reclaim the planet, or civilize the pests. Look at the mythology of human-reptile relations; either they're trying to get us to eat from trees that will give us knowledge or they're trying to blot out the sun, cause tidal waves and flood and so on. Saurian DNA experiments to reset the environment to the way it was before the asteroid impact (perhaps they have stores of such on their ship, or perhaps they're better than us as geneticists and can extract DNA from fossils more efficiently) leads to tales of dragons and *sirrush* and behemoths and what have you. However, despite their best efforts, despite superior technology (keep in mind, however, that they fear to use it against us too much, realizing how quickly we adapt and how hard it will be to keep an industrial base going without us noticing it) and their longer existence, we're too fast, too savage, too prolific in our reproduction, too talented at warfare... and we think differently than they do. We cut to the heart of the matter, whereas they tend to take their time about decisions. We go for quicker, faster, Gordian knot solutions while they try for longer term, less invasive ones. Perhaps they never developed atomic weapons, for example, because the idea of fission, of splitting the basic building block of matter, is abhorrent or even inconcievable to them. Maybe they had no way to even try to move or destroy that asteroid, maybe their terraforming processes are so slow that it takes them millions of years and generation upon generation merely to settle one planet, because that's just how they think. Now imagine how they would feel, watching us swarm over this world like cunning rats, adapting it to us instead of us to it.

It's the tortoise and the hare, the reptile and the man. (Even if they are warm-blooded saurians more akin to birds, the mindset is still alien.) To them we are impossible to anticpate. Our decisons are often arbitrary, our religions perverse and antithetical, our warfare unrelentingly awful. We are the monsters, and we rule their home. Perhaps what Icke and Barclay and Shockley see as sinister snakes trying to undermine us could just be honest saurians trying to understand us.

Then again, maybe that's just what they want you to think.

Et in Lemuria ego

Is it possible that a waning empire, sustained for so long by the magics of a hardy group of Elizabethan mystics and a fusion with the vitality of an alien land, saw itself overthrown and sought new power, new land... and new stars? The School of Night, that cabal of mystics so heavily involved in the foundation of the American colonies, populated by such luminaries as John Dee (in real life a pampered astrologer for queen and country, possibly a spy with designation 007, and the man who either received or invented the Enochian Aetheyrs. Also, Lovecraft swore up and down that the old fellow translated the *Necronomicon*, for those of you always looking for a Mythos connection), Sir Walter Raleigh (Croatoan, anyone?), Sir Humphrey Gilbert (who vanished in the mid-Atlantic), Henry Percy the Wizard Earl of Northumberland (a descendant of the same Percy family who placed Henry IV on the throne, then thought better of it), Sir Philip Sidney, Christopher Marlowe (whose death in Deptford has often been blamed on enemies of the School led by the Walsinghams, British spymasters and rivals of Dee), and of course our old friend Lord Ferdinando Strange. There is much to explore about the School: how Strange may have been one of Shakespeare's early patrons, how they owed much of their lore to the visit of Giordano Bruno to England in 1583; but for now, the School serves us mainly as an example of what English attempts to colonize foreign lands were really all about.

> By the latter part of the sixteenth century, a deepening rivalry between England and Spain in the New World was inexorably leading the two European powers towards war. The chances were heavily weighted in favour of Spain. From the mines of Mexico and Peru there came a stream of silver and gold which so fortified the material power of the Spanish Empire that King Philip could equip his forces beyond all known scales. The position was well understood in the ruling circles of

England. So long as Spain controlled the wealth of the New World she could launch and equip a multitude of Armadas; the treasure must therefore be arrested at its source or captured from the ships which conveyed it across the oceans.
*Sir Winston Churchill, **A History of the English-Speaking Peoples***

There are, of course, the desires for expansion and resources. These are real motivations, and not to be overlooked. But when America was colonized, it was as much an attempt to tame a very real (to the School of Night, at least) magical threat to the queen. The Spanish were already applying their mystical paradigm, equal parts Catholicism and Moorish thought containing within it elements of the Sufi, the ancient Persian magi, and writers like Averroes, to the land in the south. And as we know, anything the Spanish did, the English were desperate to counter. While Raleigh's old ally/rival Drake was countering them at sea, the School was doing its level best to conquer this new land magically, by wedding it to Sidney's poetic conception of Arcadia. Edmund Spenser's *The Faerie Queen* does not idly identify the lands of faerie as Virginia (named for their Virgin Queen, and thus linked to a conception of Elizabeth as queen of air and darkness) but rather does so quite deliberately. While this magical battle will ultimately end in the creation of the United States, as these rival schools of magic sublimate or consume the continent and come to a head in the southwestern US, as the clash of Arcadia and Aztlan create California out of the mythic landscape (tracing back all the way to the *Song of Roland* and the Persian enclosed place that is the root for the word paradise) we need only go to 1787, and the effect the battle had on the foundation of another new world.

The major period of English exploration in the Pacific followed the ending of the Seven Years War with France in 1763. The Earl of Egmont, First Lord of the Admiralty from 1763 until 1766, sent out John Byron in the *Dolphin* in 1764, and on its return from a speedy circumnavigation in 1766, sent the ship out again under Samuel Wallis, with Philip Carteret in the *Swallow* as consort. Wallis and Carteret were separated. Wallis went on to find Tahiti, unknown to Europeans. He named it King George's Island and his five week visit had an importance for Europeans and Polynesians that is hard to measure. Carteret

struggled on alone, and made many important discoveries, including Pitcairn. At this very time the French expedition in *La Boudeuse* and *L'Etoile* under the great Louis-Antoine de Bougainville was making its way through the Pacific, reaching Tahiti, *la nouvelle Cythre*, hard on Wallis's heels.
*Philip Edwards, **An Introduction to the Journals of Captain Cook***

By the time of the Seven Years War, England had vanquished her Spanish rival and become supreme on the oceans, only to find herself locked in rivalry again with France. While the Spanish mindset had been made hard and alien by centuries of Moorish occupation and war to reclaim the peninsula, the French were at once more familiar to the English and more inimical, their relationship one of continuous back and forth warfare since the expedition of William the Bastard in 1066. French was for centuries the language of the English court, and despite France's advantage in manpower and reputation for chivalry, the longbow and general martial spirit of England had ensured that any battle between the two would be evenly matched.

Is it to be believed that these two nations would ignore the mystical possibilities? England, home to the School of Night and later to the genius of Sir Isaac Newton, to whom science was just a puzzle and to whom Arianism and alchemy were passions? And for that matter, could any monarch who had personal knowledge of men like Cagliostro and the Comte de Saint-Germain be ignorant of what had been wrought in the New World? Indeed, when taken in that light, the French desire to involve the natives of the North American continent during the Seven Years War is clearly an attempt to gain guides into the mysticism of the land in order to sever the imported magical paradigm.

So, too, does the Anglo-French rivalry in the Pacific comes down to one idea: He who names a thing has power over it. The second major idea of Hermeticism, transferred through Rosicrucians in France and Templar refugees in England. (And indeed, could the nation that made martyrs out of the Templars have failed to gain the knowledge those worthies had liberated from Islamic sects like the Hashishin? Knowledge, even then, could be more valuable than gold, and the Templars had both in abundance.) The French and English were in a race to designate as much of the world as they could, and thus lock it into a mystical framework: ours or theirs, but not both was the mantra. However, as you may have realized, they had missed the point of Hermeticism. It would come to bite both nations on the ass, if you'll forgive my crudeness.

> He praised all the new Masonic symbols, but said that an image that represented several things no longer represented anything. Which - you'll forgive me - runs counter to the whole hermetic tradition, for the more ambiguous and elusive a symbol is, the more it gains significance and power. Otherwise, what becomes of Hermes, god of a thousand faces?
> *Umberto Eco,* **Foucault's Pendulum**

> Thus, the greatest monument of imperial statesmanship of the time was the Quebec act of 1774. Aimed in the first place at correcting some flaws in the settlement of 1763, the act recognized flatly that the French residents of Canada were not yet ready for the self government promised in 1763 as a lure to English settlers who never came. It provided for an authoritarian constitution; it recognized the Roman Catholicism of the French and permitted them to live under French civil law, though the English criminal law was retained. These concessions to the culture of a non-English people, modifying their institutions only to secure humanitarian ends, were remarkably forward looking. But to the American colonists to the south, feverishly anti-Catholic and oversensitive to any step that might seem to violate English liberties, this remarkable statute was only another and possibly the worst of the Intolerable Acts. Looking back at so profound an estrangement, we can see the Declaration of Independence as a logical and natural result. But most Englishmen could not see that inevitability, and certainly the King and his ministers had no intention of giving up without a fight. The fight they showed was not very impressive.
> *R.K. Webb,* **Modern England: From the 18th Century to the Present**

What happened was as simple as mixing petrol and fire. The English and French traditions had not excluded each other at all; a thing named may be under your power, but a thing with more than one name has more power, and both names must be accepted and understood. Those worthies who were members of the taboo-violating, elemental-alliance-seeking, cabal of cabals within the British aristocracy called the Hellfire Club (men like Horace Walpole and the infamous Lord Sandwich, who provided the only effective leadership from his position as First Lord of the Admiralty, yet invented that renowned meal of his in order that he might eat while not interrupting his gambling, whoring or drinking to do so) and who no doubt advised the king on that tragic Quebec act, thinking by it to subvert the French mystical design for Acadia, their own private Arcadia in the New World, and by so doing to fuse it to Sidney's Arcadia in Virginia, made a dreadful mistake. They did not respect both names, but instead sought to pare down to one. The result was a conflagration. (While we've discussed the actions of the British in Acadia in relation to the infamous Beast of Gevaudon before as magical guerrila warfare, their short term win in the war may have cost them dearly.) It's also interesting to note how Acadians were settled in Virginia... the alchemical marriage of Gloriana and Arcadia? Whatever it was intended to do, what it truly did was create a rebis, a union between the land and the people that demanded a unique birth. And we all know that as the king and the land are one, the king must die, or at least be separated from that land. This, as much as anything, led to the Revolutionary War; just as steam engines may come when it is steam engine time, the morphic resonance may cry out for a nation to be born when it is nation time. The French aid to this mystical separation must be seen in light of the English actions during the conflict with the Spanish. By being midwife, the French created a possible ally, avenged their own defeat, and most importantly dealt a crippling blow to the magical conspiracy propping up King George.

They did not realize how quickly the backlash would strike them, I suppose; otherwise one suspects that Louis would have thought twice about aiding the people who would place the mental virus into the bosom of his kingdom. But when you attempt to play with these forces by your rules instead of theirs, you pay for it. England would recover more quickly than the French from the backlash. And unlike the French, who took their lessons from foreigners, they had a cabal of magicians all ready to advise them on how to replace the union with Arcadia, and with what even greater power.

There is a lacuna in Australian exploration between 1699 and 1770. There were no European visits. The Dutch had lost interest and economic muscle, and the English and French were yet to regularly travel so far. So Australia remained as it always had been, an isolated land, un visited by the outside world except perhaps for adventurous Macassans in search of trepang. With the establishment of a European beachhead in 1788, the pattern of Australian exploration changed, for a frontier had been created.

Tim Flannery, **The Explorers**

From what I have said of the Natives of New Holland they may appear to some to be the most wretched people upon Earth, but in reality they are far happier than we Europeans; being wholy unacquainted not only with the superfluous but the necessary Conveniences so much sought after in Europe, they are happy in not knowing the use of them. They live in a Tranquility which is not disturb'd by the Inequality of Condition: The Earth and sea of their own accord furnishes them with all things necessary for life, they covet not Magnificent Houses, Household-stuff &c, they live in a warm and fine Climate and enjoy a very wholesome Air, so that they have very little need of Clothing and this they seem to be fully sencible of.

Captain James Cook, **The Journals of Captain Cook**

James Cook was as much a mathematican and astronomer as he was a sailor; indeed, the stated objective of his original voyage was the transport of Royal Society scientists to King George's Island, the one so hotly contested by the English and the French a mere decade before. However, while the mission (to observe the transit of Venus, which was to be most visible from the South Pacific) was indeed important, Cook's true objective was much more ambitious: he was to find Terra Australis, the great southern continent which had been postulated to exist since Ptolemy (putting the lie to the misapprehension that the ancients were unaware of the world's roundness) and which was thought to be necessary to keep the planet in an even rotation. (The theory was that the northern landmasses must be matched by southern ones, or the imbalance in weight would lead to rotational instability. So you see, the actual mistakes the ancients made were just as screwy as the ones we libel them with.) Cook was placed in charge of this incredibly sensitive undertaking with the full knowledge that not only was he to make the important journey to King George's Island, but afterwards he had the full support of the navy to find Terra Australis and make sure that he gained the consent of the natives to allow him to take possession of Convenient Situations in the Country in the Name of the King of Great Britain. In other words, when he found it, he was to claim it for His Majesty.

While there is no single continent in the South Pacific that can match the identity and dimensions of Terra Australis as the ancients conceived of it, there are two great continents. One is buried under a sheet of ice, and the other is one of the most varied continental landmasses on Earth. Boasting desert and grassland, coast and reef, this landmass was separated from the main Eurasian continent millions of years earlier when the monotreme and marsupial were still viable rivals to the placental mammals. Humans colonized it when there were still Neanderthal men living in Europe. It was a primordial land, one where nature and mankind still spoke to each other (unlike Europe, where man had long since stopped conversing with the land and started imposing his will upon it like a bridegroom who proved less than chivalrous), and it was its poor fortune to be the land discovered almost by accident by Cook while searching for Terra Australis. Having found no evidence for the great southern continent, he had arrived off the coast of New Zealand and was preparing to return as he had come, but took a slightly different course to the west and accidently stumbled upon the lower southeastern coast of what would become New South Wales. Cook himself wanted to call the cove he discovered Stingray Bay, but changed his mind and named it after the overexcited botanists on board his ship. Botany Bay it would become, and it would be the dread of English malefactors for the next forty or so years.

What many forget is that Cook's superior at the Admiralty, the First Lord himself, was the aforementioned drunkard, gambler and swine Lord Sandwich, John Montagu. In addition to these traits, he was an infamous sexual huntsman and buggerer and a member of that aforementioned group of Englishmen known to history as the Hellfire Club. Sandwich was not a particularly intelligent member of the Club, but he was forceful and arrogant, and he knew talent when he saw it. Did he recruit Cook as part of his purpose at the Admiralty, to name as much of the undiscovered (to Europe) Pacific as possible before the French beat them to it? Cook has been described as the most prodigious namer of lands in history; his titles for bays, islands and mountains are stamped into many locations. Furthermore, when we consider the strange connections from Walpole to the Comte de Saint-Germain, who claimed to be an immortal with knowledge acquired over millennia and including ancient Egyptian lore, should we remember those Egyptian coins supposedly found in Australia? It's interesting to note that when the English arrested the Comte for espionage in 1760, they merely deported him to Austria instead of having him killed. Did they know they couldn't, or did he bribe them with information about the location of *Terra Australis* culled from the mysteries of the Templars? It's known that the mystical charlatan Cagliostro claimed to have learned his Egyptian Freemasonry from Saint Germain, and that the secrets of the Temple were also those of Freemasonry. (It's also interesting to note that Freemasonry in England also claims descent from the Templars, especially those that fled to the holdings of the Sinclair family in Scotland.) Scottish-Rite Freemasonry, therefore, descends from the Templars as well. Both groups, however, are just the tip of the magical iceberg, and in groups like the Hellfire Club we see a more intense mysticism, combining elements of ecstatic (literally meaning breaking the stasis or transgressing the expected) and monastic mysticism. While the Club eventually descended into decadence for its own sake, it does seem to have served to advance its members, and sometimes the Empire as well. Were the explorations of Cook an attempt to apply ancient geomantic principles to a new land, to name and own it? Did the Hellfire Club, feeling the stress in the Americas, start looking for a new land to provide what the former Gloriana seemed unwilling or unable to?

Of course, besides all of this, another benefit of America to English eyes was that it served as a hinterland in which to dump the lowest and most embittered of Georgian society. Criminals were transported to the Americas right up to the Revolutionary War, and even while that war was ongoing, George III was heard to state that while it would take him a while to forgive the rebels, he would be willing to immediately begin transportation of convicts again upon the navy's defeat of the rebellion. Obviously, however, Georgian

England was to lose that war, and as a consequence would have to find somewhere else to dump its thieves, Irish rebels, and other assorted dregs of society. Where better than the antipodes, where the laws of nature were said to be in opposition to the accepted order, where the scum could well invert their bestial natures and become productive members of society (under the lash, of course, of governmental power) as well as ceasing to trouble the decently obedient subjects of the king? Within three years of the Treaty of Paris, the English were transporting their convicts from the dilapidated hulks moored in the Thames where they had languished since the war to the land discovered and named by Cook. There, they would serve as labor and something more.

The Hellfire Club was not composed of fools, merely transgressive magi who thought nothing of bending, breaking or inverting moral scruples and taboos. Knowing the secrets of their predecessors in the School of Night, they would have used the Royal Society (once headed by Newton, who as we know thought of alchemy as just another science and whose *Praxis* may well have encoded in its pages the secrets of the alchemical union created by the School of Night between America and England) as a mask, first sending Cook off to map the stars with the Society, and then to seek Terra Australis. The great southern continent. Was it to be found through astronomy? Well, what else is navigation? The stars lead the sailors on·and when the stars are right, what was lost can be found again. Once Australia was found by mapping the stars, what better course of action than to improve on the faulty ritual that only bound America and England for a century and a half or so? Instead of the Roanoke Island sacrifice to the land, death upon death and pain upon pain would be the cement that bound Australia to England. The System of Transportation would provide the engine for a mechanical ritual befitting the quickly modernizing English, blood and pain and death turned not only to the construction of the physical structures that would serve to house the colony but also the importation of the maritime empire of the British to the antipodes. Not merely a place to dispose of wretches, not only a strategic point on the way to India, but also the new New World.

According to Churchward, Mu was a luxurious continent

measuring 6000 by 3000 miles; its sixty-four million inhabitants, known as Lemurians, possessed an advanced technology which not only gave them a life of comfort and ease but had provided them with anti-gravity devices with which they could actually fly. They were also responsible for sending out parties of colonists who, Churchward claimed, populated all the great land masses, including Atlantis, and it was some of these people who left behind the tablets containing a pictoral record of their history.
Peter Haining, **Ancient Mysteries**

There is a certain moment in Australian exploration which has always transfixed me. It is the instant when white looks on black, and black on white, for the first time. Neither knows it, but such meetings bridge an extraordinary temporal gulf, for they unite people who became separated at least 50,000 years ago. That's 40,000 years longer than people have been in the Americas or Ireland, 20,000 years before the Neanderthals finally surrendered Europe to my ancestors, and 25,000 years before the worst of the last Ice Age turned most of Australia into a howling desert, a vast dunefield. No other cultures, meeting on the frontier, have been separated by such an unimaginable chasm of time.
Tim Flannery, **The Explorers**

That is not dead which can eternal lie, and with strange aeons even death may die.
Attributed to the John Dee translation of the **Necronomicon**

Imagine that strange aeon, on a southern continent where mankind has managed to conquer nature for the first time in history. Rand Flem-Ath and Charles Hapgood believe Atlantis to be buried by a pole shift underneath glaciers in Antarctica. What if, instead of ice, it is dream itself which has swallowed the island kingdom which was the birthplace and true cradle of humanity? Call it Lemuria, call it Mu, call it Atlantis or Avalon or the Blessed Isles; perhaps the retreat of the fae was into the myth itself. If so, how do we recall them, and worse, enslave and despoil them? How do we penetrate the web of dream and find the one place on earth where man remains much as he was tens of thousands of years ago, where the very flora and fauna are isolated from the ravages of rationalism and temporal inertia? We follow the stars. Even then, traveling by the stellar map, we need to follow the ancient Celtic suggestions and travel widdershins, passing the land entirely and then doubling back. Note that the Dutch lost interest, the Spanish were unable to stay, but Cook speared the veil of Dreamtime and brought the agony of time as a virus, withering away those it touched, to Australia.

The Hellfire Club traded an Arcadia, a Gloriana, for an Avalon, an Atlantis. They exchanged one rebis for another. I am not suggesting that Australia was Atlantis (although the time scale would be right, and they discovered ancient caches of Egyptian coins in 1963, a cache going back thousands of years to Egypt...where Saint-Germain may well have learned of it, we might as well suppose), but that it could serve as such, the same way America was made into Arcadia. The imposition of the European magic upon the land could be made easier by the fusion of ancient Celtic myths of island nations and Otherworlds onto the native terrain and the aboriginal concept of the Dreamtime. Uluru becomes Ayers Rock as the names are imposed in another attempt to redefine the land. But they should be careful where they tread, as we have seen: to give something another name does nothing to remove the first, and by piercing the veil and invading another land, they may have merely given it the potential to transcend their understanding of it. An island in the Pacific, ancient and with its own idea of time, may not have been the best graft. Untapped power lies in that desert land, power that is slow to awaken but which has all the time in the world.

Dee knew that things slept in the places between worlds. What rough beast, its hour come at last, slouches towards R'lyeh to be born? Were the first men and women, the colonizers of Atlantis, the men and women Cook saw and perceived as truly happy? Did they abandon civilization as we know it tens of thousands of years ago, because they knew better? And will we destroy ourselves by failing to understand that the more names a thing has, the greater its power? Australia, or Terra Australis, or New Holland, or Mu, or Lemuria, or simply the territory by which one enters the dream...does this island, under stars unlike those over England, serve as a source of strength to a magical conspiracy stretching back ages, or rather as the inheritor of a truly ancient way of life? As below, so above. The stars are right. Given enough time, any condition can reverse.

The Blood of a Golden Dawn

Imagine it's the 1880s. Now, what organization contained the genius of Sir Oliver Lodge, Lewis Carroll, Mark Twain, Alfred, Lord Tennyson, William James and Henri Bergson? The infamous SPR, the Society for Psychic Research. Meanwhile, not far off, another group could claim Arthur Machen, William Butler Yeats, William Wynn Wescott, Sax Roehmer, Algernon Blackwood, and A.E. White... oh, and I'm forgetting the Great Beast himself, although Aleister wasn't really that influential until the 1890s. You guessed it, I'm talking about The Order of the Golden Dawn, our favorite neo-Rosicrucian group of magi. Now the fact that two such groups should exist at the same time isn't so remarkable; after all, Spiritualism was big, the Industrial Revolution had flung England into the role of world empire and blackened her skies and buildings, promising that the entirety of existence was within the comprehension of mankind's rational mind, and Sir James George Frazer was compiling the titanic notes that would encompass his mammoth *The Golden Bough*. Clearly, this was a world on the cusp between light and dark, madness and illumination.

But did you know that Gilbert Murray, the man who drafted the Covenant of the League of Nations, was a member of the SPR? Were you aware that all the great poetry of Yeats is admittedly written with an occult current connecting Irish Myth to the Golden Key of the Order he served? And what of William Wynn Wescott's role as coroner of London during the Jack the Ripper killings? The SPR members took a hard line against psychic phenomenon wherever possible, supporting Michael Faraday as he "proved" that certain events during séances, like table tappings and levitation, could be explained as the medium using the power of suggestion on the sitters, while Aleister Crowley and W.B Yeats engaged in a magical war that led to the creation of the poem "The Second Coming" and the near death of S.L. MacGregor Mathers, Yeats' ally in the Order and the man who usurped control of it from Wescott in 1886. The two groups disagreed about everything, in this world and the next, and they were composed of the most brilliant men of their generation.

It may just be me, but I have a hard time imagining that they sat comfortably next to each other. Blackwood and Twain were notoriously hostile to each other, Yeats' ability as a poet was threatening to Tennyson, and both Bergson and James denounced the Order as pointless barbarism. For his part, Machen said, "These tinkerers try to make God obey their rules, and are outraged when He laughs in their face." (I would as well.) This is without James and Frazer duking it out as to the true meaning of religion, Gilbert Murray's political ambitions... I've said it before and I'll say it again, the Victorian era was a wild ride even if you just stick to what you can prove. And since when do I do that, I ask you?

All sorts of weird references to these groups pop up in later works; Carlos Allende's ramblings about the Philadelphia Experiment include numerous Michael Faraday references, for example. And for those of you who don't know, the Philadelphia Experiment was supposedly an attempt by the US Navy to transform the USS *Eldridge*, or at least render it invisible. Instead, according to Allende, sometime between August 12 and October 28, 1943, the ship teleported from the Philadelphia Navy Yard to Norfolk, Virginia, with all sorts of strange effects on the crew. Some crewmembers were turned invisible and intangible, some went mad, some died horribly (being trapped halfway through bulkheads or becoming frozen in time or, in a few cases, burning like the ancient bush Yahweh was said to have spoken through when addressing Moses, a fire that could not be extinguished), and so on. Of course, the US Navy denies all this. But if Faraday was involved in the SPR (and we know he was) and the Philadelphia Experiment was real and based on Faraday's work, is it possible that the SPR had a vested interest in debunking Spiritualism? Were they planning on exploiting that dimension between life and death themselves? Did the US Navy send the *Eldridge* to Purgatory? Strangely enough, Aleister Crowley's OTO, the Ordo Templi Orientis, promoted John Whiteside Parsons, a Cal Tech chemist with high Navy security clearances due to his work on the solid fuel rocket booster, to head of the Los Angeles branch of the OTO that same year, 1943. Was Crowley keeping tabs on his SPR enemies?

Also interesting is that the whole Majestic-12 debacle (yes, of course the document is a forgery, I completely agree) and Vannevar Bush's connections, both with the Navy's Office of Naval Research (officially established in 1946, the same year as the MJ-12 document was either forged or written) and the Manhattan Project can be traced back to Allende's speculations. Allende claimed that Einstein's unified field theory was somehow related to Faraday's work although he declined to explain how, and he argued that Einstein had finished it in 1923 and told only a few men, including Bush, in 1942, leading to the establishment of both the Manhattan Project and the Philadelphia Experiment. (Keep in mind that Allende wasn't even his real name-it was Carl Allen- and he was totally insane.) How does this relate to Crowley's trip into the desert with Wilfred Smith, Jack Parson's predecessor, in 1942? Is it possible that, as Robert Anton Wilson claims, Crowley's "Aiwaas" and Charles Dodgson's "Lewis Carroll" persona were indeed one and the same? That encoded in Faraday's researches and Dodgson's writings are the secrets of scientifically breaching the walls of reality and allowing for an exploration of other dimensions... even dimensions of the dead?

This leads us to some interesting questions. How do we know that the atomic bomb is in fact an atomic bomb at all? What if the wilder speculations of quantum physics are true, there is no truth to our understanding of the physical universe, and that everything is composed of superstring vibrations actoss the plane of existence? That all things are one, in life and in death? What if the atom bomb breaches the barriers between worlds, allowing Hell to enter our concept of reality for a brief moment? It was Arthur C. Clarke who said that a sufficiently advanced technology is indistinguishable from magick. Is the inverse true? Is a sufficiently commonplace magick mistakable for science? After all, magick is whatever works. Did Lodge deliberately help encode Faraday's more outré discoveries into the very fabric of modern physics? Einstein said that God didn't play dice with the universe, but is the Devil a wagering man? (I also find it interesting that Einstein was lousy at math as a child, and much of his ability with science came from what he called *Gedankenexperiments*, thought exercises. Is it possible that the Ripper killings weren't Wescott at all, but the SPR, trying to bring a sufficiently complex spirit into the world to become Einstein's muse?)

It's an obvious fact that Crowley's arrival split the Order of the Golden Dawn assunder, leaving the SPR's most intelligent and socially prominent critics at each others' throats just when they were needed most. Was Crowley, through Aiwass/Lewis, a traitor in their midst? Did Gilbert Murray deliberately help prolong the horrors of WWI and draft a weak document that wouldn't allow the League to prevent the war to come, knowing that such a catalyst was necessary to mislead the governments of the world into swallowing the Faraday model of reality and bringing about the opening of the way? First the USS *Eldridge* sails through reality, and then the atom bomb makes hell itself touch earth. Is the real reason that the nations of the world ignored the horror of the Final Solution due to the fact that they were manipulated by a sinister cabal of pseudo-scientists who needed the sacrificial energy? After all, reading through Twain, Carroll, Bergson and Lodge, one doesn't exactly miss the anti-semitism, the racism, and in Twain's case the outright sympathy with the devil. Believing the human race to be a botched experiment, might these men not make a deal with Lucifer... who, after all, as Light Bringer has often given us forbidden or dangerous knowledge? Well, it doesn't get much more dangerous than the bomb, does it?

Actually, another even more interesting idea occurs to me. Arthur Machen and Algernon Blackwood were direct influences upon the budding horror writer and amateur astronomer Howard Phillips Lovecraft of Providence, Rhode Island, my home town (or at least where I was born), and Lovecraft was in communication with Robert Goddard, the rocketry expert who refused to be involved in any research he couldn't personally control. Goddard knew J. Robert Oppenheimer, argued with him over the creation of the A-bomb, and was opposed to its use... and he died of throat cancer a few days after the atomic destruction of Nagasaki. Now, even before he died (short of the A-bomb's creation by six years), Lovecraft wrote the poem "Nyarlathotep" about sinister scientific expansion gone mad, and at the Trinity test detonation Oppenheimer was heard to quote from the *Bahgavad Gita*: "I am become Death, the shatterer of worlds." Now, I've elsewhere argued that Yahweh is indistinguishable from Yog-Sothoth and that Christ was a Dunwich Horror crossbreed... so what of their enemy? What of Lucifer, the Light

Bringer, the bearer of illumination? Is it a coincidence that Adam Weishaupt's Illuminati (founded in 1776) and the United States (also founded in 1776) both have the pyramid with the eye as a symbol? What kind of illumination are we discussing? If Yahweh is Yog-Sothoth, does that make Lucifer the Crawling Chaos Nyarlathotep? Certainly seems that way, doesn't it? It's easy to see Oppenheimer as the American successor to Lodge, the physicist of magick. After all, we don't exactly know who did the work on the Philadelphia Experiment, do we? Not hard to picture it being Oppenheimer, ultimately, while Bush kept it quiet. And pray tell, what did we need to send a destroyer into the otherworld for, anyway? Is there an American military base on the shores of the River Acheron? Have we set up shop in Hell itself?

Instead of uniting to oppose this threat, as I'm sure Blackwood and Yeats would have done, the Order was fractured by infighting. Member turned against member, *Frater* against *Frater,* and when all was said and done, the members of the Order stood separately against a menace that they needed to face together. Yeats' clues to the Golden Key, supposedly locked away inside his poetry, waits there for someone else to discover and use... and we may well want to hurry, because the tensions are rising and there is no Golden Dawn. If Lewis Carroll's works are a code explaining how to breach the barriers between realities, perhaps the works of Machen, Blackwood and their disciple Lovecraft are a warning that we know all too little about what waits for us in that darkness between realities.

If the Soul of the Elder Gods is moving to secure his power against the titan idiot overlords like Azathoth and Yog-Sothoth, can we afford to follow the tune of the Black Man with a Horn? Yet the piper plays on, and the world slides ever nearer to the day when the barriers between worlds will be shattered in nuclear fire. Aiwass must be pleased. Who, exactly, were the oysters that Carroll's Walrus and Carpenter were to feast upon? The young men dying in excrement in the trenches? The victims herded into the camps? The blasted shadows that were the last remains of the first A-bomb blasts?

Or maybe you and I, reading this now. The Great Beast has been born, and not all the *spirtus* in the *mundi* can jam that genie back in the bottle... or down the rabbit hole again. Nyarlathotep slouches towards Almagordo to be born.

It Is The Life Thereof

> The emotional impact that blood has retained upon even our
> sophisticated, space age generation is demonstrated in the
> number of people who faint at the sight of it. Surely it did not
> take long for the most primitive ancestors of our species to
> learn that when the sticky red fluid was draining from the
> body as a result of a tiger's claw or a sharp rock, the victim's
> life oozed out along with it.
> *Brad Steiger, **The Werewolf Book***

For literally two thousand years, you had a better chance of
surviving an injury or disease if you were too poor to seek medical
help. If you went to a barber (that's who did medicine back then;
those red and white poles are referring to an old tradition of hanging
the cloths used in bloodletting outside as an advertisement) he was
likely to bleed you to death or overdose you on some whacky
concoction he would shove up your ass using an enema tube that
looked like the beak of an ibis. If you were rich, like a King or a
nobleman, you were better off being injured very, very far from home
than getting sick at the castle, because then, they'd let the doctors at
you, and life was about to get painful indeed.

Responsible writers will tell you these deaths were due to a
misunderstanding of how illness and injury worked based on old
Greek ideas of the four elements and things the medieval doctors
called humors. There were four of them. The red humor was blood,
linked to fire and warmth. The yellow humor of bile was linked to
temper and arrogance and called cholera, as in the Elizabethan
description of a man of villainous temper as choleric. The white
humor of phlegm was connected to stolidness, while the black humor
led to melancholia and sadness, and was even called *melanos*, Greek
for "black." Since doctors believed these four humors could be easily
imbalanced, leading to illness, and since they had naturalists' reports
from the time of the Roman Empire describing how sick or

distempered animals would open a vein in order to calm down, they believed that by letting out some of the humors, balance could be restored. This is what responsible writers will tell you.

The great thing about being me is that I'm not even remotely responsible. I am a satirist, a fantasist, and a malcontent. So I ask you; "Is it possible that doctors for two millennia were engaged in wide-scale human sacrifice?" I think it is. Here's why.

Unless doctors were willfully stupid, they had to know what happened when someone was cut deeply. After all, they lived in medieval Europe, where people carried around long sharp things for the express purpose of cutting someone deeply, and wore suits made out of metal in an attempt to avoid being cut deeply. You see, when blood begins to come out of you, you are in danger of death. Depending on how much, of course... a pint or two is no big deal if you can get rest and staunch the flow, although it does weaken your immune system. However, four or five pints is a bit different. This causes massive fatigue, pallor, weakness, all that kind of thing. Yet the average medieval barber-physician's first recourse was to bleed the patient five or six times, taking roughly sixteen ounces or so at a time. Sixteen times six is ninety-six ounces, which in US terms means that they were taking out six pints before they considered any other options. For you metric types, that works out to two and a half litres. That is a lot of blood, especially when you are already sick.

I find the suggestion that they actually thought it was helpful to exsanguinate a man willfully ignorant, especially when exsanguination is an old, old knackerer's technique (your better class of butcher knows that you don't kill the cattle, but merely stun it so as to make slitting its throat easier; the blood drains out, and it dies without the blood rotting inside the meat) practiced since the time of the Sumerians some six thousand years ago,. Hell, the Roman cult of Mitras was all about killing by exsanguination! No, I don't buy it.

Instead, let me suggest this. Medicine derives from two sources in the west, one of them the god Aesclepius, the other the Greek thinker Hippocrates, creator of the Hippocratic Oath. Aesclepius, being the son of Apollo, was put to death by Zeus because he was saving too many mortals. What if Hippocrates learned from Aesclepius' error? What if, to propitiate the hungry sky gods, he set out on a course of deliberate blood sacrifice, offering up this precious fluid (as it says in the Bible, Leviticus 17:14, "It is the life of all flesh, the blood of it is the life thereof," and groups as widely spaced as the Phoenicians, Babylonians, Chinese and Celts all engaged in blood sacrifice) in order to divert the wrath of Olympian Zeus? This is of course not mentioning that another of the Thunderer's names was Lykaeon Zeus, Zeus Wolf-Father.

So, this secret magical brotherhood, who take oaths in Hippocrates' name, who wear to this day the caduseus of Hermes, one of the psychopomps of Greek mythology who takes the souls of the dead in the Eleusian mystery cults, set about their task of healing... but not too well, lest they draw the ire of the gods. They save some, and sacrifice others, draining their blood so that they might offer it up to their gods. Not hard to imagine the Druids (who came into contact with Greece when the Celts invaded Thessaly) being a part of all this, is it? Why was the court of King Arthur so obsessed with the Grail that had caught the blood of Christ? Were the healing powers intimated to be contained in the Grail the result of the blood of the sacrificed man-god it contained, blood that could transcend the link between the healers and their pagan overlords?

This blood harvest, as we have already seen, went the hardest on the nobles and the kings and queens of history. Was this a working of vast scale, a recreation of the unending wound of the Fisher King using the mystical link between the king and the land to preserve Europe? Remember that by 900 AD, Europe was facing invasion by the Magyars to the east, the Arab Nations to the south, and the Vikings to the north. Did this threefold threat require the blood of as many divinely ordained monarchs as possible, in order to try to recreate the sacrifice of the Lord of Hosts a nigh-millennia earlier? Was it this medical bloodletting that preserved western civilization?

Of course, one can hardly talk about blood sacrifices and the like without dragging in vampires. After all, all this blood draining can hardly have been something they didn't notice. That's like asking us to believe that Vikings weren't interested in rapine and slaughter. I mean, draining blood out of people... that's what vampires do. This of course leads one to the suspicion that at least some of the gods were, in fact, vampires. Apollo seems a poor candidate for this, however... but his cousin Hermes, winged messenger of death? Dionysus, bringer of ecstatic madness and wine-god? (And what else could he have been drinking, he asks disingenuously?) He was also the child of Lykaon Zeus, who could summon the thunder and the storm, take on the shape of animals, and sire half-divine offspring (who bring to mind the *dhampir* of Transylvanian myth... and Transylvania isn't that far from Greece, now is it?) all over the place? Perhaps there were two classes of Olympian gods, beings like Diana and Apollo and their offspring, and the hideously bloodthirsty gods like the Cthonic Hades and Zeus. As to the idea that Zeus was Apollo's father, look at their myths and you tell me. Apollo is the god of sunlight, of archery (wooden shafts; useful against vampires, no?), of prophecy and enlightenment. His sister Artemis is the goddess of wildness and freedom, also of archery, of the beasts of the forest and of the sacred hunt. Naah, they aren't Zeus' kids. Zeus' kids are like Heracles, whose rages were legendary and who killed his first wife and children in a fit of madness, or like Dionysios, whose maenads went on bloodthirsty rampages at his command, or like Pan, a hideous amalgamation of beast and man with unspeakable urges and a thirst for blood sacrifice. Apollo and Artemis were tacked on by some later writer, probably Hesiod, who was a giant apologist for the cruel, selfish, blood-drinking rapist god Zeus and his brood. It's also interesting to point out that Herodotus tells us that the Scythians were descended from Heracles. Wheels within wheels, folks. Was Hippocrates convinced that if he offered these jealous immortals the blood they craved, they would spare him? Is the Caduseus a sign to the gods that the mortal wearing it is one of their servants? Maybe. Sure would explain a lot about modern medical practices, wouldn't it now?

None of this tells us what Apollo and Artemis actually were. They bear a striking resemblance to the Morrigan and Nuada of the Silver Hand from Dannan myth, as well as in Artemis' case seeming like a good candidate for a werebeast of some kind (Apollo's connection to the Pythia at Delphi and to prophecy makes him seem less lycanthropic and more mystical)... but I'll leave that one alone for now. Because we still haven't gotten to the best part yet.

In order to get there, I'll need to set the scene. By the middle of the nineteenth century, even the most gullible were starting to notice that doctors weren't doing that well when it came to saving lives. As George Gordon, Lord Byron put it, "More have died from the lancet than the lance." Now I'll resist the urge to point out Byron's own death from bloodletting, and the urge to mention the possible vampiric connections there, and just point out how convenient it is that Pasteur developed the germ theory just when medical science needed to start getting better in order to keep people coming to the doctors. So, you may ask, what did the medical community, aside from the Red Cross, do about all that blood they needed? Did they decide to try to pull a bait and switch? (Note: If anyone reading this is a doctor, take heart. I don't think most of you guys are in on it, only the secret Aesclepian cult of the Azure Cross. Seriously, that was his symbol. Check it out. I suppose, furthermore, that it isn't fair to call it Aesclepius' cult when it is in fact dedicated to his killers, but that's occult perversity for you.)

> On the night of April 8, 1979, two Apache tribal officers were on patrol duty not far from Dulce, New Mexico, when they saw a mysterious aircraft "hovering about 50 feet off of the ground with a powerful spotlight aimed at the cattle." A third police officer in the area also observed the craft, which, he said "had to be connected with a series of 16 recent cattle mutilations in the Dulce area."
> **The Reader's Digest Mysteries of the Unexplained**

Here's where things get interesting. I assume that more than the blood is required; to some degree, the ritual is also important. But with kings gone, and it being hard to procure all the blood they need, where would the cult go? Well, black helicopters and secret medical labs are staples of modern conspiracy theory, and they serve us well here. The blood banks being constantly on the edge of collapse no matter how many times we roll up our sleeves and let them drink from us, it became necessary to supplement that intake without being noticed. They couldn't just go and buy it; in the modern world, that leaves a paper trail that could prove disastrous, and it would also mean that they'd miss the moment of death, which is spiritually important in most sacrifices. So they resort to cattle mutilation, which of course also links them spiritually to the powerful magic of the cult of Mitras, the bull-slayer, whose act of bovine sacrifice was acceptable to the gods.

Sure, it's out there. Way out there. Incredibly out there. But it explains how doctors could look at cattle who have had twenty-five-inch-square sections of their hide peeled away and decide that coyotes did it, doesn't it? In one move, they transfer the blame onto the wild beasts sacred to Artemis, the enemy of their blood-drinking lords, and they cover up their own involvement. I mean, do coyotes remove the inside of a cow's udder, then fill it with sand? No, they do not. That should be enough for now, I suppose, to put you off visiting your physician. And I didn't even get to the part about infibulation of male and female genitalia (basically, you insert hooks and wires into the foreskin of the male, closing off his penis and preventing erections, and you do the same to the opening of a woman's vagina, as a kind of sophisticated version of genital mutilation) and the link between this recent Victorian fad and the cult of Aesclepius' attempt to prevent the rise of Eleusian ritual. Although it is interesting to notice how Chronos' castration of his father Uranus took place using a flint sickle that spread his blood out, giving rise to Aphrodite as well as several other demons and creatures in Greek myth, once again proving that the blood is the life. Maybe another time.

The Devil Came Down to Jersey

Considerable sensation has been evoked in the towns of Topsham, Lympstone, Exmouth, Teignmouth, and Dawlish, in the south of Devon, in consequence of a vast number of foottracks of a most strange and mysterious description. The superstitious go so far as to believe that they are the marks of Satan himself; and that great excitement has been produced among all classes may be judged from the fact that the subject has been descanted on from the pulpit.
The Times of London, *February 16, 1855*

The first sighting reportedly took place at 2 a.m. on Sunday, January 17, 1909, when Bristol, Pennsylvania postmaster E.W. Minister saw a glowing monster flying over the Delaware River. It had, he said, a ramlike head, with curled horns, and stayed aloft with long, thin wings. It had short legs, the rear ones longer than the front ones, and it emitted cries which sounded like a combined squawk and whistle. Two other men, one a police officer who fired at it, also observed the creature. On the eighteenth a policemen at Burlington, New Jersey, spotted a flying "Jabberwock" with glowing eyes, and soon residents of neighboring towns were finding mysterious tracks in the snow.
Jerome Clark, **Unexplained!**

What has bat wings, the head of a ram, the unearthly squeal of a creature from hell, and the ability to somehow leave tracks all over the countryside with no regard for the enormous distances involved? Well, in the Pine Barrens of New Jersey and thereabouts, that would have to be the Jersey Devil. However, as to what was leaving similar tracks in England a half-century or so earlier... well, maybe that was the Jersey Devil, too. Of course, this doesn't explain what kind of critter was leaving similar hoof-shaped prints in the untouched snow of Kergulen Island, near the pack ice of Antarctica in 1840, now does it? Yet, as I'm sure you guessed by now, I have a suspicion that it may well have been that ol' Jersey Devil again. Captain Sir James

Clark Ross may not have gotten a glimpse of the devil- and that may well have been for the best- but in his *Voyage of Discovery and Research in the Southern and Antarctic Regions*, written in 1847 (some eight years before the incident in Devonshire) he wrote that the only evident traces on this island were the singular footsteps of a pony or ass.

The Devil is a curious beast, to say the least. According to that old unreliable source, folklore (which I personally always love, but not everyone agrees), the Jersey Devil has a Christian last name, and it is Leeds. The legend is as follows: sometime in 1735, at Leeds Point, New Jersey, Mrs. Leeds (no, unfortunately Mrs. Leeds' first name was not recorded in my sources) became pregnant for the thirteenth time (again, no one bothered to take down the essential information of the baby's father; I, for one, would like to narrow down the list a little here) and cursing, she stated that the baby "might just as well be a devil." Now, those of you who are familiar with the old EC horror comics can probably see that ironic twist coming, as the baby was indeed born a grotesque monster which thereafter flew into the Pine Barrens and has lived there ever since. Born in 1735, that would make it 174 as of its rampage in 1909; whatever our Devil's problems might have been, longevity does not seem to have been one of them. Since the rampage of 1909, the Devil has been seen again (in 1930 and '32, it popped up for a brief run of terror, but nothing to equal its glory appearance) which would seem to indicate that it might still be out there, not aging, a devil born of man with the power to exist in our secular age and leave signs of its presence. (Interesting side-note: the Jersey Devil's rampages in 1909 and 1930 both took place within six months of major impacts between the Earth and starstuff, the Tunguska Blast of 1908 and a smaller but still impressive blast in Rio Curaca in 1930.)

While I may be going out on a limb to include the English and Antarctic sightings (which are only of tracks, not of the Devil itself) there is a method to my madness. As is often the case, H.P. Lovecraft and his disciples are stuck right in the middle of it. F. Paul Wilson, writer of excellent novels such as *The Keep* and the Repairman Jack series, wrote a short Lovecraftian story entitled "The Barrens" about our Jersey Devil. (I know for a fact it's available in *Cthulhu 2000*; check your bookseller of choice.) Now, any Lovecraftn reader knows about Lovecraft's excellently disturbing "At The Mountains of Madness," which of course takes place... you guessed it, in Antarctica. And the English connection? Well, good ol' Arthur Machen (God bless you, Father Machen) of hideous fame as one of the wellsprings of our man Lovecraft, wrote many a tale set in those Devonshire hills, tales of stunted crossbreeds and hideous monsters. Now, as we've discussed before, Machen was a member of the Order of the Golden Dawn, started by Qabbalist William Wade Wescott in 1884. So Machen knew stuff. And I haven't even dragged in Edgar Allan Poe's *The Strange Narrative of Arthur Gordon Pym* yet. (Poe, by the way, was born in 1809, exactly one hundred years before the rampage of the Jersey Devil, and he travelled all over the country, including Providence [Lovecraft's home town] and... Devonshire. Hmm. Seems hinky to me.) Antarctica is already a hundred pounds of weird in a ten pound bag, what with the Piri Reis map and its attendant narrative of strange monsters and a hot waste where we now know pack ice to be, Admiral Byrd's little trip into self-induced oxygen toxicity, the possible connection to the Hollow Earth of the Deros and the Teros... you just can't trust the bottom of the world, it seems.

So let's look at things. We're got a mysterious demonic birth with a love of ice and snow- the Devil never appears any later than February in the barrens, and the Devonshire appearances were in that month as well, and Antarctica is, well, Antarctica- and a wild rampage or two for no readily apparent reason. We also have a Lovecraftian connection, stuff falling from the sky in two incidents; what, pray tell, is the Devil of the Pine Barrens up to? Well, one thing comes to mind: *Qlippoth*. What are those, you may ask? Well, I'm glad you did.

As a Qabbalist, Machen would know that alongside the *Sephiroth*, the emanations of the spheres that make up the tree of life, reside the *Qlippoth*, the shells. The *Qlippoth*, in *Qabbalism*, are planes containing demons, negative or disintigrating spirits, and the like. In other words, pure concentrated anti-life. As Bill Whitcomb puts it, the *Qlippoth* symbolize progressive degeneration, entropy, and disintegration. Some occultists say that the Qlippoth are, in effect, God's garbage disposal. It's interesting to note that the Qlippoth that opposes Aquarius is Bahimiron, which translates as the Bestial

Ones. Quite appropriate for our little Devil, isn't it? Now, of course Bahimiron brings to mind Baphomet, another ram-headed demonic sort, known primarily for his possible link to the Knights Templar (and it's a sure thing that rumors of said link really helped King Phillip IV of France and Pope Clement V put the Templars to the stake and otherwise wipe them out). And it is of course one of those coincidences we crazy folk so love that worship of Baphomet was said to be linked to secret Gnostic leanings in the Templars, Gnostic ideas such as the rape of Sophia, the furthest descent from the Sephiroth, by the Demiurge, who sought to create in the image of the creator of all things, the First Emanator. (Sure, it's twisted Qabbalism; what do you expect from the Templars, especially if they were worshipping one of the Qlippoth?)

Now, both William Wade Wescott and the Lovecraftian Esoteric Order of Dagon have a connection to Masonic rites (Wescott was a Mason, and the EOD is a blatant Masonic pastiche) and it's interesting to note that claims have been made linking Masonry, especially Scottish and Egyptian Rite Masonry- ah, thank God for Cagliostro, that crazy bastard- to Templar beliefs. Hell, Cagliostro claimed even more; he claimed that Nicholas Flamel, the alchemist and mystic, was one of those who transmitted secret Templar knowledge to him, and that Flamel claimed to be unkillable until six centuries had passed from his discovery of the elixir vitae, which Cagliostro claimed Flamel discovered in 1297. Flamel is of interest here not only because he was one of the few alchemists of his time not to suffer from penury (he somehow always had gold or silver whenever he needed it) but also because he was living in Paris right around the time that Jacques de Molay was burned at the stake, 1313 AD, again according to Cagliostro (granted, Cagliostro was a notorious charlatan, but once you've gone along with the Jersey Devil, why not stay for the rest of the ride?), and he helped start both Masonry and Rosicrucianism. Also interestingly enough, an unknown fellow in black arranged for the publication of Flamel's great work *The Philisophic Summary* in 1735- right around the time our boy the Jersey Devil was born, as a matter of fact. Was this fellow in black related to the mysterious figure in black who designed the Great Seal of the United States some fifty years later? Was a mysterious dark stranger, weary with his travels in the wilderness of America, entertained for a night in a tiny home near the edges of the Pine Barrens?

Flamel connects to Cagliostro and Masonry in another way, as a possible alternate identity for the Comte de Saint Germain, who is just so much fun when I need to come up with someone to connect all these kinds of things. Claiming to be an immortal and always dressed in black, Saint-Germain at times dropped hints that he was an Egyptian high priest (shades of Nyarlathotep- and here we are, back in Lovecraft country), a friend of King Solomon, a master alchemist... you name it, and the Comte will have at least claimed to have done it. He was demonstrably in London in 1743 (Horace Walpole will vouch for him) and St. Petersburg in 1762, where he invented a potent diuretic to keep the troops regular during the Crimean War. Cagliostro claimed that Saint Germain was indeed Flamel, and that he founded Freemasonry with secrets stolen from the Temple, and while his exact time and place of death aren't known (of course they aren't) a story told about him always amuses me. When a visitor asked the Comte's valet if it were true that Saint Germain was present for a marriage in biblical times in Galilee, the valet sniffed and replied, "You forget, sir, I have only been in the Comte's service for a century." Was Flamel/Saint-Germain the father of the Devil? If so, to what end? And why would the beast be so interested in wintry places and the dark mysteries of Antarctica? Was it hunting for a key to the Hollow Earth, the lost technology of the Deros, or was it merely seeking that lost meteoroid found in 1997 which contained evidence that foreign life may well have existed on Mars millions of years ago? (Remember, the Devil seems to act up when stuff falls from the sky.)

The connection between falling rocks from space and the Holy Grail shall go unmentioned for now. But I'd be amiss in my duty if I didn't mention Pelleas and the Questing Beast from Arthurian myth, the endless pursuit of the hideous monster, the amalgam of more godly animals. Perhaps the Templars were hunting Baphomet, not worshipping it? Perhaps the mysterious man in black was not the progenitor of the creature, but merely arrived too late to prevent the Qlippoth Bahirimon from recreating a physical body, like the one it had fifteen centuries ago? Hard to say, really. At any rate, we come full circle and the Devil laughs at us from the dark, his goatish features twisted in a sneer, for we do not now and may never know his true origins. And somehow, that may be for the best.

Hypatia

Her teaching appears to have been imbued with the Iambichan mystical tradition, and she may have even imparted to her students the arcana of the so-called Chaldean Oracles, a second-century collection of purported divine revelations. Judging from the evidence provided by Synesius, her best known pupil, he probably gained his knowledge of the occult sciences and of Hermeticism from Hypatia. She attracted large numbers of students, and perhaps acquired a municipally endowed chair in philosophy. Her fame was such that Synesius referred to her simply as "the philosopher."
Christopher Haas, Alexandria in Late Antiquity

At the command of Cyril his body was raised from the ground and transported in solemn procession to the cathedral; the name of Ammonius was changed to that of Thaumasias, the wonderful; his tomb was decorated with the trophies of martyrdom; and the patriarch ascended the pulpit to celebrate the magnanimity of an assassin and a rebel. Such honors might incite the faithful to combat and die under the banners of the saint; and he soon prompted, or accepted, the sacrifice of a virgin, who professed the religion of the Greeks, and cultivated the friendship of Orestes. Hypatia, the daughter of Theon the mathemetician, was initiated in her father's studies; her learned comments have elucidated the geometry of Apollonius and Diophantus; and she publicly taught, both at Athens and Alexandria, the philosophy of Plato and Aristotle. In the bloom of beauty, and in the maturity of wisdom, the modest maid refused her lovers and instructed her disciples; the persons most illustrious for their rank or merit were impatient to visit the female philosopher; and Cyril beheld with a jealous eye the gorgeous train of horses and slaves which crowded the door of her academy.
Edward Gibbon, The Decline and Fall of the Roman Empire, Volume II

In the history of the world, there have been many who have held power by force- force of arms, force of personality, force of will.

But few have held that power purely by merit of the force of their intellect, and of their number, Hypatia of Alexandria can claim a seat at the great table of the mind. In a time when one way of life was dying and another was assuming its position of respect, Hypatia was the most respected, most intelligent, most effective syncretist of the best of the Ancient World with the most useful of the newest trends. More so than even the Emperor Julian, in her lay the potential for the defeat or modification of Christianity from a bloody tenet of persecution (to steal a phrase from Roger Williams, one of my other heroes) into a philosophy of the mind and heart in union.

Therefore, she had to die. So is the orthodox view, at any rate. It isn't a bad theory as such go; it fits most of the facts of her death as we understand them, it is in line with the character of the man most likely to have orchestrated her death, the Patriarch Cyril. And, of course, I suspect it is totally wrong.

At the beginning of the fifth century AD, there were three cities in the Roman Empire so famous that the word "city" seemed to refer to them specifically. If you used the Latin phrase *urbe aeterna*, then it was obvious to all listeners that you were speaking of Rome itself, the endless city, which had (to many minds) achieved eternity by dint of its fame and its accomplishments. And indeed, of the three cities, it is the only one still called by the same name and, although rendered different by the passage of sixteen hundred years, the ancient city can still be seen and felt in the lines of the modern one.

If, on the other hand, you were of a Greek persuasion and spoke of *eis ten polin*, then you were speaking of Constantinople, the city known to many as the seat of the Byzantine Empire and the city renamed Istanbul by the Turkish armies who corrupted the Greek phrase. It is gone, and yet it remains, half asleep and half a ghost.

But to philosophers and scholars and scientists and historians and writers and poets, there was but one city in all the Empire. Alexandria ad Aegyptum, home of the fabled Museon which today we know as the Library, the most glorious city of the Alexandrians. And in the years between A.D. 395 (Gibbon's official end point for Volume I of his *Decline and Fall*) and A.D. 415, the year of Hypatia's murder, Alexandria was the most important city for matters of theology, philosophy and scholarly debate. As is pointed out in the quote by Haas, Hypatia was a master of all these fields, so famous that she usurped the ancient prerogative of Aristotle and Plato and was known as *the philosopher*. She knew science and theology and mysticism, she was the greatest mathematician of her time (and like Archimedes, another great mathematician, she would die before she could complete her work) and more than any other figure since Hermes the Thrice Great, Thoth of the Ibis himself, she was a syncretist. She combined numerous fields of learning into one body of work, whose purpose was the elucidation of and understanding of all existence.

And *that* is why she had to die.

> Since the "face on Mars" is related to the issue of extraterrestrial intelligence and visitation, it should be noted that hyperdimensional physics is noted in *The McDaniel Report*. McDaniel explains that Hoagland and Torun have interpreted some of the mathematical relationships around objects on the Cydonian area of Mars around the face in terms of higher-dimensional geometry.
> *Charles F. Emmons, **At The Threshold***

> The Sephiroth are often thought of as intermediary states or stages between the First Emanator (godhead) and all things that exist, though some sources also view the Spheres as divisions of existence within God. These ten fundamental attributes (or modes of) God together compose the unified universe of the Life of God and are usually imagined in the form of a tree (Otz Chaim) or of a man (Adam Kadmon, the "Primordial Man").
> *Bill Whitcomb, **The Magician's Companion***

> At first sight this particular type of superstring theory might seem to have an insurmountable drawback in that it deals with a space-time of ten dimensions instead of the three dimensions of space and one of time that are perceived in the everyday world. It seems, however, that six of the ten dimensions may be "compactified," or "curled up"—i.e., so small that they are unnoticeable.
> *Encyclopedia Britannica, **Superstring Theory***

Michio Kaku, the author of the brilliant *Hyperspace*, argued that whoever first discovered the means to manipulate hyperspatial reality would become "Lord of the Universe." Sounds an awful lot like our old pal Yahweh, that proto-Lovecraftian universe-creating Sephiroth-manifesting maker of all things seen and unseen, doesn't it? If the Sephiroth are in fact the map of the mind of God, the Adam Kadmon or primordial man as it were, then doesn't it seem interesting that there are ten dimensions to superstring theory, the mathematically predicted, new physics attempt to explain all of existence? Well, it does to me, anyway. (And anyone remembering our pal Lovecraft's "From Beyond" or "Dreams in the Witch House" right about now has been paying attention, and gets the gold star.) Especially interesting, in the light of the fact that Hypatia was a master of Hermetic thought, is Hermeticism's long-standing debt to the Qabbala. Alexandria had a very entrenched Jewis community which naturally looked to the pagan Hypatia and her toleran ally Orestes for protection from Patriarch Cyril, who considered them "most deranged of men, senseless, blind, uncomprehending, demented, foolish God haters and killers of the Lord." One should note that these were some of his more gentle exclamations regarding them, which means they would have been fools not to support his enemies. This they did both through alliance with Hypatia and by arranging on several occasions to set fire to Christian churches in order to ambush Cyril's followers, the parablani, the most fanatical of the Christian sects then in Alexandria. It is also interesting to consider Hypatia's combinatiosn of Pythagorean mathematics and Iambichan mysticism, which might well have derived from her study of Iamblichus' biography of Pythagoras, containing stories of the great man's ability to exist in different physical locations at the same time.

Hypatia was instrumental in the development of the concept of IAO, the Gnostic term for the formula that would explain all things. It consisted of three words, reflecting the influence of the Qabbala's Tetragrammaton upon her thinking: Like the constantly unfolding mathematically predictive name of God, the IAO consisted of a constantly mutable series of interactions between Iota, symbolizing the eternal present, Alpha, which represented the creation of all things, and Omega, which was of course the end. Sound familiar? *I am the Alpha and the Omega, the first and last.* Like a certain Hebrew carpenter who Cyril followed, Hypatia was very interested in the relationship between what had been at the beginning and what would be at the end. However, what he seemed to find in a sacrificial ordeal, she sought to reveal through the application of a whole new kind of mathematics.

In short, Hypatia sought hyperspace. And in so doing, she threatened Cyril's boss, who was already in the Lord of the Universe business and who had in Cyril the perfect tool to ensure that she never finished her calculations. (Like Archimedes, like Pascal, like Turning, like von Neumann; just as the mind turns to the more interesting paths where science and magick seem the same, the path is truncated, diverted, or otherwise sabotaged. A familiar pattern, no?) One of her followers was Synesius, a heretical Arian who would end up as a bishop and follower of the teachings of Origen and who was at least sympathetic to the Gnostic ideal of the True God, of whom the universe was made, and who was approachable by the Tree of Life, as opposed to the Demiurge, the unclean spirit who made this world and who was afraid of perfection and knowledge. (In case you're wondering, the Demiurge is explicitly linked to Yahweh in the Gnostic gospels, and also bears a great resemblance to Satan, who one might notice is a servant of the God of the Old Testament yet an enemy of Jesus in the new. Did Lucifer fall, or did he keep on serving the same God he always did?) It wouldn't take much to get Cyril, who was violently opposed to both Arianism and Gnosticism, to move against both (as he did in his attacks on Orestes, a baptized Catholic who opposed Cyril's more Nicean faith) and even less to move him to assassinate a pagan philosopher who threatened the status quo and who had more political influence and acumen than he did, especially a woman.

The actual death of Hypatia is simple enough: a mob, most likely led by Cyril's parablani, dragged her from her carriage one day while she made her way from her residence to the Museon and tortured her to death inside the great church of the Caesarion itself. The religious significance of her death severed the alliances of Cyril's enemies (Orestes and the Arians, the Jews of Alexandria, the Imperial bureaucracy) and established the supremacy of Cyril's church in Alexandria. He also unwittingly helped shatter Alexandria's standing as a great city and may well have left it open to Muslim conquest a mere two centuries later, for with Hypatia's death any certainty as to the role of the Museon in the city proper departed.

Today, we do not even know where the Library of Alexandria was. Hypatia's father Theon was its last official head, and it is likely that she herself assumed the power and responsibilities, if not the title, upon his death. Yet after her death, we hear little of the Museon. While the accumulated wisdom of the Museon was transmitted, in some small detail, to the later Islamic authorities of al-Iskandariyyah, the greatness of the Library was lost following her death. Its mythic destruction is lamented as a great loss, and indeed it would be, if the library had been destroyed. But was it?

> So far, no one has managed to work out the mathematics to prove or solve how the electromagnetic, strong and weak nuclear forces, plus gravity can be combined in hyperspace. Nor can a human possibly visualize in any material sense more than three spatial dimensions (with time as the fourth dimension.)... As Kaku explains, "The key step in unifying the laws of nature is to increase the number of dimensions of space time... so that we have enough 'room' to unify all known forces." As it turns out, according to superstring theory, all forces can be unified if there are 10 dimensions.
> *Charles F. Emmons, **At The Threshold***

Hypatia, like Archimedes, was no fool. She would have hidden her knowledge from her enemies as best she could. Recently, a palimpsest with lost works of Archimedes was found. Is it possible that Hypatia was even more skilled than the great artificer, and created a far more cunning kind of palimpsest? Did she fold space-time, compacting the dimensions of sections of the Museon itself? Well, why not? We've already established that had she succeeded in her quest, Hypatia may well have become as close to God as we frail mortals can be, and the compacting of dimensions is a key component in superstring theory, the scientific Qabbalism of space-time. I propose that more than a millennium before Newton and Liebniz invented the calculus, Hypatia of Alexandria came as close as any human being ever had to working out the hyperspatial math, using the Iambichan version of the Tree of Life as a mentalization shortcut, and hid the truly inspirational sections of the Library in hyperspace. There resides forever all the lost plays of Sophocles and Eurpides, the lost work of Pindar and Hesiod and Sappho and Aristotle and Democritus and Demosthenes, all that was shorn from us in a moment of uncaring brutality.

Sure, it's probably just me being weird again.

So, who's up for a hyperdimensional book-salvage? I'll drive.

Noon Blue Apples

This entry exists because I was looking through one of my books, and the heading *Noon Blue Apples* caught my eye. That's basically it. I wish I had a more profound reason, but I don't. Just noon blue apples. Please note that I make no claims to the accuracy, historical value or even entertainment value of this entry.

> *A Dagobert II roi et a Sion est ce tresor et il est la mort.*
> To Dagobert II King and to Sion belongs this treasure and it is death
> *From the **Rennes-la-Château** manuscripts*

If you've read *The Invisibles* or are a big fan of Baigent, Lincoln and Leigh, you've heard all about the Priory of Sion, the Merovingian kings, the secret bloodline of Christ, the Arcadian secret and all that. But have you ever noticed the alternative translation of the above message? Usually, when someone translates that passage, they translate it to read, "This treasure belongs to King Dagobert II, and to Sion, and he is there dead." But what if the version above is correct? What if the treasure is not hidden with Dagobert's body, but rather, has some more esoteric and sinister meaning? What could it be?

> BERGERE PAS DE TENTATION QUE POUSSIN TENIERES GARDENT LE CLEF PAX DCLXXXI PAR LA CROIX ET CE CHEVAL DE DIEU J'ACHIEVE CE DAEMON DE GARDIEN A MIDI POMMES BLEUES.
> Sheperdess without temptation to which Pouissin and Teniers hold the key peace 681 with the cross and this horse of God I reach this daemon guardian at noon blue apples.
> *From the **Rennes-la-Château** manuscripts*

For thrice seven years he poured over these perplexing pages, until at last his wife suggested that a Jewish Rabbi might be able to translate them. As the chiefs of the Jews were principally

located in Spain, to Spain went Flamel, and there he remained
for two years. From one of the Hebrew sages he obtained a
hint which afforded a key to the patriachal mysteries, and
returning to Paris he recommenced his studies with a new
vigour. They were rewarded with success.
Lewis Spence, An Encyclopedia of Occultism

Alchemy is a strange art, practiced in secret for centuries by
people who did not care to tell others what it was they were doing.
They had good reason for that... they tended to end up dead when
they let fly with that little secret. As a result, alchemists are supposed
by folks like Fulcanelli to have learned to encode their secrets in
such a way that it takes a lot of doing to discover them. Indeed,
some would argue, it becomes more important to learn how to
decipher those secrets than it actually is to successfully do so: the
journey one takes to become capable of such a feat is the means to
enlightenment itself. So, then, if that is the case, then what was
encoded at the Church of Mary Magdalene? Well, if you listen to
Gerard de Sede, you'll end up scratching your head at the voluminous
amount of information he'll throw at you without connecting it or
explaining it. However, he does hint at strange connections to bear
gods and goddesses, to the star Sirius (shades of the Dogon tribesmen
and their Nommo spacemen, and of course old Oannes and the
Babylonians, but we'll get to that) and the murder of poor King
Dagobert II on December 23, A.D. 679 in the Ardennes Forest. (It's
worthwhile to note that Dagobert II is often referred to as Saint
Dagobert, and also interesting to note that he spent time in an Irish
monastery, and that the town of Stenay where Dagobert is often
said to have died has a Satanic head in its coat of arms.) de Sede's
one of those people who seems to be constitutionally incapable of
telling you what he means straight out, always obfuscating his
message, and yet if it weren't for de Sede, then Lincoln, Leigh and
Baigent wouldn't have had a book at all. It was de Sede who provided
Lincoln with the original cipher that led to the translation of the
Rennes-le-Château manuscripts. Why, we may wonder, would de
Sede want to do that?

Most of Paoli's book tries to show, from the few issues of
Circuit he managed to get his hands on, that the group behind
the magazine, the Priory of Sion, wrote in a kind of code (wine

making=a very specialized eugenics, because wine=human
"blood," i.e., human genes in modern language) and that they
seemed concerned with the special "blood" (genes) of the
French Royal Family and of some related noble families in
Spain, England and elsewhere.
Robert Anton Wilson, **Everything Is Under Control**

To answer that question, I suppose we need to go into a bit
more detail on what is known about Rennes-la-Château. The basic
events are as follows: In 1885, a man in his thirties came back to his
home town region. That man was named Berenger Sauniere, and he
had returned as a poor curé to tend to the small church in the area.
In 1891, while restoring the altar of the church, he discovered in a
hollow pillar four parchments. Two of the parchments were
concerned with the genealogy of local families, and the other two
were texts from the New Testament written down without the gaps
between words we are accustomed to. Sauniere believed the first
text to contain an encoded message, and working diligently he
transcribed those letters that were raised, and came up with "*A
Dagobert II roi et a Sion est ce tresor et il est la mort,*" as we
discussed above. Most believe that Sauniere came to view the
messages as concerning a secret Merovingian treasure. It is also
generally accepted by those that have studied this mystery that the
documents were left behind by Father Antoine Bigou, who was curé
of the church at the time of the French Revolution some hundred
years earlier. Sauniere brought what he had found to Bishop Felix-
Arsene Billard of Carcassone, who for whatever reason sent Sauniere
to Paris to consult with scholars and cryptographers. These included
Abbe Bieil of St Sulpice, that worthy's nephew Emile Hoffet, and
Hoffet's acquaintances Mallarme, Maeterlinck and Debussy. Debussy
himself introduced Sauniere to Emma Calve, who was at that time a
famous soprano. Somehow, from Calve, Sauniere got the idea to
visit the Louvre and purchased three reproductions, one of which
was Nicholas Poussin's *Les Bergers d'Arcadie*. Yes, the infamous
Et in Arcadia Ego painting.

Upon his return to Rennes-la-Château, Sauniere set to work.
He raised the slab of the altar with the aid of local workmen and
discovered that it was carved on the underside with a bas relief of
mounted knights that dated to about the time of King Dagobert II,

the unlucky saint who died with a lance piercing his brain. Underneath that were two skeletons and a pot of what a worker described as worthless medallions. Sauniere sent away the workmen and remained there alone for an unknown amount of time. He then began to wander through the region, collecting stones which he used to build a grotto out in the church's garden. What else he did is unknown. What is known is that during that same time he defaced the tombstone of Marie, Marquise de Blancheforte, apparently because her tombstone had been designed by the same Abbe Antonine Bigou who had left the encoded documents. Despite this strange act of vandalism, the tombstone's message has come down to us because it was recorded by a local antiquarian, unbeknownst to Sauniere. The tombstone was framed with a mixture of Greek and Latin letters that spelled out *Et in Arcadia Ego* and the center of the stone was inscribed with the phrase *Reddis Regis Cellis Arcis*. The inscription of the headstone seems deliberately written to suggest two words by means of its errors: CT GIT NOBLe MARIE DE NEGRe DARLES DAME DHAUPOUL De BLANCHEFORT AGEE DE SOIX ANTE SEpT ANS DECEDEE LE XVII JANVIER MDCOLXXXI REQUIESCAT IN PACE (P.S.) PRAE-CUM If you take the lowercase letters out of that inscription, the only word that can be spelled is the French for sword, while the misspellings in the inscription can only form the word *mort*, French for death. According to the cipher that de Sede provided Lincoln, these two words are keywords that allow for the translation of the second manuscript Sauniere found. (If you're interested, look up the Vigenere process, which is the encoding used in this case, or the book *Holy Blood Holy Grail* which tells the story from Lincoln, Baigent and Lee's perspective.)

Somehow, after he defaced the tombstone, this formerly poor parish priest suddenly came into money. Enough money to build a road leading to the village, to pipe in water, to build himself a villa with fountains and gardens, and a gothic tower to hold his collection of manuscripts, to collect rare china and antiques, to entertain Emma Calve (again with Emma Calve, he mutters to himself) and Archduke Johann von Habsburg of Austria. However he came by this money, he was able to convince his immediate supervisior (Bishop Felix-Arsene Billard of Carcassone, who had sent him on the quest in the first place and who had assigned him to Rennes la Chateau as a young curé as well) that it was best kept secret. This lasted until Billard was replaced, and when Sauniere declined to explain, he was ordered to another parish. He refused, and though a new cure was appointed to the area, none ever came and the people of the town considered Sauniere their priest (and why not, when he had done so much for them?) until his death in 1917. (All of this misses the little touches Sauniere made to the church itself when he restored it... touches like a demon, supposedly the demon Asmodeus from the apocryphal The Book of Tobit, who now guards the threshold- and Asmodeus, as we recall, was also the guardian of King Solomon's treasures- or the legend *Terribilis Est Locus Iste* which is taken from the mass of dedication for new churches, although the church at Rennes-la-Chateâu was an old, old church. Not a new one. These are clues we will return to, I swear.)

So what did Sauniere find? Various arguments have been proposed: that he discovered the lost Templar treasure buried in a nearby Cathar stronghold (remember, many prominent Templars were of the Pure Ones, as the Cathars were known; Bertrand de Blanchefort was the fourth Grand Master of the Order, and a Cathar), or the seized gold of the Merovingian dynasty. But remember what I said about alchemists before; they love to encode their mysteries, so that one must endure a journey of self-discovery, of enlightenment, before one can grasp the literal meaning, as much of alchemy is metaphor for the transformative purification of the process. Furthermore, as Fulcanelli pointed out, they loved to use their mastery of mathematical encoding on the very structures around them, building into them clues that would reveal their secrets if one could master their method. So what secrets, actually, were to be found at Rennes-la-Chateâu? Let us consider the suggestion that Lincoln, Baigent and Lee make. Was the Merovingian dynasty truly related to Christ?

And therefore, through Christ, rightful claimants to the bloodline of David, and thus the Throne of Israel? "*A Dagobert II roi et a Sion est ce tresor et il est la mort.*" Another way to translate that would be as "In Dagobert II King and of Sion is this treasure and it is death." Was Dagobert II attempting to claim the throne of Jerusalem as well?

Lincoln eventually came to feel that de Sede was being less than candid with him, and traced the man to a secret organization called the Priory of Sion, which according to a dossier Lincoln found at the Bibliotheque Nationale was composed of the inner council of the Knights Templar. According to Lincoln, Hugh de Payens built the Knights Templar in 1118 on the site of the old Temple of Solomon on Mount Sion as part of a grand scheme. The Templars grew wealthy and powerful, allying with mystics like the Cathar Pure Ones and the Hashishin. The Cathar Pure Ones were strict Gnostics, believing that the God of Genesis was in fact a demiurge, a demonic entity who created this world in mimicry of the true God of the New Testament, who then was forced to redeem our creation by direct intervention. Using Qabbalah, the Cathar traces the emanations of the True God up the Sephiroth, or spheres, as well as came to understand the Qlippoth, or cracked shells which once imprisoned spirits of negation. The Hashishin, meanwhile, followed the Old Man of the Mountain (the mountain, in this case, was the Mountain of Paradise, the enclosed place of ancient Persian thought where Ormazhd and Ahriman would do final battle) and used drugs to achieve a level of consciousness whereupon they could do anything.

Among the names listed on Lincoln's dossier as Grand Masters of the Order were Claude Debussy (who Sauniere, as we recall, met in Paris and who introduced him to Emma Calve), Victor Hugo, Isaac Newton, Leonardo da Vinci... and our old buddy Nicholas Flamel. Now, we know what Lincoln did with these documents; he used them to come to the conclusion that Sauniere had discovered the Priory of Sion, discovered the fact that Jesus had not died on the cross at all, and used this information to blackmail the Priory and those descendants of the Merovingians (Lincoln suspects the Hapsburgs, who did assume Merovingian rights by marrying their descendants) into supporting him. Lincoln cited that the documents argued that Sigisbert, Dagobert's son, had fled to Languedoc and inherited the titles to the Rennes-la-Château region from an uncle, making the region a hotbed of Merovingian plotting, and that Godfrey de Bouillion, leader of the First Crusade and cousin to Baldwin, who later became King of Jerusalem, was a direct descendant of the Merovingian line. As such, both Godfrey and Baldwin would be sympathetic to the Templars, who as Catharists were natural allies.

(Languedoc was the Cathar heartland.) A serviceable theory, I suppose.

But is it correct? In 1973, a Swiss journalist named Matthew Paoli published *Les Dessous*, a book prompted by his discovery of the internal newsletter of a Freemasonic order called Grand Loge Alpina. At first, Paoli thought the magazines were about horticulture, specifically the raising of grapes for wine. Soon, however, Paoli came to believe that this group was talking in code, and all this talk of wine and grapes was in fact encoded discussion of specific eugenics programs. Soon, he noticed that the supposed publishers of these magazines were (you guessed it) the Priory of Sion. (The publisher hid under the name the Committee to Protect the Rights and Privileges of Low-Cost Housing, but when he went to the address listed for it, there was of course no one to be found.) Paoli connected the document to the Committee for Public Safety (of which Robespierre was once a member) and found among the membership such worthies as Andre Malraux and Pierre Plantard de Saint Claire, who was at once a resistance fighter and yet supposedly sympathetic to the Nazi juggernaut during WWII. Now, in case you were wondering why I brought it up, Pierre Plantard de Saint Claire claims direct descent through the Saint Claire family (also known as Sinclair in Scotland, the same family so prevelant in modern Freemasonry) to Dagobert, and thus to the Merovingian line itself. Interestingly, Paoli was killed by the government of Israel when he took an assignment there, because they believed him to be a spy.

Confused yet? To try and get through this thicket causes one to snag on a mass of thorns. We have Pierre Plantard de Saint Claire and Gerard de Sede, both supposedly members of this shadowy Priory of Sion, who each give Lincoln puzzling or contradictory answers. These answer guide him to purportedly ancient documents in the Bibliotheque Nationale leading him to the idea of Jesus' survival in Palestine and his foundation of a royal bloodline in the Merovingians, which Lincoln takes to be the secret of Rennes-la-Château... and henceforth, ceases to pry any further. What if, however, he has been tricked? What if we all have?

It occurs to me that the first place to resume digging is in those two geneological documents that Sauniere found. It has been argued that they were used to determine who in the region was of the proper bloodline to serve in the Priory. Well, Sauniere was from the region. Is it possible that he discovered his own ancestry on those pages? And then he sought out his old mentor, the Bishop of Carcassone, who had assigned him to the area in the first place, and the Bishop merely smiled, and nodded, and encouraged him to work out the mystery of the building. *Complete your researches, my son.* When in Paris, he met with those who were at that time the most important members of the Priory of Sion, including Debussy himself, who also provided him with tidbits enough to solve the mystery and return to Rennes-la-Château. When there, he completed his studies, unearthed the truth of the Priory... and thus became a member, as it was always intended that he should. Thus, his sudden wealth did not come from hidden treasure, or from blackmail, but was a privilege accorded someone with the special wine the order so seeks. In other words, Sauniere could claim descent from the Merovingians. Dagobert II's death in A.D. 679 has all the hallmarks of a sacred king killing, similar to the death of Jesus. Was it an attempt to establish a connection which was not actually there? Were the Merovingians (who never claimed descent from Jesus, but rather from a merman named Merovech) attempting to become the rightful heirs to Sion?

It obviously didn't work out too well for them. By A.D. 720, Pepin was writing to the Pope, asking him for permission to take the throne and getting it. But why would the Merovingians think they could, or should, attempt to usurp the divine prerogative? Perhaps because of their links to the Cathars. The Cathars believed in gnosis, or secret wisdom. But is it possible that both the Cathars and the Hashishin who would later inform Templar belief were simply incorrect? That they'd done the math wrong? That there were not two gods locked in combat, but only one... One God, who was Three at once?

Paradise, in old Persian, is an enclosure. In the Old Testament, the Jews build an Arc to hold the Covenant with God sacred. It is an enclosed box. If you look at ancient Persian scripture, neither Ormazhd nor Ahriman made the universe; that was the work of Zurvan, a being totally unconcerned with mere physical reality. Now, if you consider many of the myths of the Near East, from Sumeria to Egypt, from Greece to the Hittites, there is always a three-leveled arrangement of gods, a three-generational struggle among unconcerned deities who make all that is, their corrupt successors who batten upon their creation in an attempt to flatter their own egos, and a class of guardian deities who can be supplicated. What if all this is an alchemical encoding of the truth? What if there are always three: a maker, a protector, and a destroyer similar to the Brahma, Vishnu and Shiva of India? What if the reason Christ mentioned the Father, the Son, and the Spirit was to attempt to bring this condition to light?

In other words, what if God is schizoid? From the very first in the Bible, God (who is supposedly but one God) is heard to say things like, "Now he is like Us, with the knowledge of Good and Evil." What if, in order to have knowledge of Good and Evil, it was necessary for our detached, uninterested Creator to create in Itself the potential for both, literally to incarnate Good and Evil as beings inside of it? In order to know Itself, division was necessary. This is the event that creates what the Cathars call the Demiurge, what the Magi call Ahriman. At first, the experiment is allowed to proceed apace, with Good and Evil doing battle on the mortal plane. But the Creator creates; if Good and Evil progress unchecked, they will hinder creation itself. So direct intervention is necessary.

Have you ever noticed how the great heroes of the Bible often have strange nativities? Moses is floated down the river Nile and found by a princess of Egypt. David is seen killing lions with a sling, alone of all his brothers. Joseph can interpret dreams. Jesus, alone of all of Joseph's and Mary's children is considered to be divine. Outside of the Bible, there are beings like Hercules, Gilgamesh, Zoroaster, Krishna; chosen ones, beings as much of the gods as of men. Is it possible they all come from a common source? That these images of angels and showers of gold and the like are an attempt to understand what cannot be understood, or could not be then? The blood is the life, the blood is wine; the blood is the source of DNA, and DNA is what makes us. Creates us. What if the Creator simply reached down and re-created a favored servitor over and over again, manipulating the genes of infants so that a selected pattern would emerge? In other words, what if in the genetic line of David is a replication of Moses? What if Jesus were simply a clone of David, who was a clone of Moses, who was a clone of Abraham of Ur, who may well have been a clone of Gilgamesh himself? Magic, science-all are the same to the All in One. And why, you ask, did the Creator create a DNA pattern that would replicate itself?

Consider again the Ark of the Covenant. To touch it unbidden was death. To possess it, and not be the Chosen of God, was to invite disaster. The Phoenicians placed it in the Temple of Baal... and the Temple of Baal was destroyed. The Babylonians took it when they conquered Israel... and the Persians conquered Babylon. Now supposedly lost, it lay at one time in the Temple of Solomon, guarded by the demon Asmodeus (yes, that same demon who Sauniere carved into the walls of the Church at Rennes-la-Château). Why did God create this enclosed place? Well, in Zoroastrian myth, Paradise was the enclosed place wherein Good and Evil would do battle, and decide the fate of the universe. In the Bible, Adam and Eve learn the nature of good and evil and are driven forth from Paradise. In the Qabbalah, one takes the *Shem ha memporash*, the seventy-two fold name of God, and through Gematria one applies mathematics until one can walk the path up the Tree of Life, past the Burning Sword and into Kether, the Crown.

Paradise is a tesseract, and it lies inside the Ark of the Covenant, where the Creator has imprisoned Good and Evil forever. This is the treasure of the Temple of Solomon, protected by the demon Asmodeus... and what is a demon but a terrible Angel, fallen forever from Heaven?

Why is it that the Israelites were always triumphant in battle so long as they held the Ark? Because those with the proper DNA can resonate with the energies of the prison, and tap the power of the Protector and Destroyer forever sealed within it. That is the covenant the Creator, YHWH, I AM made with Israel, that they would forever be the keepers of God's own prison. By manipulating the Urim and Thummin, the high priests of Israel (descended from Moses' brother Aaron, and thus claimants to the sacred blood, the DNA pattern made by the Creator for the purpose) could discern the will of the Creator and use the Ark.

Were the Urim and Thummin a series of lots, as many people argue? A mystical unfolding of patterns, like the I Ching or the runes of the Norse? Or was it their DNA itself? Can those with the right bloodline tap the power of the box inherently, as if they were magicians? Does the tesseract itself draw upon the power of the spheres of the Sephiroth, allowing for those who resonate in sympathy with it to manipulate hyperspatial relationships by mere will? It's interesting to note how much of Qabbalistic mysticism is involved in the manipulation of number and designation, as if the entire universe were a massive multidimensional computer, and all that is needed to access the Creator's power is the right file in His database. Does the Ark serve as an interface? Are the Urim and Thummin its passwords, and the constant play of Notariquon and Gematria the language of the machine?

From the time that a Greek became king of Israel, and thus the rulership passed to someone not of the proper bloodline to harness the power of the tesseract, trouble began. The rebuilt temple was destroyed, and the treasure of the temple stolen by Visigoths... who were defeated by the Merovingians at what would become Carcassone. Seeing what they had, and being mystically inclined, the Merovingians sought by placing Dagobert II in the charge of an Irish monastery to ensure that he would be spiritually pure enough to become a sacrifice, allowing them to harness the power of the Ark. Instead, the Ark ensured their destruction at the hands of the Carolingians. From there, the Merovingians sought to reclaim their power from their base at Languedoc, using their Cathar allies as sounding boards for various plans on how best to make themselves suitable. Not understanding the triple nature of the divinity, they decided that a side had to be chosen, and that by becoming king of Jerusalem, a chosen Merovingian could claim the proper bloodline. And so the formation of the Templars, the launching of the Crusades... but in the end the Merovingians failed. Starting to understand the curse they had called upon themselves, they hid the Ark in an out of the way place and studied, trying to discover where the true descendants of Jesus had gone. For years, men like Flamel and da Vinci tried to crack the operating code of the box, and even their failures were world-shaking. Upon the coming of Sauniere, they felt they had one with the right blood at last.

The coming of WWI and the death of their candidate for the Davidic bloodline was a bitter pill to swallow. By the 1940s, they were quite fed up with the Ark, so they arranged for the Germans to acquire it through their pawn Pierre Plantard de Saint Claire. The result was a crushing defeat for Germany. Plantard and his other allies in France after the war then arranged for the box to be returned to Jerusalem, where its presence can be felt today in the Jerusalem syndrome as the box resonates endlessly, seeking those of the proper heritage to harness its power. That is the treasure of Rennes-la-Château. A box full of stars, a world everlastingly enclosed, where Good and Evil fight forever.

"To Dagobert II King and to Sion belongs this treasure and it is death."

If the universe is made by a Creator, who is to say how many levels it has? (Interesting side note: "blue apples" is Victorian slang, I am told, for testicles that ache for lack of sex. Make of that what you will.)

And, Bound in Flesh, I Find Myself a Beast

So, I was reading through my strangely expurgated copy of *The Dictionary of Imaginary Places* when I came upon an entry for a place named London-on-Thames. Seems that it made its appearance in Edgar Rice Burroughs' *Tarzan and the Lion Man* and it was a strange parody of London of the time of Henry the VIII, populated with apes that thought they actually were the people of sixteenth-century London. One ape called himself Henry VIII, and he had various gorilla wives with the same names as Henry's wives, although unlike the actual Henry our ape king didn't bother with divorce or beheadings, simply keeping all his wives at once. It all turns out to be the work of God, an ape with long white hair who lives among the strange society of London-on-Thames. He's a scientist who fled England years before with cell samples from various notables (no, I don't know how he got them; I freely admit that I don't remember having read this, despite the fact that I read Tarzan stories as a child) and built himself a paradise of sorts. He then injected himself with cell samples from young apes, transforming himself into a gorilla-but a young one, thereby extending his life.

Weird, even for Burroughs, and that's saying something. This is a guy who positioned a continent named Pellucidar on the inner surface of the Earth, the mind behind Barsoom and Amtor, a man who populated Africa with at least six lost cities (Pal-ul-Don, Onthar, Thenar, Castra Sanguinarius, Castrum Marinus and Opar... I may be forgetting more), tiny foot-tall men and so on... but this is the only story of his I know of with such a strange theme. There's also some mention of human-looking girls who are, or were, apes who have been extensively modified by God. It reminds one of *The Island of Doctor Moreau* with its theme of animal uplift (although Wells' surgically-enhanced beasts would be unlikely to dress up as the Tudor court) and another, darker tale.

The reason why Arthur Jermyn's charred fragments were not collected and buried lies in what was found afterward, principally the thing in the box. The stuffed goddess was a nauseous sight, withered and eaten away, but it was clearly a mummified white ape of some unknown species, less hairy than any recorded variety, and infinitely nearer mankind, quite shockingly so. Detailed description would be rather unpleasant, but two salient particulars must be told, for they fit in revoltingly with certain notes of Sir Wade Jermyn's African expeditions and with the Congolese legends of the white god and the ape-princess. The two particulars in question are these: the arms on the golden locket about the creature's neck were the Jermyn arms, and the jocose suggestion of M. Verharen about certain resemblance as connected with the shriveled face applied with vivid, ghastly, and unnatural horror to none other than the sensitive Arthur Jermyn, great-great-great-grandson of Sir Wade Jermyn and an unknown wife. Members of the Royal Anthropological Institute burned the thing and threw the locket into a well, and some of them do not admit that Arthur Jermyn ever existed.

H.P. Lovecraft, *"Facts Concerning the Late Arthur Jermyn and His Family"*

"Arthur Jermyn" was written a decade and a half before *Tarzan and the Lion Man,* and in fact the two stories are almost certainly unrelated... but one can create a relation for them in the mind. Imagine one of God's twisted test subjects, deformed and albinized by injections of British stock (perhaps Elizabeth I herself? The tinkerer certainly showed her father no reverence) escaping from his mad kingdom. Infected with the powerful will of England's greatest queen, this horrid creature stumbles upon Sir Wade Jermyn and learns from him the current state of affairs in England. Knowing herself to be royal, she forces her will upon the explorer and compels him to take her to his manor. Given Elizabeth's love for dashing adventurer types, is it so hard to see this simian re-creation finding herself attracted to this intrepid plumber of the secrets of the dark continent? She died not long after giving birth to Robert. Perhaps her transfigured simian body could not handle the strain, or perhaps she died happy, free of the burdens of state and wed to a man who reminded her of her long-ago Raleigh and Esses. And as for him, well... it's hard somehow to imagine anyone being able to resist that cold yet powerful mind.

Elizabeth ruled an entire nation. I think, even in reduced circumstances (if that's the right term for being recreated in the body of an ape) she could rule one man. Lovecraft tells us of Wade Jermyn: "Learning was in his blood, for his great-grandfather, Sir Robert Jermyn, Bt., had been an anthropologist of note, whilst his great-great-great-grandfather, Sir Wade Jermyn, was one of the earliest explorers of the Congo region, and had written eruditely of its tribes, animals, and supposed antiquities."

Indeed, old Sir Wade had possessed an intellectual zeal amounting almost to a mania; his bizarre conjectures on a prehistoric white Congolese civilization earned him much ridicule when his book, *Observation on the Several Parts of Africa*, was published. In 1765 this fearless explorer had been placed in a madhouse at Huntingdon. Madness was in all the Jermyns, and people were glad there were not many of them. The line put forth no branches, and Arthur was the last of it. If he had not been, one cannot say what he would have done when the object came. The Jermyns never seemed to look quite right; something was amiss, though Arthur was the worst, and the old family portraits in Jermyn House showed fine faces enough before Sir Wade's time. Certainly, the madness began with Sir Wade, whose wild stories of Africa were at once the delight and terror of his few friends. Why, pray tell, did Wade go to the asylum? Why do his tales of ape-haunted ruins remind one of the stories of London-on-Thames, that stone and brick parody of the city he would have known so well? I am also somewhat intrigued by the Jermyn family's love of knowledge, and for the accumulation and exchange of it. It's easy to imagine Robert Jermyn, despite his unattractive features, sitting in some London club, smoking cigars and sipping brandy while telling of his anthropological work and his own father's interesting theories about the Congo. Furthermore, scientists (and the Jermyn clan, despite their dark secret, were certainly that) publish their theories, in places where others can find and make use of them.

Lovecraft, of course, was using the theme of Lady Jermyn and her influence on the family line as a thinly veiled don't-mess-with-the-lesser-races metaphor, while Burroughs was more interested in a ripping yarn than anything else. But it makes one think. Did a young Dr. Moreau, working on his strange theories, come upon one of the Jermyn journals and so discover the secrets of God? (Well, no, of course not, Wells' novel predates both of them, but play along and see where we go.) God the once-human, God the intelligent anthropoid ape. (Which of course makes one think of the strangely intelligent apes that found and raised young Lord Greystoke to begin with. Were they descended from one of God's test subjects, an ape with human intelligence?) Did our mad doctor decide that God's problem was that he hadn't gone far enough, that he'd stayed with only one species, that he'd attempted to recreate specific personalities rather than allowing the subjects to develop as their natures would prompt them? Rather than making apes that thought like man, Moreau created beasts that thought as well as man. Were the beasts of Noble's Island the beginnings of a sister civilization to that of London-on-Thames? Moreau himself died, but his notes may have survived him... and if those notes contained the Jermyn family secret, perhaps even now there prowl through the world men and women who are not what they seem, who contain the essence of the beast. Remember, God knew how to so extensively modify an ape as to make it indistinguishable from a human being. Who is to say that the animal-men of Noble Island, formed like men, smart like men, could not have found a way to complete his work and hide in plain sight?

> It would be impossible to detail every step of the lapsing of these monsters,—to tell how, day by day, the human semblance left them; how they gave up bandagings and wrappings, abandoned at last every stitch of clothing; how the hair began to spread over the exposed limbs; how their foreheads fell away and their faces projected; how the quasi-human intimacy I had permitted myself with some of them in the first month of my loneliness became a shuddering horror to recall.
> H.G. Wells, **The Island of Doctor Moreau**

It's hard to say how fair Prendick was to the beast-men, considering how he loathed them and longed to escape (shades of Arthur Jermyn, although it was worse for that worthy, knowing himself to share blood, not mere intimacy). But even he, later, admitted to occasionally feeling as though all who were around him could be more beast than man. "I know this is an illusion; that these seeming men and women about me are indeed men and women,— men and women for ever, perfectly reasonable creatures, full of human desires and tender solicitude, emancipated from instinct and the slaves of no fantastic Law- beings altogether different from the Beast Folk. Yet I shrink from them, from their curious glances, their inquiries and assistance, and long to be away from them and alone." Was this mere paranoia, or was he being followed by the very creatures he had dismissed as having denegrated, seeking to use him to understand the world of the most savage creature of all? Were they feigning their devolution in order to ensure that Prendick would not call in any more of his kind, while at the same time leaving him alive because he was the only model for humanity they had left? (The physical signs are hard to ignore... but even in that, is it necessary to believe that they all made the same choice?)

Are you an animal? I'm not so sure about myself.

The World Below

Say, does anyone remember Atvatabar? You know, that continent lying exactly under North America and mirroring it in outline, accessible through the hole in the North Pole? Why am I not surprised? I suppose, what with all the troubles we've had with China, and the tensions in the Middle East, the Hollow Earth has to be low on our list of priorities. But perhaps it shouldn't be: as early as 1891, Commander Lexington White and his boon companion Captain William Wallace (yes, William Wallace... hey, I didn't name him, William R. Bradshaw did) discovered the people of Atvatabar were capable of manipulating their weather, creating railroads underneath their oceans and magnetic wings that allowed each soldier in their army to become a kind of one-man aircraft. Oh, and lest we forget, they also had gigantic steel ostriches that they rode into battle. And that was a hundred and ten years ago, so who knows what marvels they have created since?

Sure, you say it's unlikely that the Atvatabari have any plans for conquest; after all, they have many rivals in the eternal sunshine of the hollow world. The endless dark of Tsalal resides within the boundaries of the Antarctic gateway to this place, guarded well by its inhabitants who fear what might crawl out of the depths of the caverns. The Vril-Ya plot in their cavern, half-way between our world and the world within, as Lord Lytton warned us. Was it they who convinced Guy Warren Ballard that he had spoken to the Comte de Saint-Germain and a cabal of Tibetan masters and Venusians who used the gateway between worlds at Mount Shasta, or did Ballard indeed meet the mysterious Comte in 1930? For all we know, the navies of Atvatabar and Pellucidar skirmish in the Lidenbrock Sea as I type this. Of course, if they do, they'll have to be on the lookout; the Deros, detrimental robots who are somehow descended (so they claim, anyway) from the Titans of myth lurk in the tunnels that shoot through our world, and either world is up to them.

It's a man's life in the Hollow Earth. Of course, first you have to be sure which side is the skin, and which side the core, don't you?

> They considered it helpful to locate the British fleet, because the curvature of the Earth would not obstruct observation. Visual rays were not suitable because of refraction; but infrared rays had less refraction. Accordingly a party of about ten men under the scientific leadership of Dr. Heinz Fischer, an infrared expert, was sent out from Berlin to the Isle of Rugen to photograph the British fleet with infrared equipment at an upward angle of some 45 degrees.
> *Popular Astronomy, June 1946*, as quoted by Dusty Sklar, *Gods and Beasts*

Before you get to laughing, keep in mind that at around that same time we in America were apparently trying to make battleships invisible and were definitely trying to build a bomb based on splitting an atom, and we weren't sure that same bomb wouldn't cause a chain reaction that might rip the atmosphere from the planet. Makes a few upward cameras seem a lot less goofy, doesn't it?

The Nazis got the idea for this particular bit of lunacy from two sources: the writings of English writer Lord Edward Lytton (amazing how often the Nazis took inspiration from Englishmen; unlike Houston Stewart Chamberlain, however, Lytton's role was inadvertent) who wrote *The Coming Race* in 1871, and Cyrus Teed, an American religious fanatic who, after having a visit from the Mother of the Universe (she was probably upset that the Universe never calls... and would it kill the Universe to get its hair cut?) realized that he was the savior of the world. Therefore, Teed moved to Fort Myers, Florida, changed his name to Koresh, and began preaching that the world is hollow and we live on the inner surface, that the sun is at the center and all of the planets and stars as well as the moon exist inside the hollow earth.

Generally speaking, however, most Hollow Earth theorists or fantasists tend to assume that we live on the outside of the orange peel. Makes it easier to explain how the sun rises and sets. (To my knowledge, Teed/Koresh never did explain how that little bit of solar prestidigitation works if we live on the inside of a hollow globe.) Let's trace some of the more interesting or notable ideas and see how they connect.

In 1692, the Astronomer Royal of England, Dr. Edmund Halley, who gave his name to probably the most famous of all comets, affirmed his conviction in an address to the Royal Society of London. "Beneath the crust of the earth,' he said, 'which is 500 miles thick, is a hollow void. Inside this space are three planets. They are approximately the size of Mars, Venus and Mercury."
Peter Haining, **Ancient Mysteries**

Symmes believed that the earth is made up of a series of concentric spheres, with 4000 mile wide holes at the north and south poles. In spite of massive ridicule, Symmes wrote, lectured and lobbied vigorously for funding to mount an expedition through the poles to the interior, where he and his party would meet the inner-earth people and open "new sources of trade and commerce."
Jerome Clark, **Unexplained!**

Worlds within worlds. In this model of the Hollow Earth, not only is there a world inside this one, but another one inside that one, and so on. While certainly an interesting idea, it didn't really catch on; even Symmes' own disciples would eventually reject it. (Of course, one of those disciples, John Reynolds, would use the good captain's ideas to bilk the credulous out of their money.) When Marshall B. Gardner published his book *A Journey to the Earth's Interior* in 1913 he returned to the inner sun conception of Teed, although he argued that the inner sun created the aurora borealis by shining through the holes at the poles. Gardner also argued that the center of earth's gravity existed within the crust of the planet, in the solid portion of the earth and not in the hollow center, so that the inhabitants could walk on the inside of the planet the way we walk on the outside. (Symmes had simply argued that Newton was full of it and that objects on this earth are subject for their movement to an aerial plastic fluid invisible to the eye, whatever that means... sounds like our old friend the Ether again, doesn't it? Wonder if Lord Kelvin ever read Symmes' book... in 1818, Symmes managed to catch Czar Alexader I of Russia's interest, but it didn't last long and the Russian Expedition fizzled) and Gardner's cosmology of the inner world has been the one, generally speaking, to hold the interest of authors and occultists ever since. However, while it is Gardner's vision of the inner world that has triumphed, you'll note that most authors (Verne, Poe, Bradshaw, Lytton, Burroughs) tend to model their heroes after the adventurous Captain Symmes. (Poe's narrator is almost certainly modeled after Symmes, and Poe wrote his narrative after reading about the captain.) The Allan Quatermain of Hollow World theory has managed to hold on, at least somewhat, I'm glad to say.

Of course, even after they determined that we aren't living on the inside of the planet, the Nazis hardly gave up on the hollow world, packed as they were sure it was with Agarthans and Vril-Ya who were tall, blond, and gifted with supernatural powers and intellect. Madame Blatavsky and the Theosophists had primed the pump with talk of the White Brotherhood, and Himmler was hardly about to let go of the idea that a society of magical white men was going to come up from under the earth and haul the Werhmacht out of the fire. Seems silly to me to trust in allies vouchsafed by a Russian countess who may or may not have been in contact with Czar Alexander I, but maybe that's just me. The Nazis were so interested in Lytton's book that they sent dozens of squads down into mineshafts and caves throughout Fortress Europe, looking for the entrance to the caverns of the Vril-Ya. Is it a coincidence that throughout the 1920s and '30s the US Navy sent Richard E. Byrd (you knew he was coming, so don't try to fight it now) to the North and South Poles? Symmes and his colleague and friend Richard M. Johnson had petitioned Congress for just such an expedition a century earlier (Johnson, by the way, would eventually become vice president of the United States, not that it made much difference to Symmes) and had been shot down, but that same Congress would promote Byrd to Lieutenant Commander and send him to fly over the North Pole. Were they worried by all this Nazi talk of Vril-Ya and Agartha? Was it considered in the national interest to make contact with the peoples inside the earth?

Maybe, but to me, the best hollow world is the fictional one, where we don't have to worry about things like *what the hell would that inner sun be made of* or *how would a biosphere of eternal day function*, and *what adaptions would living on the surface of a bowl constantly lit require of living beings*? To be honest, the racist assumptions of the Theosophists and the Nazis bore the hell out of me, and I don't really care so much about Agartha and the White

Brotherhood as I do Richard Sharpe Shaver's Dero (hoax or not, it reads like fiction, and so I shall treat it as such) or Burroughs' Pellucidar, where the vicious Mahar pterodactyloids enslave Sargoths (shades of Lovecraft's shoggoths, who as we know echoed Poe's "tekeli-li" cry first heard by Arthur Gordon Pym) and herd humans into cruel vivisection laboratories... and there we curve recursively back to the Nazis, don't we?

In all the fiction set in the hollow world, surface worlders come to it with adventure or exploration or even conquest in mind. Who is to say that the beings living under the fire of the endless sun don't view the surface world the same way? It's interesting to note that so many of the occultists who tell tales of the world beneath our feet present the inhabitants as advanced, enlightened and powerful (Ballard, M.L. Sherman, H.P. Blavatsky, H. Spencer Lewis) and willing to come to the surface to aid us poor, wretched throwbacks. Sound anything like, oh, I don't know... the English in India and Africa, or the United States talking to its victims during the western expansion? *We come in peace. We bring you a more advanced way of life.* Were folks like Cyrus Teed and Gardner (who wrote of the paradisiacal tropic conditions in the inner world) dupes of aggressive Mahar? Serpent folk again, you might say if you read Howard as a child, as I did. And isn't it interesting that as Ballard spread his tales of Secret Masters beneath our feet and the Nazis prepared to ally with the Vril-Ya, Lovecraft and Howard died? *Tekeli-li. Ka nama kaa lajerama.* Are these phrases we should all commit to memory?

> Despite the failure of mission after mission, Hitler and his cohorts refused to be shaken in their belief. The Fuhrer even believed he had seen one of the members of the super race, as he told Herman Rauschning, the governor of Danzig. "The new man is living amongst us now," he is reported to have said. "He is here! I will tell you a secret. I have seen the new man. He is intrepid and cruel. I was afraid of him."
> *Peter Haining,* **Ancient Mysteries**

> Most Pellucidarians share the belief that Pellucidar rests on a burning sea known as the Molop Az. Pellucidar itself is imagined to be flat and to be protected by a wall which prevents the earth and water from falling into the flames. Any dead who are buried in the earth are carried down piece by piece to

the Molop Az by the wicked little men who live there.
*Alberto Manguel and Gianni Guadalupi, **The Dictionary of
Imaginary Places***

Imagine if you will, a subterranean triparate alliance. the Atvatabari, with their magnetic technology and military demeanor, the Deros with their rapacious cruelty and ancient society, derived from destroyed/sunken Lemurian devices that allow them to harvest power from death and suffering (and isn't it interesting that Shaver tells us that his Deros are of Lemurian origin just as H. Spencer Lewis is telling us that under Mount Shasta is a colony of Lemurians and Ballard is telling us that the inner world contacted him on the slopes of Mount Shasta?) and the Mahar, with their ability to mesmerize victims so that they walk calmly to their deaths at the hands of the Sargoths.

All three seek new territories and new conquests, yet to attack each other may well mean mutually assured destruction, so evenly matched are they. So they hit upon a plan. The Dero and the Mahar will pose as advanced societies (the Secret Masters, the Vril-Ya) and manipulate dupes upon the surface into instigating a savage war. The Atvatabar, for their part, will supply those same dupes with just enough information to make new advances in the fields of military engineering, while misleading them enough as to the nature of that information and of the world in general to keep them weak enough to conquer after the surface war is over. It takes a while to find the proper dupes (Dero assassins go so far as to eliminate Symmes and Poe because they either know or might learn too much; Teed went mad and mixed everything up in his head; Blavatsky and her ilk were receptive but not directly useful, serving mainly as seeds to flower later) so they begin manipulating groups such as the Futurists to move outworld society towards a destructive conflict. World War I is their testing ground, allowing them to learn exactly what our capabilities in war are, and it convinces them that it would be a bad idea to invade the suface world. They decide to continue with their two-pronged attack, manipulating the extreme fringes of occult and nationalistic thought, till they manage to create a fever pitch even stronger than the last one.

In 1922, the Secret Masters have infiltrated those occult

organizations that have gained any inspiration from Theosophical writings or teachings. Since the death of Poe, they have managed to shepherd and protect spiritualism, converting many influential people with demonstrations secretly pulled off by Dero thoughtech or Mahar psi powers. However, their use of manipulation and trickery and their thinly-veiled anti-Semitism (is this due to some ancient conflict between the Hebrew people and the Mahar? Is the tale of the Serpent in the Garden some twisted memory of the long-ago battle between reptile and human? Are the Jews the descendants of the Valusians? Well, probably not that last one) angers a man of clever and unorthodox thought and great means. He begins an anti-Spiritualist crusade, despite the fact that many of his own friends think he possesses occult powers that he uses unconsciously to escape repeatedly from certain death... in order to entertain crowds of spectators. In 1926, a college student (another Dero assassin?) strikes him in the midsection, causing him to rupture his appendix and die. With him out of the way, the work continues, but once they have what they need, a group of die-hards like the Thule Gescehllenscaft and the Germanenorden to manipulate into a structure more pleasing to them, things begin to take off.

However, all is not yet lost. Byrd's flights over the poles were scout missions, taking him deep into the hollow world and charting it. Learning of the inner world's plans, the US Government responds as quickly as it can. They send a commando mission to the hollow earth, to take action behind enemy lines. These men, instructed by the nephew of Commander Lexington White, a pulpish novelist living in the American Southwest at that time, include a reclusive New England bibliophile, a Texan as talented with the word as he was with gun and fist, and the real spymaster of the United States, a man who faked his own death in the 1920s to oppose the Secret Masters and their Aryan stooges. Together with a company of kill-crazy misfits (and really, would the mission have been complete without a company of kill-crazy misfits?) they storm off into the hollow world to create as much havoc and disrupt as many of the Subterraneans' operations as possible. This motley crew surges forth to defend the surface world against the hidden threat from within. They foment rebellion among the human slaves of the Mahar and use their chemical based firearms and explosives (chemistry being a science the Atvatabari never mastered) to great effect. They create a kind of French Resistance in the heart of the earth, and direct American bomber wings led by Admiral Byrd to strike the heart of the Atvatabari and Mahar cities. The Deros are driven into their cavernous cities and sealed inside, where they will only trouble the dreams of men like radio operator Richard Shaver.

Their mission done and the world saved, the leaders of the expedition eschew the thanks of a greatful world, knowing that the secret must be kept. Atvatabari must be reconstructed, Pellucidar explored and the Deros monitored. Their researcher and translator, Howard Phillips Lovecraft, is buried on an island in the Lidenbrock Sea. Robert E. Howard takes a machine gun and a sword and stalks off for the uncharted depths of Pellucidar to investigate, explore, and perhaps even to rule a kingdom won by his own hand. And the driving will of the expedition, Ehrich Weiss, returns to the surface to settle down into obscurity, looking on with wry amusement as a name he never uses again becomes synonymous with illusion.

The Habits of the Universe

This assumption that the laws of nature are eternal is the last great surviving legacy of the old cosmology. We are rarely even conscious of making it. But when we do bring this assumption into awareness, we can see that it is only one of several possibilities. Perhaps all the laws of nature came into being at the very moment of the Big Bang. Or perhaps they arose in stages, and then, having arisen, persisted changelessly thereafter. For example, the laws governing the crystallization of sugar may have come into being when sugar molecules first crystallized somewhere in the universe; they may have been universal and changeless ever since. Or perhaps the laws of nature have actually evolved along with nature itself, and perhaps they are still evolving. Or perhaps they are not laws at all, but more like habits. Maybe the very idea of "laws" is inappropriate.
Rupert Sheldrake, ***The Presence of the Past: Morphic Resonance and The Habits of Nature***

The known is finite, the unknown infinite; intellectually we stand on an islet in the midst of an illimitable ocean of inexplicability. Our business in every generation is to reclaim a little more land.
Thomas H. Huxley

What is reality? What is thought? Do we exist in a state of equilibrium between the evolutionary process that governs life and the immutable laws of physics that govern the universe and therefore serve as a meta-structure governing evolution itself, or does the universe itself change over time? Are what seem to us bedrock laws of physics really just those axioms which have endured through repetition and hold force today through the sheer inertia of their long existence?

I've repeated before the old argument of the philosophers that the reality each individual inhabits is subjective, because in great degree it is only revealed to us through the interface of our perceptive faculties and our intellect and thus is subject to the limitations of both. But is it possible that even the reality we all inhabit together is also slowly changing, expanding and altering in response to the chaotic impressions of our senses and minds as well as the impressions of potential other minds existing everywhere in the universe? Do crystals grow in certain formations because they must, or merely because they always have, guided by fields of energy that bear more similarity to those proposed by a dissolute French excommunicate to explain the behavior of elemental spirits than those one may have heard about in ones' earth science class? (Isn't it fascinating how much like an elemental god a morphic field can seem?)

> There is no reason why the universe is perfect; there is indeed, no reason why it should be rational.
> *Julian Huxley,* **What Dare I Think**

> The Qabalah makes the primary claim that the intellect contains within itself a principle of self-contradiction, and that, therefore, it is an unreliable instrument to use in the great quest for truth.
> *Israel Regardie,* **A Garden of Pomegranates**

Studying the history of life on earth- the long period between the formation of the planet and the first proto-cells formed in the oceans, the wait between that and the rise of unicellular organisms, then the slow crawl between that and the rise of the plants and animals of the oceans, and then the wait till the invasion of the land began- we note that each step, though still consuming vast stretches of time, takes less and less of it. The rise from amphibian to reptile was more rapid than that of fish to amphibian, or arthropod to fish. Even when mass extinctions take place, the rejuvenation of the ecosphere occurs with startling speed and diversity, and within the deoxyribonucleic acid of each arising life form is contained that of all its ancestors.

Is it possible that this process takes place on all levels of existence, not merely the biological? After all, biology is just another form of chemistry to some, ultimately to be governed by the same rules, and for the past hundred years or so it's been assumed that the laws of chemistry provided the immutable framework that allowed biology to behave as a mutable evolutionary process. But what if that mutability is in fact a consequence of the chemistry and ultimately the physics underlying our biology? The universe can be best pictured, although still very imperfectly and inadequately, as consisting of pure thought, the thought of what, for want of a better phrase, we must describe as a mathematical thinker.

James Jeans argued this upon first contemplating Einstein's theory of relativity, and it echoes the Neoplatonist view of existence as a constantly unfolding equation as well as the Qabbalistic view of reality as a series of emanations from *Ain*, or Nothing. If the universe itself is evolving, what is it evolving from... and what is it evolving into? Evolution itself is usually explained in a Darwinist or neo-Darwinist framework as survival of the fittest, a process wherein life is constantly adapted by environmental pressures and chance into forms most suitable for the niche in which they exist. Those that are suitable thrive, and beget offspring who share their characteristics... those that are not die, and do not. As the environment changes, it forces change upon the life within it, which responds by either adapting and thus being selected by blind chance, or by being unsuccessful and dying out. Within this framework there is no room for design, and no overarching goal towards which evolution proceeds. Indeed, evolution itself is not a moral process, it does not make for better life forms, merely ones which are more suited to the environment they find themselves. Human intelligence may be the product of an evolutionary process, but it is not the goal of that process, merely a happy accident.

However, if one accepts the premise that the universe itself, and all the perceived laws by which the universe is governed, are constantly undergoing a process of selection of their own and this process creates axioms that exist only so long as they are suitable and which are discarded when they no longer function effectively, one has to question the idea of evolution as a blind series of selections without design or goal. God, or some seemingly divine presence at any rate, seems to have found a way to creep in the back door of the evolutionary party He'd been invited to leave not so long ago. (Feel free to impart your own preconception of the gender of divinity here. I was raised Catholic, and there are hooks within my soul that will never extract themselves; And then again, there is the matter of my father.) Of course, if there is a mind evolving here, then we come back to the idea of intellect... and how it can be self-deceptive.

> The nothingness "before" the creation of the universe is the
> most complete void that we can imagine-no space, time, or
> matter existed. It is a world without place, without duration
> or eternity, without number-it is what mathematicians call
> "the empty set." Yet this unthinkable void converts itself into
> a plenum of existence-a necessary consequence of physical
> laws. Where are these laws written into that void? What "tells"
> the void that it is pregnant with a possible universe?
> *H.R. Pagels, **Perfect Symmetry***

> To become conscious of itself, or to render itself
> comprehensible to itself, Ain becomes Ain Soph (infinity),
> and still further Ain Soph Aur, absolute Limitless Light (the
> Daivapraktriti of the Brahman Vedantists, and the Adi-Buddha
> or Amitabha of the Buddhists); which then by contraction
> (Tsimtsum, according to the Zohar) concentrated itself into a
> central dimensionless point-Kether, the Crown, which is the
> first Sephirah on the Tree of Life.
> *Israel Regardie, **The Tree of Life***

Of course, just because we suspect the universe may be undergoing evolutionary change of its own is no reason to suspect that it is alive, especially not as we define life, exactly because of that pesky tendency we have towards self-deception through the application of our limited intellect to a limitless expanse of matter, energy, time and space extending outwards through dimensions we've only recently come to realize must exist, even though we can't perceive them. One could argue, in fact, that the reason our intellect seems to deceive is that we are dependent on our perceptions to gather the evidence we need to make determinations, and those senses do not and are not designed to take in information from those physical dimensions that transcend the three of which we are consciously aware.

But there is plenty of evidence of higher dimensions in human history; it's simply evidence we tend to ignore. I'm sure we're all familiar with the Australian concept of the Dreamtime, or the old Celtic Otherworld, or the astral plane of the Theosophists and it makes one wonder at the similarity of these ideas (The astral plane, of course, was hardly a new concept, just a restatement of the ancient

Greek and Roman concept of otherworldy realms where the dead dwelled as do the living, borrowed from the Egyptians and Sumerians... and then there's the concept of the Platonic Ideal Forms, the conceptual perfect versions of all gross physical existence, which existed as pure thought that transcended this universe... and suddenly we're back to the idea of the universe as thought expressed in mathematics, whether it be the Pythagorean solids or the theories of Kaluza-Klein and their successors). Of course, it's possible to explain that underlying symmetry of thought as a result of our evolving minds being exposed to the variety of morphic fields in existence. Does inspiration come when individual mind interacts with group mind, which then interacts with universe mind? Is it possible that the intuition that mystical groups seek to weld to the intellect is in fact the voice of the universe speaking back to us in the only language we share?

Sheldrake argues that evolution is a universal constant, that all things from subatomic to cosmic scale are under the influence of individual morphic fields that resemble the habits of the universe. That these fields, or forces, are created as the universe progresses, and that they become more rigid and more seemingly immutable the longer they exist and the more reinforcement they receive. This brings to mind the work of Georg Bernhard Riemann, who on June 10, 1854, managed to mathematically show that forces are really simply the effect of dimensional interface.

> To Riemann, "force" was a consequence of geometry. Riemann then replaced the two-dimensional sheet with our three-dimensional world crumpled in the fourth dimension. It would not be obvious to us that our universe was warped. However, we would immediately realize that something was amiss when we tried to walk in a straight line. We would walk like a drunkard, as though an unseen force were tugging at us, pushing us left and right. Riemann concluded that electricity, magnetism and gravity are caused by the crumpling of our three-dimensional universe in the unseen fouth dimension. Thus a "force" has no independent life of its own; it is only the apparent effect cause by the distortion of geometry.
> *Michio Kaku,* **Hyperspace**

Imagine our three-dimensional universe, crumpled into the fourth.

Now imagine that four dimensional universe, crumpled again into the fifth, and so on... each universe emanating from the next, each one a reflection of the last, just as described in the Tree of Life, or in the nestled solids of Pythagorean theory, or the Ideals of Neoplatonism. Reflections, each deceptive, none truly expressing the nature of reality, and each being taken in by the limited senses of a race of recently sentient hominids on a small ball within one of those crumpled spheres. The universe evolves, and it does so in levels of existence we can only grasp through the brute application of math. But by doing so, we slowly alter the universe itself by our efforts. These changes may be small, but there's a butterfly effect at work here, and the inertia of these universal habits indicates that over the course of billion of years, what once was hotly disputed becomes axiomatic, and almost a law. If there are forces directing the growth and evolution of everything we can grasp with our minds, including our minds themselves, it is likely that those forces are nothing more than the effect of the interaction of dimensions themselves and that the mind of the universe is, ultimately, to be found within the brains of small, limited beings like ourselves, who may be separate beings and who yet have access to a mind that transcends our deceived conceptions of what space and time are. We lie to ourselves, and yet, we are not fooled.

It's a concept so old it is shared by the ancient Vedic writers of the *Bhagavad Gita* and the long-isolated tribesmen of Australia, the natives of the North and South American continent and the nomadic pre-Celtic inhabitants of Europe as well as the primordial civilizations of Egypt, China and Sumeria: as above, so below. Contagion and sympathy seem to be hardly the relics of a bygone age, as many would tell us, but instead the building blocks of a new reality, wherein every particle in existence is connected by an existence that transcends what can be seen and grasped and reality itself is as shifting and transient as our temporary and yet infinite lives. The known is finite, the unknown infinite.

If we're supposed to try to equalize that vast discrepancy, I suppose we'd best get to work. Me, I have my eye on a homestead somewhere between sanity and madness.

And What Is Past, or Passing, or To Come

According to Plato's *Critias*, a great war between an island empire in the Atlantic Ocean and a people who lived on the site of the city of Athens was taking place around 9600 BC or so, which would have meant that it was certainly possible for that aforementioned island empire (Atlantis, that is) to have existed in the year 10,000 BC. Robert Temple, in his book *The Sirius Mystery*, argues that aliens from Sirius (natch) were visiting our planet and imparting mystical secrets to the peoples who would become Egyptians and Sumerians right around that time. Meanwhile, proto-Celtic peoples seem to have been migrating into what would eventually become China and Mongolia, where they would be buried in sophisticated tombs complete with vast amounts of gold and tartan cloths (although this date is on the extreme end of things, I admit), and someone walked across the land bridge onto the British Isles from Europe and built Stonehenge. The Baltic Sea was an inland ocean and, according to the author of the mysterious *Oera Linda* book, home to yet another advanced civilization. Meanwhile, if you buy into the Piri Reis map of Antarctica, someone had both the nautical skill to sail around the southernmost continent in the world charting the coast, and the ability to either see through glaciers in order to map the land beneath... or to see it without an ice cover that some argue has been in place for millions of years.

I've said before that the past is a busy place where by definition everything that has happened took place, but even so it would seem that 10,000 BC was a very busy time, especially considering that much of the world was in the thick of an ice age at the time.

> The Wheel turns and nations rise and fall; the world changes, and times return to savagery to rise again through the long age. Ere Atlantis was, Valusia was, and ere Valusia was, the Elder Nations were. Aye, we, too, trampled the shoulders of lost tribes in our advance. You, who have come from the green

> sea hills of Atlantis to seize the ancient crown of Valusia, you think my tribe is old, we who held these lands ere the Valusians came out of the East, in the days before there were men in the sea lands. But men were here when the Elder Tribes rode out of the waste lands, and men before men, tribe before tribe. The nations pass and are forgotten, for that is the destiny of man.
>
> Robert E. Howard, *The Mirrors of Tuzun Thune*

How many times has man risen out of barbarism and tried to forge a civilization? The gap between the rise of the modern human and the rise of the first known culture, that of ancient Sumer, is tens of thousands of years at the most conservative guess. Was it merely a case of overcoming inertia before the slow march forward could become the torrential changes we have grown accustomed to, or is there truth to the various stories that say before the nations familiar to us, there were others not known today?

Consider the lost cultures of Minoan Crete and the Hattusa, both only rediscovered in the last two centuries. Before Arthur Evans' work on Crete, the seafaring culture of the Minoans was totally unknown outside of a few myths involving Zeus' origins on the island, the tale of Theseus and the Minotaur, and little else. Likewise, the empire of Hattusa was remembered mainly in Old Testament passages in Genesis and the Book of Numbers. Until the language of the Hittites was rediscovered and sites like Ugarit excavated, no one knew of this nation, which had rivaled the empire of Ramses and left behind several ruined cities. If two Mediterranean superpowers from a mere three thousand years ago could nearly vanish from our sight, if cities like Harrapa and Mohenjo-Daro could be forgotten until people began using their bricks to construct a railroad despite the fact that they only rose around 2500 BC, who is to say what we have lost from further back?

Of course, the very fact that we don't know means that, well, we don't know. It also means that rampant speculation sets in: according to Graham Hancock, for instance, an encoded astrological text was created at some point in the distant past, a text that contained information about the precession of the sun through the various constellations of the zodiac some six thousand or more years before conventional wisdom holds the Sumerians invented the first constellations, much less noticed that if one watches long enough (long enough being roughly 2,160 years) the wobble of the earth's orbit would cause the sun to rise in a different house of the zodiac. (Basically, if you've ever wondered why this is the dawning of the Age of Aquarius, here's a quick and dirty explanation. If you watch the sky before dawn, you will notice that the sun appears to rise against one of the twelve constellations of the zodiac, depending on what day it is. At present, the constellation that the sun rises against during the spring equinox is Pisces, but as the earth orbits the sun, the axis wobbles. In essence, every 25,920 years, the earth's pole makes a small circle, and as it does, the constellations seem to shift behind the sun from equinox to equinox and solstice to solstice. At present, Aquarius is poised to take over the spring equinox from Pisces, and 2160 years after it does, Capricorn will take its place.)

In order for the Sumerians to have even been aware of precession, Hancock argues, they must have been watching the stars since at least six thousand years before Christ. (He actually argues that somebody was doing so a lot earlier, as typified by a painting on the walls of a cave in Lascaux, France. This painting, called the Hall of the Bulls, is generally agreed to date from more than 17,000 years ago. It is a painting which represents the relationship between the constellation of Taurus the Bull and the stars of the Pleiades. Now, it's unlikely that two cultures separated by thousands of miles and twice as many years would independently create the exact same constellation in the same location in the sky, one would have to agree.) The reason for this ancient stargazing was an ancient cult of death and rebirth that existed before any culture we now know of, and which was disseminated to South America and Mexico as the cult of Quetzalcoatl, to Egypt as the rites of Osiris, to Cambodia and Easter Island and the islands of Japan as various solar and stellar cults. He marshals quite a bit of evidence for his theory: ancient monoliths in the Sea of Japan and mathematical elements in the ancient temples of Malta and Uxmal in Mexico which seem hauntingly similar, various aspects of the cults of Osiris and Quetzalcoatl which resemble each other, reams of astronomical observation and more. Hancock, and others with similar views like Rand Flem-Ath, ultimately argue that before the year 10,000 BC a great culture or cultures dominated the planet, and that after a calamity of some sort- a meteor, or possibly earth-crust shift, or what have you- all that was left behind was various monoliths and temples which were designed to serve as a kind of document on a global scale, built to exacting standards so that as human culture was reborn we would become able to understand the message of a higher culture existing tens of thousands of years ago, an age when man was on the cusp of unlocking even the secrets of life and death.

> In their immense study *Hamlet's Mill,* published in 1969, they argue that a body of scientific astronomical knowledge was in existence in the world at least "6000 years before Virgil" (i.e. at around 6000 BC) and that this lore used precise, idiosyncratic and widely disseminated mythological conventions to describe celestial events that have been proved by astronomical calculations to have occurred in the skies in the epoch of 6000 BC. The evident maturity of these conventions even at that early date troubled Santillana and von Dechend, who at length, rather hesitatingly, ascribed the origins of the astronomical lore to "some almost unbelievable ancestor civilization" that "first dared to understand the world as created according to number, measure and weight."
> *Graham Hancock and Santha Faiia,* **Heaven's Mirror**

Another option, however, is suggested by Robert Temple. Temple argues that relics like the Lascaux Bulls, the Antikythera Device (an ancient mechanical calculator found in the Aegean in 1900, dating back some three to four thousand years) and advanced astrological knowledge in the hands of an African tribe called the Dogon (including, it would seem, knowledge of the composition of the Sirius star-system we are only just now beginning to match) prove that while there certainly may have been an advanced civilization before any we know of, it certainly wasn't human. Temple connects the ancient Sumerian tradition of Enki, the amphibious trickster god and semi-patron of humanity (described at length in the *Enuma Elish*, the Sumerian/Babylonian creation myth) to the fragmentary tales left to us of the historian Berossus.

> This is the history which Berossus has transmitted to us. He tells us that the first king was Alorus of Babylon, a Chaldaean; he reigned ten sari [a saros equals 3600 years]: and afterwards Alaparus, and Amelon who came from Pantibiblon: then

Ammenon the Chaldaean, in whose time appeared the
Musarus Oannes the Annedotus from the Erythean sea.
Apollodorus as quoted by Robert Temple, **The Sirius Mystery**

Of course, I'm giving both men's theories short shrift here,
partially because I really can't do justice to such dense and well-
argued portraits of the time before history (Temple's book is 440
pages long, and packed with references to sources ranging from
modern astrophysics to Neoplatonist authors like Proclus to Robert
Graves' *The Greek Myths* and *The White Goddess* and so on, and
Hancock has written two books of similar size) and also because
they cover a lot of the same ground. Basically, both men (and many
others besides, like the infamous Madame Blavatsky of Theosophist
fame, Zecharia Sitchin, Lewis Spence and others) are arguing that
there was something here before those civilizations we know of,
something that left behind sophisticated astrological information,
artifacts, cultural traditions, and even the occasional building or
megalithic structure. And indeed, even if you cull the most outlandish
elements from the basic theory and look only at real live tangible
evidence like the Antikythera Device, the Lascaux cave-paintings,
Stonehenge, the strangely carved heads of what appear to be Africans
that are scattered all over the territories that once held the long-
vanished Olmec culture of Mesoamerica, and other such oddities...
you start to get the feeling that there may well be a kernel of truth
here. Somebody painted that cave. Somebody built Stonehenge, and
Avebury, and the megalithic monuments of Malta.

Of course, we haven't really discussed the very myths and legends
that so many speculations have been founded upon. The fact is, even
in their fragmentary state, the epics of many cultures refer to ages of
man that pre-date this one. The time of slavery endured by ancient
humanity at the hands of the gods in the *Enuma Elish*, the seemingly
advanced technology used in the war described in the *Mahabhrata*
of India, the decadent races of giants and human-angel crossbreeds
destroyed by God with the flood in Judeo-Christian traditions... the
same flood which appears in the *Epic of Gilgamesh* and Greek myth
and the *Enuma Elish* and at the end of the Fourth Sun in Nahuatl
mythology, one wonders? The flood the Egyptian priests at Sais
told Solon about, according to Plato?

For example, these genealogies, Solon, which you just now recounted of the people of your country, are little better than children's tales. For in the first place ye remember but one deluge, whereas there had been many before it; and again ye know now that the fairest and noblest race among mankind lived once in your country, whence ye sprang, and all your city which now is, from a very little seed that of old was left over. Ye know it not, because the survivors lived and died for many generations without utterance in writing. For, once upon a time, Solon, far back beyond the greatest destruction by waters, that which is now the city of the Athenians was foremost in war and all besides, and her laws were exceedingly righteous above all cities.

*Plato, **Timaeus***

Pro-Athenian jingoism aside, what can we take from that passage? Well, for one thing, it argues not merely for one great civilization-wrecking catastrophe, but a series of them. It's as if humanity has risen only to be knocked back into barbarism again and again and again, as if someone keeps erasing the chalkboard and sending a recalcitrant humanity back to its seat in the classroom to try again. And in the myths, that someone has been the gods, as some divinities (Prometheus, Enki, Thoth, Quetzalcoatl) bring mankind knowledge while others bring various calamities, be it Zeus or Yahweh dispensing floods and cursing us for aspiring to heights of knowledge reserved only for the divine or the Annunaki deciding to rid the Earth of man. You get a picture of a fractious, divided divinity, squabbling like Ahura Mazda and Ahriman in Zoroastrianism. The gods are unpredictable, showering gifts and punishments with equal frequency.

So who are the gods, exactly? Are they from another planet, as Sitchin and Temple argue? I think it unlikely, mainly because the idea of alien beings who act like human beings is so unsatisfying. I could accept the concept of alien beings who arrive on earth and accidentally screw with our development just by virtue of their presence- and indeed, that could very well be what happened- but the idea of advanced and, more importantly, alien beings who brave the distances of the void (however they do it, be it generational ships, relativistic time dilation, traveling through hyperspace in order to side-step distances, or even taking advantage of the effects of quantum synchronicity to affect change on earth without travelling from their worlds at all; whatever floats your boat) and then begin acting like human beings the second they get here just doesn't work for me. An alien, by definition, would be more unlike us than anything we have ever met. We have more in common with anaerobic unicellular organisms that live on undersea volcanoes than we would with an alien. The idea that they could understand us well enough to impart any sort of civilization seems wrong to me, somehow. So while I think it possible that there was some sort of non-native influence on our earliest culture, I don't necessarily think it came from space.

I think this, in part, because it is still with us to some degree, helping or hindering the development of our society, steering us in directions it wants us to proceed, editing our past in order to create our future. Therefore, it would seem to imply an understanding of human nature I just don't believe an extra-terrestrial of the type Sitchin and Temple describe could have, not even if it considers us livestock (as our old friend Charles Fort used to say, "I think we're fished for"), although I freely admit this is a bias, and I could well be incorrect. For now, though, let's assume that it isn't beings from space, at least not the space we can see by looking up at the sky. Who the hell is it, then?

What if it is us?

> Once upon the throne of kings, there shall never have been a tyranny to equal ours, no despot shall ever have put a thicker blindfold over the eyes of the people; plunged into essential ignorance, it shall be at our mercy, blood will flow in rivers, our Masonic bretheren themselves shall become the mere valets of our cruelties, and in us alone shall the supreme power be concentrated; all freedom shall go by the board, that of the press, that of worship, that simply of thought shall be severely forbidden and ruthlessly repressed; one must beware of enlightening the people or or lifting away its irons when your aim is to rule it.
> *The Marquis de Sade,* **Juliette**

Forget the sexual perversion: the real heart of sadism, as the marquis himself envisioned it, is to be free, free of all concerns or doubts or hesitations, so free that society itself adapts to service you. In the eyes of Sade, freedom is a rare thing, and one can only have it if he is willing and able to deny it to almost everyone else in the world. The true sadist is aware that a populace will almost always create a society with strictures and laws, and in order to be free, he or she must therefore pervert that society while standing atop the pyramid of those who make the decisions. Since first expressed by François Rabelais in his *History of Gargantua and Pantagruel* in 1535 (a farcical and perverse tale of giants that served as an enormous satire of European history and development) the doctrine of the Abbey of Thélème, "Do what you will," has been expressed over and over again by groups like the Hellfire Club and the disciples of Aleister Crowley, but Sade was the first to look at it from a pragmatic and entirely unsentimental viewpoint. How does one make it possible to do as one wills? To Sade, in order to be truly free, one must be free from fear, from conscience, and from any possible repercussions for ones actions. The only truly free individual would be one who could control the very laws of society, directing to whom punishments accrue and always exempting him- or herself.

> The contrast between the abortive mediation of Prometheus and the legitimate mediation of Hecate emphasizes the fact that the regime of Zeus changes the relation between men and gods. Prometheus' intervention in the destiny of mankind begins "when gods and man came to Mecone to settle their dispute" over the division of the sacrificial animal (lines 535-36); at this point men and gods intermingle on a basis of equality. The wrath of Zeus against mankind is provoked by Prometheus' resort to trickery in the division of the sacred animal, that is to say, by his attempt to settle the issue between men and gods as though it were between men and other men.
> *Norman O. Brown, **Introduction to Hesiod's Theogony***

Imagine, if you would, the dawn of humanity itself at some dim juncture hundreds of thousands of years ago. Instead of supposing that, after the Neanderthal and Cro-Magnon strains of humanity either merged into one or the Neanderthals were wiped out, nothing at all happened to move humanity into any sort of culture for at least 97,000 years or so (and that is a conservative estimate; it could be more like 197,000) and then, bang, we have Sumeria and the beginning of history, let's assume that it took 20,000 years to develop something like a culture. That would take us to 70,000 BC if we use the most conservative estimate of how far back one can trace modern man. So, assuming a bronze age culture existed in some form by 70,000 BC, and assuming it took them ten times as long to go from the bronze age to what we laughingly call modern civilization, we would arrive at some form of technological society by 20,000 BC.

Plenty of time. There's no reason to assume it would, in fact, take so long. Assuming that it took them twice as long as did the most recent push from Bronze Age to modern day, that's only 10,000 years. (From ancient Sumeria to right now is roughly 5000 years.) So one could plausibly put an advanced human civilization somewhere on earth around 60,000 BC and not really be stretching things too much, and it would fit right into the mythical pattern. (Of course, with the eruption of Toba around 73,000 years ago causing massive climactic changes- hey, a catastrophe, just like those wacky Egyptians said we'd see!- it might make more sense to push things back a bit, but let's assume they weathered that or that it was all part of the reason it took so long for their society to develop in the first place.) Now, assuming we accept the idea of such a society existing at all, where did it go?

Maybe nowhere at all, or at least nowhere in a physical three dimensional sense. Maybe, seeing the Ice Age coming and disinclined to let their society be buried under the ice, they began exploring higher mathematics and found a way to doppler shift their society along the ten dimensional axis. So, in essence, they're still here and they're still occupying three physical dimensions... just not the same three we occupy. There are other possibilities, of course. They may well have been working on a way to use quantum synchronicity, that strange superluminal communication between all matter and energy that superstring theory attempts to explain with the idea that all matter and energy is in fact a three-dimensional cross section of the superstring, which enters and exits our perception as subatomic particles but which, in a ten-dimensional sense, is really continuous. Any society that understood such would be able to tap near-limitless power from anywhere in the universe without traversing the intervening distance, since that distance wouldn't exist in a different cross-section of reality. Testing such a science could well be fraught with peril. Perhaps they didn't leave our reality so much as they were pushed, and in the pushing left behind a cataclysm that created ice age conditions across the globe. Eventually, they managed to realign themselves and could re-enter our world; either by choice or through calamity, they'd pierced the veil between levels of existence.

As such, and with the power to enter and leave our reality at will along any point in space, they could well appear as gods to those they left behind, as they began the slow climb out of the killing ice. But they wouldn't be gods; they'd be men and women, with the same pettiness and jealousy and love and hate and all the other elements of humanity we have. At first, they may well have tried to explain to their post-ice kinfolk what was happening. Then, frustrated by their lack of comprehension, they decided to accept the mantle of divinity, and over time have even come to believe it. No more would man and god mingle as equals; one would adapt to service the other.

Of course, no human society is monolithic, not even one that has managed to outpocket itself into a seperate dimensional status, and there would be dissidents, those that would want to directly uplift those left behind (especially if the calamity was of their own making) and who would attempt to impart their advanced knowledge to us. Also, there may well have been those who fled from their advanced society, perhaps feeling that it was too restrictive, and sought to create one more to their liking, one that allowed them all the freedom to do whatever they liked by creating in us a blindfolded, shepherded state similar to the one on which the Marquis de Sade ruminated. This results in the constant conflict between those who wish to enlighten humanity and those who wish to keep us in darkness and ignorance... the war between Prometheus and Zeus, between the gods of the Annunaki and Enki, between Quetzalcoatl and Tezcatlipoca, between Lucifer the Light Bringer and Yahweh the Forbidder. Meanwhile, the mainstream policy is to selectively edit the historical record, to destroy any evidence of their existence, cull any references from epics that mention them, and create a climate where any such evidence would be laughed off or dismissed, hoping that we'll manage to redisover the same scientific principles they did without the possible near-disasters they experienced.

Of course, it could well have been biotech instead of quantum tunnelling. Maybe it took them longer to develop a society because they grew their technology, and they then retreated physically rather than otherdimensionally. There are a few places in this solar system where a colony of precursors could conceivably head off to, like Mars. For that matter, if we accept a more radical timeline (say, 200,000 years ago instead of 100,000) and combine that with the Egyptian idea that there were multiple disasters, volcanic eruptions, floods, et cetera... suddenly, there can be multiple waves of precursors, each possibly interefering with the other, and with us. The wars of the gods described in the *Theogony* and *Mahabhrata* suddenly become the wars of our forebears, trying to ensure that they have a monopoly on the worldview of any successive society. Some trying to teach us, some trying to use us; some viewing us as their children, others as cattle; some wiping us out when they can, others who started out as refugees from a previous attempt at world-scouring and then rebelled against their attempted destroyers.... So Zeus and the Olympians making war on the Titans, and Enki and the Annunaki making war on Apsu and Tiamat, become the story of different precursors realizing how they were manipulated, and rising against their oppressors- before going right ahead and manipulating us for their own various reasons.

Which, of course, leads us to wonder: are we sheep, or are we gods in embryo, about to rise up and punish our forebears as they punished theirs, in an endless cycle of revolution dedicated to the premise that we must be free to find our own fate? And do our ancestor-shepherds see this danger, which is why they edit or delete the epics, why they hide the evidence, attempting as did the Aztecs with their blood sacrifices to avoid or even avert the end of this, the Fourth Sun, and the beginning of the Fifth, and to keep us blind? It's interesting that so many of the supposed wild and libertine thinkers of the past five hundred years, those that picked up the standard of Rabelais, never really got anywhere. Despite their political influence, the Hellfire Club degenerated into a group playing at petty politics and perversions. Lord Byron, who started out as a firebrand voting in the House of Lords to defend the Machine-Wreckers who followed the mythical (and re-imagined Celtic god) King Ludd, bled to death while fighting to free Greece, the home of so many of the epic poems that deal with this very subject. Crowley died feeble and addled, his grand re-statement of the law of Thélème ("Do what you will, yes, but know that your will should, nay, must be in alignment with your most true and worthwhile inner purpose") ignored by many. The idea of absolute freedom combined with absolute knowledge of oneself has been tossed aside, and pointless lust for more and more replaces it. Is this the hand of one, or perhaps many, or our predecessors trying to mire our development in things that are of no consequence, sidetracking our best and brightest so that we never rival them?

If so, they may be too late. On December 23, 2012, some say the Fifth Age will begin. Terrence McKenna argued that Timewave Zero would commence, and all of recorded history would come to an end. Is it the destruction of all we know, or the step through the door into elsewhere, and the beginning of our war with our makers, they who think of themselves as gods and us as sheep? Do we die... or ascend?

The Mind War of the Great Khan

In 1294, Roger Bacon (almost certainly the most intelligent man in the world at that time) and Kubilai Khan, ruler of China and nominal head of the Mongols (thus the most powerful monarch on the whole of the Eurasian continent) both died. At first glance, that seems to have been all one could possibly say they had in common. Of course, as in all things, there may be more going on under the surface than we can see at a superficial glance.

Both were possessed of a ruthless intellect, although in Bacon's case it was channeled into fields of inquiry such as science and alchemy, whereas Kubilai used his to become a ruler over half the world. (To put the vast size of the Mongol domains into modern perspective, imagine if one nation ruled China, Russia, all the former Soviet republics, the Middle East, and Asia Minor. It was the largest empire the world had ever seen.) But what common acquaintanceships could an English student of natural philosophy and a Tartar Khan have?

A prolific penman, he was forbidden to write, and it was not until 1266 that Guy de Foulques, the papal legate in England - subsequently Pope Clement IV - hearing of Bacon's fame, invited him to break his silence. Bacon hailed the opportunity and in spite of hardship and poverty, finished his *Opus Majus*, *Opus Minus* and *Opus Tertium*. These works seem to have found favor with Clement, for the writer was allowed to return to Oxford, there to continue his scientific studies and the composition of scientific works.
Lewis Spence, *An Encyclopedia of Occultism*

When the Great Khan, whose name was Kubilai, who was lord of all the Tartars in the world and of all the provinces and kingdoms and regions of this vast part of the earth had heard all about the Latins, as the two brothers had well and plainly declared it, he was exceedingly pleased. He made up his mind to send emissaries to the Pope, and asked the two

brothers to go on this mission with one of his barons....
Thereupon the Great Khan had letters written in the Turkish
language to send to the Pope and entrusted them to the two
brothers and to his baron and instructed them what they must
say on his behalf to the Pope. You must know that the purport
of the letters and his mission was this: he sent word to the
Pope that he should send up to a hundred men learned in the
Christian religion, well versed in the seven arts, and skilled
to argue and demonstrate plainly to idolators and those of
other persuasions that their religion is utterly mistaken and
that all the idols which they keep in their houses and worship
are things of the Devil - men able to show by clear reasoning
that the Christian religion is better than theirs. Furthermore
the Great Khan directed the brothers to bring oil from the
lamp that burns above the sepulchre of God in Jerusalem.
Marco Polo and Rusticello of Pisa, **Description of the World**

So we have Bacon, a genius equally learned in church doctrine
(he was a Franciscan friar) and science, freed from punishment and
set to work producing his great masterworks by a man who would
become Pope. Subtracting the Polos travel time (in *Description of
the World* it is claimed that Niccolo and Maffeo, the aforementioned
brothers, took three years to return to Acre, in 1269) we find that at
that very moment the Great Khan was sending to Europe for a
hundred men just like Bacon. What, one asks, was Kubilai's purpose
in inviting Christian missionaries into an empire torn apart by religious
struggles between Tibetan and Chinese Buddhism, not to mention
Taoism and Confucianism? Within the territories claimed by his family
were Eastern Orthodox, Nestorian and Jacobite Christians, as well
as much of the Dar-al-Islam. It would seem on the surface rather
unintelligent... but Kubilai Khan didn't overcome all of his close
relatives to become the Great Khan by being less than razor keen.
And, in point of fact, Kubilai didn't require much instruction in
Christianity anyway, for his mother Sorghagtani Beki was a Nestorian
Christian (a sect of Christianity viewed as heretical by the Church of
Rome) and he was hardly ignorant of the tenets of the faith.

Indeed, perhaps far from ignorant...

From Ayas they went on to Acre, which they reached in the
month of April, in the year of the Incarnation 1269. There
they learnt that the Lord Pope, whose name was Clement,

was dead. They went accordingly to a learned clerk who was legate of the Church of Rome for the whole kingdom of Egypt, a man of great authority named Tedaldo of Piacenza, and told him of the mission on which the Great Khan of the Tartars had sent them to the Pope. When the legate had heard what they had to say, he was filled with wonder, and it seemed to him that this affair was greatly to the profit and honor of Christendom.

Marco Polo and Rustichello of Pisa, **Description of the World**

No kidding. A pissant promontory of Eurasia being singled out by the Great Khan? And why, by the way, did he seem so eager to get his hands on the oil of the Holy Sepulchre? What was Kubilai really up to? And why did he seem so sure that he would find the Pope a willing ally? For that matter, what was Clement up to? Why free a dangerous man, possibly a heretic, in 1266? Four hundred years later Galileo would recant and Giordano Bruno be put to the stake for less... what leverage did Bacon have?

The character of later recruits changed. Many went out to the East to avoid paying their debts; judges gave criminals their choice of jail or taking the cross. After the defeat of Saint Louis in 1250, preachers of a crusade were publicly insulted. When mendicant monks asked for alms, people would summon a beggar and give him a coin, not in the name of Christ who did not protect his own, but in the name of Mohammed, who had proven to be the stronger. Around 1270 a former master general of the Dominican order wrote that few still believed in the spiritual merit promised by the crusades. A French monk addressed God directly: "He is a fool who follows You into battle."

Morris Bishop, **The Middle Ages**

To understand what the underlying theme was, we have to look at Europe from the millennium forward to the time of Clement, Bacon and Kubilai. Europe at the year A.D. 1000 was beset on all sides by ideological enemies. To the north were the Vikings ("from the fury of the Northmen, oh Lord, deliver us"), who would be broken in two climactic battles (1014, as the Irish managed to keep the Norse from conquering their island, and 1066, as Harold of Wessex managed to drive Harald Hardradi out of York in a battle that would come to seem anticlimactic very shortly) but who had up to that point basically made Christendom their bitch. To the south, even holding much of Spain and Sicily, were the hated Moslems (and part of that hate was envy; Islam had come out of nowhere in the eighth century and burned up half the Mediterranean, swallowing Christian territories whole), and to the east, as had been the case since Atilla drove Germanic tribesmen like a thorn into the side of Rome, were nomadic horsemen like the Turks and Magyars, ready to attack. A siege mentality and an apocalyptic faith combined with a society designed around a nobleman's obligation to provide mounted military service to lead Europe into a situation with more heavily armed horsemen than they knew what to do with. The Crusades had seemed an inspired solution, but ultimately the western European knight could not hold the territory he could take: it was a battle of tanks against skirmishers, and while the "Franks" (as they were called by the writer Usamah ibn Munqidh in his *Book of Reflections*, no matter where they were actually from) were capable warriors, they were outnumbered and unfamiliar with the territory. (I'd love to get into the Knights Templar here, and maybe I will later, but for now they're a diversion to our course.) By the middle of the thirteenth century, Christendom was reeling under the failure of its attempt to take the Holy Land from the "followers of Mahomet" and was feeling the pressure. At this point, a hoax begun in the 1180s by an unknown hand began to sweep Europe... the legend of a great Christian king in the Far East. He had fifty sub-kings under his banner, and his reign was so dazzling that it shamed the twin courts of Christendom, Rome and Byzantium. Pope Alexander sent a mission to the East to find him which failed.

Of course, I'm talking about Prester John, the greatest delusion of the middle ages. The so-called priest king of the East appeared like a mirage to a desperate man, and seemed as elusive. In time, when Asia was sufficiently familiar to the men of the West that they could no longer delude themselves into believing he could be hidden there, they simply moved him and his legend wholesale to Africa. But it's interesting to note that the rise of the legend, and its fullest flowering, would begin in the thirteenth century... during the reign of the Oceanic Ruler, Temujin, better known to history as Genghis Khan.

But insofar as my calling is high, the obligations incumbent

upon me are also heavy, and I fear in my governance there may be something lacking. To cross a river we construct boats and rudders. Likewise, we invite sage men, and choose assistants, to keep an empire in good order. Ever since I came to the throne, I have constantly taken to heart the ruling of my people, but I could not find worthy individuals to occupy the offices of the three and nine. With respect to these circumstances, I inquired and heard that you, Master, have penetrated the truth, and that you walk in the way of right.
Chinggis Khan, **Letter to Changchung**

The whole dynasty of Temujin had a strange mystical strain from day one. Temujin (later Chinggis Khan, better known to westerners as Genghis Khan) overcame the odds and rose from a seven year old boy exiled from his father's clan to become the leader and unifier of the Mongols and the conquerer of just about everyone who crossed his path. A shaman as much as a horseman, he knew how to alternate naked power with reasoned statescraft, how to flatter and how to best use honesty, to threaten or cajole or argue as best seemed fit at the time. While he crushed the Chinese states in open battle, subduing the Jin and the Song (although it would be left to his grandson Kubilai to complete the subjugation of the Chinese) as well as the Tangut, he also used spies in his battles with the Kwarzim and showed he knew how to conquer by subverting an enemy's ideals. His practice of reaching out to the intellectual elite of his own conquered lands, assimilating their best and brightest into his new state, was an example of his brilliant pragmatism. If the Chinese would not accept a ruler who did not behave in certain ways or who seemingly lacked the Mandate of Heaven, Chinggis would simply provide himself that mandate. He was also interested deeply in the ideas of the Taoists, especially the idea that alchemical immortality could be achieved. He died without finding it. (Indeed, it was the mission of the aforementioned Changchung to instruct Chinggis in the ways of preserving life.)

His son Ogodai was a throwback to older Mongol ways, brutally efficient in battle but not a tremendously subtle ruler and certainly not nearly so affected by Chinese ways. His death in 1241 prevented another Mongol, Batu Khan (lord of the Golden Horde) from completing his march through Russia and arriving in Europe. The halt of that advance must have seemed heaven-sent to a Europe that was experiencing a series of aftershocks. Batu had seemed yet another hammer from the East; now, in that land rose a Great Khan who might just be reasoned with. Between 1253 and 1255 William of Rubruck, a Franciscan Friar, made his way east from Constantinople to Mongke Khan's court, which lay in Mongolia at Karakorum. Mongke, Kubilai's uncle and Great Khan until his death in 1259, was not entirely convinced, but he did make sure to let the Westerner see his people, for reasons unknown to us.

Imagine, if you will, a young Kubilai at his uncle's court, already preparing to take control of the Mongol Empire. Like his dead grandsire, a man who planned ahead and made use of those with talent, no matter who they were, he takes the opportunity to make contact with William of Rubruck, using his knowledge of Christianity and his gift for putting people at ease to create a dialogue between them. Of course, William is of no use to Kubilai... yet. But Kubilai either learns from William or already knows of a piece of folklore that will serve him well, and creates an inroad from which the Mongols can gain a great deal.

Prester John.

> The Emperor Prester John always marries the daughter of the Great Khan, and the Great Khan likewise marries Prester John's daughter. For they are the two greatest lords under heaven. In Prester John's land there are many different things and many precious gems of such magnitude that people make vessels, such as platters, dishes and cups out of them... this Emperor Prester John is Christian, as is a great part of his country as well.
> *Sir John Mandeville, **The Travels***

Perhaps wily Chinggis planted the seeds (the dates are about right, although the earliest rumors of the Presbyter King date back to a Moslem defeat in 1148, four decades before Chinggis' rise to power) or simply fostered them, or perhaps it was Kubilai's idea to make use of this fictional Christian king. By linking himself to the greatest Christian monarch in the world, Kubilai makes himself an irresistable object to the Pope and Patriarch alike. All of Christendom, already pleased to see Islam reeling under the attack of the Mongols (and somewhat afraid of the awesome power of the Golden Horde that so recently smashed its way through Russia) was very willing to ally with the Great Khan, especially those elements in European society at that time who had lost prestige when crusading had taken such a downward turn. Were the Franciscans Kubilai's Fifth Column into the soft underbelly of Europe?

Perhaps. If so, then what could have possibly stopped the greatest imperial power in the world from forging an alliance with the papacy? Who could have seen through the mask of alliance offered through secret Franciscan channels to the greedy, vicious streak in the Timurid Dynasty, which sought to live forever through twisted alchemical means?

Only the most intelligent man in the world, a Franciscan friar, a man who managed to somehow convince a Pope the Great Khan felt he had in his pocket to release him from prison. The man Europe credited with the invention of gunpowder (which we know existed in China before this time) and who mastered the arts of alchemy and cryptography. Roger Bacon, whose *Opus Majus* was somehow so persuasive that Clement read it... and sent him back to Oxford and his laboratory. What was encoded in that book for Clement to read? And how would a man in a Franciscan prison cell know anything so potent that even the Church, that known burner of heretics, kept him alive?

> His name is for ever associated with the making of gunpowder, and if the honor cannot wholly be afforded him, his experiments with nitre were at least a far step towards this discovery. His study of alchemical subjects led him, as was natural, to a belief in the philosopher's stone by which gold might be purified to a degree impossible by any other means, and also to a belief in the elixir of life whereby on similar principles of purification, the human body might be fortified against death itself.
> Lewis Spence, *An Encyclopedia of Occultism*

Imagine the following scenario: Kubilai Khan convinces the Franciscans that he speaks for his kinsman, the Christian monarch Prester John, and that the two of them seek an alliance with the West for purposes of crushing the "followers of Mahomet" between them. Wishing to prevent the Byzantines and other heretical Christians as well as rival monastic orders from reaping the benefits of this alliance, the Franciscans become secret allies with Kubilai (and, unbeknownst to them, pawns in his games of deceit and death... and yes, some of you see where I'm going with this, don't you?), serving as the intelligence agency by which the Great Khan can reap Europe. At the same time, like his grandsire, Kubilai seeks to live forever. What good will it do him to gain the Mandate of Heaven if he will be dead within a decade or two? In his lifetime there had already been two Great Khans. So, using his grandsire's notion of subverting the intelligentsia of every conquered land, he has his Franciscan allies look for an alchemist who might be able to succeed where Changchung and the Taoists failed. Soon, tales of a boy who achieved preeminence in many fields at Oxford reaches the Franciscans, who recruite this young prodigy and bring him in on the plot. At first, perhaps Roger goes along with it. But it seems likely that his agile and somewhat devious mind (he was, after all, a master of cryptology and is often mentioned as the author of the *Voynich Manuscript*, a book that has gone unread for hundreds of years) saw through Kubilai's constant requests for various exotic oils and other alchemical components (why would any Christian king, especially the great Prester John, want the oil from the Holy Sepulchre to be moved from that holy edifice?), and he eventually balked at providing the Great Khan with eternal life.

Of course, Kubilai would have wanted Bacon punished while keeping him alive (hoping he would change his mind and provide the elixir vitae he sought) but Bacon's years in the conspiracy had provided him with secrets... secrets he encoded in his trilogy, secrets he knew would be seen only by Clement. Terrified at the prescience of the young friar and aware that an embattled Europe might well need such terrible explosive weapons if it was to survive while surrounded by more advanced and powerful cultures, Clement sent Bacon home to England to work. Kubilai, of course, would have moved the Franciscans to assassinate Clement and sent his cat's-paws to Acre to continue his alchemical researches. You'll note that the Polo brothers seem to have simply arrived in the Mongol Empire and been embraced immediately by the Great Khan, up to and including his giving them various crucial tasks to fulfill. Part of this can be explained by his tendency to make use of talented men, but even so, how often do foreign merchants just arrive in a nation and begin immediately working for the government?

The shadow war between Bacon and Kubilai no doubt continued- Bacon's matchless intellect versus Kubilai's vast power and political acumen- and if the Great Khan could have brought all of his might to bear without constant rebellions to suppress and family members to deal with, who knows? For that matter, if he hadn't been imprisoned again from 1278 to 1292, perhaps Bacon could have brought Europe further along towards modern weaponry.

Shades of Weyland Smith (whose name is, of course, a play on a mythical forger of weapons) and the great Doctor, Fu Manchu? If you want. Pulp adventures in the thirteenth century seem damn cool to me.

The Endless Knot

I'm a nut for King Arthur. I believe in him, despite all the evidence to the contrary. I want to believe, so I do. However, I'm hardly a rigid, doctrinarian sort of guy, and I can disbelieve what I believe and then turn right around and believe in it again. I'm good that way.

Furthermore, I don't believe in causality. I believe that sometimes, cause can follow effect. That the power of will and focused belief can reach back or forward along time, since time is simply one of at least ten dimensions written of in Qabbalistic documents as emanations of the Sephiroth, or spheres, and thought of today as the continuum of hyperspace, wherein many things are possible. Did Hypatia of Alexandria banish the contents of the Library to hyperspace to preserve them from destruction? Is the Akashic record accessible by the minds of men from its location at the end of what we would perceive as time and space? Is the universe an Ouroboros, swallowing its own tail? You've got me there, I have no freaking idea.

Yesterday, along with my lovely and talented companion, I traveled to various bookstores. Hardly a surprise there; trips to the bookstore are as common as dirt around my corner of reality. For whatever reason, I ended up purchasing Gregory of Tours' *The History of the Franks*, Gerald of Wales' *The Journey through Wales* and Geoffrey of Monmouth's *The History of the Kings of Britain*. The day before, after eating dinner at a lovely Italian restaurant on Irving Street in San Francisco, I stopped in a bookstore and bought a copy of Bede's *Ecclesiastical History of The English People*. All of these were Penguin Classics, which have a special place in my heart, right up there with old comic books, Norton Critical Editions and anything from Adventures Unlimited Press, masters of things freaky. All of these books will receive places of honor in my bookshelf, next to my trade paperbacks, my Moorcock and Robert E. Howard novels and short stories, and the stacks of role playing games I never play.

But of all of them, the one I shall treasure is Geoffrey of Monmouth's book. Because I am a nut for King Arthur, and this book is the foundation. From the vernacular stories of Arthur in the Welsh and English countrysides around A.D. 1300 or so to the earlier French romantic stories of Marie de France and Chretien de Troyes, Wolfram von Eschenbach and Sir Thomas Malory and Sir Richard Blackmore and Tennyson... if it mentioned Arthur and came after 1136, it draws from this book. (The only book that really predates it and discusses Arthur much would be *Nennius*, I believe.) This doesn't do much to prove the historical existence of Arthur; after all, Geoffrey was writing his book some six hundred years after the fact. It would be like trying to prove the historical accuracy of Marco Polo's existence and exploits using only books written in the twentieth century.

Sure, I know Polo existed. And he probably did go to China, although how much of his book is fact and how much is fabrication based on the fertile imagination of Rustichello of Pisa, a writer of romantic tales he met in prison, I don't know. Similarly, while there may have been someone who stood up after the death of Aurelianus Ambrosius and led the Britons to victory over the Saxons and Angles in battles like Badon Hill, it is beyond the scope of possibility to imagine that the events resembled those that Malory or Tennyson or de Troyes wrote about. If there was an Arthur, son of Uther and Ygerna, descendant of the imperial line of Constantine, he wouldn't have looked familiar to anyone who read the romances.

But somehow, it's not hard to imagine him looking somewhat like Geoffrey's rendition of him.

> Arthur was a young man only fifteen years old; but he was of outstanding courage and generosity, and his inborn goodness gave him such grace that he was loved by almost all the people. Once he had been invested with the royal insignia, he observed the normal custom of giving gifts freely to everyone. Such a great crowd of soldiers flocked to him that he came to an end of what he had to distribute. However, the man to whom open-handedness and bravery both come naturally may indeed find

> himself momentarily in need, but poverty will never harass
> him for long. In Arthur courage was closely linked with
> generosity, and he made up his mind to harry the Saxons, so
> that with their wealth he might reward the retainers who served
> his own household.
> *Geoffrey of Monmouth,* **Historia Regum Britanniae**

Even filtered as it is through the pen of a Norman-era churchman who would become a bishop and a signatory to the Treaty of Westminster, this was obviously a recollection of the Celtic tradition of generous hospitality their kings were famous for upholding. Geoffrey's King Arthur, deciding to raid the Saxons as much for loot as for his own personal right to rule all Briton, reminds one of the hard kings and queens of Irish myth, Aelil and Medbh of Connachta and Conchobar of the Ulaid, monarchs who raided each other and then feasted with their retainers. Likewise, in his battles with giants and his daring in war Arthur bears a strong family resemblance to Cuchullain of the Ulster cycle and Llew Llaw Gyffes of the *Fourth Branch of the Mabinogion* (and the later romances, with their tales of Arthur's marital misfortunes, solidify that link still more) as well as Bran the Blessed.

It's certainly possible that Geoffrey made him up. That he took the few scraps of information available in Nennius and Bede about the period, grabbed as much Welsh myth as he could from his friend Walter, Archdeacon of Oxford and a Norman of Breton descent who could understand Welsh and who loved to collect fables, myths and stories, and set down to weave out of whole cloth a history of the British and their kings. He may have been inspired to point out subtly to his squabbling overlords the dangers of disunity and civil war (the fact that he dedicated his book to Robert of Gloucester, the illegitimate son of Henry I and the chief architect and general of Matilda's attempt to enforce her claim to the English throne of their father against their cousin, points to this as a possible motivation) as well as how such activities eventually cost the British people their island, first to the Angles and Saxons, and then to the Normans who were now seemingly emulating their dangerously fractious behavior. But I somehow doubt that. There's too much genuine affection and sympathy in Geoffrey's British history, too many great and glorious deeds, too much tragedy. King Leir first appears in Geoffrey, along with his three daughters and the tragedy of his mistaken affections, and while that tale could serve as another parallel to the tumult wracking the kingdom that Geoffrey lived in, it also served to show the human side of the people he was writing about. Geoffrey was born in Monmouth, lived in Caerleon-on-Usk, and spent much of his life working at Oxford (before it was a university) as a canon of St. George's. His sympathies were not with the Normans, no matter that a careful reading of his book might well have served to show them the dangers of their civil broils.

Furthermore, mentions of Arthur in stories like *Culhwch and Olwen* and the ancient triads would seem to point to the idea that Arthur, or someone like him, actually existed in some form, that he was more than a churchman's idealized plea for unity in the face of civil war or an embroidered fantasy made up like a quilt from mythological leavings. God knows, I prefer to think of him that way. So here's an idea.

Maybe Geoffrey made him up... and then *made him real*.

> I was marvelling at this, and looking about me, when my wife came to a dead stop and gave a gasp. I ran smack into her. Then she went speechless for a time while I begged to know what was wrong. Finally she took my hand and, pointing, described to me exactly what I was seeing. At which point, I became speechless. Finally pulling myself together, I blurted out something like "What do you think's happened?" but my wife's reply startled me even more. I remember it only too well: she said, "How did we get to Paris five hundred years ago?"
>
> *Ivan T. Sanderson,* **More "Things"**

The phenomenon of time slip makes me wonder. Along with its clear relative pschometry (the ability to detect psychic impressions on objects that reveal past events) it's one of the most fascinating weird talents ever reported. Since Geoffrey lived in one of the more fascinatingly weird *times* ever in English history, time sip doesn't seem so far-fetched. Green children were popping up in the Suffolk countryside and being written about by Abbot Ralph of Coggeshall, lights were appearing in the sky, King Stephen and Matilda were each half a great king and were tearing the kingdom apart in a rejection of the traditional alliance of Sacred King and Divine Queen (and let's not forget that Matilda's son Henry, the future king, was descended from Satan on his mother's side), and in Oxford, Geoffrey of Monmouth was studying everything he could get his hands on about Merlin. Merlin, the man T.H. White would much later argue was unstuck in time, living his life backwards. Geoffrey translated the man's prophecies into Latin, wrote obsessively about the lost British past, the Celtic twilight. Time slips indeed.

Oxford even has a kind of backwards precedent for time slip. In August of 1901, two women from Oxford who were principals at a college of the university, Eleanor Jourdain and Annie Moberly, took a trip to Versailles and ended up in the same garden they were visiting... except that it was apparently 1789, and Louis XVI was still on the throne. Their book on the subject provoked controversy, but few people called them liars or charlatans due to their unvarished reputations for honesty. Since we're discussing a faculty that violates space-time and causality, I feel safe in describing an incident in 1901 as precedent for one in 1136. (To be honest, when the hell have I ever let a little thing like the logical fabric of forward temporal progression stop me from proposing something absolutely lunatic?)

> Uther, the King's brother, who was hunting for the enemy army, was just as terrified as the others. He summoned his wise men, so that they might tell him what the star portended. He ordered Merlin to be fetched with the others, for Merlin had come with this army so that the campaign could have the benefit of his advice. As he stood in the presence of his leader and was given the order to explain the significance of the star, he burst into tears, summoned up his familiar spirit, and prophesied aloud. "Our loss is irreparable," he said. "The people of Britain is orphaned. Our most illustrious King has passed away. Aurelianus Ambrosius, the famous King of the Britains, has died. By his death we all shall die unless God brings us help. Hasten forward, most noble leader! Hasten forward, Uther, and do not put off for a moment making contact with the enemy. Victory shall be yours and you will be King of all Britain. The star signifies you in person, and so does the firey dragon beneath the star. The beam of light, which stretches towards the shore of Gaul, signifies your son, who will be a most powerful man. His dominion shall extend over all the kingdoms which the beam covers."
> Geoffrey of Monmouth, **Historia Regum Brittaniae**

Geoffrey claimed that he didn't write anything attributed to him, but merely translated a book his friend Walter, Archdeacon of Oxford, had given him, *quendam britannici sermonis librum vestustissimum*, "a certain very ancient book in the British language." Now, knowing about weirdness and Oxford, one is drawn to the character of Roger Bacon, monk, scholar and alchemist who lived between 1214 and 1294. Obviously, Roger lived after Geoffrey by some fifty years... and just as obviously, that no longer really matters here, because I'm referring to Roger as one of a field of candidates for the creation of a book now called the Voynich Manuscript after the American book dealer Wilfred Voynich, who rediscovered it in 1912. The Voynich Manuscript is written in a strange alphabet all its own, and has proved resistant to cryptographers and translators for hundreds of years. Adorning its pages are illustrations of plants and astrological sketches. The book is known to have been studied by Jesuit scholar Athanasius Kircher in 1666. It is also known to have existed in the library of Holy Roman Emperor Rudolf II and was probably brought there by our old friend Dr. John Dee, member of the School of Night, scryer, discoverer or inventor of Enochian, and Dee may have gotten it from the Earl of Northumberland, who pillaged monasteries on behalf of England's King Henry VIII when that monarch broke with the Pope over his much-sought divorce from Catherine of Aragon. Various scholars go from there to attribute the book to Bacon, who was a monk, a genius linked to various subjects from gunpowder to occultism, and who taught and lectured at Oxford. But what if the manuscript isn't Bacon's work, merely something he studied?

What if it is that mysterious ancient book in the British language that Geoffrey mentions? After all, most scholars who study Geoffrey have no idea what he means by the phrase "British language," exactly. Does he mean Welsh? Breton? No one is sure. Now, we know of Geoffrey's obsession with Merlin, legendary magus and Druid. We know what Diodorus said of the Druids, that they were "certain philosophoi and religious interpreters, men highly honoured... it is their custom not to make any sacrifice without one of these philosophoi, since they believe that any offerings should be rendered to the gods through the agency of those well acquainted with the divine nature" (on speaking terms, one might say, and Strabo called them experts in justice and natural philosophy. Caesar said that the Druids believed in the immortality of the soul and reincarnation, and it is generally accepted that the Celtic Otherworld was a timeless place, where one could go forward or back without understanding what had happened. This could well be the root of the idea that Merlin was somehow unstuck in time, and the base of his prophesies. And it could well have been that infamous Druid and magician's book of prophecies that turned up in the hands of John Dee, having been liberated from a monastery that inherited it when Roger Bacon finally died some eighty years after he was born (an incredibly long lifespan for the time). Did Bacon, for his part, find the book in Geoffrey's papers while studying at Oxford? It may have lain there, unreadable to anyone else. It's poetic to imagine Bacon studying, even at that distance, at the feet of Merlin. Is the reason the Voynich Manuscript is unreadable due to the fact that it is written in the secret language of Druids, illustrated with its stellar and vegetative designs as a clue to the nature of its author, a Druid, concerned with the stars and portents of the heavens and the plants and animals of nature?

> Finally, there is the archaeological evidence, the fact that strange light has been thrown upon certain of the alleged fancies of Geoffrey of Monmouth by subsequent archaeological discoveries. The connection of Vortigern and his son Pacentius with Ireland is, for example, allegedly supported by the Ogham stones with Vortigern"s name on them which have been discovered at Ballybank and Knockaboy. As fate caught up with him, Vortigern, in Geoffrey"s account, fled to the fortified camp of Gonoreu, on the hill called Cloartius, in Erging, by the river Wye. Here "Gonoreu" is Ganarew and "Cloartius" a mispelling for the modern Little Doward, with its hilltop camp, all of it very near to Monmouth. There is the remarkable story of how Merlin brought Stonehenge piecemeal from Mount Killarause in Ireland to Salisbury Plain and its resemblance to the parallel account of the carrying of the bluestones by sea and overland from the Prescelly mountains which is given by modern archaelogists. Geoffrey tells how the Venedoti decapitated a whole Roman legion in London and threw their heads into a stream called Nantgallum or, in the Saxon language, Galobroc. In the 1860s a large number of skulls, with practically no other bones to accompany them, were dug

up in the bed of the Wallbrook by General Pitt-Rivers and others.

*Lewis Thorpe, **Introduction to the Historia Regum Brittaniae***

Furthermore, I find myself imagining Geoffrey bending himself to the study of the manuscript, feverishly working to decipher and translate the lore and wisdom of Merlin, discovering as he goes along that the more he works on it, the more visions of the places around his hometown of Caerleon-on-Usk he sees. Soon, he finds himself vouchsafed more and more visions, feels himself almost being pulled in and out of places at once familiar and vastly different than any he knows. He witnesses Merlin's famous prophecies as they are being uttered, the way the famous magician intended all along. Indeed, the meeting of Merlin and Geoffrey might well have been a two-way communication across time and space, Geoffrey imparting his knowledge of the future and Merlin his knowledge of the past, of past lives some thousands of years earlier, when a previous Merlin helped move the stones of Stonehenge to their location on the Salisbury Plain. Eventually, Geoffrey realizes what he'd only suspected: he is Merlin. It was his mind reaching backward that warned Uther to act hastily, it was his decision to aid Uther in his seduction of Ygerna; it was he who set into motion all the actions that created Arthur, he who lived life after life in Celtic and even pre-Celtic Britain, he who wrote the very book he had studied for so long. In essence, he was the translator of his own imagination, the creator of the saga he had lived. Time no longer mattered to him; he knew it curved back on itself, he had lived it backwards and forwards, and he would live it again. When he died in 1155, he merely stepped out of the stream of time... and who knows when he stepped back in? In 1214, as Roger Bacon? In the 1500s, as John Dee? Perhaps earlier.... Critics have compared *Historia Regum Brittaniae* with its battles of kings and giants to *Beowulf* and Homer's *Odyssey*.

Of course, the date of his death is notoriously hard to pin down. It seems odd that a man who was privy to many of the most notable events of his time, a signatory on the treaty that would eventually place the first Angevin monarch on the throne of England, a man who inspired hundreds of years of literature, would find his death only mentioned in one source, and that a somewhat unreliable Welsh chronicle. Perhaps, instead of dying, he even stepped back to just before the birth of Merlin himself. Most legends argue that the magician was born of a demon... and would a man materializing out of nowhere not appear to be a demon to a young woman in newly-Christianized Britain? Perhaps he was a demon, or one of the fae folk who populated the time-lost Otherworld... or perhaps a man unstuck in time, who slipped back into the legends he loved and the past he sought to understand in order to ensure that they happened as he remembered them. Merlin seemed awfully nonchalant about dressing up Uther as Gorlois in order to trick Ygerna. Maybe he thought what was good enough for him was good enough for Arthur, too.

Like I said, I'm a nut for King Arthur. He is one mess of oddities, wound up in my own private endless knot, the symbol so beloved in ancient La Tene designs. Time and space are not a straight line, but a hyperloop in ten dimensions, like a man walking widdershins around a barrow at sunset, or a strip moving through the emanations of the ten Sephiroth.

Yule

Snowmen are pretty damn weird, you have to admit. It seems like some sort of wintry Caedmus ritual, as these strange entities rise up like fangs of ice and snow from the hoar-shrouded earth. All over the world, wherever it snows, humans (especially children) gather together and make these effigies, bedeck them in our cast-off clothing, and even tell stories of magic that can make them come to life.

Snow golems, that voice in the back of my head that gets me into trouble and which has been remarkable silent for the past few months, whispered. They're making snow golems. But what kind of world could sustain a snow golem indefinitely? And then more thoughts came to me, thoughts of snow and ice that have been plaguing my mind recently.

> The world-tree, Yggdrasil, emerged from the sacred body of Ymir (the frost giant whose body formed the mists of Niflheim when the universe originated). Ymir represents primordial chaos, destroyed by Odin, just as Tiamat was slain by Marduk in Assyrian mythology. Like the qabalistic Tree of Life, the cosmic pattern of Yggdrasil springs from the soil of the ultimate void.
>
> Bill Whitcomb, *The Magician's Companion*

Christmas is a pre-Christian holiday, with roots in the ancient Roman festival of Saturnalia, dedicated to the Roman equivalent to the ancient Titan Chronos, lord of time and father of the Olympian gods as well as the one who attempted to destroy them. Much like Tiamat and Ymir, Chronos was and is a godslayer, a Titan.

Always, before there are gods, there are beings so massive and inhuman that the authors find themselves unable to fully describe them. To the Greeks, these beings were the children of the earth and the sky, and were called "strainers" for their appetites and ambitions, which strained the boundaries of their vast parents. The word comes down to us today as Titan. Before the gods of Babylon and Sumer, there was Apsu and his mate Tiamat, vast and potent and utterly unconcerned with anything like worship. Before the coming of Odin, Villi and Ve came the *jotun*, the great giants born of titanic forces like Ymir, the embodiment of endless ice, and Surtr, he who was and is eternal flame. Always, in every religion, there is formless chaos that must be defeated by the gods. Even in the religious base that would become the monotheisms of Judaism, Christianity and Islam, God divides the primordial chaos with His Word. "In the beginning God created the heavens and the earth, and the earth was without form and void; and darkness was upon the face of the deep. And the spirit of God moved upon the face of the waters. And God said, Let there be light, and there was light." Compare that to, "Verily at the first, Chaos came to be, but next wide-bosomed Earth, the ever-sure foundation of all the deathless ones who hold the peaks of snowy Olympus, and dim Tartarus in the depth of the wide-pathed Earth, and Eros, fairest among the deathless gods."

There is always chaos before order. And Chronos, as a Titan, is chaos' archetype, of an order and a power beyond and unlike that of a god. Saturnalia did not exist to honor the lord of endings, merely to propitiate him. As the nights grew longer and longer, culminating in the winter solstice, the Romans ate and drank in a frenzied, entirely undisciplined, entirely un-Roman manner, attempting by their exertions to hold back the rising tide and please this wild and untamed being.

It fascinates me to think of the formation of Christianity, and the origins of its most showy holiday, pieced together like a mosaic out of the fragments of vanquished faiths. Out of Zoroastrianism it steals the three Magi (for as we know, the Magi were the high priests of Ahura Mazda, those Persians most responsible for keeping the mysteries of the faith), out of Greek mystery faiths like that of the followers of Dionysus it steals the manger full of beasts, it is placed in December so that it might steal Saturnalia's pride of place. So syncretic a holiday is paradoxically ideal for the religion that displaced so many pagan faiths, I suppose.

Let's look at its modern aspects, however. The Christmas tree itself, bedecked in tinsel and ornaments and crowned with a star or an angel, is a modern recreation of a Saxon classic: the decapitation and evisceration of an enemy, whose head would be placed atop the tree and whose internal viscera would be garlanded about its boughs. Likewise, Yule logs once held humans writhing along their lengths, screaming as they were delivered to the flames. And mistletoe! Must we even comment on this plant, the slayer of Balder, the killer of the light? That Christmas stalwart, Santa, is often described or depicted as an elf and is served by elves... but elves, call them *alvar* or *sidhe* or what have you, are old pagan standbys who are often indistinguishable from divinities (beings like Lugh and Mannannan are hard to tell from gods) and who serve their own chaotic aims, not those of the White Christ (as the Norse called him).

Yule, the holiday of the Celts and, later, their Germanic and Norse supplanters and rivals, was no meek celebration. It symbolized the eternal battle between darkness and light, between the chaos of the Titans and the order of the gods, and while the Celts believed it to be the birth of a new sun, the triumph of the light, the Norse believed that all such victories were fleeting. In the end, the gods would die, the ice would return (and isn't it interesting that chaos is often water or ice, in the minds of man? Shades of watery Cthulhu ever dreaming in dead R'yleh for the stars to finally be right... like the stars on the converted blood trees, perhaps?) and all that lives will be destroyed as the world screams back into chaos.

It's interesting to muse on what, exactly, those early Christian missionaries could have done, when they were trying to sell Christ to the Wotan-obsessed German tribes that would become the Frankish kingdom, Christianity's early bulwark and the shield that would protect Europe from Muslim and Pagan alike, to convince men like Clovis to come in under the banner of the Christ. What would make them take the cross?

How about the potential aversion of Ragnarok? Christmas, by that time, had absorbed the attributes of a dozen faiths. The holiday served to celebrate the birth of the Son of God and Light of the World, making it heir to the Celtic festival celebrating the birth of the sun itself. It contained the festive propitation of Chronos, the mantle of Ormazhd, the union of man and beast of Dionysus and Pan... no wonder the medievals often held Christmas over the course of twelve days! By accepting Christ, the pagans accepted a power that could hold back the Titans, maintain the division of chaos and order in the firmament, hold back the darkness forever.

Obviously, if you were on the side that was expected to win Ragnarok, you might object to its endlessly postponed state. You might come to view Christianity, especially its winter festival, as a stake in the heart of Yule, that great and terrible night wherein the ultimate battle for the annihilation of all things of form was scheduled. But how to defeat the White Christ? How do you uproot a faith that subverts all it comes into contact with, absorbing elements of other beliefs into itself? It would take a truly great deceiver, a trickster without par, to come up with an answer.

Somewhere, lashed to the ground while snake venom drips in his face, a great trickster came up with the answer. Make the strength of your enemy his weakness. To Loki, the White Christ is just another Balder gleaming in his light... but the humblest plant eats light, and misteltoe worked once.

Like the roots of the humble god-killer, elements wholly un-Christian have wormed their way into the cracks of the stake driven into the night of darkness. Led by Loki, the chaotic rivals of the gods have worked to supplant the last, greatest divinity. Blood trees, like small Yggdrasil-seeds erupting from the corpse of the primal ice. Yule logs. Mistletoe. The creation of endless effigies of Ymir, that primordial giant, the first titanic being of whom all things were made... and to whom all things shall return. When the world is frozen, when Ragnarok rages and the gods are dead, then and only then will there be a world in which a living snowman could possibly exist. The sun will rise no more, and all will be winter forever.

It comes, the end of all that is, and it will have its way if it must debase a million holy days.

Painted

That "Cruithne" or "Qrtanoi" signified "Tattooed" is clear enough from another passage in Herodian, who says that the Northern Britons tattooed upon their skins the figures of animals. This notice of the practice is doubly valuable, as it is written at least a century before the name of the Picts or tattooed people is mentioned in classical literature. It is upheld by a rendering of the early Gaelic writer Duald MacFirbis, who says that "Cruithneach (Pictus) is one who takes the cruths or forms of beasts, birds and fishes on his visiage, and on his whole body."

*Lewis Spence, **The History of Atlantis***

One of the earliest arts of mankind is the visual. Cave paintings and skin markings are ancient indeed, and can be found among almost all human societies if one looks back far enough in time. From paintings of the *bunyip* of Australia on the side of cliff faces baked by the relentless heat of the sun, to etchings of men with the heads of beasts stalking herds of powerful Aurochs cattle; from carved chalk representations of giants and horses in cliff faces in England to the Nazca lines rendered in the deserts of South America, women and men have been transforming any surface available, even their own skins and the bodies of their dead, into representations of the beasts of the field and serpents of the den for thousands of years. Art marks the caves of Aurignac in France, the skins of bog-people dug out of the peat in Wales, the walls of impressive tombs in Egypt and temples in ancient Mexico, and indeed even our earliest forms of written language are pictographic.

Of course, it could easily be said that this is just a consequence of humanity's unique position as an animal that can think, and the combination of our ability to reason and our hominoid manual dexterity provides us with an opportunity to make these artistic representations. I don't deny that, nor that through art, many women and men throughout history have sought to express themselves, to create a lasting and tangible connection between humans, allowing us to experience the world as they do by showing us what they see, or how they feel. Furthermore, some of our near-relatives in the hominid superfamily have been taught to paint, and the results have been interesting if not entirely successful. I still think it fair to say that the creation of visual art is an almost unique human attribute, and that it is almost as old as human civilization itself.

Instead of being a byproduct of the human march out of the Stone Age and into the modern era, is it possible that art is the only talent that has made humanity the masters of the world? Everywhere you look, humans have shaped stone, painted on wood and even bone, marked their own flesh with sigils. Is it merely a desire to share with one's fellows, or rather something else entirely... a defining impulse that makes life as we know it feasible in the face of chaos and madness?

This would seem to fly in the face of the idea of art as an expression of the self and the limitless possibilities that seem inherent therein. But art is a selective activity: in order to create it, one must choose what one will incorporate and what one will exclude. In this way, it seems to mimic the march of the human worldview, from a vast and boundless animism wherein all things have spirit and life of a sort, and the world is not set into any one form but is the product of a series of chaotic and orderly principles in constant conflict towards a gradual winnowing away from infinite spirits, to one overarching divine presence who created all things. From chaos to order. That order might not be especially regimented... anyone who has ever seen the backstage area of a play in production would be glad to recount that there can be a great deal of chaos involved in the creating the illusion of order- but it's just barely possible to conceive of the early visual representation of daily events in cave paintings and skin art and the building of monumental architecture as an attempt to learn how to select reality moment by moment, to focus only on a limited piece of creation rather than attempting to take it all in at once. In essence, one cannot take the action necessary for the establishment of a culture beyond the Paleolithic without first learning how to seperate oneself from the great chaos of all that is and imposing individual will on the world, and the artist creates through her or his own will a microcosmic rendition of the world around him. As above, so below... and as through the brush, so too in the world.

> With the last retreat of the ice, only twelve thousand years ago, the Peninsula received new waves of immigrants. Unsung pioneers and prospectors moved slowly out to the west, rounding the coasts, crossing the land and the seas until the furthest islands were reached. Their greatest surviving masterwork, as the Age of Stone gave way to that of Bronze, was built on the edge of human habitation on a remote, offshore island. But no amount of modern speculation can reveal for certain what inspired those master masons, nor what their great stone circle was called.
> Norman Davies, *Europe: A History*

As the Stone Age passed away, man became a builder as well as a painter and carver of his own flesh and the bones of his dead. From the megaliths of the British Isles to the cyclopean structures of Malta, the pyramid complex at Giza, mounds and barrows and Atrean treasuries... the world's skin is itself dotted with the such structures, and the tracks between them, like the lines of a Maori islander's tattoos.

I'm reminded again and again of the stories of the creation of the world that mankind has told over the past few thousand years. Of how a time of chaos and titanic beings was slowly overcome by a new order, how a firmament between wildness and humanity was created by (fill in the name of your gods here) and so mankind was granted dominion over the earth. To a modern eye, which has experienced the rise of the Internet and heard the phrase "information overload," the chaos of Hesiod takes on a new shape, and the Otherworld of the Celts can be rendered as an endless web of data that threatens to overwhelm. Taken as such, the ancient drive of humanity to render, to create, to encapsulate, becomes a kind of harnessed monomania, a refusal to experience too much of the world at once for fear that it would be impossible to take action in the face of so vast and indistinguishable an entity. In a world where all things have spirits and are in essence alive, equals to humanity, what right do we have to hew down a forest and build a city?

We experience the world through our senses, and process it as best we can inside our own individual minds. The continuum between us is a spectrum, and it is far vaster than we can make sense of if we attempt to see it, hear it, smell it, taste it and feel it all at once. But art is selection. Through art, we learned how to, in essence, tune out the static and harness our minds to our own individual aims. We formatted the world to create in ourselves an illusion of order we needed if we were to get anything done.

Then again, perhaps we didn't so much filter out what we couldn't bear to see as we sealed away what we couldn't compete with. In the Otherworld, humanity is far inferior to our *sidhe* rivals; beings like the Tuatha de Danann and the Formor are nearly gods, with vast powers and insatiable appetites, and we are food and sport to them, unable to cope as they change the seasons on a whim, alter our forms to suit their fancy, and set us to tasks that we cannot possibly accomplish without death. Julian Jaynes wrote of the age of Homer as a time when humans took the voices of their own unformed egos as the voices of gods. Perhaps he missed the point, and those voices were those of the animistic infinity surrounding man... and only through the forced isolation of our harnessed creative impulse could we weed them out of our psyche's garden and take action on our own terms, safe from the terrible glories they were capable of inflicting on our all too frail and human flesh and minds. Suddenly the obsession with tattoos among those peoples who most spoke of the Fair Folk makes a bit more sense- seeking mastery over one's own body by self-expression, rather than allowing some alien being to inflict her or his opinion of what you should become upon you, makes a lot of sense.

And as the body of a man, so too the body of the world. Was the frenzied and ultimately self-destructive construction of statuary on Easter Island an act of self-sacrifice, an attempt to aid in the creation of the barrier between us and those who came before, the fluid ones who view us as prey? Like Sarah Winchester and the ghosts of those slain by her father in law's firearms, are we engaged in an endless cycle of expansion and construction and creation that at once beguiles and ensnares those beings of pure chaos in a cage of constantly changing form?

Probably not. But I make no promises.

The University of Ares

> In April 1097, the crusading army crossed the Bosphorus unopposed. The Turkish Sultan, Kiliji Arslan, lured into a false sense of security by his earlier victory over the army of Peter the Hermit, attacked the crusaders outside Nicaea. He learned too late that he was up against something more formidable-the heavy cavalry made up of Western knights. Anna Comnena, the daughter of the Emperor Alexius, was to write in her memoir of her father that 'the irresistible shock' of a charge by Frankish knights "would make a hole through the walls of Babylon."
> *Piers Paul Reid, **The Templars***

The birth of feudalism depended on many factors... and one of them was superior technology. The thirteenth-century soldier was in every way superior to the Roman Legionnaire, armed better, armored better. The development of heavier and heavier armor and more lethal weaponry culminated in the armored knight riding a warhorse, capable of bringing to bear all the power of his steed as well as his own skill in a charge that could easily tear a standing man apart. However, any technology has its limits, and that of armor in Europe was limited by two factors: the strength of a man to wear it, and the power of the steed to carry it into battle. Furthermore, as the battles of Crecy and Agincourt would show a credulous Europe, the power of the longbow to pierce even the heaviest armor at ranges no continental archer could match would mean that French military superiority (which depended on the large levy she could call out for war and her surplus of nobles, who were the only ones who could afford the expense of arms, armor and horses) would be severely tested. Eventually, the advent of the pike and gunpowder would mean the end of the man on horseback. Technology gave, and then she took away.

However, it is possible to re-imagine the past. Indeed, that's one of the chief pleasures of knowing anything about it. twisting it out of its charted passages and into a new direction, where it never flowed but could have. We view our lives as uncertain, the future as a series of unknowns, and so it was for those who came before us. They did not know what was to come yet, and many pivotal events came and went, setting the limits of what would be. Those limits are ours to alter. We can make the past our sandbox, carve rivers in the gritty medium, free to cause them to jump their banks and see where they take us.

> Arming a knight was a slow process. In time, as the weight and complexity of armor increased, the chevalier was unable to prepare himself for conflict unaided. He had to sit down while a squire or squires pulled on his steel-mailed hose, and stand while they fitted the various pieces, fastening them with a multitude of straps and buckles... defensive armor steadily became more elaborate, with coifs to cover the neck and head, elbow pieces, knee guards and greaves. Because the face remained vulnerable, helmets increased in weight and covered more and more of the face until they came to resemble cylindrical pots with slits for the eyes. As usual, security was gained at a cost. The knight had to bandage his head, for if he took a fall, he might easily sustain a brain concussion. William Marshal, a famous English champion who lived at the end of the twelfth century, won a tournament and afterward could not be found to receive the prize. He was finally discovered at a blacksmith's, with his head on the anvil and the smith hammering his battered helmet in an effort to remove it without killing the wearer.
> *Morris Bishop,* **The Middle Ages**

Hard to imagine what that must have felt like. At the time of the greatest dominance of the armored knight over the battlefield, the era of the Crusades, when vastly outnumbered armies from Europe would repeatedly crash onto the Holy Land and briefly deal the Islamic world defeats that would forever redefine the relationship between Christendom and Islam, mechanized warfare was beginning to evolve. The crossbow, the catapult, the siege tower- these were all common and part and parcel of medieval warfare.

So it interests me that no one ever looked at a trebuchet or a crossbow, and then at an armored knight fallen from his horse and drowning in the mud of a battlefield, and thought about how to use the first to improve the second. In the court of Frederick II, Holy Roman Emperor (known to us as Stupor Mundi, the wonder of the world), learning and the sciences were prized, as was exploration of all sorts. Frederick somehow captured and transported a polar bear to Syria as a gift to the Sultan of Damascus... and he founded the University of Naples in 1224 in order to train bureaucrats for his empire. Although Frederick was an evil-tempered, sneaky, sadistic little man, he was a brilliant one. Writer, poet, anatomist, who was willing to experiment, Frederick is tailor-made for any thought experiment in changing the course of history.

One of the reasons for this is his association with thinkers and philosophers and mystics. One of the greatest at that time was an Oxford-educated Scotsman named Michael; in fact, in one of those displays of unoriginality that plague the human race, he was named Michael Scot. Among his accomplishments were translations of Aristotle and of Averroes, the Islamic author so inspired by Moses ben Maimun's doctrine of rationality. From his days at the Sorbonne to his refusal to take the Archbishopric of Cashel (an Irish post he declined entirely because he didn't speak Irish, which most men would have simply ignored because of the money available to an Archbishop), Michael Scot cut a wide swath through the fields of academia and mysticism. According to Roger Bacon (and we'll get back to him later), Scot returned to Oxford just before his death in the 1230s, bringing with him a translation of the works of Aristotle that was at that time unknown in England. Scot was welcome, indeed, at the court of Frederick II, and also esteemed by Frederick's sometime enemies at the Vatican.

It's not hard to imagine the fevered mind of Frederick II turning itself more fully to matters of war than it did. While certainly unafraid to use war to achieve his aims, Stupor Mundi was just as likely to turn that magnificent brain of his to diplomacy, since he had such an advantage over others in that arena. But it wouldn't have taken much; merely endowing a university somewhere in Italy or Germany for the study of combat tactics and technology would have been enough. Imagine one of Frederick's infamous dinner parties, where Saracen dignitaries could be found seated next to Christian churchmen, and razor-sharp minds like Scot's jousted with the Wonder of the World. Attention is brought to bear on the Crusader defeat at Hattin a generation before and how Frederick managed to reclaim Jerusalem through diplomacy. Someone a little too much into his cups declares that Frederick, being a stunted little snake of a man, couldn't have led an army there anyway. Frederick smiles tolerantly and orders that person taken away, to be killed after he regains sobriety in one of his strange experiments. (Frederick once had two prisoners fed rich meals, took one hunting with him and left the other to rest at leisure, and then had them both killed so that he could study the contents of their stomachs and so discover which one digested his meal better. It was the one who he'd left behind.) He then turns to Scot, a strange gleam in his eyes. "We will improve war so that the stature of the man matters less than his mind."

> It was to be expected that a man who thus immersed himself in the depths of thought, should be an enemy to noise and interruption. He dashed to pieces an artificial man of brass that Albertus Magnus, who was his tutor, had spent thirty years in bringing to perfection.
> *Lewis Spence, **An Encyclopedia of Occultism***

Using his alliance with Hermann of Salza, Grand Master of the Order of the Teutonic Knights, his own prestige, and the reputation of Michael Scot, Frederick could easily have forged an institution dedicated to the reforging of war. Scot, for his portion, could easily bring such geniuses as Albertus Magnus (a young man teaching within Frederick's German possessions at the time, who would write *Of Things Metallic and Mineral*, the maker of the aforementioned man of brass that St. Thomas Aquinas had felt the need to destroy) and Roger Bacon (fellow Oxford alumnus, fellow mathematician and scholar, the man who most likely helped create gunpowder in the West, writer of *Opus Majus*, *Opus Minus*, and *Opus Tertius*, a young but brilliant scholar by 1235, around the time Scot died) to his project. The goal would be to transcend the limitations of the individual knight: the strength of the man, the ability of the horse to carry him and his extremely heavy panoply. Since Frederick's predecessors had tasted defeat at Bouvines, he would no doubt have seen this project as a way to check the growing power of France, which had the most nobles and thus the most knights of any European nation. By Frederick's death in 1250, the University of Aresia (so named for Ares, Greek god of war) could well have made significant gains in the production of self-powered armor.

Imagine the combination of Albertus Magnus' skill at creating armatures that somehow triumphed over the difficulty of mimicking the human form, similar to the one that Aquinas destroyed, a radical elaboration of the devices used to make crossbows and catapults functional, and Bacon's chemical genius. To us, gunpowder is an explosive used to propel slugs through soft tissue, but Bacon the alchemist always saw other uses for it. Uses possibly inspired by the gunpowder rockets of the Chinese, whose Mongol masters were already known in Europe (Marco Polo would be born by 1254, some four years after the death of Frederick II), or perhaps simply imagined by the brilliant Bacon. Gunpowder is a chemical fuel; when created as flash powder, it burns rather than explodes. Knowing of steam engines, of hydraulics, and being exposed to the machinery of Magnus, it's not hard to imagine Bacon creating a gunpowder engine.

The Aresian Armature would change the face of war. Capable of carrying armor heavier than ten men, of moving around the battlefield independently of the horse, and totally immune to the longbow, the crossbow, and infantry, this massive device would have limits. Battlefield conditions such as mud could significantly slow its progress, it would be unable to climb hills, and siege weapons like catapults would probably be useful against it. However, with primitive cannon and this colossus at their disposal, the armies of Frederick's successors would be able to do what they were unable to in our history and check French power. Also, let's not forget that both Roger and Michael were Oxford educated, proud of their school and its traditions; it's quite possible that the university would come into possession of some of their works on the subject. Indeed, one could not effectively make war in Europe- or against it- without technology of this kind. The mounted knight would no longer be a man on a horse. Rather, he would be a man strapped into a metal coffin that moved, a collection of gears and pistons powered by black powder. The knightly orders of the time, the Temples, the Teutonic Knights, the Hospitable, would be forced to embrace the Aresian Armature or be swept aside.

It's hard to imagine the sophisticated and technologically savvy Islamic nations being far behind once the Aresian made its appearance on the late thirteenth-century battlefield. But the balance of power would shift as the Franks (all Europeans were Franks to the Saracens, just as men from Arabia or Egypt or Asia Minor were all Saracens to the nations of Europe) walked their clanking machines into battle. Likewise, Byzantium would want to try to make up their loss at Manzikert by investing in armor of this sort... and they have would Greek fire to add to the mix.

In this history that never happened, Brusa becomes a Byzantine victory, allowing them to reclaim their lost farmlands in Asia Minor and destroying the Ottoman Empire, allowing the Mongols defeated earlier that century to make another push into the Middle East... only to report back to the Great Khan that the men of the West had developed machines of war unlike anything seen to that date. The Polo brothers, servants of the Khan, are sent west to make an alliance... and to procure the secrets of these great armored men for the army of the Khan. English and French knights at Crecy do battle from within their clanking armors, firing cannonballs at each other, and the Oxford connection gives Edward III control over the territory he claims through his mother, finally winning back the Angevin lands lost by King John, backed in part by Knights Templar who escaped to Scotland and England with their heavy war machines rather than accept the papal bull of 1307, due to their more scientific inclination.

It is a world at war, just as our history has it… a world strode by colossi of clanking metal, where a knight's physical strength is far less important than his tactical knowledge, his ability to calculate the trajectory of his cannonballs, his endurance. It becomes important to educate a knight precisely in mathematics, in the natural sciences, in order that his service as a young squire can keep up with the technology of battle. Knights become soldier-technicians, understanding the working of their armor, how to maintain and repair it, how to keep it and best use it. Imagine the ripple effect this has, as the nobility of Europe must learn if they are to survive, and their rivals outside Europe must keep up. The Great Khan in China, the states of Islam, Byzantium... all changed. By the middle of the fourteenth-century, the ripples are already being felt, as geniuses like Nicholas Flamel pick up the work left behind by Bacon when he died in 1294, working to combine the mechanical with the mathematical to provide precise targeting for the Aresians, to improve their carriage to make them more surefooted and maneuverable, to lighten them while maintaining their protection or increase the amount of armor they can carry. Whole lines of armor, from scouts to heavy assault and siege armatures, are developed.

I admit it, I just wanted to get the Knights Templar into mecha. To me, the idea of a feudalism forced to become highly materialistic and overly rational tickles me. Imagine the crusades that never happened, with Saracen and Crusader battlesuits charging each other outside Jerusalem, Mongol warsuit cavalry taking India in advance of Babur and the Timurids only to be forced to hold it from the natives and a resurgent Byzantium seeking territory and allies from which to mount assaults on Baghdad, as well as trying to recreate the glories of Alexander the Great. Greek fire versus cannon, giant swords crashing into giant shields, and the beginnings of computer science being born out of a need for accurate artillery calculations in an individual context.

Technology created the knight, and then defeated him. But it could so easily have recreated him instead, in a world that never happened.

Black Blood of the Earth

Imagine an international network of businesses dedicated to the exploitation of petroleum, working hand in glove with totalitarian dictatorships and seeking to curry influence in Iraq, Peru, Europe and the United States, giving money to political candidates and borrowing money from banks in vast quantities as it constantly sought to expand, lining the pockets of its highest executives while it operated constantly and secretly in a precarious position, concealing its own possible insolvency with creative bookkeeping and obfuscation from those politicians it had helped come to power. Doesn't seem that hard to imagine, does it?

Only I'm not talking about any recent entity, but rather the complex web of holdings created under the umbrella of *Europaische Tanklager und Transport A.G.* by the American oil speculator William Rhodes Davis in the 1930s, a corporate entity that helped the Vatican and various banks to move their funds out of frozen accounts in Nazi Germany while allowing the Reich to gain the oil it needed and the refineries necessary for it to exploit that oil in order to wage world war. It's hardly a recent phenomenon that a large, multinational oil concern could attempt to subvert the law and reap profit by working with people and ignoring what they might do with the service provided them, you see.

Oil. The industrial world is a junkie, and oil is the black tar heroin it must inject into its slowly rotting veins. Oil is the opiate of the automotive-bound, electricity-craving Western nations, and the United States is one of the biggest, nastiest, most desperate-for-a-fix bastards in that writhing chain of smackheads. The USA, in fact, is the kind of junkie who doesn't get all needy and pathetic when its supply is threatened. America is that rare junkie who is also a dealer, and if anyone threatens the supply, they get taken out at the knees. However, I'm not just pointing fingers at America here; Britain, Japan, you name an industrialized nation and I'll show you a quivering, gotta-have-it addict.

What is the deal with oil? Why do people who would define themselves, if asked, as decent church-going folk (remember Mrs. Kenneth Lay's teary tales of woe?), who take part in their communities and support local causes, seem helpless to keep from bankrupting their companies, creating rampant energy speculation that increases the burden on the communities that depend on them, and even taking unethical or even illegal actions in its pursuit? For every well we drill that comes up with oil, dozens fail. Many have been bankrupted in its pursuit, and yet we reel blearily on like drunkards, still chasing after it. If you've been paying attention to the news lately, you can't get away from the effect of oil on our world... whether it be fighting in the Middle East (why do you think we care?) or abortive totalitarian coups in Venezuela possibly supported by my nation (*Legitimacy is something that is conferred not just by a majority of the voters,* however. Say what you will, but the Bush administration knows how it got to the White House, doesn't it?) or the collapse of enormous energy concerns in a blaze of bad bookkeeping and highly-placed employee suicides.

> Though this religion would seem tailor-made for *Weird Tales*, it is quite real. The Middle Eastern sect shares the apocalyptic world view of the New Testament writers whereby God has abandoned the world to the control of Satan for the time being, hence all the pain and evil of the world, though one day He will resume hands-on control. The Yezidis made the common-sense inference that if Satan (Shaitan) is in charge, one had better learn to get along with him. Use a long spoon, yes, but you're going to have to dine with him if you want to eat. So they render him worship as Melek (or Malak) Tous, which means "the Peacock Lord," an epithet denoting his Luciferian pride.
> Robert M Price, **Introduction to 'Dig Me No Grave',** *from* **Nameless Cults: The Cthulhu Mythos Tales of Robert E. Howard**

> Petroleum: complex mixture of hydrocarbons that occur in the Earth in liquid, gaseous, or solid forms. The term is often restricted to the liquid form, commonly called crude oil, but as a technical term it also includes natural gas and the viscous or solid form known as bitumen. The liquid and gaseous phases

of petroleum constitute the most important of the primary fossil fuels.
Encyclopedia Britannica

Imagine a world that ran its elaborate infrastructure by using dead beings as fuel, dead beings whose very presence as fuel created choking fumes, could poison the waters, often caught fire when being harnessed and would burn unless extreme measures were taken to cap the means of their extraction, and which when rendered into other forms (some of which could even be made into durable physical forms that served well in various constructions) could cause types of cancers and birth defects.

Welcome to that world. Oil is the compressed corpses of those beings killed by mass extinction, according to most theories. Fossil fuels. In other words, it's dead beings, compressed by geological action into a fuel. It's concentrated mass death on a scale almost impossible for us to understand, the slurry of mass extinction, sealed away from us by the earth itself. So we drill gaping wounds into the land that feeds and sustains us, pull this fluid up to the surface, and render this black toxic gunk into even more concentrated forms that we burn and lubricate and even used to build.

Current theories of the mass extinction phenomenon indicate that it was probably the result of our planet colliding with comets or meteoroids, fallen masses from space that created vast craters and explosive releases far greater than the suspected impact at Tunguska or the one that our crazy conspiratorial buddies Christopher Knight and Robert Lomas argue created the Noah's Ark-Great Flood myth in their *Uriel's Machine*. A great flaming rock from space that smashed into our world, killing whole species. A mass of death that gave birth to more death. If you're into Rupert Sheldrake's morphic field/laws of physics as universal habits theory, then let me bring to mind two other observations: this would have happened more than once (the fossil record contains numerous mass extinctions, after all), and habits are made stronger by repetition. A child repeatedly beaten may grow up to be an abuser him or herself. What kind of morphic resonance does the death of millions upon millions of beings create? Remember the identification of the rock from the sky, the *lapis ex caelis*, with the solar cult of El-Gabal and the flaming mountain from Revelations that was Satan falling like fire from heaven? Satan, Malak Tous, as the Yezidis who live to this day in one of the most abundant oil-producing regions on this planet style him... a region that is at this moment at the precipice of disaster as it as been so many times before. A region made rich by trafficking in a fluid created from death. I mean, seriously, think about this. Flaming rocks fall from the sky and wipe out whole species, and then millions of years later we come along and pump their liquified remains out of their mass graves to make fuel and plastic out of them. For all we know, the dead were even sentient creatures. I mean, if *Homo sapiens sapiens* was wiped out a mere millennia ago by an asteroid impact, how much evidence of us would be left in sixty-five million years?

Oil obsesses. It has replaced its sister, Coal, and become the primary source of power in the world. Nations go to war over it, and its influence has illuminated (and perhaps even Illuminated) the world. One thinks of Ahriman, lord of the lie; Lucifer, the Lightbringer; Nyarlathotep, the bearer of starry wisdom; figures who seek to impart a progress that kills. A promise of peace and prosperity and power that leads mankind, stumbling, addicted to the ease and everywhere dependent on the effects of the compacted sludge made from the repeated wounding of our planet's biosphere, the repeated killing of the earth's children. And indeed, since we became servants of oil, we have increased the rate at which extinction comes for other species, have created chemicals that are swimming in our tissues to what effects we cannot say, have made plastics that gave the workers who helped create them cancers and their children birth defects, have poisoned the waters and choked the skies. A man-made emulation of the effects of those rocks from the sky as they lanced the earth? Some Islamic nations call America the Great Satan, while we demonize them as well. Are we both really just pawns to an entity that was born out of mass death, a being that lives in the black fluid which we drink like vampires out of the veins of our world?

Oil is undisputedly necromantic, and our society is run on the energy created by death. Death, which converted the sun's light (and again we have that overlap between the sun, giver of life and light, and death), stored in the matter of the living, into the fuel we today use to light our homes, power our machines, and transport ourselves worldwide. And it destroys as we do so, as if it were infused so thoroughly with the death-agonies of those beings who became it that it cannot but punish us for disturbing its rest.

Oil, it sometimes seems, is the real lord of this world, and its specter makes for a convincing Satan. It corrupts the just, maddens nations, brings forth plagues, tempts us to sloth and gluttony and wrath... and if it weren't for this lightbringer, I couldn't be writing this now.

Tunguska I

Whatever it was that struck the Tunguska region of the Siberian forestland had exploded with a force never before imagined. Its shockwave traveled around the globe twice before it died out, and its general effect on the weather in the northern hemisphere was far-reaching. During the rest of June it was quite possible to read the small print in the London Times at midnight. There were photographs of Stockholm taken at one o'clock in the morning by natural light, and a photograph of the Russian town of Navrochat taken at midnight looks like a bright summer afternoon. For some months the world was treated to spectacular dawns and sunsets, as impressive as those that had been seen after the great Krakatoa eruption in 1883. From this, as well as the various reports of unusual cloud formations over following months, it is fair to guess that the event had thrown a good deal of dust into the atmosphere, as happens with violent volcanic eruptions and, notably, atomic explosions. Perhaps the strangest aspect of the Great Siberian Explosion was that no one paid much attention to it.
Colin Wilson, **The Great Tunguska Explosion**

Tunguska.

It fell from the sky. Most people can at least agree on that. Like a morning star fallen from the grace of God, on June 30, 1908 something slammed into the taiga in Tunguska, Siberia, exploding with a force estimated at between ten and forty megatons of TNT, depending on the source. In so doing, it created a mystery that has stood the test of the following ten decades. What force caused the Tunguska blast? Most modern researchers argue for the meteor theory, although there are still astrophysicists willing to champion a comet or even a small black hole. Still others argue for more esoteric culprits like Nikola Tesla (broadcast power experiments gotten out of hand), aliens (a UFO whose antimatter power core exploded before impact) or even an anachronistic atomic bomb. I myself postulate elsewhere in this collection the fancy that a failed attempt at time travel caused the blast... the basic idea was that a time machine appearing in our time would be attempting to materialize in a location that already contained matter, and that inevitably some of the atoms of the materializing time machine would inhabit the same location as oxygen atoms or what have you, causing an explosive annihilation similar to that of a matter/anti-matter contact.

Tunguska could be any of those things. Certainly, if one is a believer of Koestler's bisociation, at this point it's become all of those things. It exists like an iceberg, bobbing in the waters where fantastic ideas calve off from fact like a glacier into the unknown. All we know is that something blew up. So let's play with the idea. What can we make out of Tunguska? If our ideas contradict, it shouldn't concern us too much; after all, Tunguska has many faces now, and we can play with the idea from many angles, like the gemstone of the strange that it is, faceted for our revelation.

The Soviets are a lunatic's best friend, sometimes: they spent money on the most interesting things, like psychotronic warfare and ESP research and time cameras and UFOs and yes, Tunguska. We've been told that Chernobyl was a nuclear reactor that was poorly maintained and which had a bad accident. Certainly, that would be bad enough. But what if it was more? Indeed, what if the whole history of Tunguska as we've been given it is all a cover story, a great mask for something truly beyond our understanding, something that sent the Soviet Union chasing down alleys of weirdness for years and which caused them to bite hard on the most improbable bait we could have extended, even though it bankrupted them? The Soviets were always more interested in space than anyone else. We wanted to beat them up there, but they didn't give two hoots in hell about us, they just wanted to get up into the void. Why? What was it about space that so compelled and terrified them?

Let's look at some unrelated issues first and see how they fit. Isn't it interesting, for instance, that the word *Chernobyl* means 'Wormwood'? So, if you start in June of 1908 and travel forward to 1986, you have the whole Book of Revelations happening in Russia. Furthermore, if Tunguska had happened with the earth having rotated even slightly differently than it had, it would have come down upon St. Petersburg, where Grigori Efimovich was living at the time. Even that worthy might have found a multi-megaton explosion a bit hard to survive... even if, eight years later, he would endure the most prolonged assassination this side of St. Sebastian, finding himself on the receiving end of cyanide-laced cakes, poisoned wine, bullets (he was shot three times), a beating and finally, a drowning attempt in the Neva River. (He died not from the drowning, but from exposure.) Grigori Efimovich is of course more famous to us as Rasputin, the so-called Mad Monk who appeared around Halloween of 1905 with the ability to cure the hemophilia that afflicted Czarevitch Alexei, inherited from Queen Victoria of England. Eventually, afraid that Rasputin had too much power over the Czarina and thus over the nation, fellow lover of whores and drinking Felix Yusupov had Rasputin assassinated in that extremely difficult manner alluded to above. Yusupov, who had connections among Madame Blavatsky's Theosophists, considered Rasputin to also be in the service of Greens who he never really defined. Shortly after Rasputin's death at Prince Yusupov's hands, the Romanovs fell from power and the Soviet Union came into being, soon to take up the study of many of the things Rasputin could be said to exemplify.

Imagine this - a war that used the heavens as a kind of artillery platform? In the years before the development of the atomic bomb, the only way one was going to see mass destruction on the scale of a Tunguska was either by tapping into the earth's geothermal potential (as was seen in the volcanic eruption of Krakatoa in 1883) or a hurricane or other massive storm. The only other possibility was meteor impact. A stone from the sky (the *lapis ex caelis*, one of the guises of the Holy Grail) makes for a devastating weapon in the right hands. To a magician, who lives (and perhaps dies) in a world of microcosm affecting macrocosm and vice versa, the stars are always right.

> As above, so below. The truth that lies at the heart of the occult school of Hermeticism, and the key, in the eyes of some, to almost unimaginable power. For it is, of course, a truth that may be invertible: as above, so below... as below, so above. The earth mirrors what takes place in the heavens... and the heavens mirror what takes place on earth. A ritual performed on earth will influence the heavenly bodies. Heavenly bodies such as mirrors.

Simon Whitechapel, **Guts and Roses: The Coming Apocalypse
of the Ripper Millennium**

Yusupov, even Blavatsky, are mere ciphers in this magical war,
I would suspect. Neither of them possess enough real knowledge to
try to drop a meteor on St. Petersburg... but Rasputin, the man who
can arrest hemophilia (the blood is the life, and it obeys his will) and
resists death with the power of a Christian martyr (and who claimed
to be a starets, a Russian mystic of the Orthodox faith) and who
may have engaged in heretical orgies in order to conceive a god on
earth... he seems more genuine, more capable of seeing things others
cannot, more capable of deflecting the attack from above. Is it
possible that Rasputin was the real thing, an agent of mysterious
powers? Yahweh, the Great Old Ones, whoever the Theosophists
meant by the Greens. Was Rasputin the avatar of the Gaia-Mind?
Perhaps so; such a man could well have considered himself
bridegroom to Mother Russia itself, a modern day Druid of sorts,
and such a man could well have used the earth's power to deflect an
errant meteor summoned by a dark cabal serving Aghartans or
Hollow Worlders or whatever shadowy cult you prefer. One wonders
if, perhaps, Yusupov and his controllers miscalculated when they
removed the Mad Monk. Perhaps the power that directed his actions
then decided to take direct control of the Soviet Union, as evidenced
by their researches into all things wild and wonderful, all
investigations strange and dark. But who were the ones dropping
the rock? Were they, perhaps, a strange branch of the Rosicrucians?
Whitechapel's thesis is not that the Tunguska blast was caused by
the Ripper. He mostly argues that the cult of Elah Gabal, a meteorite
cult inspired by the very stone of Cybele we remember from our
mention two paragraphs above, inspired the Ripper (it's a very
involved theory, referencing Hebrew numerology, a painting entitled
Roses for Helioglabus, and good ol' Prince Eddy, this time as
sacrificial victim rather than Ripper candidate) in an attempt to draw
down the Leonid meteors and destroy the earth entire. But what if
he was off? What if the Ripper didn't want to kill everyone at all?
What if he was simply attempting to draw a new god down from the
heavens, much as the sun god Elah Gabal, consort of Cybele, came
down from the sky centuries before? Tunguska was a blast of fire
and force that twice circled the world- and isn't it interesting that

within forty years, mankind would be emulating it, setting off devices of mass destruction that would almost seem like an explosive equivalent of a small child copying an adult? Tunguska as a lesson, and one we learned. Furthermore, the relation of the painting *Roses for Helioglabus* and the Ripper, and the presence of sunlight in London at midnight after the blast, almost forces us to think of the fingers of a rosy-colored dawn... or perhaps one of purest gold.

After all, it's interesting to note that the Order of the Golden Dawn had but recently fallen apart... and that the Ripper killings were twenty years before, in 1888, a mere five years after Krakatoa. Was the Order acting in accordance with a directive that wouldn't take shape for another twenty years, attacking Russia from the skies? Or perhaps Aleister Crowley would later claim the Ripper killings were a working because the Order feared that someone else was at work, using the prostitutes of Whitechapel to stab at a man who would be more than acquainted with such. Perhaps even as a counterattack to the working that destroyed an island east of Java. Of course, the Ripper might well have been trying to hit London and simply miscalculated his sacrifices, but Tunguska as badly aimed attack doesn't have the same appeal, somehow.

Of course, there are other possibilities. The very fact that the destiny of the Soviet Union seems predicted by Tunguska, a falling object from heaven, and destroyed by Wormwood (Chernobyl), points to another idea, another conception of Tunguska. Perhaps it wasn't an annihilating stroke intended to kill an unkillable man (shades of Koschei the Deathless there... perhaps Rasputin was merely his most recent name) so much as the return of an older being. A far, far older one.

> And the third angel sounded, and there fell a great star from Heaven, burning as though it were a lamp, and it fell upon the third part of the rivers, and upon the foundation of waters. And the name of the star is called Wormwood, and the third part of the waters became wormwood, and many men died of the waters, because they were made bitter.
> **The Book of Revelations,** *8:10-11*
>
> I beheld Satan fall as lightning from heaven.
> **Luke** *10:18*

The Romanovs were the monarchs of a nation deeply in the grip of the Russian Orthodox Church, a faith seeded by the Eastern Orthodox brand of Christianity, and saw themselves as the emperors of the last holdout of Byzantium, God's kingdom on earth. I'm not saying that they were especially religious; I'm just pointing out that within a decade of the fall of the Tunguska fireball, the faith of the Russian people was completely suppressed by communism and the birth of the Soviet Union. It's often been said that faith requires doubt in order to be of merit, that those that do not see, and yet believe, are more blessed than those that must be shown in order to believe, those that commit the sin of Thomas. Isn't it interesting that atheist Soviets were the first to penetrate the heavens, and did so in part to prove there was nothing there? Why did they fear the possibility of a divine afterlife so much that they needed to visit in order to prove it wasn't there, like children afraid of the monster in the closet so deeply that they have to have the light shone inside to prove its nonexistence?

According to the official story, nobody checked on an explosion so powerful that its shockwave twice encompassed the earth until 1927, when Leonid Kulik finally convinced someone that it was worth looking into. So for nineteen years, the site supposedly lay fallow, with no one visiting it. Granted, between Russia's defeat in the Russo-Japanese War and Rasputin's arrival in 1905 (yes, both of those events occurred in the same year) there was a lot going on in St. Petersburg. But still, the idea that an explosion unlike any ever seen before could happen, and then no one would notice it for almost two decades, kind of shakes the bounds of credibility more than the idea that a babbling lunatic from out of nowhere could cure hemophilia. Indeed, another possibility is that Rasputin didn't deflect Tunguska at all. If one could summon rocks from space via the medium of sacred prostitutes in the ritual at Whitechapel... how much better, then, to embody the god from on high and create a sympathetic vibration? Literally turning himself into a magnet to draw the holy one down to himself, to finally bring the god he sought to earth? Many of the ancient meteorite cults have the same basic mythos, one familiar to anyone who has read the story of Lucifer: a divine being of great beauty and power rides from the heavens down to earth in a stone of fire. Sometimes the meteor-gods are seen as bringers of gifts and culture, and others are destroyers. It almost seems to vary depending on what those who witness it value.

Imagine yourself as Czar Nicholas in 1908. Everywhere beset by traitors, at the head of a state pinned between the past and the future, hemmed in by political maneuvering that would make the Empress Irene of Byzantium look petty. Your heir is sickly, your wife convinced this dirty whoremonger can cure him. And when you go to confront the bastard, what does he do but promise you a wonder? The sky shall fall, and with it, the old Russia. You can control this... or be destroyed by it. Even as this happens comes news of the blast. Of the blast, and what was at the center of it, which cements your willingness to accept Grigori Efimovich and his presence at your court. Something that so shocks Lenin and his advisors when they kill the Romanovs that they have to suppress it at all costs.

Several possibilities come to mind. One of the more fun ones would be an angel, fallen from heaven. Perhaps *the* fallen angel; after all, we've already referenced the prophecies that speak of the fall of a star burning like a lamp, and a lamp is one means to bear light, *lux ferre*. Lucifer. The ultimate enlightener, he who convinced our ancestors to eat of the Tree of Knowledge and know Good and Evil... and isn't it interesting that God didn't seem to want us to know? (Shades of Weishaupt's Illuminati and the old Hellfire Club, with their unconscious aping of Rabelais' law of Thélème, put forth later by Crowley as "Do what thou wilt shall be the whole of the law," enlightenment as will to power, as Nietzsche put it in his *Thus Spake Zarathustra*... and we'll be getting to Zoroaster himself shortly.) But what would our nascent dictatorship of the proletariat do with Satan himself? One remembers how Rasputin prophesied that if he was slain by a noble, then the nobility itself would fall. We then remember the *lapis ex caelis*, the stone from the heavens, which seems odd when we contrast it with Satan falling as lightning from heaven.

The original root of the Christian concept of Satan, however, comes from the Hebrew 'adversary', he who does the work of God on earth. The temptation in the garden, the torment of Job, the Babylonian captivity... these are all the work of God's prosecutor, he who brings charges against humanity. Satan wasn't God's antagonist; he was ours. He's literally administering a test, advising God as to our sinfulness and misdeeds. It's interesting to note that he doesn't become evil in the Hebrew conception until the Babylonian captivity and its aftermath, when the victorious Persians (you knew it was going to be the Persians) released the captive Israelites and sent them home, unwittingly introducing the Zoroastrian concept of dualism into the Hebrew faith, which had recently become fully monotheistic. They took to it, and sought for a figure to cast in the role of Ahriman.

They found Satan, the Adversary, just waiting for them. Just as did the czar and his troops in 1908, just as did the Bolsheviks when they eliminated the Romanov family and seized power less than a decade later, just as Stalin did when he took control and began his series of infamous purges to ensure that no one could emulate him and overthrow his rule. We could debate the purges as blood sacrifices, of course, but I think they were more like tests that Stalin, who'd attended seminary and wanted to be a priest, failed utterly. After Stalin, as the USSR entered the atomic age, they became paranoid and hid their benefactor under (of all things) the Chernobyl reactor, nuclear power being a fulfillment of the old alchemical search for primordial matter and thus an excellent deflector of any possible magical search. For that matter, if we apply the Zechariah Sitchin/ Erich von Däniken lens, Satan could well be an advanced alien or technological artifact- perhaps the *lapis ex caelis* is an artificial intelligence inhabiting an alien craft of some kind, The Russian space program becomes a desperate attempt to create some sort of early warning system in case other angels come looking for the Fallen One, who might well be powered by a quantum synchronicity tap that exists on a dimensional scale transcending time, sending out vibrations that create the very prophecies that lead one to the falling rock and the blighted waters of the Book of Revelations, the various cults of gods falling from the sky and so on. A distress signal that reaches out into the supersymmetry of the universe and behaves acausally? Why not? When dealing with the Devil, many things are possible. Were the Magi inspired by the scream of a trapped supercomputer some thirty centuries after they were created?

Tunguska II

On June 30, 1908, the Tunguska event took place in the wilderness of Siberia, near Lake Baikal. I have no idea what took place, athough I speculate elsewhere in this collection about what it might have been. But for now, let's consider a somewhat delusional spin on the events. (Hey, it's what I do.)

Edward Elmer Smith was born in 1890. In his life, he earned a Ph.D. in chemistry, ran the inspection staff for an ordnance plant, and worked as a lumberjack, chemical engineer, blacksmith, photographer and cook. His interests included rifle drill, light opera and guitar, and he created the first epic space opera/generational science fiction classic, the series of tales known today under the umbrella of his *Lensman* stories. In their own way, Smith's stories of the Lens are as influential as the cosmic horrors of H.P. Lovecraft, his contemporary, and at the time they were afforded a great deal more respect and admiration. Smith's epic was nominated in 1966, the year after his death, for a special Hugo award for Best All Time Series…although they have suffered a bit as time has passed and their sexism and assumption of human inequality have become less accepted in our culture. Still, without *Lensman* someone else would have had to create a two billion year epic SF masterpiece so that others would have known that it was possible, and with that delay we may well have lacked tales like Asimov's *Foundation* novels, the classic comic book *Green Lantern*, George Lucas' *Star Wars* series of films or J. Michael Straczynski's "Babylon 5" television show, to name a few.

Don't worry, I haven't forgotten Tunguska, I promise.

Smith's epic begins some two thousand million years ago, when two galaxies pass through one another, and it shows the conflict between the advanced beings of Arisia and Eddore. Eddore is devoted utterly to conquest and domination of all sentient beings; Arisians are more reasonable, rational beings who seek to create a kind of union of all sentient beings under their benevolent guidance, what they call Civilization. To oppose the Eddorians (whose actions can only be predicted so long as they are unaware of Arisian influence, which would prompt them to change tactics), the Arisians seed the galaxy. An Arisian calling himself Mentor shepherds these seeded races as they evolve into the peoples who form first the Triplanetary League, then the Galactic Patrol. The goal of Civilization is to create beings who can use the totality of their minds, who are in essence at the same level of existence as the Arisians and Eddorians, and in so doing usher in an age of cooperation and unity. It's a ripping yarn for all that, with great starships using inertialess drives and vacuum tubes to plot their way through space, and with battles involving thousands of ships and planetary-scale weapons.

However, it's a little neat. The idea of the totally Machiavellian and evil Eddorians and the completely benevolent (in a time-scale we humans might have problems with... Mentor has no problem allowing World War III, with its attendant deaths, as long as he's sure it will benefit Civilization in the long run) Arisians works for the story, but it kind of fails the reality check for a modern audience. However, when one looks at the technology of Smith's Galactic Patrol, with its strange mixture of death rays and vacuum tubes, with its lack of computers and its ability to contravene the laws of gravity and inertia, one starts thinking almost inevitably about Nikola Tesla. (I promise, at no time during this essay do I speculate that he was from Venus.) The year the future chronicler of Civilization was born, Tesla was at the height of his fame in New York, lecturing on alternating current as part of the so-called battle of the currents, making demonstrations of new inventions that often baffled and amazed those he invited to his luxurious parties (paid for with the money he earned from Westinghouse for his patents on alternating current) and in general acting more like a stereotypical pulp genius than a scientist. Soon, however, a disaster at his lab rendered him penniless and reduced him to funding his experiments with donations, and an unaccountable lack of interest in his patents made it harder and harder for him to get any new money. By 1908 he was desperately trying to convince someone, anyone, that broadcast power was the wave of the future. But why did so unarguably brilliant a man find himself suffering penury and isolation so soon after having been the darling of New York?

Let's look at Civilization and Eddore a little more closely, and from a subtly different point of view. In the *Lensman* stories, Lensmen are telepathic (thanks to the Lens itself, an artifact of Arisian technology) and indeed, they invade minds with no compunction, even in court cases to establish guilt or innocence. None of that pesky right to avoid self-incrimination in the Patrol's tyranny of the mind. (You could be accused of a traffic offense of which you were entirely innocent order that you could be mind-probed and proved guilty of a more serious offense.) Furthermore, the Lensman has the power to enforce the law, decide on guilt or innocence, and pass sentence. Smith envisioned the Lensmen as totally incorruptible, of course, so they would always use these powers for the greater good. But I can't help but think of an elite corps of interstellar vigilantes with the power to control and violate the mind, to take the law into their own hands, that act at the behest of an alien race that thinks nothing of plunging the entire earth into a destructive atomic war as long as things work out on a scale that measures time in billions of years, as a little daunting. Granted, Boskone, the syndicated criminal organization that Eddore creates to oppose the Patrol, is a pack of drug dealing miscreants in Smith's stories. But when one considers the long use of chemicals to open the third eye and create psychic sensitivity in humanity (as opposed to the slavery human Lensmen are yoked to, forever dependent on the Lens, an Arisian technology), and looks at the Eddorian drive to dominate contrasted with the human drive to do likewise... suddenly, one realizes that Eddore might well view the machinations of a sterile galaxy-wide cadre of dictatorial behind-the-scenes conspirators (after all, what else do you call it when a group spends two billion years subtly opposing you with the aid of organizations it secretly created?) with alarm, and seek like-minded allies. Like, say, humanity.

It doesn't matter if you re-envision the Patrol and Arisia as tyrannical and despotic or accept Smith's rendition of them as benevolent, with their ends (Civilization) justifying their means (anything at all) in such graphic ways. Either will suit our purpose, which is to imagine E.E. Smith as Civilization's apologist on earth... and Nikola Tesla as the reason Civilization had something to apologize for.

Imagine these two unfathomably advanced alien cultures engaged in a wide-ranging galactic game of chess, a cosmos-wide equivalent of the Great Game Rudyard Kipling wrote about. Neither group is entirely sure who it opposes... the Arisians hide behind their agents, and the Eddorians do likewise. Both groups operate on Earth behind agencies like the Theosophical Society, the Society for Psychical Research, the Order of the Golden Dawn, the Illuminati, and so on. They give Edgar Cayce visions. They are behind the electrical people of Victorian London. They meddle with us, use us as tools, and are completely unconcerned with our welfare when it is contrasted with the greater scope and scale of their conflict. It's possible that their endless machinations are responsible for the legends of Oannes (a serpent from the sea who brought information and culture-Civilization- to ancient Sumeria; was Oannes a Velantian Lensman, using his telepathy to spread the message of his unknowable masters?) and Lucifer (a Boskonian infiltration of the primordial Arisian experiment remembered today as Eden?), and they support and oppose new developments among their human pawns as the need arises. The battle of the currents becomes a struggle between them, using their human proxies, to control the development of human small-c civilization and technology. Did Tesla's triumph mark him as a threat to one, or perhaps even both groups? His influence, had it gone unchecked, might well have leapfrogged humanity past the current information age and into the age of limitless power, broadcast telluric currents along the lines of Umberto Eco's menhirs from *Foucault's Pendulum*. (It's also interesting to note that in Smith's stories, earth is called Tellus and humans Tellurians.) After all, Tesla could think about as well as any human on the face of the planet at the time.

> War cannot be avoided until the physical cause for its recurrence is removed and this, in the last analysis, is the vast extent of the planet on which we live. Only through annihilation of distance in every respect, as the conveyance of intelligence, transport of passengers and supplies and transmission of energy will conditions be brought about some day, insuring permanency of friendly relations. What we now want is closer contact and better understanding between individuals and communities all over the earth, and the

elimination of egoism and pride which is always prone to plunge the world into primeval barbarism and strife... Peace can only come as a natural consequence of universal enlightenment.
Nikola Tesla, **My Inventions**

It's easy to imagine one or both sides of the galactic cold war fearing the emergence of a new rival, especially one who would have no need for either the Lens of the Arisians (having technology of its own that would equal or surpass it) or the drugs of the Boskonians (having eschewed such crude manipulations of the self for a more sublime mastery of the surrounding world) as well as having attempted to set a course of universal enlightenment, a course that would run counter to both the Eddorian drive to conquer and the Arisian ideal of Civilization as a realm of rigid controls and order. However, it's just as easy to imagine Tesla as an agent of either side; if you take Smith's word as gospel, Tesla and the Patrol are bedfellows of philosophy. If you view Smith as a yellow journalist in the service of Arisia, then Tesla's goal of enlightenment and Eddore's search for freedom from Arisian meddling dovetail nicely. For our purposes, it doesn't matter. One of them works to ruin him, the other seeks to recruit him.

And that's when things get interesting. Because whoever Tesla doesn't work for would begin stepping up plans to move their agenda into operation. Perhaps Rasputin was the choice of whichever group Tesla doesn't join, the Green Brotherhood another in a series of fronts for an alien agenda to push the earth into their mold. All very fine, you may well say, but what about Tunguska?

It was clear now that the Tower of Babel had been simply an attempt, however hasty and deservedly a failure because of the pride of its architects, to build the most powerful menhir of all. But the Babylonians got their calculations wrong.
Umberto Eco, **Foucault's Pendulum**

Modern field theories are rooted in the work of Michael Faraday, who through his investigation of magnetism came to the conclusion that "lines of force" extended around a magnet. These were states of strain and were physically real. But they were not made of ordinary matter. So what sort of reality had they? He was not sure, and suggested alternative

interpretations. Either they have physical existence as states of a material medium "which we may call aether," or else they have physical existence as states of "mere space."
*Rupert Sheldrake, **The Presence of the Past***

Had Faraday concerned himself about the mag field surrounding an Electric Current, We today Would NOT exist or if We did exist, our present Geo-political situation would not have the very time-bombish, ticking off towards Destruction, atmosphere that Now exists.
Carlos Allende (Carl Allen) to Morris K. Jessup

Here's where things get weird (that's right... so far, at least by my standards, they've been basically normal), so hang on. Sir Michael Faraday came closest before Tesla to developing alternating current, and while doing so he stumbled upon field theory (inspiring both Lord Kelvin's vortices and modern superstring theory), which in its more developed state argues that all matter and energy are illusions created by the interaction of space and dimension. Forces, like gravity and eletcromagnetism, are phenomena of the way spacefold and matter/energy/spacetime affect each other. In essence, there is no distance, and everything is made of interrelated vibrations along the superstring, which leads to the fields of morphic resonance being able to control the development of matter in vastly distant places, to photons interacting in separate labs at speeds faster than light, all that kind of thing. Now, Faraday was at the merest beginnings of discovering this... but if you listen to Tesla's ranting about the annihilation of distance you start to wonder. Furthermore, how will such information create universal enlightenment? Well, what is telepathy, exactly? It's the ability to know what someone else is thinking. If there is no distance and all matter and energy are the same, then your brain and my brain are connected. There's telepathy for you. Imagine, therefore, that Tesla and his alien backers decided to engineer an enormous telluric menhir, to create a kind of quantum-state mass-mind among all human beings. In one shot, they'd eliminate all differences and create a world that wasn't ticking towards Destruction, as Carl *"The Philadelphia Experiment* was more than just a bad movie starring the guy from *Eddie and the Cruisers*, or was that Ken Wahl? I forget"* Allen so colorfully put it. Tesla was poised to leapfrog the atomic age to the quantum filament age, an age where time and space were one, distance was an illusion, mankind was enlightened and anything was possible.

Clearly, he had to be stopped. Ignoring the chaos that might have resulted had every mind on the planet suddenly been opened to every other mind- honestly, do you really want to know everyone at once, and have no secrets from them all?- you can easily see why either, or possibly both, groups would have balked at the idea of humanity become like unto gods. Their elite club of two would suddenly have had a new member, and one with an atrocious track record at that. Perhaps Tesla went further and faster than anyone expected, or perhaps he merely misled his benefactors about his intentions. At any rate, one night in June his lab in New York, site of his infamous released energy at a distance experiment, is raided and his inventions destroyed, and half-way around the world, the power is released. Distance, after all, is an illusion. Tesla's device destablizies the telluric currents, sending vibrations along the superstring, and Tunguska is the result. It could have happened anywhere: perhaps Tesla himself managed to redirect the blast to someplace relatively isolated before it blew up New York instead. At any rate, the agents of one or both camps go into high gear to prevent Tesla from ever getting the proper funding for his experiments again, leaving him to die in obscurity some four decades from the night of the blast. From there, Civilization decides to try and spin things to its benefit while Eddore entrenches itself even further into the countercultures of the earth, waiting for the stars to be right... oh, wait, that's a Lovecraft reference, and any resemblence between Smith's omnipotent alien meddlers and Lovecraft's otherworldly gods is left as an exercise to the readers.

The Choir of Our Minds

These are practiced in different forms by many people, from
the fire-dancing Navajo Indians to the Hindus, and even occur
within a nominally Christian tradition in Europe. To this day,
on the feasts of St. Constantine and his mother St. Helen, the
villagers of Langadas in Greece dance on glowing coals,
clutching icons of these saints.
*Bob Rickard and John Michell, **The Rough Guide to
Unexplained Phenomena***

Statistical tests have shown that sick people who have taken
"sugar pills" - tablets with no drugs in them - but who are told
that they have taken drugs often seem to recover, even though
their diseases have not really been treated. In "blind trial"
experiments, some patients are given healing medication,
and others are given tablets with no healing value. The patients
do not know that some of the tablets have no drugs. A
significant number of those receiving the placebo recover
anyway, apparently just by taking what they believe is
medicine.
*William F. Williams, ed, **Encyclopedia of Pseudo Science***

I'm sure most of us know about the placebo effect, in which a
person who is taking completely non-medicinal substances can show
an improvement in health merely because he believes the substance
will cure him. (There is, of course, debate as to how much of a role
hypochondria can play in this. Then again, hypochondria is in its
own way an example of the flip side of this phenomenon, wherein a
person's sincere belief in an illness can actually manifest symptoms
of that illness.) Then there are those who walk on hot coals, or
manifest stigmata, or cause blisters to rise on their skin, or who can
emit electricity from their bodies or magnetically lock themselves in
place. What mechanism allows for all this? Doctors refer to the
placebo effect as a psychological one, but how can a mere
psychological process, in effect a delusion ("these pills are curing

me"), bring about real healing? How can the inverse delusion ("I have an illness") actually cause sickness in some cases? How does one human being walk across burning wood or coals that would kill another?

> Harrison's book, which gathers together the result of many studies, leaves no possible doubt of the reality of spontaneous combustion. But what causes it? At present it must be confessed that the phenomenon baffles medical knowledge. But Harrison offers some interesting clues. He speaks of the researches of an American doctor, Mayne R. Coe ,Junior, who was interested in the study of telekinesis - mind over matter. Coe was able to move aluminim strips pivoted on the points of needles by moving his hands over them... he began various yoga exercises in an attempt to develop his bioelectricity; sitting one day in an easy chair, he felt a powerful current passing downward from his head throughout his body.
>
> Colin Wilson, *Mammoth Encyclopedia of the Unsolved*

I once argued that spontaneous human combustion was quite possibly caused by a moment of transcendence similar to the concept of *samhadi*, a state of fixation, wherein the person in question comes to that moment of clarity so familiar to those who dabble in mysticism (and which is often called hitting bottom by addicts, which many SHC cases seem to be, addicts to alcohol) and at that moment of clarity, when the addict's brain chemistry is at its most fervid, self-loathing takes over and the victim literally burns him- or herself to death. Obviously, just as Harrison does, I see a connection between SHC and the psionic, although in my case I argue that the person who burns is causing himself to burn. Admittedly, it would take a great deal of self-loathing, but subconscious self-immolative suicide is just the beginning of what I'm talking about.

There are innumerable examples. Mircea Eliade reports that the Dogon of North Africa (the ones who tell tales of Sirius B, the ones who may or may not have been contacted by fish men from space in Robert Temple's *Sirius Mystery* cosmology) can handle red-hot metal and often do in order to ritually repeat the actions of the smiths who forged the universe. Anna Monaro, a patient suffering from asthma, found herself glowing from within in May of 1934, and we can all decide if we think the official explanation that electromagnetic radiation from certain compounds in her skin was actually an explanation, or simply a way of saying "She's glowing and I don't know why." Or if we want a psychiatric evaluation of her case, we can always use the one handed down, that electrical and magnetic organisms in the woman's body developed in eminent degree. If you're wondering what organisms those would be, or how psychiatric training would allow one to perceive them, you aren't alone in that. There are cases of supposed saints or mystics who display such luminous fields, of course, but in many cases it seems that pain and/ or ecstasy play a key role.

It makes me wonder. Pain, whether it be the suffering of an addict unable to bear what his life has become or the self-inflicted pain of one walking on fire, can often serve as a great focusing agent. Distractions melt away when one is in agony. Even the anticipation of pain can serve to clear one's mind, and the desire to avoid pain is one of the most primal emotions a human can experience. We know from our dabbling in neurological circles that all human thought is rooted in the paleomammalian brain and its emotional drives, that our powerful neocortical "computer" is really secondary to the urges of the paleomammalian, that it is in effect enslaved by it. We rationalize. So the idea that pain, or the desire to avoid or end it, has an effect on these related phenomenon- the healing of the body thorugh belief in worthless medication, the ability to transcend fire, to end the suffering of a life one cannot bear, to create symptoms of imagined diseases for treatment, the shedding of light from diseased or wounded portions of the body to illuminate their position, the display of strange powers of attraction or repulsion following psychological or physical trauma (as did Angelique Cotton and Vyvyan Jones)- becomes something to consider.

Pain focuses thought. But what is thought, that focusing it should have such an effect? Objectively, we think every day and I would be fairly certain that most of us can't lift iron bars with magnetic fields or cause objects around us to burst into flame. Is it merely the extremity of pain? If it were, wouldn't our terminal wards be filled with beds that contained naught but ashes or people emitting strokes of lightning as they thrashed about? It would seem to me that were pain enough to cause these kinds of effects, we'd have no assisted suicide cases in our courts and Jack Kervorkian would merely be a doctor with a morbid taste in art. Also, it's clear that in many cases; the mystic who levitates himself, glowing like a torch, above a crowd of believers; the stigmatic who manifests gaping wounds on her body- that at times pain is totally irrelevant to the situation. And there are other factors to consider.

> **psychogenic death** Literally "mind-caused death," the possibility that a person can die as a result of a psychological process was first considered by social scientists under the name voodoo death. Researchers observed in many cultures that individuals who were cursed, or who violated a taboo, frequently died shortly afterward in the absence of obvious physical causes. The classic description is that of Basedow (cited in Cannon). He observed the reaction of an Australian aborigine who had just had a cursing bone pointed at him by a sorceror. The victim: "stands aghast, with his eyes staring at the treacherous pointer, and with his hands lifted as though to ward off the lethal medium which he imagines is pouring into his body. His cheeks blanch and his eyes become glassy and the expression on his face becomes horribly distorted... he attempts to shriek but usually the sound chokes in his throat, and all that one might see is froth at his mouth. His body begins to tremble... he sways backward and falls to the ground... writhing as if in mortal agony. After awhile he becomes very composed and crawls to his [shelter]. From this time onwards he sickens and frets, refusing to eat and keeping aloof from the daily affairs of the tribe. Unless a counter-spell is done quickly, death may be imminent."
> *Leonard George, **Alternative Realities***

But if we adopt an organismic rather than an atomistic perspective, there seems to be no good reason why organisms at levels of complexity should not have characteristic fields. Indeed, de Broglie's original idea of matter waves implies such a view: entire atoms and molecules were wavelike quanta, as indeed were all forms of matter. It might not be absurd to think of an insulin molecule, say, as a quantum or unit in an insulin field: or even of a swan as a quantum of unit in a swan field. But this may just be another way of thinking about morphic fields: any particular insulin molecule is a manifestation of the insulin morphic field; any particular swan is a manifestation of the swan morphic field. Morphic fields may indeed be comparable in status to quantum matter fields. If atoms can be said to have morphic fields, then these may

well be what are already described within quantum field theory. The morphic fields of molecules may already be partially described by quantum chemistry. But the morphic fields of cells, tissues, organs and living organisms have so far been described only in vague and general terms.
*Rupert Sheldrake, **The Presence of the Past***

Imagine thought. Thought, at its most basic chemical description, is an encoding of neurological signals which are transmitted by chemicals known as neurotransmitters. Therefore, thought is chemical. Therefore, thought is made up of matter. Therefore, thought may be described as a wavelike quanta, a characteristic morphic field of its own, the thought field. Any particular thought can be said to be a manifestation of the morphic field of thought. Are there, therefore, multiple morphic fields of thought? Just as individual cells may have their own fields, and the organs they make up may have discrete fields of their own as well as the fields generated by their components cells, which may have fields generated by their component molecules, which may have fields generated by their component atoms, which may have fields generated by their component electrons, protons and neutrons- and so on, and so on- does each kind of thought generate its own morphic field? Is there a field for hate, a field for love, a field for disgust... all of these fields separate, and yet overlapping with the larger field of thought itself? And how does the thought field intersect with the field for the brain which generates the thoughts? We know that fields of force such as morphic fields are generated (in general quantum superstring theory, anyway) by the interaction of dimensions on matter. So there is no actual gravity as such, just the effect of a concentration of matter or energy on three-dimensional space, a kind of space warp.

Consider, then, the morphic field of thought. It's a manifestation of the same means by which all matter and energy are created, the way three-dimensional space interacts with the ten (or twenty-two, or however many dimensions are ultimately postulated) dimensions of the superstring. The superstring could be said to generate the morphic fields of all fundamental matter and energy, which then combine to create the ascending fields- the morphic fields of electrons, protons and neutrons, in varying combinations, creating the various morphic fields of all elemental atoms, which then combine to create the various morphic fields of all molecules- all the way up to the ultimate morphic field for the universe. Everything is a vibration of the superstring, or more accurately stated, everything is a different variation of the vibrations of the superstring, just as music is different variations in the vibrations of air. The universe is a symphony played on the string, and the morphic fields are the notes. (Compare this to the Celtic concept of *Oran Mor*, the world-music, and you get some interesting ideas.)

Thought and its sub-fields, therefore, are a component in that symphony, and a very interesting one. Imagine a symphony in which none of the performers have the sheet music, and are improvising as the music progresses. Now, into that symphony, introduce an instrument which is even more mutable, one that can mimic almost any other sound and can range forward and back over the score, making itself felt in ways subtle and gross. We know thought can be translated into action. When a woman picks up a rock and throws it into a crowd, or spends a day planting a garden, she is translating thought into action. There is always resistance to this translation, whether it be the weight of the rock or the consistency of the soil, but this interaction of forces has a myriad of daily effects we experience. The sweep of a clock's black wing. The smell of a human hive, exhaust fumes and sweat and food's explosion of odors, the literal chaos of interacting forces. Chaos can be seen as the fields that make up existence coming into resonance, the hand (as it were) of morphic resonance itself.

But is it possible that the thought fields can interact more directly, without needing to use the body as an instrument? Field theory would seem to argue that it is; morphic fields are habitual. A crystalline structure forms, and then it becomes easier for those crystals to form in that manner again. The fields are generated by repetition, as if the fold of three-dimensional space wears a crease in it. So it becomes possible to imagine that as the thought fields interact, they can create regions in which the universe is more or less disposed towards their interference. Consider, for example, the terminal ward mentioned above: if thought fields, focused by the stimulus of the pain field (like a catalyst dropped into a solution) can cause spontaneous human combustion, why don't we see explosions every day in these storehouses of the dying, suffering and wounded?

Because there are multiple fields at work, and they are worn into place by the general conception of an area. A terminal ward is a place of great suffering, yes; but it is also a place of hopelessness. One only goes there when there's nothing more that can be done. The weight of that much belief, pointed in one direction, becomes a counterforce that only the strongest focus could overcome.

It helps if you imagine the thought fields as electrons for a moment. We know that the reason our bodies don't just pass through other matter (despite the fact that, in atomic terms, there's plenty of empty space that would allow solid matter to pass through other solid matter) is the repellent charge of our electrons. In this conception, both electrons and thought are essentially just fields, the electron field and the thought field. What if the reason that our sorceror in Australia can kill a fellow who grew up in the same belief system with a bone but can't even make a sociologist nervous is that their thought fields are not sympathetic, but rather repellent? Electrons bind atoms, yet also repel them. Until the sociologist's and the sorceror's cultures come into close enough contact for there to be (for lack of a better phrase) morphic infection between them, the two cultures simply bounce off of one another. Their thought fields are not composed of the same sub-thought component fields. If you take it further and imagine that the collective of humanity is composed of the thought fields of all humanity together, there would be many, many places where these thought fields were in morphic dissonance with each other, many places where the wave of thought is in flux, and can more easily be swayed in one direction or another by sufficient focus of thought by one individual, imposing her own will with an effect like ripples in a pond.

So we have two competing mechanisms by which thought fields can have direct affect on the fields of rocks, flesh, light and so on. One is through infection, as the morphic field of thought creates resonance with the morphic fields of other aspects of reality- the symphony taking on a new rhythm, or a new tempo- and the other is through dissonance, as morphic fields clash and possibly create new patterns. But how does a thought field create sufficient resonance to overwhelm or infect another? The easiest way is through sympathy (as magicians have known forever, it seems, with their fetish dolls and bits of primal matter), as the personal thought field of one being contains enough of the sub-thought component fields to, in effect, tune itself to match the fields around it. The sorceror points the bone, and like a tuning fork, matches his field to the field of his intended victim's expectations. They both know what will happen; they both expect it to happen. The sick man is given a pill with no medicine in it, and he tunes his thoughts towards the possibility of recovering. He does not consider that it will not happen, and his focus is sufficient to allow him to override the fields of his own body.

All sorts of possibilities come to mind. Are the legends of shapeshifters endemic to our species cases in which someone manages to tune his thought field such that his image of the body merges aspects of another species with his own? Does a werewolf think strongly enough that it is both beast and man, and thus become both? One imagines Tarzan and Mowgli as humans who managed to go halfway, and at least think of themselves as beasts strongly enough to achieve some of the power of their chosen totems. Does the ancient Qabbalistic idea of emanations of God, of the descent and ascent of the divine lightning flash, symbolize the quest to conceive sufficiently of the *Ain Sof Aur* that one may tune one's thought field to the highest possible frequency and encompass everything? Does it follow that, as world society becomes more and more intertwined, the set of sub-thoughts that make up the thought field of individuals will become more susceptible to morphic infection, allowing old ways to start working again? Is this what is behind the seemingly constant similarities between quantum physics and ancient mysticism, the almost hermetic nature of the superstring and superspace theories? Is is because of the effort it must take to force the fields of so many disparate components into alignment with our own that these things don't seem more readily apparent, or is it the result of misappliation? Should we be attuning ourselves to the universe rather than attuning it to us? And for that matter, are we deliberately creating a world in which the mental focus, be it esoteric or simply personal, is harder and harder to generate?

This doesn't even address the idea that thought fields are contagious, that our conception of the past, present and future is created and revised by them. Historical revisionism can actually revise history. Enough people set to believing the same "truth" about an event can cause that truth to manifest itself, changing what was into what we think it was and erasing thoe things in which we no longer believe. Elves may have been wiped out by the backward-travelling wave of "There are no such things as elves" told by parents in years that hadn't happened yet, or transformed into stunted pre-human cave dwellers by those that read and adopted Arthur Machen's little people hypothesis. Did the Dogon create the very star-pisceans they preserve today in legend by repeating those legends to others? Everything is fluid in the great music. Dragons, demons, magical lands and drowned islands, the position of the poles, gods and angels; all are summoned into and out of existence again and again as the thought field changes pitch and tone, as it grows resonant or dissonant.

Some see the universe as math. Music, one might respond, is inherently mathematical and yet resonant. Are we at once notes in a grand song and potential composers? How closely is thought bound to perception, and perception to reality? Hell if I know, but if everything is a vibration of a string, I'm happy just to get to hear some of it.

Heading Towards the Plain Vigrid

> Burning ice, biting flame; that is how life began.
> *Kevin Crossley-Holland,* **The Norse Myths**

Sixty-five million years ago, the world changed. The great beasts died, named long after their passing by a species descended from creatures that feared to thrust quivering pink snouts outside their warrens when these thunder demons trod past. This is obvious. What is less obvious is that our world has been cooling since that time. The average global temperature in the Cretaceous period was 26 degrees celsius (around 70 degrees fahrenheit) and since that time it's fallen to roughly 14 degrees celsius. That's colder than it was during the time of the great grasslands (16 degrees) and colder than it was when the Antarctic ice sheet began to form roughly thirty-five million years ago (18 degrees). In short, our Pleistocene age is the coldest age the world has seen since the Cretaceous Extinction, far colder than the Palaeocene upswing (when the worldwide average was 28 degrees celsius and there were forests throughout the world, most of them rain forests; Antarctica was covered in conifers). We live in a cold world.

This is not a holdover from the Cretaceous. The decline in temperature following the end of our saurian rivals was a dip that lead to a peak in the Palaeocene. Some time between 50 and 40 million years ago, however, the world rainforest began to see the first signs of a cooling trend. For millons of years, the temperature fell unabated, and although it has seen some reversals since the Eocene, the general direction has been one sloping towards glaciation. The world gets colder. At present, we live in a lull between ice ages.

The dragons died. When they did, the heat went with them, and the ice rolled up. It's a strange fact that in addition to living in a cold world, we live in a small one, at least so far as big animals are concerned; even our titans are miniscule in comparison to their ancestors, save the whales, and they have the advantage of an ocean habitat. Is it because of the constant back and fourth between ice and temperate climes? Possibly, for while it's true that animals tend to grow larger in colder climates (where the larger mass of their bodies has less proportionate surface area to disperse heat), it's also true that swift alteration to the habitat tends to be hardest on big creatures. For whatever reason, as the millions of years passed and our world froze, the big beasts drifted into oblivion. We think of an elephant as massive, but an indricotherum was three times its size. And when you think of the creatures that died out.... Consider one ton Andrewsarchus, an ungulate unlike any hoofed animal that lives today, with a skull 33 inches long (yes, almost a yard long) absolutely packed with triangular teeth that could crack bone with ease, a giant wolflike animal 16 feet from end to end. A predator of the mesonychians, closely related to whales and pigs. Unlike anything you have ever seen in your life. There were birds as big as horses that ate horses the size of cats. Strange to think that some 50 million years later, humans would tell tales of great birdlike beasts named griffons that hunted horses, completely unaware that it had actually happened before their ancestors had even thought about branching away from the lemurs, lorises and adapids. The dragons and the giants died. A pack primate slowly rose out of the chaos of shifting climates, changing ecosystems, whales that swam in the Sahara and ate elephants, and creatures that had the teeth of hyenas millions of years before hyenas existed.

It sometimes seems strange to me, that in a world of parallel and divergent evolution, where great reptiles grow bodies like those of fish and great mammals grow bodies like those same reptiles, where several different species of saber toothed cats arose and shared existence with a marsupial lookalike, we are tol believe that the humanoid form has only arised in primates. Ichthyosaurs followed by Dorudon. Dinofelis and Smilodon. Gastornis and Phorusrhacos. Again and again, these are the phoenix impulses of evolution, yet we are to believe that only hominids, and to a lesser extent our simian relatives, have developed this combination of manipulator and motivator limbs, the forward-facing eyes, the scanning sensory package and the large, unusually complex brain.

We remember, twisted and deformed, experiences we could not have had. Before the fossils were found, we told tales of dragons and giants. Is it possible we've forgotten parallel predecessors? Forget the Paluxy tracks, forget metal spheres found in ancient rock strata, forget whether you believe in morphic fields creating evolutionary habits or simple natural selection creating a series of similar forms via environmental pressures like fractals spinning in time. Just confining ourselves to what little we can see in the fossil record, we know that the same forms repeat in very different species. An ancestor of whales and goats takes the form of a giant bear. A bird becomes a horse-killer, and another bird repeats the act almost forty million years later. Titaniotheres and rhinos both fill the role the triceratops once occupied. What of man? In a world once entirely forest, a world populated by dragons and giants, did a manlike being walk before we ever did?

Evolution, however it works, has proven that it loves to play the same numbers over and over again. We have so few clues to the world that came before our own. So few remains, a few fossils, some of which we can't even interpret properly. In the past we've placed Iguanadon's thumb on its nose, assumed that Apatosaurus couldn't even move due to its size, and named the king killer whale of the distant past Basilosaurus even though it was a mammal, not a reptile or a dinosaur. We know very little. There's room for all sorts of prodigies in the past. It is by definition the place where everything happened. Did the forces of natural selection bring about another warm-blooded omnivore millions of years before us, one that lived in the aftermath of the great Yucatan impact, in which fire from heaven began the process of declining warmth, the slow ice death of our planet? Would ten million years have been enough? Twenty? Imagine these beings, not human, not even primates; yet just as Andrewsarchus and Hyenadon shared a physical kinship, these beings suggested in their form what we would one day become. They built their kingdom on a planet that was entirely forest, a world-tree unlike anything humans today could possibly imagine. Were they even the first? Is it possible that they, too, were merely a reprise, an encore of sorts? After all, those metal spheres were billions of years old. That predates Vendian times, predates anything we know about the history of life on earth. How many times have we been down this road?

> Yggdrasil itself will moan, the ash that always was and waves
> over all that is. Its leaves will tremble, its limbs shiver and
> shake even as two take refuge deep within it. Everything in
> heaven and in earth and Hel will quiver.
> *Kevin Crossley-Holland,* **The Norse Myths**

It becomes possible to imagine in scales of time that seem ludicrous to poor temporary humans like us. But the facts are there to be seen; again and again, life on earth is dealt a savage blow and must crawl back from the abyss. We imagine that the cause is enormous rocks from space- and perhaps it is. But we've covered that song before, Tunguska and our old friend Jack the Ripper in Simon Whitechapel's "Guts and Roses," and we know that the Hermetic ideal can be inverted, that "as above, so below" contains implicitly the idea that "as below, so above." Did nations of amphibious "men" do battle in the Early Cambrian? Did saurians use magic to drop the Yucatan rock on themselves at the end of the Cretaceous? Did seemingly human yet actually inhuman mammalian precursors do something to push our world away from its temperate climate and towards this icy phase we endure today? Have we somehow in our racial mind "memories" twisted beyond all understanding, thoughts from other "men" on other "earths" that we tell each other as myths?

Probably not. The truth, as is so often the case, is probably way stranger than that. But it's pretty chilling to imagine that seemingly suicidal, fratricidal warfare might not merely be a human trait. That indeed, the blood that best fertilizes the roots of the World-Tree is mixed with ashes, just as the Norns knew so long ago, and that men that were not men may well have walked the road to Vigrid and the plain of Ragnarok before us. Was Andrewsarchus a Fenris? Did Basilosaurus play the role of the Midgarthsomr? Was Gullinbursti an entelodont? What do we hold in our myth webbing, and what does it mean, and why does it seem that everything repeats itself? Hell if I know. But making up my own versions is more satisfying than knowing anyway.

When Mongo Attacks!

Okay, it's 1934. Hitler's been in power in Germany for a year, Stalin has been engaging in a systematic purge of his enemies, and Mussolini is ignoring the League of Nations and marching through Ethiopia. Manchukuo is the beginning of the end for the Last Emperor of China. Despite the best efforts of many, the prophetic doomsaying of Churchill is coming true, and the world is slouching towards war.

Meanwhile, a TV reporter, an ex-football player, and a demented genius are headed to a planet named Mongo. At least in *some* worlds-worlds in which Alex Raymond's cartoon strip was drawn from life. But, as excellent as Raymond's vision was, I feel compelled to ask. Could Flash Gordon have actually prevented the invasion of Mongo?

Nope. C'mon, an *ex-football player?* As excellent as Dan Marino and John Elway may have been, I'm fairly sure that if you put one of them, Richard Feynman and Jane Pauley on an alien world, it wouldn't be *Feynman* who committed the inevitable mistake that got them all dead. (Okay, originally Flash was a polo player. *A polo player.* He's a corpse waiting to happen, he is.) No, Flash wouldn't last ten minutes, and I don't care how much a man of action he was. Let's be charitable, however; what with alien princessess digging his mojo and what not, let's assume that Flash actually managed to sabotage Ming's effort to bring Mongo to the earth system and use the tidal effect as a weapon. Cool.

Ming then kills Flash, enslaves Dale, and has Zarkov thrown in a dungeon until the old man either dies or co-operates. Sure, the invasion is pushed back (let's say three years)... but it's hardly *off.* Ming's got plenty of those cool movie serial rocket ships; he'll just invade earth the old fashioned way. Imagine the fleet of old-time starships, seemingly ludicrous to us, but each bristling with exotic energy weapons that may well work by a physics we can't understand, and protected by energy screens that make them invincible by the standards of the earth forces of 1937, their hulls scintillating and exotic, ringed and sleek like art-deco valkyries. Ming, in his great flagship, would no doubt chortle at the thought of his fleet ambushing the helpless primitives of the earth, even as he conquered the many races of Mongo so long before. Aura, at first despondent at the death of the exotic earth man, is now once again Ming's loyal daughter. Everything is going according to plan. Soon, the fleet will launch, and earth will tremble at the name of *Ming The Merciless!*

Of course, Ming has never been good at understanding women. Aura and Dale, both enraged at the death of their shared love-interest, have joined forces, and together they manage to steal a ship and escape the flagship, after inflicting enough damage on it to slow Ming's fleet. (The grandiose Ming would be enraged if his fleet went ahead without him; likewise, he'd hardly be likely to leave the *Crusher Of Mongo* behind.) Using the ship's communications array and Dale's journalistic smarts, the two women warn the earth of the coming of the Mongo fleet and crashland at Zarkov's old lab.

At first, the nations of the world (set on annihilating each other) ignore the warning. But there are those who know a bit about the wider world, men like Robert Heinlein, a naval officer and wide thinker, who manages to convince Roosevelt (by the simple expedient of bringing the president to see the wrecked flier) that the two women are sincere. Soon, Roosevelt has a team of his best and brightest working on the secrets of the flier, men like Oppenheimer, Einstein, Goddard- and of course Clark "Doc" Savage and his allies, who know a little something about science and a lot about action.

However, these are hardly the only people who would stand up and take notice. Once Bundist spies informed their Nazi masters that Roosevelt was taking the alien threat seriously, could the Austrian painter allow his Third Reich to fall behind? While many of the "Jew physicists" had already left (Einstein in '35) the rest would be put to work on coming up with a way to counter this threat. Russia would likely follow suit. However, these two brutish nations would not be the most likely rival to Oppenheimer and Savage. That would be the Mad Doctor himself, *Fu Manchu*, with his diabolical genius and his ability to outthink anyone, and *Shiwan Khan*, the reincarnation of the great Chinggis himself, with his warrior heart and strange powers of the mind, who would doubtless ally with the Doctor in the face of the Mongovian threat. These two madmen, while hardly friends to the civilized world, would have no desire to see it enslaved by barbarous aliens.

By 1938, the War of the Worlds begins, and the first stroke no doubt belongs to Mongo. Despite the warnings, the Fascist nations saw no reason to turn from their course, and Ming would no doubt see them as the strongest rivals to his rule. So the skies of the world are suddenly flooded with the great shells of the Mongo fleet, and in one startling strike the powerful armies, navies, and air forces of Germany, Italy and Japan are blasted into submission in a battle that no doubt takes only minutes. October 29, 1938 sees the annihilation of the Axis Powers, and no one celebrates, evil madmen they had been, but human, and what has befallen the earth now would seem to be subjugation from beyond the stars! Then, from his flagship, the face of the *Merciless One* beams forth in holographic projections across the skies of the world.

"People of the pathetic planet earth! Know that you, as many greater peoples also have discovered, are totally helpless before the stupefying power of Ming! I have defeated your mightiest nations in a matter of moments, and if any resistance continues, I shall do the same to the rest of your meaningless race! If you display the wisdom of the vanquished and offer me your necks, you may yet survive, cringing curs though you be! So speaks your future emperor, Ming!"

Little does he know that in secret meetings, Roosevelt and Chamberlain have agreed to assemble their greatest minds, men like Wayland Smith and Alan Turing, the elderly yet still dangerous Moriarty, the American Oppenheimer/Savage group... with the Si Fan brotherhood's Dark Doctor himself, for at stake is the fate of the world! And not only these mind have turned themselves to the idea of how to engage the invading forces, for from the ranks of his secret network, Kent Allard has managed to place one of his own among the number of Clark Savage's group, the absent-minded but brilliant Reinhardt Lane. While Shiwan Khan suspects his nemesis, and Savage knows from bitter experience that Lane and the Shadow are somehow connected, for their own reasons each turns a blind eye. Soon, with the date of the invasion at hand, they concoct a desperate bluff, based upon their researches on the crashed flier and a suggestion by Dale Arden.

Actor Orson Welles is engaged to conduct a radio address of *another* sort, a deliberate bluff that mankind is being invaded by *another* alien conquerer! While Ming and his fleet scan desperately for signs of this strange new complication, the Doctor of the East and his old nemesis Wayland Smith, working alongside Doc Savage, engage a *disruption beamer* that disengages the shielding technology of the Mongo fleet. Then, before the shocked aliens can comprehend what is happening, Shiwan Khan, using ancient magics to conquer space and time, leads an attack on Ming's flagship, knowing full well that among his men is an imposter, his enemy *The Shadow!* Ming's men could deal with pure force,but the strange mind-tricks of the Asian Khan and "He who knows what evil lurks even in the hearts of alien men" are too much for them, especially when combined with the limitless brutality both men are all too willing to dispense upon their foes.

Even as Ming attempts to respond to this new threat, he is jolted by another surprise, for piloting a reconstructed flier is Robert A. Heinlein, of the newly constituted US Naval Space Force! Heinlein ferries Doc Savage and his men aboard the craft (ramming it, which is the most expedient way to get on board, especially since *his* shields still work) and the two contingents meet in Ming's command chamber! Despite the loyalty of Ming's personal guard, the savagery of the Beast Men of Mongo, and their superior weapons, the two-fisted heroics of Savage and Wayland and the relentless stone deadliness of Khan and the Shadow lead to the death of the Merciless One... who erred in thinking the earth bereft of that particular quality itself!

And as our saga ends, with the death of Ming and the retreat of the Mongovian Fleet, we know that while not one but *two* evils have fallen in short order- the madness of the Axis Powers and the cruelty of Ming- there is still much to be done. For what of Zarkov, still a prisoner on Mongo, which will now no doubt revert to barbarity until a new warlord arises, if the powers of the earth do nothing to prevent it? And what of Shiwan Khan and Fu Manchu, allies once but now deadly threats with access to technology far superior to any seen before? What will the new Allied Space Force do? And what of the Shadow, who was forced to reveal the depths of his network? Will he be hounded by the governments of the world, or courted as the only man capable of standing against Shiwan Khan? Will Fu Manchu head to Mongo, seeking to replace Ming as a more capable and ruthless warlord? The future, as always, is as yet unwritten.

Postscript: *Kansas, November 1938*

After the invasion was over, and the people of earth had a chance to take stock of the new, larger universe of which they were a part, a curious event happened. In a Kansas wheatfield, Jonathan Kent, who'd spent his whole life being a typical isolationist American, saw a streaking red and blue *something* blast across the sky. Without thinking, he hopped into his Ford and rolled down after it, knowing it would come down in his back forty.

"Holy sweet jumping Jesus, I ain't but thinking that's a rocket ship. One o'them Mongo boys?" He gets to the edge of the crater the ship- curiously undented- has plowed in his field. Staring over the edge, he looks down...

And beholds a small, squalling infant, also strangely unhurt.

"Well, according to that Dale Arden reporter-lady, them Mongo folks is people too." Ignoring his fear, Jonathan climbs down to help the child.

Remember, it's 1938. All sorts of things happened that year....

Cattle of the Mind

Man is a plural being. When we speak of ourselves ordinarily, we speak of "I". We say "I did this" or "I think this", "I want to do this"-but this is a mistake. There is no such "I" or rather there are hundreds, thousands of little "I"s in every one of us.
G.I. Gurdjieff, **Beelzebub's Tales to his Grandson**

In his book *The Origins of Consciousness in the Breakdown of the Bicameral Mind* (of which, sadly, I no longer have a copy) Julian Jaynes argues that, over the course of thousands of years of human mental evolution, the ego developed from an agglomeration of separate fragments of self into a fused singular entity, an "I" if you will, that ran and directed the mind as its sole occupant. During that period of evolution, according to Jaynes, the nascent self was bombarded by voices and visions that it interpreted as the will of various entities- call them spirits, call them gods- that were in effect nothing more than shards of the self, not integrated into a singular being. Even to this day, Jaynes argues, the process is incomplete and can be undone by a significant enough trauma, leading to the formation of psychoses, split personalities and the like. It's an interesting, albeit controversial, theory. Jaynes' theory argues that as recently as the Trojan War (1200 BC) mankind was in the habit of evoking these framentary selves ("Sing, oh Muse, of... ") as *gods,* such as Zeus and Athena. A very interesting theory.

What if the truth is exactly inverse? What if, instead of our minds forming slowly while we misunderstand these separate voices as gods... what if they were gods? What if the reason the pagan dieties fell into disrepute is that we subconsciously *knew* that they weren't going to be answering any of our prayers, *because we tore them apart and used them as mortar to connect our minds?* And what if it is this very subconscious understanding that leads to the Frazerian concept of "eating the god?" (Oh, sure, snicker. But eating the god in a sexual connotation has much the same effect; see Robert Anton

Wilson's *Shroedinger's Cat* series for details of fellatio and cunnilingus as sacred rites.)

> From this interesting passage we learn that the ancient Mexicans, even before the arrival of Christian missionaries, were fully acquainted with the doctrine of transubstantiation and acted upon it in the solemn rites of their religion. They believed that by consecrating bread their priests could turn it into the very body of their god, so that all who thereupon partook of the consecrated bread entered into a mystic communion with the deity by receiving a portion of his divine substance into themselves. The doctrine of transubstantiation... was also familiar to the Aryans of ancient India long before the spread and even the rise of Christianity.
> *Sir James George Frazer,* **The Golden Bough**

Almost every religious system on the face of the earth has had the concept of transforming gross physical matter into pure, perfect, divine and glorified stuff. From the ancient myth of Tammuz being subsumed into the corn to the story of Mitras, slaying the divine bull that we might all live on in it (and how similar is that to the tale of Gilgamesh and Enkidu slaying the Bull of Heaven, he asks?), and the apotheosis of Heracles, man has dreamed of somehow absorbing or becoming a god. (Hell, that's what *apotheosis* means, after all.) But over time, as the human mindset has developed and become increasingly more sophisticated, our divine landscape has become ever more sparse and bare.

We have moved from being a species in a world *teeming* with signs and wonders and portents and spirits and gods to a species that can't even decide if there's *anything* out there. We have broken down the gods, chewed them up, and swallowed them into ourselves. Why else would we respond so to archetypes? Those tiny fragments of the divine we've used to prop us up are still there, still resonating with each other. *We still hunger to be everything and nothing at once.* (To be interconnected yet fragmentary. To be more than mere humans, locked together in solitude, yet to be one with all things.) Humanity's spiritual development, paradoxically, has taken the opposite tack from most creation myths, wherein out of nothing more and more complexity forms. From vast complexity, we've distilled our gods down to One, and now we argue as to whether or not even *He* exists.

Look at Christianity, which to me seems to infest the Western mind like a disease. It's all about the god-eating, and we know it. "Take, and eat... this is my body, which will be given for you, and the forgiveness of all sins." Christianity could be said to be a Western way to try to eat that last unswallowable God, or a means for Yahweh, alone amongst the heavens, to prevent us from doing so by *giving us a substitute.* Is Christ just the bait and switch, the inverse of the Frazerian king for a day? Did Yahweh deliberately set up this young Jewish carpenter, creating him out of the womb of a virgin, so that we wouldn't suspect the trickery and would take him as a surrogate god for our divine consumption?

> One of the authors of this emerging view was Nobel physicist Wolfgang Pauli. In particular, he was fascinated by parallels between his own quantum theories and Carl Jung's description of the collective unconscious. Just as probes into matter had led to the discovery of a subjective principle in the form of the observer-participator, so the deepest study of human consciousness had led Jung to an objective principle in the form of his universal ideas, or archetypes, which structured human understanding. Thus, on the deepest levels of reality mind and body, matter and psyche, observer and observed, particle and wave seemed potentially linked by abstract codes and patterns. Though these could not be directly perceived, they could be deduced from their impact on more accessible levels and expressed symbolically. In the scientific field the symbolism used was mathematics. In the field of consciousness, it was image and myth.
> *Sylvia Fraser, **The Quest for the Fourth Monkey***

Rupert Sheldrake, the daddy of morphic resonance, argues that there is a field effect created by living beings that helps steer and direct their evolution and development, telling an embryonic chick's cells, for example, which ones are to become a wing and which ones are to become a heart. In mankind's case, it would be morphic resonance that told our ancestors "It is gigantic frontal lobe time." Morphic resonance, or the morphogenic field if you prefer, could also be called by the name Dylan Thomas gave it, "The force that through the green fuse drives the flower."

Maybe that's too long and poetic for some, but I like it. Just as

The Force drives our physical evolution, I believe it drives our mental evolution. Ever notice that inventions come in clumps? People struggled for years to develop a heavier-than-air flying machine- da Vinci probably designed a working one- but it wasn't till the Wright brothers actually did it that the explosion of competing ideas suddenly resulted in dozens of different kinds of airplanes. There's also the case of the Pascal calculator and the Babbage engine. Does "good" fear certain kinds of invention because they require the consumption of gods? "Steam engines come when it's steam engine time," as a teacher of mine once said (he was quoting Sagan, who was paraphrasing Jung, and so on), and perhaps that's what inspiration (from the Latin meaning 'to breathe in' is all about.

Imagine gods not as creators, but creations. Archetypes, generated by the human mind as the morphic resonance produced that splendid brain of ours (and it truly is an epic feat of evolution to have so quickly produced such an efficent conceptual engine), become gods and spirits and move through the world, until we, knowing that they are but waste energy generated by us, reabsorb them into ourselves in an attempt to recycle that terrible, powerful pure thought essence. We farm the gods. We grow them like wheat in the fields of the astral plane/collective unconsciousness/quantum universe/morphogenic field, and then we reap them and grind them into the spiritual bread we need to inspire us to feats of creativity. Some of us, like Leonardo da Vinci and Pascal and Babbage and Newton and Leibniz and Archimedes and Jules Verne- some of us are getting the bread earlier or more often, but we all partake in the great god feast. We eat them. We are the predators of the gods.

No wonder "good" views the spread of knowledge with such alarm; no wonder "God" burns Galileos and tries to calcify the world with empty cataloging, to divert science from what it can be, the love of knowledge and wisdom, to mere statistical number crunching. To separate magick from it, when the two are wedded and should be always one. To keep us ignorant, that we might not aspire to newer, greater feats of invention- and so need a greater source of the divine infusion. We eat archetypes to dream, and we dream to create, and we create to become divine ourselves. We stalk the gods like ravening wolves falling upon kine.

Here There Be Dragons

Thank God for Yale University's obsession with strange books. If not for them, where the hell would the Voynich Manuscript be? Well, probably nowhere, since if they hadn't been willing to pay ol' Voynich for the damn thing, he'd probably not have bought it in the first place. However, as useful as that is, today I'm actually wondering about another book of theirs, *The Vinland Map and the Tartar Relation.*

Actually two books discovered together, this strange tome is the key to a whole new past, and strange aeons for the American continents. The Tartar Relation is an undisputedly geniune handwritten book dating back to 1440, but discovered within a copy of the book in 1957 was a world map showing what looked to a curator at Yale to be the coast of Canada, labeled Vinlanda Insula. Wormholes between the two seem to line up, indicating that a third book, now lost, was bound together with them. This would seem to indicate that someone in Europe knew about the Viking trips across the Atlantic some fifty two years before our boy Christopher got rolling.

However, little problems keep popping up. For instance, if you go to L'Anse Aux Meadows and look around the Viking settlement, you'll notice no sign of something important- namely, grape vines. There are none there. So, since we're supposedly in Vinland... shouldn't there be such? Well, yes. But that's not the only dissonant note in all this. Here's another one for you... what, pray tell, was the book that somehow brought together The Tartar Relation and Vinlanda Insula? The two would seem damn unrelated on first view, wouldn't they? What the hell do Tartars, the Turks of the North Caucasus mountains, have to do with Vinland?

Maybe a lot. In 1513, Muhiddin Piri al-Din ibn-Hajji Mehmed drew a map for his master, the Ottoman Turkish Sultan Selim I, father of Suleyman the Magnificent (who at the time was a nineteen year old princeling in his father's house), and this map would come down to us as the Piri Reis map, Reis being Turkish for "admiral." This strange map seemingly (after a great deal of adjustment by geographer Charles Hapgood) represents the coast of the South American and Antarctic continents... save that the Antarctic of the Piri Reis map has no ice. Furthermore, Piri describes the land of his map as "a land of ruins, filled with white-haired monsters and also six horned oxen... The country is a waste. Everything is in ruin and it is said that there are large snakes here. For this reason the Portugese infidels did not land on these shores and these are also said to be very hot." Okay, I could almost buy that Piri got lucky enough to draw Antarctica's coast without ice, but to describe it as a hot wasteland packed with snakes and ruins? Doesn't sound like any Antarctica I know. Our Tartar admiral assures us, however, that he drew these maps based on those used by Christopher Columbus on his expedition, as well as older maps left behind by Alexander the Great himself.

Okay, so now things are getting weirder. We have a Vinland with no vines, and an Antarctica that rivals the Sahara, and both connect up with the Tartars of the Caucasus Mountains. But wait, there's more!

In the 1370s, Sir John Mandeville wrote his Travels. Now, it's not widely known, but this is the book that Columbus used to draw up the plans for his journey, and to bone up on his Chinese. The Travels are a fascinating read, filled with Amazons in Azerbaijan (stolen from Herodotus, of course, who also placed them in the Sauromatae north of the Caucasus- in Tartary, as a matter of fact) and cyclopean Arimapasians and canine Natumerians, off on distant isles past India, which is of course where James Churchward argues up and down that Mu can be found, that ancient homeland for all humanity. Past India is also where Ctesias, Herodotus' Persian-loving rival for the title of Father of History, felt that magical creatures like the griffin, manticore and unicorn could be found. Which reminds one of the Persian mountain of paradise, Kar-i-Farn, which mutated into 'Calyferne' when the Hashishin tried to invade France via the Pyrenees and their Spanish conquests- and thus, we come back to Columbus, whose patrons were the Spanish monarchs Ferdinand and Isabella who'd so recently ejected the Moors from Spain. Was Sir John really a simple liar and teller of tall tales, or was he the maintainer of an ancient tradition that linked the peoples of the Caspian Sea with another, far more distant land?

Still, while the linkage is suggestive, we haven't yet discovered how it is possible for Leif Erikson to find vines where there were none, or for the Turkish admiral to write of a superannuated wasteland filled with heat and seething with serpents, when there is naught but ice where he placed them. At least, naught but ice on our world. We know the Hashishin were creatures of alternate states of consciousness, their arts passed down from the very Persian magi who Alexander the Great so thoroughly destroyed in his mad rush to power. Is it possible that these travelers' tales were not narratives of simple physical journeys, but of hybrid expeditions both on the ocean-sea of our world and of others? Let us look very carefully at this paradox from the other angle.

The pre-Columbian American civilizations seem to exist from some point in the distant past to the time of the mariners with ageless dignity. From the theorized crossing of the Bering Strait to the invasion of the Spaniards they changed and grew yet maintained themselves. However, while there is evidence on the American side of the migration, there is less concrete evidence for the Asian half, which is odd, as Asia was their starting point. However, if you look at the supposed previous communications between East and West, you will be struck by one salient fact: in each case, when myths of strange gods from the East are passed down, they are almost always benevolent in aspect. Quite a contrast from the reality brought to America by Cortez and Pizarro, eh? Similarly, in narratives like St. Brendan's on his travels to the isles of the West, while many strange and wonderous events take place, one doesn't hear much that reminds one of the Cahokia Mound Builders of North America, or the Toltecs of Mexico and South America. Brendan would have been within a hundred years of the Maya empire of Shield Jaguar Lord- yet we hear of nothing that is even remotely similar to the distinctive society of the Maya as he would have found them. Instead, we get tales of unnatural beauties and timeless days spent in ageless comfort, and warnings that to return to Ireland from the Western Isles is to court instant death, as to step off of the mysterious "steeds" of the Western Ones is to age into dust. Hy Brazil is a dangerous place from which to return, it seems.

And so it goes. What if, before the Columbian mission to the "New" World, these voyagers were traveling not merely in space, but across space-time itself? What if the Piri Reis map is not of any Antarctica we know now, but of the Antarctic as it looked hundreds of millions of years ago? The adjustments that Hapgood made were not merely corrections, but rather allowances for geological drift over millions of years. The snakes were not mere snakes, but enormous reptiles from the Jurassic or Cretaceous. Similarly, Leif Erikson found vines in Vinland because he traveled back before the Ice Age, his Aesgaardian religion prompting the unstable region in the Atlantic to transport him to a land similar to the Midgaard of the sagas. In this conception, the Atlantic itself was somehow temporally "unstable," perhaps due to the great devastation of the ancient cataclysm so imperfectly preserved by James Churchward's ridiculous Mu theory or Ignatius Donnelly's antediluvian world, perhaps due to the actions of Persian magi seeking to escape Alexander the Great along the web of magickal exploration that branched out from Kar-i-Farn to girdle the whole world, or even perhaps due to the efforts of the wise "strangers from the east" who advised the Maya and Cahokia to work powerful magicks in order to ensure that the east and the west would be unable to make contact. For that matter, who is to say that the Persians were not, in fact, the very people who came to America from the east, desperate for an escape the American culture was only too happy to provide them?

Of course, the ones who were left behind joined with Alexander rather than suffer his wrath, and are the ancestors of the Hashishin of the Arab world and the Iberian mages who attempted to graft Kar-i-Farn onto California- never realizing that it was already here. Perhaps, in fact, the magi of the Americans convinced certain tribes- the Cahokia, the Inca descendants of Viracocha (who, like Ormazhd, was a sun god), and the Anasazi- to depart with them for the past... or the future. Is the end of the Maya calendar in 2012 a harbinger of their return? For that matter, how did Columbus manage to breach this effect? Was it slowly shrinking, or did his studies of Mandeville lead him to The Vinland Map and the Tartar Relation, and the mysterious master tome they were both linked by... and to secrets of otheworldly navigation? Columbus took being becalmed in the Sargasso very well; was that because he knew he was inching his way around time-space portals like icebergs in the Atlantic?

Well, probably not. But I guess we'll see, won't we? For that matter, there's no reason to limit the time displacement to just a time displacement; perhaps it's a series of shattered gateways to all sorts of universes. Perhaps Piri Reis' map is of an Antarctica in a universe where the poles of our planet shifted, creating an ecological catastrophe? Perhaps the Bermuda Triangle is nothing more than the still-healing scab of reality, attempting to grow back over the wound left behind by the ancient catastophe, a rip in space and time itself, and the various pirate treasure maps left behind are not revealing pieces of eight and doubloons at all, but boltholes in the firmament of existence. It would explain why there's less evidence of the migrations in Asia than in America: in the reality in Eurasia, fewer people left for the land bridge, but the distortions caused a different migration from a different universe to end up in the Americas. Either that, or perhaps the same group simply showed up from multiple realities.

So, which universe were *your* ancestors from?

Lord of the Etheric Vortex

In 1867, one of the most brilliant physicists of the day came up with an entirely new theory to explain how atoms of hydrogen and oxygen behave differently. This was at the tail end of a career that had begun when he was a young man of fifteen whose papers had to be read to the Royal Society by others, because it was felt he would embarrass the grown men who populated that august body. In the fullness of time, that young man had grown into the person who discovered the second law of thermodynamics, first postulated absolute zero, and who developed the moving coil galvanometer, all of which have made his reputation one that exists to this day. (Of course, Kelvin also predicted that heavier than air flight was impossible, so it wasn't all peaches and cream.)

Yet William Thomson, Lord Kelvin, had some problems with the established order of physics as it had come down to him, and like Michael Faraday before him, Kelvin was fascinated with the properties of energy and matter. This would lead him to the vortex. And the vortex would lead us... nowhere.

> The dazzling idea that struck him in 1867 seems to have developed from his observation of smoke rings. A simple way to produce these is to introduce smoke into a box that has a round hole in one of its sides. If you give the opposite side of the box a vigorous slap (particularly if that side is made of some soft material like toweling), a smoke ring will shoot out of the hole. But if you try to stop the smoke ring with your hand, it will not dissolve like a bubble as you might expect. It will simply bounce off your hand like a rubber ball. If you make two smoke rings collide head on, they vibrate from the impact like two charging bulls meeting head on, then bounce away from each other. In short, they behave like solid objects.
> *Colin Wilson, **The Mammoth Encyclopedia of the Unsolved***

Kelvin's explanation of atomic behavior was that each atom was a vortex of energy, capable of forming different substances because each vortex was capable of great variation in size, speed, and so on. This answered the question of why an atom of hydrogen behaves so differently than an atom of oxygen, if they are composed of the same primordial particles. Kelvin's theory of atomic vortices had a certain similarity to superstring theory, in that he argued that atomic vortices resembled strings, and that the rotational and linear strains in these strings produced variations that were, in effect, the atoms. However, one of the greatest limitations in Kelvin's theory was that it required etheric motion; in effect, the vortex is an eddy in the universal ether. Of course, we all know there is no ether. Vortex theory suffered its most crippling blow when another scientist named Thomson, who had previously distinguished himself in vortex theory, discovered the electron in 1897. The knell sounded for the vortex.

Or did it? It seems strange to me that the magnetic vortex theory is in essence an exact inversion of atomic vortex theory (instead of vortices of energy producing atoms, atoms produce vortices of energy) with the electron at center stage, especially since it was Alfred Mayer who helped convince Kelvin of the existence of the vortex with his experiments involving magnets suspended in a fluid. So, if there is no ether to act as a fluid medium for the energy vortex and electrons, which supply the necessary atomic cohesion by means of electrostatic repulsion,the electrons in the atoms of the table repel the electrons in your hands, thus keeping all the empty space in each from just sliding past the other, like galaxies collding. That's what they tell us.

I've mentioned elsewhere the strange synchronicity of subatomic particles; how, in an experiment involving a beam of light and two pinholes, rings of light will be cast on a far wall. These rings will have black lines where the photons passing through one of the pinholes interefere with the photons passing through the other. Now, if you dim the light so that only one photon at a time can pass through one of the pinholes and slowly expose a photographic plate- well, once you develop the plate, guess what? *The black lines where the photons interfere with each other will still be there.* Despite the fact that there can only be one photon passing through one possible pinhole at a time- thus, no intereference- the black lines continue.

Those black lines. Hugh Everett argued that they resulted because we misunderstand the nature of photons. In other words, the "wave-particle duality" is a misnomer, resulting from our brains' inability to understand potentiality as opposed to reality. There is no actual wave; there is no actual stream of photons. There is only one photon, and it exists in what Everett calls "the wave of possibilities." If there is one photon passing through the hole, and yet it intereferes with itself despite the fact that there is no other photon passing through the other hole, then all possible paths in the photon's track must be accessible by the photon at once. In other words, the photon is in two places at once.

Is that possible? It does not seem so, but we have to remember Robert Anton Wilson and his brief explanation of neurolinguistic programming, as William S. Burroughs and Korzybski detailed it. It seems impossible because we are using the word *place* in an all-too-limited way. Likewise, when we look at Kelvin's vortex, we dismiss it because it was conceived before the existence of the electron (another subatomic particle, like the photon) was known. But does the existence of the electron (if it even exists at all... but I'll assume, for now, that it does) invalidate the vortex? There is one photon, yet it interferes with itself. How?

Because there was only one photon, ever, and it exists in all places at once. Our definition of place is a limited, temporally fixed point in three dimensions. If you've read about superstring theory, or read the Qabbalah for that matter and seen the emanations of the sephiroth, you know about the interconnected layers of reality. (As an aside, isn't it spooky how well the Qabbalah and superstring theory coincide? It always catches me off my guard.) These extradimensionally extruded *strings* exist as a web, constantly slipping into and out of our limited universe at levels both macro- and microscopic; we cannot truly see them. They seem to be particles because that is how we have chosen to describe them, and neurolinguistics creates a feeback loop in our minds, so that how we describe reality becomes how we percieve it. But think of the particles not as particles at all, but as filaments traveling an ouroboros path through levels of reality too compressed to be understood, constantly tangling and weaving and knotting, forming vortices in the incredibly dynamic, *fluid* medium of the superstring continuum. Hell, call it ether if you want; we may not see it, feel it, or be able to detect it, but can we do any of that with empty space? The way we define a physical object is that it has mass and takes up space, but what *is* space? Nothing. And the ether is just nothing on a bigger scale.

All very fine, but what does it have to do with anything? Well, I'm getting to that. Because one of the things the vortex allows for are the *electrical people*. You know, like Angelique Cottin of La Perriere, France, who began to display strange symptoms in January of 1846?

> Whenever she went near objects they retreated from her. The slightest touch of her hand or dress was enough to send heavy furniture spinning away or jumping up and down; and no one could hold an object she also was holding without it writhing from her grasp. A study group was appointed by the Academy of Sciences, and a famous physicist, François Arago, published in the **Journal des debats** (February 1846). He noted that her power seemed to be like electro-magnetism - compasses went wild in her proximity - that it was stronger in the evening, and seemed to emanate from her left side, particularly her left wrist and elbow.
> *Bob Rickard and John Michel, **Unexplained Phenomena: A Rough Guide Special***

I don't think I even need to point ou that the left side of the body is controlled by the right hemisphere of the brain, the one that controls our more creative and intuitive impulses, although I will anyway, just in case the connection between Kelvin's vortices, superstring theory, the Qabbala and strangeness like our electrical friends wasn't enough. Not to mention all the reports of people who could glow with light from within, burn themselves to death, ignore intense heat... all of which are effects that could be achieved by control over photons, electrons, etc- the electromagnetic spectrum. The Gordian knots we call atoms are made up of bunched strings, and what if some people can intuitively pull on those strings? After all, we are all just collections of the same strings; we're nexuses of vortices. All we have to do is unlearn what our programming tells us is impossible. *As above, so below.* A hoary old chestnut, true; but in the etheric macrocosm, just possibly a good guide.

Massive

Hubble's sharpness allowed us to make this remarkable new
type of observation, successfully demonstrating our ability to
see very small objects....
CNN Online, June 21ˢᵗ, 2001

In this case, the very small objects were merely 80 times the size
of the planet earth. The next time my ego begins raging out of control,
I'll try to keep that in mind. This herd of "small" objects make up 10
percent of the mass of M22, the globular cluster they currently reside
in, although only six of them were actually photographed. Ten percent
of a *globular cluster*, a damn *galaxy*. Just... wandering along,
untethered by gravity. If there really are so many of them, it would
seem unlikely that they were rogue planets.

This is the fun part of being me. Because, while astronomers
and physicists have to seriously sit down and wonder what these
things are (nonbaryonic matter? embryonic stars or planets? loosely-
packed swarms of cometary matter? gravitational eddies creating
occlusions in stellar dust, creating the effect of mass where there is
none?), I can sit back and think to myself, "Hey, a herd of whales!"
Because that's what they remind me of, a pod of whales, swimming
through space. Imagine these enormous beasts, the smallest of which
must have a gravitational field that puts our planet's measly 1G to
shame; with a size approaching gas giant ranges, and a density more
like a terrestrial world, they could bend whole solar systems just by
passing through them. Hell, planets the size of Earth could well be
pulled from their orbits by such behemoths and dragged into the
void. That could be exactly what Hubble has taken a picture of,
here: a creature surrounded by worlds that it has stolen from solar
systems throughout M22. If the quote in the article about 10 percent
of M22's mass turns out to be accurate, then we suddenly come up
with an image of a massive ecosystem of stolen worlds orbiting beasts

that dwarf them. (And it is possible to think that those planets need not become lifeless; Jupiter gives off a great deal of energy, perhaps enough to support life, so one of these creatures might do so as well.)

Why would this benefit the behemoths? Well, perhaps it doesn't: perhaps the planets are unnoticed by them. On the other hand, it is equally possible that the creatures are composed on nonbaryonic matter, or perhaps something even more exotic, and they require orbiting companions to stablize them as they travel through space. Or perhaps the tidal stress of orbiting companions serves to scrape dead matter from their bodies the way birds do for rhinos on the savannah. And, for that matter, we're ignoring the possible benefits for the behemoths in having the ecosystems of those worlds accompany them into empty space. Societies of intelligent beings could inhabit the outer skin of the behemoths much as they would a planet; indeed, entire ecosystems could support themselves there. In other words, as they grow mature (which leads us into the interesting supposition of how they reproduce at all) they acquire companions to aid them in their travels through space.

And imagine the intelligence such a being could possess. If Sheldrake's theory of morphic resonance is true, and intelligent beings are affected by it, then this behemoth could well kidnap planets in order to gain from the overlapping of their own unique morphogenic fields, using them to become even more intelligent, more varied. It becomes possible to conceive of deliberate selection of those worlds with the most varied and robust ecosystems, the ones most likely to survive being torn away from their original orbits and the catastrophes that would cause, in order for the behemoth to grow ever more diverse. These beings are like hunter-gatherers, and those planets with the most interestingly widespread systems, with life branching out to fill a variety of niches- these are the ripe fruits that they pluck from the vine and make use of. Inhuman, titanic, as concerned with the individual types of life on these particular worlds as we are with the microbes on an apple. Is it possible that the force that through the green fuse drives the flower drives *their* green age as well? (With all love and respect to Dylan Thomas, of course.) Do they *eat* the collective existence of Gaia-beings?

Gardeners of the galaxies. And we aren't even bugs to them -

we're like mold. Perhaps we are the ergot that poisons them, drives them mad with new thoughts that they cannot bear or understand... or the penicillin that cures them of diseases and helps fight off infection. It may be possible to interact safely with the great beasts of space. Then again, maybe they are the ones who should be worried about us.

Anyway, just something that came to mind. Have a nice night. Oh, and on the subject of how they reproduce, well, the first thing that comes to mind is spore-release, and the first idea for a good incubator would be one of those worlds caught in its gravitational web. Perhaps these beings die when they spawn, and when the world-eggs hatch, they batten upon the immense corpse of their mother before scattering. Unpleasant consequences for all the other forms of life involved, I suppose.

Men of Peace

In the fear known through the Far East as "Koro" - for the Malay word for turtle - the sufferer imagines his penis is withdrawing into his body; in females this applied to breasts and labia. Koro is not a trivial phenomenon; the outbreak in Singapore in 1967 resulted in the hospitalization of 446 men and 23 women in a single day. Medical studies of the phenomenon are full of tales of victims' bizarre attempts to prevent their genitals being seized by "fox spirits" or vanishing forever, including the application of special clamps. The novelist Anthony Burgess, in his autobiography *Little Wilson and Big God* (1987), describes the desperate behavior of a terrified Chinese koro victim in Kuala Lumpur: "He stole a superfine jeweller's knife and rammed it in, screaming on the sunlit street."
Bob Rickard and John Michell , **Unexplained Phenomena: A Rough Guide Special**

First off, yes, he stabbed himself in the penis. In order to prevent it from retracting into his body, at that. I don't pretend to know why. Before we get to feeling smug, there have been plenty of outbreaks of strange coordinated dementia in the West (I don't use the term "mass hysteria' because, in my opinion, it has been totally dishonored by those that use it to explain any and all weirdness that they stumble upon) like the case of the Mattoon, Illinois strangeness often referred to as "The Mad Gasser." In the summer of 1944, as World War II rolled towards its grim conclusion, a town of some 16,000 or so souls experienced something that defies conventional explanation. Either the town magnified a few disconnected reports into a surge of lunacy that swept them along its flood channel, or something else entirely happened that would require us to believe that a strange person was sneaking around a town in Illinois anesthetizing people with gas while wearing high-heeled shoes.

No, seriously.

> Even in the face of this official denial of his existence, the
> gasser made one last house call. On the evening of the
> thirteenth a witness saw a "woman dressed in man's clothing"
> spray gas through a window into Bertha Burch's bedroom.
> The next morning Mrs. Burch and her adult son found
> footprints of high-heeled shoes under the window.
> *Jerome Clark,* **Unexplained!**

Okay, we'll make a quick effort to round up the partygoers in Mattoon, because believe you me, we've got plenty of stops on our tour of the crazy that men do. Starting on August 31 and ending on September 13, residents of Mattoon began reporting feeling dizzy, nauseous and even paralyzed. Soon, Mrs. Aline Kearney reported that she saw a tall man dressed in black wearing a tight cap standing outside her bedroom window. The local paper reported that Mrs. Kearney was the first victim of a mysterious assailant. One report led the police to discover a tube of lipstick outside the window of a family who reported symptoms like "sensations similar to coming in contact with an electrical current" and also "burning, swelling, bleeding and vomiting." By the twelfth, the police were ready to blame the press for overreporting and sensationalizing the events at Mattoon, although this announcement didn't prevent the apparition or what have you that gassed the Burches on the thirteenth.

You probably think that this is an anomaly, the kind of event brought about by a kernel of truth (a strange prowler) and blown all out of proportion by hype and fear. Well, if it is, there are a lot more of these anomalous events than you'd expect. A mere decade earlier, a similar panic had occurred in Botetourt County, Virginia between December of 1933 and January of 1934. Unless one suspects the people of Mattoon of *plagiarizing* their panic, which would have been difficult, since the events of Botetourt were only reported outside of Virginia by a brief mention in the *New York Times* in one article on January 22, 1934, it seems we must accept both as geniune. Basically, the occupants of an isolated farm reported three incidents of gas being introduced into their house on December 22, with symptoms including "nausea, headaches, facial swelling" and suchlike. Sounding similar to Mattoon? And, as at Mattoon, the only evidence in this incident was again *a woman's high-heeled print.*

What does this mean? Are armies of androgynous

anesthesiologists attacking our heartland? And what, you may ask, does this have to do with the Halifax panic of 1938, where a phantom with a razor appeared out of the dark and cut people, only to vanish as quickly as he came and evade the police as if they were standing still? As this case endured, it too took on the trappings of hysteric delusion, with press headlines becoming more frantic and both police and citizen groups helpless to prevent the attacks, and eventually the police ended the whole thing by declaring it "imagination at work." This despite the fact that several of the victims had corporeal wounds. Or, for that matter, the sheep panic of Berkshire, wherein thousands of sheep were found panicked over a wide area for no obvious causes on November 3, 1888. Maybe Jack the Ripper stopped in Berkshire on his way into the mists of mystery and they fled for their lives. Somehow, I doubt it. Let us not leave unexamined other cases where the intersection of Real Avenue and Fantastic Boulevard got snarled up.

> Until 11 P.M., when all concerned packed into a car and roared at top speed to the Hopkinsville police station seven miles away, the witnesses repeatedly saw and shot at the creatures, which would roll over and escape, propelling themselves with their arms and hands. Their legs, skinny and inflexible, seemed to have no other function than to orient them vertically. If the creatures were in a tree or on the roof when hit, they would float, not fall, to the ground. At no time did they display overt hostility. The observers had no idea how many of the creatures there were. They could be certain only that there were at least two, because they saw that number at the same time.
> *Jerome Clark,* **Unexplained!**

Other cases of mysterious attacks abound, like the one at Cape Ann, in Massachusetts (which is a pretty damn weird state anyway, all things considered) in 1692, where Ebenezer Babson saw two men leave his house and flee into the cornfield, only to find that his family inside the house had seen no such men. He saw them twice more and eventually got the local garrison to travel with him in pursuit, who had now grown to a party of six. Upon engaging these men, they found them to be strangely invulnerable to their muskets, and capable of returning their fire. Upon surrounding and shooting down one of these strangers, the garrison group moved in for the kill... only to find him vanished. Later, after having gained an additional five men, these odd intruders apparently engaged in some sort of mystical ritual which was interrupted by another salvo of arms from the garrison. This, of course, led to the dispatch of an additional sixty-man party of reinforcements to Cape Ann from Ipswich, yet sighting of these strange men continued, and their reported activities became more bizarre. They attacked empty barns, threw rocks, and in one incident deliberately walked into an ambush laid for them by Babson and greeted him with disdain as he attempted to shoot them, only to have his gun misfire. And then they were gone. Cotton Mather, that noteable writer and participant in witch trials, figured they must have been demons. Yet they harmed no one.

A similar outbreak of strangeness froze the French countryside just after July 14, 1789. (Happy Bastile Day, everybody!) Similar attacks also occurred in Michigan in 1978, two decades after the noteable incident in August of 1955 wherein the Taylor family of Kelly, Kentucky experienced the case quoted above, with the odd creatures as resistant to gunfire as the Cape Ann strangers had been 250-plus years earlier. Police Chief Russell Greenwell, upon investigating the case, found little hard evidence of anything but stated that he had "a weird feeling. It was partly uneasiness, but not entirely. There were men that I'd call brave men, and they felt it too." Despite their best efforts, even Project Blue Book (never shy to declare something a weather balloon, a reflection off of Venus, or even a bit of undigested beef) had no answers, although a few die-hard skeptics argued that the attackers were a horde of escaped monkeys.

Yes, bullet proof glowing escaped monkeys. In rural Kentucky. That makes sense.

There's more going on here than mere panic. Granted, real panic is pretty uncanny already: it's named for the fear the goat-god Pan could spread, and anyone who contemplates that connection for long has to see its roots in the belief that certain emotions were spread by divine proxy. Which makes one wonder if the police were simply mistaking the footprints of a being with the feet of a goat (which, of course, would make no sense) for those of a woman in high heels. It seems pretty absurd, I'll grant. The idea that Pan is wandering around the world causing people to freak out is, on the face of it, absolutely ridiculous. After all, Herodotus reports to us that the great god Pan is dead. Besides, we have other possibilities to explore. (I've covered the notorious *Springheeled Jack* elsewhere... so I'll just touch upon the idea that a being with the legs of a goat could make some prodigious leaps, if he was of a mind to, and leave it at that.)

Ever heard of Jerusalem Syndrome? This is the condition that overwhelms hundreds, if not thousands, of people every year upon visiting that most disputed, most holy of cities, whereupon the visitor becomes convinced that he or she is a figure from the Bible (Old or New Testament) or the Quran. Or Stendahl's syndrome, where fainting or hysterical blindness attacks a person upon witnessing a profound work of art that overwhelms the senses. While not as gruesome as Koro or as easily dismissed as the phantom attackers at Mattoon, Halifax and Botetourt, both of these are widely reported. Almost as widely reported, and rivaling any for pure weirdness, are the repeated outbreaks of dancing madness that broke out in Europe for almost a century, starting in Aachen in 1374. Or the poison terrors of the sixteenth and seventeenth centuries in France and in Italy. In many cases, these manias led to the conviction, torture and death of suspected "witches" and "poisoners" who probably were neither. Whether or not these cases were caused by the spread of ergot fungus on the grains these people fed upon, I'll leave up to the reader. After all, it is certainly unclear if such could explain the outbreaks of Koro that plague the East to this day, or the belief in Chongqing, China that an enormous American robot was on its way to destroy the town and eat the children who dared to wear the color red unless those same children had managed to lay in a supply of cruicifixes and garlic. This happened in 1993. I don't want anyone to feel left out, so I'll also mention the similar panic that swept Houston, Texas in 1983. Just replace "rampaging American robot" with "army of Smurfs with guns and knives" and the color red with the color blue, and you've got the Texas headline down.

Is it just me? Am I the only one who sees the hand of a capricious and demented prankster in all this?

My original theory when I started this ramble a few paragraphs ago was that human brains generate energy, like all electrochemical processes, and some of that energy is radiated out. Call it the Kirlian aura, call it waste electromagnetism, whatever you would like. These electrical fields or auras intersect, creating mild dissonance, the way your laptop can interfere with the picture on your television screen, and since we have been steadily increasing the number of people who share this planet, we have been generating more and more of what you could call *static*. This static interacts with the human mind, which attempts to resolve it into something it can comprehend, the way your TV tries to make a picture out of the static your laptop generates and gets a fuzzy picture for its trouble. The mind, being a whole lot more intricate and sophisticated than a TV, tries to make sense of this static by means of the cultural information already stored in the brain. So, in Kuala Lumpur, the static of all those human minds in close proximity becomes a belief that the penis is crawling up into the body, and in Jerusalem, it become a certainty that the Bible is literally true and you are Moses. It seemed elegant enough.

But now I wonder.

Because this seems more than just random impulses being interpreted by the brain. This seems *directed*. Oh, it certainly seems tailored to the beliefs of the observers, I will admit; in 1692, you get mysterious demons, in 1955, you get glowing space monkeys, and in 1993, you get giant American robots. But something as mindless as static seems insufficient.

> Thought-Form: A mental image solidified in astral substance by will applied to visualization. Supposedly, an adept may build up an objective image through intense concentration, producing seeming actualities. A thought-form may also be made into a "magical body" as a vehicle for the consciousness during astral projection. Some say that thought-forms can also embody the collective will of a magical group.
> Bill Whitcomb, *The Magician's Companion*

Then it hit me. Jung's collective unconscious. Terrance McKenna's hyperstatial entities, contacted through various hallucinogens. (A hallucinogenic or psychedelic drug can only do what the mind can, ultimately. It is like training wheels for the brain.) Aleister Crowley's Aiwass. The *kappa* of Japan, the manifold Celestial Bureacracy of China, the Dreamtime of Africa... many names for beings and places beyond this one. Entities from elsewhere- and that elsewhere is like the Celtic Otherworld with its strange fae who can bring pigs to Britain. Why not spook sheep? Pan was a satyr, one of their Greek cousins, and while the Great God Pan may be dead, must his people be? What McKenna called machine elves (imagine what a machine elf would look like... perhaps a shining silver being with elongated ears, *resistant to gunfire?*) the ancient Irish called the Tuatha de Dannan, with their silver-handed man-gods and wondrous craft. It's easy to imagine one of Pan's kin playing a horn and making the folk of Europe dance- perhaps even Puck, old Robin Goodfellow himself? Are these beings like us, or are they entities of pure mind, interacting with our brains and using the overlapping thoughts to create form for themselves? And if so, why? Looking to the definition for a thought-form above, I will say only this: the collective will of six billion humans is not to be ignored or underestimated, and the perversity of humankind is an established fact.

Perhaps because the two theories overlap. There are more minds than ever before, more complex and contadictory human thoughts pushing their way out into astral space, taking up areas that were once created by the much less complex minds of our non-human kin. No more are the fae nature spirits, or spirits of the hearth... they are becoming spirts of man, made mad and strange by the warping of their very nature by the rising tide of mankind. And it's not like the fae folk were ever all that nice. They've often been called names couched in irony, names like the Gentry and "men of peace" which were similar to the old Greek trick of calling the Furies the "Kindly Ones." They are often viewed as baby stealers and demonic lovers.

They do not like us, they never have. Have they become media saavy? Do they watch anime and Saturday morning cartoons, or experience them as we watch them, seeing through our eyes? Have they become more and more like us as we have spread across the globe in ever-increasing numbers? Do they seek to prune our out-of-control growth like a tree gone mad, or do they enjoy the ever spiralling dementia of mankind's contradictory thoughts and impulses? It seems to me that in the borderland between what is and what has never been, imagination is a terrible swift sword, and it is dangling over us like Damocles'.

Or maybe you believe that it's all in our heads. Which would mean that you agree with me, in a way. See you later. Try not to do anything rash with any superfine jewler's knives or shotguns, okay? I'd miss you.

Life in the Claws of the Dragon

> On leaving, Confucius told his disciples, 'I know a bird can
> fly, a fish can swim, and an animal can run. For that which
> runs a net can be made; for that which swims a line can be
> made; for that which flies a corded arrow can be made. But
> the dragon's ascent into heaven on the wind and the clouds
> is something which is beyond my knowledge. Today I have
> seen Lao Tzu who is perhaps like a dragon.'
> D.C. Lau, Introduction to the Penguin Classics *Tao Te*
> *Ching*

Life has existed on this planet for hundreds of millions of years
at the least. According to my very nifty *Atlas of Life on Earth*
(snagged on the cheap from the remainder section, with divers hands
such as Dougal Dixon, Ian Jenkins, Richard T.J. Moody and Andrey
Yu. Zhuravlev contributing) the first molecules of primordial RNA
arose some 3,900,000,000 years ago or so, during that time period
we call the Archean and it has continued to change ever since.
Somewhere along the way, those few molecules managed to give
birth to a massively diverse biosphere we've not yet managed to
wipe out, no matter how assiduously we work at it. I suspect all we
humans will really manage to do is render earth uninhabitable for
ourselves.

The spread of life throughout Earth's long history means, by
necessity, that more things have died than are currently alive. Even
as the *human* population attempts to buck this trend and maintain
some sort of perverse equilibrium where there are as many living
members of the species as have died, the fact remains that in terms
of total biomass the dead far outweigh the living. Like the Yezidi
who view their Malek Tous (the Peacock Lord) as the Adversary, a
potent spirit of fire and earth who rules this world and must be dealt
with, so must we all recognize the power and omnipresence of death.

Indeed, evolutionary theory is very respectful of the power of death. After all, it is death that prunes and directs the otherwise boundlessly chaotic, mutable explosive flow of life. Death is the mechanism of selection, death the means by which certain mutations are deemed fit to survive and be passed on to future descendants. The tension between the urge to procreate and the possibility of dying before passing one's genetic information forward to be combined and developed is what, according to Darwin and his disciples, helped create that massively diverse biosphere in the first place. Taken still further, there are schools of thought that regard evolution as punctuated by bursts of sudden adaptation which may well be explainable as the influence of sudden drastic shifts in environment placing additional selective pressure on life. The death rate goes up because a rock falls from space or continental drift changes the climate. As the deaths pile up the remaining life forms are pared down to a few hardy forms, which then explode into novelty as soon as the playing field is stable enough to be exploited. It becomes clear that death provides a necessary service in simultaneously producing fodder for future expansion and allowing room for new development by carving stagnation away.

When contemplating this alignment between death and life, one thinks of the various metaphors life has been expressed in over time. One is that of the tree, whether it be the connotation of the *tree of life* from the book of Genesis, also found in the Qabbala. The Axis Mundi can also be found as Yggdrasil, forever chewed upon by the serpent Niddhog and forever growing in response. Yggdrasil and Niddhog together form an almost perfect tension between life and death, between potential and negation, that seems to spur on the development of life on earth. However, even as we consider this arrangement, it behooves us to consider the fascinating idea that life itself may not only be affected by death, but may well affect it as well. If the laws of physics are habitual then life's development changes the rules that life develops under even as those rules develop life itself. You cannot tell the dancer from the dance.

> The *Sefer Yetzirah* likens this to a "flame bound to a burning coal." A flame cannot exist without the coal, and the burning coal cannot exist without the flame. Although the coal is the cause of the flame, the flame is also the cause of the burning

coal. Without the flame, it would not be a burning coal. Since Cause cannot exist without Effect, Effect is also the cause of Cause. In this sense, Effect is the cause, and Cause is the effect. Since beginning and end are inseparable, "their end is embedded in their beginning, and their beginning in their end."

Aryeh Kaplan, **Sefer Yetzirah - The Book of Creation: In Theory and Practice**

The implicate order can be thought of as a ground beyond time, a totality, out of which each moment is projected into the explicate order. For every moment that is projected out into the explicate there would be another movement in which that moment would be injected or "introjected" back into the implicate order. If you have a large number of repetitions of this process, you'll start to build up a fairly constant component to this series of projection and injection. That is, a fixed disposition would become established....Moreover, such a field would not be located anywhere. When it projects back into the totality (the implicate order), since no space and time are relevant there, all things of a similar nature might get connected together or resonate in totality. When the explicate order enfolds into the implicate order, which does not have any space, all places and all times are, we might say, merged, so that what happens in one place will interpenetrate what happens in another place.

David Bohm, **Nature as Creativity**

If we're ever going to find an element of nature that explains space and time, we surely have to find something that is deeper than space and time-something that has no localization in space and time. The amazing feature of the elementary quantum phenomenon-the Great Smoky Dragon-is exactly this. It is indeed something of a pure knowledge-theoretical character, an atom of information which has no localization in between the point of entry and the point of registration.

John Wheeler, Interview in **The Ghost in the Atom**

But the dragon's ascent into heaven on the wind and the clouds is something which is beyond my knowledge. As Confucius spoke of Lao Tzu, leave it to quantum physicists (those shamans of modern science) to look at the unfolding nature of reality, the conflict between forces, and see the snout of a dragon. The Dragon, in this case, is the Young Experiment, wherein light falls on two slits in a screen and creates interference enabling one to demonstrate that light is a wave- even when we're in that undiscovered country Bohr told us we had no right to talk about, when the particle of light, that photon, is on its way to interfere with itself. Wheeler's dragon, Bohm's implicate order, Sheldrake's morphic field, Lao Tzu's Tao (the way which begets one that begets two, begetting three, begetting the myriad) or the Qabalistic *Ain* all trail towards that ultimate understanding of the burning coal that is life and death. Without life, nothing would die. If not for death, there would be no potential for life. And as the two wind about each other, they drag each other into a more complicated series of emanations (for those of us still hanging from that Sephirothic tree) and feed back from explicate reality to implicate order, where all things are in totality. Consider, therefore, how the implicate order exists as a palimpsest behind the reality we perceive, covered over by it *and* rewritten by its own constant interaction with it. The morphic field creates all we see and sense and interact with; and as everything we see and sense interacts with everything else, including us, new creations are written onto the baseline set of existence. *The most submissive thing in the world can ride roughshod over the hardest in the world - that which is without substance entering that which has no crevices.* Lao Tzu's reminder of the erosive power of water should be considered when thinking of the life-death interdependency, the truth of the implicate order forming the explicate world only to have the explicate world redact the implicate order right back. It's like considering Plato's cave, with the shadows cast upon the wall; the shadows may appear to be merely thrown, helpless before the fury of the light, but they reach back by creating impressions in the minds of those who may well extinguish and rebuild that fire somewhere else entirely.

Life began simple, a chain of atoms into a molecule that contained none of the characteristics we now consider to be symptomatic of living things. Slowly, with great care, life took on more and more of those attributes. And as it did, life eroded itself into the implicate order, projected and introjected back, a constantly more sophisticated and elaborated series of associations. Then came the hammer of death, of mass extinction...and that death, instead of the purity of universal void, death as the harvester of life (remember, single celled organisms don't die as such...mitosis creates two cells with identical DNA, neither the original, neither distinguishable from each other) and its gardener, became etched as well into the palimpsest of existence. After each extinction comes a new explosion of life, new orders, new kingdoms. When they reach their choke point, a new method of pruning the garden is manifested, projected out of the implicate order and chaos and destruction become explicate again, and death reigns. Each time, variations on the theme carve their way through introjection into the DNA of the universe, the emanations of the Sephiroth, the tree that is the Axis Mundi, the ever sophisticated *Ain* that grows and changes as it divides to learn itself and creates always something new to learn, in the process throwing shadows that become the Qlippoth. The clash of sphere and cracked shell brings forth ever more fertile soil for creation by bringing death into life itself, making death a part of it, so that life itself is dependent on its own unmaking.

The dragon rises. Grows ever more complex. Created and creating, pinned by its own exertions, defined ever more furiously by that which it removes. Does the dragon think? Indeed, as the Yezidi argue with Malek Tous, who is destroyer and creator at once (shades of Shiva the Nataraja and Kali his bride) the Great Smoky Dragon both makes and destroys, cures and kills...has the furious imposing of habit upon the implicate order created a nurturing mind which culls the weak, and has it imposed a form upon it based on our nightmares by forging our nightmares from it, as the burning coal is both cause and effect, effect and cause? If, as Sheldrake argues, the past is everywhere with us at once, being rewritten and rewriting, could it be that the serpent has grown, that separating the tree and the snake into halves is inaccurate? If one thinks of the tree as the implicate and the explicate intertwined, the implicate becomes DNA and the explicate RNA, and the interaction of replication from one to the other creates whole new patterns on introjection. The snake descends the tree from kether to malkuth, and climbs back up again.

One considers the effect of fossils on the imagination. Looking at these reconstructed effigies seems to bring a sense of power and grace to the scaffolding of petrified bone, the implicate order of a once-living being. Then when one considers the fossil wars of the American Southwest or the curious coincidence between the fossil hunting expedition of Roy Chapman Andrews and the outbreak of the Chinese Civil War and Japanese invasions; and is it a coincidence that just as we manage to get back into the Gobi and begin digging again that tensions rise worldwide? Or, for that matter, that we discover Spinosaurus in Egypt only to see the fossils destroyed in WWII, or that our efforts to rediscover this prehistoric Apophis coincide with ascending chaos in the region? These are the bones of dragons. These are the remains of the primordial serpent gods, the Midgarthsomar, the lords of creation, those that could not be snared in a net nor speared with an arrow, the brood of Tiamat. Do we think we can disturb their rest so easily, that their long mesozoic reign etched no new wrinkles into the implicate palimpsest, that their ruthless tyranny and explosive finale did nothing to impress the Great Smoky Dragon? They ruled the planet for more than a hundred and eighty million years, enforcers of the endless rule of death over life, perfectly positioned to exploit the land and seas they found themselves in. Even after death came for them in fire and ruin, one must be impressed by so long a rule. And, with our knowledge of how all space and all time interpolate each other, we know that all time is no time, and what is past may well interpenetrate what is now.

The bones are charged with the death of the reptile kings, the chosen brood of the dragon. They resonate forward, manifesting in our dreams as legends of the serpent and the rainbow, the feathered serpent (Archaeopeteryx via Mesoamerican morphic resonance?), the chaotic Tiamat at the well of Apsu, Typhon the hundredfold dragon bursting forth from the earth...the great celestial dragons of the bureaucracy of heaven itself and wearing its mandate, gnawers at the tree. The Peacock Lord is their descendant, the lines of force that riddle the Earth the ancient tracks of their feet, the legends of serpents bringing knowledge and dragons ravaging mankind one in purpose, the brood of Niddhogg, the raging wings of the Great Smoky Dragon. We should tread lightly on the Earth, for where we are now, mighty ones have walked before us. It says so in the Bible. They bring destruction in the service of the way, they are the mechanism of evolution made manifest, the will of that which kills and cures.

> A mythic image among many peoples, the dragon is a living, fantastic hybrid creature that frequently has many heads. In many religion, the dragon (often akin to the serpent) embodies primordial powers...It grants fertility, since it is closely associated with the powers of water and thus with the Yin principle...yet at the same time it primarily represents the masculine active powers of the sky and thus the Yang principle; as a demiurge, it produces the waters of the primeval beginning or the world egg.
>
> *Udo Becker,* **The Continuum, Encyclopedia of Symbols**

Imagine the world of the reptile kings, so long lost to us, so little but bones remaining, once a world jungle inhabited by the penultimate god-beasts. From tiny flyers smaller than modern birds to paleocrocodilians as vast as their dinosaur rivals, festering with life, slowly drifting into a more temperate environment as vast plains began their creep across the land, as the continents methodically drifted apart. Who knows now, looking back, what kinds of mind might well have existed in that world? Whatever we postulate, we can never truly know. We do know that those minds rose and fell and rose over the course of one hundred and eighty million years, methodically carving themselves like hieroglyphs into the morphic field. Then flashed the *lapis ex caelis*, the stone from heaven, the talon of the Great Smoky Dragon as the impulse to cull flashed into the explicate world. Who is to say what effect that mass death had on the implicate order? Did death, the gardener of evolution, take on the aspect of his most successful creations as he brought them fully over into that timeless, spaceless backdrop to space and time? Do their bones still bear the resonance of their awesome reign and titanic death? Do they come together in the shape of their creator and killer, gestalts of themselves, and drive the human race forward as an implement of ideas and concepts hatched from the cosmic egg of their unknowable brains? Serpents gave us the knowledge of good and evil, serpents were the ones Berossus attributed with mankind's rise to prominence, serpents shaded the lord Parshva from demons, the dragon-titan Typhon made war on Zeus for Earth's sake...serpents terrify and awe us, be they the rainbow serpent of Uluru, the world-girding serpent Midgarthsomar, the divine dragons of China who hold the secret of immortality lightly in their powerful claws (tree of good and evil, Axis Mundi, tree of life), the sun-swallowing Apep (a manifestation of the spirits of countless Spinosaurs seeking revenge on the sky that destroyed them?) and so on. The reptile kings, they are dead.

And yet they live.

Index

About the Author

Matt Rossi was born December 7, 1971. Yes, Pearl Harbor Day. He's already heard all the jokes, thanks. He's a native of Prudence Island, Rhode Island, and resides wherever the wind takes him, having lived in London, Chicago, Washington D.C. and San Francisco before stopping to rest in Seattle. He has four tattoos but they're all in relatively accessible places, so if you ask politely he'll probably show them to you. He refuses to stop reading strange fiction, crooked history and comic books even though everyone thinks he's got to grow out of it sooner or later. He earned his BFA in Creative Writing in 1996 at Roger Williams University in Bristol, Rhode Island. He has no desire to be more than he is, but he would like to be better at what he does. If he died tomorrow, he'd have a hard time finishing any of the stories he's currently working on. He finds it really odd to write about himself in the third person, and he's pretty much out of anything interesting to say.